Bill Gillis was head of Dumfries and Galloway C.I.D. for the last six years of his service. He spent two thirds of his career as a detective and had a well earned reputation in our region and beyond for treating crime as a personal matter and something not to be tolerated. He instilled this attitude into his detectives, ensuring Dumfries and Galloway was not just one of the safest places in Britain to live but the local force always had one of the highest detection rates in the country, especially for serious crime. On a personal level I can confirm just how dogged and determined he was in ensuring those responsible for committing such crimes were brought to justice.

His police experiences were put to good use when writing his first crime novel, 'Stable of Touts' which I and many others have read and thoroughly enjoyed. Now he has put the main character, Detective Inspector Jimmy McBurnie, centre stage again in his second novel, 'McBurnie's Awakening'.

We can now get a real insight into the complex world of serious crime investigation and the pressures detectives face. I for one cannot wait to see how McBurnie tackles the 'neds' and the 'system'.

Signed ...*Ronnie Nicholson*...

Leader of Dumfries and Galloway Council.

'I am indebted to John for his assistance and advice with regards to legal procedures and practices described in this book'

HE001991

McBurnie's Awakening

By

Bill Gillis

Published by Gallus Press

Gallus Press is an Imprint of Olida Publishing established
January 2013 www.olidapublishing.com

First printing: January 2015

For more information, e-mail all inquires to Allan
Sneddon –
allan.olidapublishing@gmail.com

Printed in the United Kingdom

Cover Design: Scott Wallace and Joe Murdoch
ISBN: 978-1-907354-35-9

'I dedicate this book to Fiona Jane McKenzie the bravest and most inspirational young lady I have ever met'

REFLECTION

Jimmy McBurnie was brought up in a Scottish coal mining community in the 1950s and '60s. He left school with only a rudimentary education but still managed to get employment as a blacksmith in a Clydeside ship yard. His grandfather and father, who were both miners, repeatedly told him, coming from the background he did, he would never beat the class system.

In the 1970s shipbuilding on the Clyde was in decline and now with a wife and child to support McBurnie needed to get secure employment. One of the few options available to him, especially with only having such a basic education, was the police service.

Much against the wishes of his family, who saw the Police as agents of the state, he joined the neighbouring police force. Like many members of the public, McBurnie believed the police operated within an egalitarian system based on meritocracy. Under this system he felt he could get promotion purely on merit, and prove his family wrong about class and privilege.

Not long after joining, he found he could 'speak' to neds and recruit them as informants(touts). In keeping with his earlier penchant for horse racing and gambling he supplied each tout with a 'stable name' and appointed himself their trainer. This paradigm worked well. His team were invaluable in not only helping him detect many serious crimes, but got him promoted to the rank of Detective Inspector, which he was sure was well beyond the expectations of his grandfather and father.

Detective Inspector(D.I.) Jimmy McBurnie gave his heart and soul to the Police and was addicted to crime fighting. He was convinced with his 24 hour a day work ethic and success on the crime front, other chances for promotion would soon come along.

His early days in the service should have convinced him otherwise...

When he joined the Police he found there was indeed a class system operating within the service. Officers with little experience were being promoted because they fitted the stereotype required by the ruling elite, or had friends in 'high places'.

With him being from the working class and 'outside' this elite, promotion would prove to be an uphill struggle, but one which he felt was not insurmountable. After all he had achieved two promotions to get to the rank of Inspector by purely hard work. What he didn't fully appreciate was now he was a 'Detective' Inspector he was regarded in some quarters as a 'bad boy' and a manager of 'bad boys', by some senior officers with no C.I.D. experience.

Those with this view didn't want to become involved in dealing with criminals. Many saw the detectives who dealt with these 'neds' as little better than criminals themselves. However, when there were nasty crimes to be dealt with and pressure coming from local representatives and the media to get early
detections, some of this elite took a step back and let the detectives take the flak.

As D. I. McBurnie had been in this position many times, he increasingly found it almost impossible to have any respect for these members of the police hierarchy. With his background in a mining community and while working in a ship yard, respect was something that had to be earned.

He certainly didn't hide his feelings and his loose tongue and attitude to discipline meant he made a few enemies at senior level, who would ensure any further promotion for him would be difficult. Further advancement became almost impossible when he had witnessed a senior officer, Chief Supt. Scott, being assaulted by Jimmy's boss, Detective Chief Inspector Chambers, and then denied it.

Scott was always part of the Force's promotion panel and 'marked' McBurnie's card when he applied...

At the next promotion panel interview no allowance was made for McBurnie having been the Senior Investigating Officer (S.I.O.) to investigate a murder just days before the promotion panel sat. Meanwhile, all his competitors for the post, most with 8-5pm. Monday to Friday jobs, had plenty of time to prepare.

He got a torrid time at interview and was marked down because 'ironically' he didn't have enough uniform experience for the position of 'Detective' Chief Inspector! McBurnie knew this was just an excuse to make sure he was not the next D.C.I. He knew the real reason he didn't get the job was because of him denying he had witnessed Scott being assaulted...

He was in no doubt Scott was behind the knock back and he swore revenge on him...

He was sure with his touts, both within and outwith the police, he could, again referring to racing terms, get Scott 'pulled up' permanently.

However, there was also a problem with another member of the panel...

A.C.C. Ramsden like many of his peers had never been a detective and saw them as 'chancers', not much better than the criminals they locked up. McBurnie was convinced he too would always be a 'hurdle' he would have to overcome.

Just after he was informed he hadn't been successful at the promotion interview McBurnie left the C.I.D. office and went straight to his local pub to drown his sorrows and formulate a plan for Scott to take a 'fall'...

The D.I. was now a truly embittered individual...

REVENGE

McBurnie entered his local pub and unusually for him he didn't socialise with the regular drinkers who all knew him, but sat in a corner by himself. He was in an internal rage and downing pints and whisky as if they were going out of fashion. By the time he got home he could hardly stand and his wife, Doris, in her wisdom decided the best place for her was in bed.

She made Jimmy his supper and headed to the bedroom.

The next morning he woke up on the couch in the living room never having gone to bed and with a thumping head. His recollection of the previous night was vague and he was hoping he hadn't told anyone in the pub what he was actually thinking or planning.

The big issue for him now was to return to work and not show his true feelings about Scott, and his disappointment at not being promoted, to his colleagues. He knew he would need to try and be his normal, 'gallus' self but this was not going to be easy.

On reflection he had seen one of his ex D.S.'s getting no favours from the Force yet still remaining totally loyal. This guy just got on with it and continued to focus on what he saw as the true role of the police i.e. getting the bad people of the street.

Jimmy thought he should put on a similar display of loyalty at least for the benefit of his peers and the bosses. This would show Scott and his cohorts they were not going to get him down.

His first day back was a bit of a drag and it took all his determination to get through it and keep up appearances. To be honest he was more than glad when he got back home to Doris and the kids and away from the C.I.D. office.

After the evening meal and the children were packed off to bed he apologised to Doris for the state he was in the previous night. She was understanding and accepted his frustration and anger about Scott's deviousness and Jimmy's disappointment of not getting promoted, especially when he gave 24 hours a day to the police. She knew this was going to be a difficult time for the whole family and how he managed the disappointment could have a real impact on their family life, and maybe even their marriage.

Being the worldly wise woman she was, during their conversation that night she referred back to the happy times of their youth. In particular in the 1950s when they both grew up in the mining village of Auldburn.

Jimmy initially was dour and said he didn't want to engage in any sort of conversation. He was totally absorbed with hatred and revenge and it was eating away at him. He kept telling himself how stupid he had been not to accept what his father and grandfather had told him about the class system.

However, Doris was nothing if not determined and after some coaxing he eventually found his tongue. It wasn't too long then before they were reminiscing about life in the miner's row where they were both brought up.

They started to share childhood experiences...
It had been tough in small houses with no running hot water and no fitted baths. Nevertheless, they both agreed, the community spirit was great and Jimmy and Doris had many

'adopted' aunties and uncles in the rows of 'pit' houses, who ensured no one went short. A lot of the 'aunties' worked as school dinner ladies and they made sure the kids were well fed and got second helpings at meal times if they wanted them. Every kid in the village took school dinners and at least here they were sure of a good nourishing meal. This was not always something their parents could provide because of their low incomes, ill health, or lack of benefits.

Poverty was indeed a shared experience, but comradeship, community and caring, were unsurpassed...

The more they reminisced the more Jimmy relaxed and recollected events; like his mother boiling a huge black kettle on the fire to fill the zinc bath which was kept in the coal shed till it was needed for bathing. Once it was filled it was ready for his dad, returning, black from head to toe, from the pit.

This was a daily occurrence and quite often Jimmy, when he was a child would follow his dad into the bath coming out dirtier than he went in. Doris too could relate to this picture and they laughed about it. Both of them had memories of miners sitting on their 'hunkers' against the Co-operative Store wall, discussing football and what were the chances of the bets they had placed on horses and greyhounds.

Each clearly remembered the gambling at the pitch and toss schools behind the 'bookies' shop, where the miners placed their bets using their nom de plumes.

Sometimes at the pitch and toss, arguments broke out, as did allegations of cheating, which often resulted in fall outs and fights between the miners. Once the fights and fall outs were through, mostly they were forgotten. Miners knew there would always be a time, when you lived in such a close community and worked in a dangerous, low paid work environment as theirs, when you would need help from your neighbour.

The more Jimmy and Doris talked the more they remembered about their youth. They had vivid memories of when they were eight years old, how common it was for them, and other miners' kids, to be sent by their fathers to the bookies with their 'lines' (bets). These pieces of hand written paper contained their fathers' chosen horses, their nom de plumes and the money for the bets. Both could recall being in the bookie's when it was raided by the police, checking up on the bookie. Looking back they found it hilarious when thinking about this event because all the 'punters' in the bookmakers were under ten years old:-

All there putting on their dad's line...

For Jimmy this was not only an early exposure to gambling and horse racing, but his first real contact with the police. He asked Doris, somewhat jokingly if she thought this had been an omen for things to come?'

She just gave him a wry grin and shook her head.

He then told her he remembered, when he was eight or nine he would regularly hang onto the back of the coal lorries which were collecting coal from the pit and taking it to the railway depot some two miles away. At the depot, he and his friends would hide until the lorries had deposited their load and then they would covertly hang onto the rear tailgate and get a 'lift' back to Auldburn. As a kid Jimmy said he thought this was a real adventure, but he told

Doris he would be in the horrors if he thought any of his kids did similar things now.

It was well after midnight before the couple went to bed and Doris was praying that sharing their recollections had taken his thoughts away from his frustrations at work.

If Jimmy was honest with himself he would have agreed...

It had taken his mind, temporarily, away from constantly thinking about Scott and to some extent Ramsden, and seeking revenge.

Later that week the couple received an unexpected call from their old minister, Sandy Morrison, who had heard through the grapevine Jimmy had not been promoted. Once he had a cup of tea and a blether with him and Doris he asked Jimmy to accompany him, while they had a walk across the field adjacent to their house.

As they were walking Morrison managed to get him to open up...
Jimmy expressed his true feelings about how angry and vengeful he was, in particular in relation to Scott and others in the police hierarchy who he had no respect for. He told the minister he was going to plan Scott's downfall but did not go into detail about how we would achieve this.

Sandy Morrison having been a miner earlier in life, knew only too well the miners' code about respect having to be earned. He also knew, to dwell on revenge and getting 'even', was similar to a cancer which festered away in your system eventually spreading and eating you up.

He told Jimmy it was not his place to seek revenge. This was a matter for God and if Jimmy was a true believer he would leave it to God. Morrison knew personally just how hard it was to forgive someone who had wronged you but he believed Jimmy had it in him to do it.

Before they finished their stroll this old sage guaranteed Jimmy God had a plan for him and he might be surprised just how this plan would pan out.

After he left, McBurnie sat for a while on his own, mulling over what Mr Morrison had said. He decided, for the sake of his wife and family, to try and follow his advice. He then told Doris and his kids, Derek and Stephanie, they were going out for a meal to their favourite eatery. The kids were excited and couldn't wait to get their teeth into burger, chips, coke and ice cream.

Outwardly, it was a happy family who went for this meal but in Jimmy's case, still a man caught in the dichotomy existing between revenge and listening to the advice of his old clergyman.

In his heart of hearts he hoped the latter would prevail...

FRIEND OR FOE?

After a week back at work McBurnie was introduced to the new D.C.I., Louis Johnston. He had been the successful applicant at the same promotion panel as Jimmy.

Initially there was a bit of trepidation on both sides when they met in the C.I.D. office, but Jimmy just kept calm and didn't let his guard down. D.S. Martin Green, a keen supporter of Jimmy, was watching how the D.I. would respond to Johnston, and was hoping he wouldn't let himself down.

He shouldn't have worried because McBurnie was nothing if not astute, and just played it cool. He made a point of shaking hands with his new boss in front of all the C.I.D. staff and assured him he would have his support.

Jimmy knew little about his new boss because Johnston had spent quite a bit of time in uniform. To be honest other than identifying him by his strange accent, he didn't know very much about him at all. It turned out, as they engaged in conversation, Johnston had transferred from an English Force some ten years before. His last three years in Jimmy's force had been as a uniform Inspector in the neighbouring division of Burnfoot.

Once the niceties were passed Johnston asked Jimmy to come into the D.C.I.'s office and once there, he closed the door.
Now they were alone...

Johnston told McBurnie he knew how disappointed he must be at not being promoted and he sympathised with him. He assured him he would have his full support and hoped they could work together as a team.

Initially, Jimmy had difficulty understanding what Johnston was saying as he couldn't identify whether his accent was part English, part Scottish, part Irish or a combination of all three.

Irrespective of the accent, he had heard it all before and being the cynic and sceptic he was, he treated Johnston's comments with a pinch of salt. For Jimmy, actions spoke louder than words. He would wait and see how Johnston's actions related to his words...

They remained in Johnston's office for more than an hour and Jimmy was quite shocked, but pleasantly surprised. His new boss knew all about his 'Stable of Touts', but not their identities, and his prowess as a detective. He was even more taken aback when he learned that Johnston, before joining Jimmy's Force, had spent three years as a Detective Sergeant and had worked on some high profile cases.

All in all McBurnie left the office thinking it could have been a whole lot worse. His new D.C.I. could have been a right plonker, and with Jimmy's suspicious mind, possibly a 'plant' by some of the bosses. The D.I. knew to get a true account of anyone you had to, in keeping with his favoured horse racing analogy, 'study the form'. As a result he would do just that, and watch how Johnston performed on the job, before he decided to come to a decision of whether he was a friend or foe.

In the next few weeks Johnston neither said nor did anything which caused Jimmy any concern. However, Jimmy being as paranoid as he was, decided he needed some assurance his new boss was as serious about crime detection as he was. He hoped Johnston was not just in the C.I.D. to get his 'card stamped', to show like some other favoured cops, that at some stage in his career he had spent time as a senior detective.

McBurnie thought long and hard about how he could achieve this assurance and of course it all came back to the use of one of his touts...

He had been receiving a constant supply of information from Delicate Girl, a long term member of his tout stable. She was responsible for putting another of his touts, Wise Archie, out to pasture. She was now telling him about a planned break- in at the chairwoman of the Police and Fire Authority's home.

McBurnie knew her information was always reliable, but he was always in a dilemma about her involvement as a tout, because of her background and her addiction to heroin.

When he first got to hear about her she was seventeen years old, classed as a bit of a wild child, and very promiscuous with male junkies. Initially Jimmy thought she had no children, but some years later after he recruited her, he found when she was fifteen she had given birth to twins.

On the advice of her 'well to do' parents she handed them over for adoption and she always regretted this decision. Sometimes while under the influence of drugs, drink, or both, she would tell him how much she missed seeing or having any contact with her twins. She said she often thought about them, what was happening in their lives and whether or not their adopted parents were good to them. On these occasions she would become quite morose and start crying uncontrollably.

Jimmy, being a parent himself, felt for her, and always did his best to tell her she was not to blame for giving up her kids. At the age of fifteen, he reasoned she was only a child herself and her parents probably thought adoption was the best course of action at the time.

Privately he wondered if this traumatic experience was one of the reasons Delicate had started mixing with druggies and become one herself...

He was always concerned for Delicate but knew if you looked beyond her appearance, and her addiction, there was a young woman, who given the right circumstances would have made a good mother. She had a kind heart and doted on her friends' and neighbours' children, but only 'when she wasn't out of her face on smack'.

He worried constantly about the baddies she mixed with who fuelled her addiction and abused her. She looked in a terrible state, in fact every time he met her she seemed worse than the time before. He repeatedly tried talking to her, offering her help to get her into rehab, and putting her in touch with drug workers and agencies he knew well.

All to no avail...

Every time she met him she promised she was getting rid of her habit and becoming 'clean' but she never did.

Whenever she supplied information, which she did on a regular basis, she was looking for a cash payment. This left McBurnie in a real dilemma as he suspected he knew where the cash went. It certainly wasn't on clothing or food for herself because she wore the same clothes every time they met, she was more unkempt, and was getting thinner and thinner.

He had in the past, instead of giving her cash, got vouchers for clothing and grocery items, which could be used at different shops. It wasn't long after he gave her these vouchers he heard through the grapevine she was trading them with other druggies for cash or gear...

Two weeks after Johnston was appointed she contacted Jimmy and gave him information which led to the arrest of two heroin dealers who had been on his radar for some time. On this occasion McBurnie passed the information and the subsequent collar to D.S. Green, while taking a step back to see if Johnston tried to claim any of the credit for the arrests with the bosses, which he didn't.

Delicate was also keeping him up to date about the planned break-in at the home of Mrs June Gillespie the chairwoman of the Police and Fire Authority. Initially McBurnie kept this information to himself to ensure no 'glory hunters' could get themselves noticed, or tell the chairwoman and spook her. This was a risky strategy, but he was sure he would receive confirmation from his tout when the job was on. This would be the time to tell Mrs Gillespie and it would ensure he could catch the neds on the job.

He had a bit of trust in his new D.C.I. now and at his last meeting with Delicate he told her if she couldn't get hold of him she should speak to D.C.I. Johnston, using the pseudonym he had given her. To further test his boss he told her any information she had, if he couldn't be contacted, she was to insist it was passed to Johnston.

If the D.C.I. passed the information to him and didn't keep it to himself, or pass it to somebody else, it would be another positive indicator he could be trusted.

Two days later Delicate phoned the C.I.D. office trying to get Jimmy. When she was told he wasn't contactable she asked to speak to D.C.I. Johnston. When he came onto the phone, she used her pseudonym and provided him with the names of two neds who were planning the break-in at the chairwoman's house.

Johnston noted what she said and she told him to make sure D.I. McBurnie was given this information. He confirmed he would pass it on to the D.I. when he came to work the next day.

When McBurnie arrived for his early shift the following day the D.C.I. asked him to come into his office and when he entered Johnston closed the door. He told Jimmy a tout using a strange pseudonym had phoned with information for him the previous night. He then went on to tell McBurnie, almost word for word, what Delicate had said to him. He also confirmed he had done nothing about the information and the only person he had discussed it with, was now Jimmy.

McBurnie was impressed and gave Johnston another mental tick in his 'friend' box. However, in his way of thinking no one was ever to be fully trusted, and Johnston's real test would come when they worked on a case together and saw it through the courts.

He then contacted Delicate and arranged a 'meet'...

When they met she told Jimmy exactly what she had told Johnston. She named the two neds who were planning the break-in at the chairwoman's house and confirmed she had passed this on to Johnston. Jimmy said he was grateful but he doubted the neds she named had the bottle to do the break in. Delicate said they were desperate for cash, for kit, (drugs) and they thought this woman was well to do. They had seen her driving a flashy car and knew she lived in an expensive house. She was rumoured to be very rich and was now a widow and living on her own. They believed she was bound to have cash or valuable items in her home.

Jimmy could see the state his tout was in again and handed over some vouchers with a face value of £100, telling her she should use them to clothe and feed herself. As usual she was looking for cash, but he left her in no doubt her well being was more important than cash. Perhaps the vouchers would be of more benefit he told her.

She didn't look pleased when she took them...

He should have been relieved his boss passed the 'trustworthy' test he had set for him, but being suspicious of everyone, he decided he still needed to find out more about Johnston. Next time it would be away from the police environment.

When he got back to the office he asked the D.C.I. if he would join him for a pint after work some time. Johnston was only too happy to have been invited and the following night they headed to

Jimmy's local pub.

On the way there Jimmy gave Johnston another tick in his 'friend' box...

McBurnie was well aware it would do Johnston no favours with some senior officers if they learned he had been socialising with Jimmy. Then again he thought, "Maybe Johnston has an ulterior motive and only agreeing to join me for a drink to be able to report back to Scott or Ramsden."

Talk about paranoia!

In the pub McBurnie introduced Johnston to his fellow drinkers. After a few pints, Johnston, because of his outgoing personality and ability to be 'one of the boys' was given the thumbs up by them. He even took all the ridicule about his accent, on the chin and gave as good as he got.

The more Jimmy saw of Johnston the more he liked him but that still didn't mean he trusted him...

Three days later Delicate contacted Jimmy again and told him the job was on and the break-in would happen early the next night. From somewhere, the crooks had learned the chairwoman would be at a function that night and not home till late.

Delicate confirmed again the names of the two junkies who would be breaking in and told a somewhat surprised Jimmy, they were even more desperate for cash and were getting 'strung out'. Delicate said she was worried what would happen if the householder disturbed them. There was no saying what they would do then. She told McBurnie she had heard them talking about this and agreeing to shut the 'old bat' up permanently if she turned up.

The D.I. knew both neds and still could hardly believe they had the bottle for this, but he had to admit, they certainly had the know how. One of them, before he became caught up in the drugs world had worked for a company installing alarms. He had the knowledge to overcome most alarm systems and he could no doubt use this experience to overcome the security of Mrs Gillespie's house.

Jimmy thanked Delicate and then contacted Johnston who decided both of them should meet with Mrs Gillespie, alert her to the danger, and put a plan in place to get the two neds.

Mrs Gillespie was a seventy year old widow who lived on her own, in a beautiful, detached bungalow, in a sought after and secluded area of Newholm. Her late husband had been convenor of the local council before his death, and they were indeed a wealthy couple.

Jimmy knew her well. When she had been a Justice of the Peace. (J.P.) he had often called at her home to get her to sign and authorise search warrants. She was always interested in what he was investigating and there was never any difficulty getting her to sign these warrants.

Her house was always immaculate, filled with paintings and antiques. Anybody entering there would know this old lady was rich.

When McBurnie and Johnston turned up at her house, Jimmy introduced Johnston as his new D.C.I. She ushered them in and offered them both coffee and biscuits, which they accepted.

She asked Jimmy how things were on the crime front and he said they were still putting a lot of the bad people away. In response she smiled and said, "That's great, the people of Newholm should be grateful they have such dedicated officers making their town a safe place to live."

Johnston smiled and then said the reason they were visiting her was to put more bad people away. He asked Jimmy to tell her about the information he had received concerning a potential break-in at her home the next night.

She was taken aback when she learned her house had been targeted. She also confirmed the following evening she would be attending a civic reception at the council offices, and didn't expect to be home before 11.pm.

When asked about her valuables or any money she kept in the house, she told the detectives she kept quite a bit of money and jewellery in her wall safe. Other high value items like paintings, ornaments and antiques were displayed throughout the house. She also confirmed she had a good alarm system protecting her house and wondered how these housebreakers would overcome it.

Jimmy said he had a good idea of who these housebreakers would be. If he was right they had plenty of experience in getting past alarm systems.

She then asked the two detectives what their plans were to deal with this break in, and what did they want her to do. Johnston, being keen to impress, took the lead. He said he would like to put four officers in her house and she should go to the civic function as she planned. She should secure the house as she did whenever she was going out, so nothing would appear abnormal.

Jimmy then told her the likelihood was the crooks would already have been watching her house and taking notes of her coming and goings. When she was to attend the civic function there would be no doubt they would be watching again, ensuring she had left. To reassure her he said more cops would be positioned in hidden locations around her house, long before she went to the function and guaranteed no harm would befall her.

She thanked him but said she wasn't worried, she could look after herself...

Johnston then confirmed if the four cops could get into her house quietly that afternoon, they could hide themselves inside and wait the arrival of the housebreakers. These officers would be supplemented by two surveillance trained officers in an observation point. They would give notification of the imminent arrival of the neds to the other cops on the inside and plain clothes detectives plotted up around her house. These detectives would be situated in positions where they could respond timeously once the intruders attempted to enter the house.

Mrs Gillespie was concerned someone could have been watching her, but she was also excited. She said she would love to be there when the baddies turned up, but she was sure they would be dealt with appropriately.

Both Johnston and Jimmy nodded and Johnston said "You can be assured they will."

Both detectives then left this resilient old lady and because of who she was in the community, and her role as chairwoman of the Police and Fire Authority, Johnston briefed the Chief Constable on the planned break-in. The Chief, who had little hands-on experience of dealing with crime, was more than a little perturbed when he heard this news. He told Johnston he had better catch these neds or maybe he would be on the move. He confirmed he was attending the same civic function as Mrs Gillespie and told Johnston to contact him with any developments, even if he was still at the function.

Johnston assured the Chief the plans were sound and he would provide any updates, promptly. He then returned to the C.I.D. office and shaking his head told Jimmy about his meeting with the Chief.

On hearing the details, McBurnie, being the cynic he was, said the only reason the Chief would want updated, was if there was good news, the housebreakers had been arrested. He could then score brownie points with Mrs Gillespie directly, and indirectly with the Police and Fire Authority, by telling her, and them, how well his officers had performed under his direction.

Johnston, tongue in cheek said, "Why would you think that?"and laughed.

Johnston then dropped a bombshell by stating he and Jimmy would be two of the four officers who would be hidden in Mrs Gillespie's house, awaiting the arrival of the housebreakers. Jimmy was delighted he would be on the inside, but never thought for a minute Johnston would accompany him. The more he thought about it the more suspicious he became and the more he questioned Johnston's motive for being 'on the job'. He asked himself, was it because he would get the adrenaline rush of catching neds in the act, or was it to prove to the Chief he was leading from the front? If the latter was the case he would get the credit if the neds were arrested and charged with the break in.

What Jimmy didn't know was the Chief had threatened Johnston with a move if he didn't catch the housebreakers. If he had known this, and been in Johnston's shoes, then perhaps he too would have insisted being in Mrs Gillespie's house...

The next day things went according to plan and the four detectives, including McBurnie and Johnston, got into the chairwoman's house early in the afternoon without being seen.

By 5p.m. the observation post was staffed by the two surveillance trained cops. D.S. Green and D.S. Allan had been briefed and they and their troops were in unmarked cars, close enough to the targeted house to respond, if and when required.

Everybody was now in communication with each other and ready for the arrival of the neds...

At 7.pm. Mrs Gillespie was picked up by a car driven by another member of the Police and Fire Authority. As she was leaving the house she said a quiet 'Good Luck' to the cops inside and gave them the thumbs up sign.

It was now just time to sit and wait...

Darkness fell at 8.10.pm. and at 8.30.pm the obs. men radioed Johnston stating two men wearing dark clothing were heading up the driveway to Mrs Gillespie's house.

Shortly thereafter the cops inside the house heard wires being cut on the outside wall and the two men whispering to each other outside a rear bedroom window. Adjacent to this window was a large patio door which provided great views over the countryside from the house's elevated position.

McBurnie, Johnston, and the other cops then heard movement at the patio door followed by the noise of something being pushed under the door runner. Immediately thereafter the sliding part of the door was lifted off the runner and removed.

The two neds then entered through this opening, one carrying a crowbar and the other a screwdriver. Before Jimmy could move, Johnston had smacked the one with the crowbar across the collarbone with his baton. The ned let out a squeal and his mate dropped his screwdriver and tried to jump back out the patio door, only to be rugby tackled by Jimmy, and pinned to the ground by the two hand picked 'bears' Jimmy had selected to join them in the house.

The lights were switched on and the two neds, with their startled expressions, looked like rabbits who had been caught in the beam of a car's headlights. Johnston took great delight in cautioning them and telling them they were under arrest.

None of them could speak...

The cavalry were summoned and before too long the two housebreakers were bundled, unceremoniously, into police cars and taken to Newholm Police Station.

Once back at the station Johnston went into his drawer and brought out a bottle of malt and shared it with Jimmy and the other troops. He then phoned the concierge at the civic function and asked him if he could get the Chief Constable to phone him urgently.

Two minutes later the Chief phoned and Johnston told him two men had been arrested after breaking into Mrs Gillespie's house. They would be appearing at court the next day charged with housebreaking with intent to steal.

The Chief asked if any damage had been caused to the house and Johnston said other than some alarm and telephone wires being cut and a patio door removed the property was still intact. It looked likely repairs could be carried out quickly.

The Chief didn't wait to ask if anybody was hurt or even congratulate Johnston and his team for the good work. He was in too much of a hurry to break the good news to Mrs Gillespie and the rest of the Police and Fire Authority committee members who were at the civic function.

When Johnston came off the phone Jimmy asked him what the Chief had said and after a pause he told Jimmy, "You are not the only only sceptic now."

Jimmy just gave him a knowing look and Johnston smiled in return...

The two housebreakers eventually pled guilty at court and each was sentenced to six months in prison.

Mrs Gillespie asked Johnston and McBurnie up for tea once the necessary repairs had been carried out. When they arrived she couldn't wait for them to tell her everything about the job.

Johnston described the excitement of waiting in the house for the intruders and about their delight in catching the neds 'On the job'. Mrs Gillespie was all ears and she said she would have loved to have been there and both detectives believed her...

She later wrote a nice letter to the Chief Constable asking him to pass on her regards to all the officers involved, but particularly D.I. McBurnie and D.C.I. Johnston.

When the correspondence eventually found its way to Johnston and McBurnie to note and sign, before it was returned to their personal files, Jimmy said. "This will go in my personal file but maybe you will get a commendation."

Johnston laughed and then said, "Cynic" which caused Jimmy to burst into laughter.

McBurnie put another tick in the 'friend' box...

He then met up with Delicate and provided another £300 in vouchers, paid for from the tout fund.

HORSES FOR COURSES

McBurnie and Johnston were now working well together. Regularly, they shared the shift briefings, and in private, some of their thoughts about certain senior officers. Jimmy was always guarded about what he said about them.

Being the D.I. he was still getting out and about meeting his stable of touts and getting information. Johnston meanwhile was becoming more and more office bound, dealing with the ever increasing amounts of administration, bureaucracy and what McBurnie saw as 'drivel', being foisted upon the C.I.D.

Jimmy was beginning to think he was glad he hadn't got the D.C.I.s job because he couldn't suffer being stuck behind a desk for most of the day. Having said this, had he got the position he was sure he would have tailored it to ensure he kept his touts, and he remained actively involved in getting the baddies off the street.

What happened next was to involve both Johnston and Jimmy becoming 'hands on' again, dealing with some real 'nasties'. This would give McBurnie another opportunity to assess Johnston's reliability and trustworthiness, and see if he deserved another mental tick in the 'friend' box...

Joseph Symington was a very private, fifty-five year old divorcee, of diminutive stature, slightly overweight, and with a receding hairline. He was father to a ten year old daughter, Samantha, whom he doted on. He had built up a small fortune in the oil and gas distribution businesses and just over a year earlier he bought 'The Laurels', a nineteenth century, six- bedroom mansion for an undisclosed sum, rumoured to be in excess of £1,000,000. The mansion had a long tree lined driveway and was set in eight acres of grounds on the outskirts of the village of Glenrigg.

When he moved in, he employed local tradesmen to complete an extensive refurbishment, thought by the locals who spoke to the tradesmen, to have cost a small fortune. This had set tongues wagging in the small village and it wasn't long before rumours were circulating that Symington must be a multi-millionaire.

Shortly after the renovations were complete he brought six Shetland ponies from his previous home near Stratshall and had a bespoke stable built for each of them. The ponies had been given as a gift to Samantha on each of her birthdays from age four to age ten. No expense was spared. Each stable had modern lighting, heating, hot and cold running water and each pony had its own bedding and blankets with their names embroidered on them.

Shetlands were both his and daughter's shared passion and he gave substantial donations to charities which re-homed these small horses, and to other organisations who cared for them.

After the divorce Samantha lived with her mother when she was not in a private boarding school. Symington did have visiting rights, but they didn't allow him to spend as much time as he would have liked with his daughter. When she visited, which was normally every third week-end, they both spent a great deal of their time with the ponies. Samantha had given each of the ponies a name. In their new stables the individual names were shown on a brass name plate above the stable door, together with a photograph of Samantha and her dad.

Most days he could be seen entering the stables and the adjoining fields, feeding and tending to these cute little animals, and obviously looking forward to Samantha's next visit. When he wasn't going to be at home he always made arrangements to have his friend, and retired farrier, Doug Murdoch, from Stratshall, come and feed them and check to see they were OK.

Locally, he was thought to be a bit of a recluse because there were never many comings or goings at the house. He hardly went into the village other than to pick up a newspaper or some milk from the local village shop. Even when he went to the shop, which was only a mile from 'The Laurels', he never walked, but always took his silver Mercedes car so that he could get in and out of the premises as quickly as possible.

Like most small communities, Glenrigg's residents were keen to know as much about an incomer like Symington as possible, especially one rumoured to be as wealthy as him. This proved difficult when they tried to engage him in conversation and found he confined it mostly to the weather. There was never a mention of any girlfriend or wife or of any other interest, and Symington certainly wasted no time on idle chit chat.

The only local person who went to his home on a regular basis was his cleaner, Sheila Campbell, who classed herself as his 'house keeper' not his cleaner. She was forty five years of age, born and bred in Glenrigg, and had gained the job through replying to an advert in the local newspaper.

Sheila was intensely proud to have this job which paid £3 per hour above the minimum wage, and to be working with someone of some standing. Her work place was now a mansion and a world away from the rest of the houses in Glenrigg.

She was divorced with two grown up sons who had left home to get work. Before the divorce she had been her husband's secretary, in what was a very profitable building business. Locally she was seen as a bit of a jumped up snob because she could always afford expensive clothes and holidays. She drove a nice car and loved to parade around the village with her nose in the air.

After the divorce, some three years previously, she had become depressed and let herself go a bit. For a woman who had enjoyed a wealthy lifestyle and then to be hit with a double whammy was almost too much to bear. Firstly, her husband's building firm was declared bankrupt and they had to sell their five- bedroom villa. Secondly, he left her for a younger woman who he been spending most of the business profits on.

Sheila was left without a job, no income, few prospects, and now living on her own in a council house in Glenrigg, among those she once looked down her nose at.

As a result, she rarely went out or socialised with anyone in the village. She still retained a certain pride in her appearance whenever she did leave the house, and could be seen by the Glenrigg residents. As a means of coping on her own, when money allowed it, she resorted to cheap drink, which she purchased at Stratshall, well away from local wagging tongues.

Thankfully, now with a job as 'house keeper', with Joseph Symington, she had a sense of purpose, self worth, and importantly, an income.

With the benefit of this income she could be found some nights in the only local village pub 'The Maze', as usual, always well dressed. After a few drinks, she took great delight in telling the regulars in the pub, who had been gossiping about her fall from grace, and her husband leaving her for a younger woman, about the fantastic mansion she worked in, as Mr Symington's 'personal assistant'.

She wasn't slow to let them know about the beautiful furnishings he had installed in his home, the four sports cars he kept in the old stable block, and his love of horses. Sheila boasted that her boss, although quiet was of a different class to them. He knew how to behave like a gentleman. Unlike them he had impeccable manners and treated her like a lady.

Privately she hoped her relationship with Symington could go beyond that of employer and employee, but he gave no indication this would change.

The more drink she consumed the more she told them you didn't become a millionaire by being silly with your money, and Mr Symington was certainly not silly with his. In fact she said he had the biggest wall safe she had ever seen mounted in his bedroom. She teased the locals by asking them how many millions did they think her boss had, because they, a band of no hoper's, could never achieve his success.

Her comments had not gone unnoticed...
A fairly recent incomer to the village by the name of Alfred (Alfie) Eastly who had a strong west country accent, wasn't slow to pick up on the details of Sheila's conversations.

Eastly, a twenty eight year old, very plausible, well dressed 'ned', had met a Glenrigg girl, Mary Armstrong, when she was working as a carer in Sunderland. She regularly drank in his local pub and not knowing many locals she was looking for company.

Alfie, did not have a local Wearside accent, was always well turned out and was a shrewd judge of character. In Mary he saw an opportunity for some free drink and maybe more. Accordingly, with his line of well rehearsed 'patter to flatter', he paid her many compliments. He confirmed he too was a relative newcomer to Sunderland, which he was, and also in need of friendship.

Mary was taken in by him and it wasn't long before he was getting her to buy him drink, always with the promise that he would pay her back. As expected this never happened and Mary in her naivety soon let Eastly into her life, her home, and they became an item.

She had always wanted to return to Glenrigg and through her sister she heard that a job was coming up at a care home in nearby Stratshall. She applied and got the job, and Eastly was only to pleased to move north with her. This move would get him away from the attention of the local bizzies(police)in Sunderland, who had their eyes on him when he arrived there the year before, and started associating with some well known local neds. He was in no doubt Mary, who was now besotted with him, would continue to supply him with a space in her bed, the use of her car, and money for a few drinks.

If an opportunity came up to get some extra cash by crime he would take it...

It wasn't surprising then, Eastly, who had become something of a regular at The Maze, since moving to Glenrigg, identified Sheila, like Mary, as naïve and vulnerable. Using money he got from Mary for drink, he started to buy Sheila a few drinks and as he had done with Mary he turned on the 'patter'. He was soon complimenting her on her appearance and quietly agreeing with her about the 'country cousins' who were The Maze patrons.

Before too long, and out with Mary's knowledge, he was going to Sheila's house armed with a bottle of gin, which was Sheila's favourite tipple. After a few drinks and more flattery he was soon in bed with her, even though at forty five she was seventeen years older than him.

With his criminal mind and cunning he wasn't slow to introduce questions into the conversation with Sheila about the mansion she worked in, and the comings and goings of its owner.

Sheila, especially when she had a few drinks, supplied all this information innocently. For her it was only conversation, and like Mary, she had fallen for the Eastly charm. He had asked her more than once if she truly believed that Symington was a multi millionaire. When she confirmed she did, and described how fantastic 'The Laurels' was, Eastly said surely Symington was paying her a good wage, with her being such a good 'personal assistant'.

Comments like these boosted her ego and she wasn't slow to confirm Mr Symington did give her bonuses and often told her how much he appreciated and trusted her. Alfie, buttering her up again, said he wasn't surprised when she was such a professional. This continued flattery did wonders for her feeling of self worth but also encouraged her to disclose more about her boss. Unwittingly, she was soon resplying to specific questions Alfie raised about Symington and where he kept his cash. Sheila responded innocently, confirming Mr Symington was not careless with his money and never left any lying about the house. Any monies he had she was sure, were always kept secure in his wall safe in his bedroom. She had never seen him open the safe in her presence but she was sure it contained plenty of money and high value, precious articles.

When Eastly asked her what her boss' hobbies were, she told him his only love other than his daughter was for horses, but she didn't state what kind of horses.

Eastly knew now he had identified an excellent target in Symington for a robbery, and in Sheila an unwitting source of information. He was shrewd enough to know he could not get to Symington on his own. He would need assistance and a well thought out plan...

He contacted Dale Lochans, a thirty two year old career criminal from Sunderland who was built like a brick shit house and had a well earned reputation for violence, but not brilliance. Alfie had befriended Lochans about four months before meeting Mary. They had worked together on a couple of break-ins in Sunderland, not long after Lochans completed a five year sentence for armed robbery.

Eastly returned to Sunderland in Mary's beaten up Ford Escort to tell Lochans about Symington and his wealth. He told his potential partner in crime he now knew all about this wealthy guy's movements, and the distinct possibility he would have a lot of cash in the house, which they could easily get their hands on.

To impress Lochans, which wasn't difficult, he explained to be successful in getting the cash they would need a well thought out plan. He said he had already given it all his attention and smugly said 'failing to plan' equated to 'planning to fail'. These comments went right over Lochans head, all he wanted to hear was the plan and when they could get their hands on this wealthy guy's cash.

Alfie told him his plan…

Firstly, they would go to 'The Laurels' when they knew Symington was home alone. That part would be easy because Sheila would unwittingly give him this information.

Secondly, they would need some disguises to appear legitimate when they were approaching The Laurels front door. This shouldn't be too difficult because Alfie said he knew some of the punters in the Maze Pub were road workers from the north of Scotland. They were doing contract work on the roads and the motorway near Stratshall. Quite often they would be in the pub, still wearing their fluorescent jackets complete with company logo, having a pint, before they went to their digs in two rented cottages in Glenrigg.

He said he knew the workers had a portacabin situated next to the motorway, where they stored their work gear. It would be easy to break-in to the portacabin and nick a couple of jackets and safety helmets and they could then use them as their disguises. The jackets had huge pockets, suitable for them to stash a couple of stocking masks, some rope and some strong tape in. The skips on the helmets were long and they could be pulled down a bit to hide their faces.

Thirdly, once they had their disguises they would both go to the mansion posing as legitimate road workers, with the stocking masks on top of their heads, but underneath their safety helmets. Eastly said he would hide a knife in one pocket and he told Lochans he could easily hide a baseball bat underneath the bulky fluorescent jacket. This brought a smile to Lochans' face...

Fourthly, when Symington opened the door they would quickly remove their helmets and pull the stocking masks over their faces. Then they would jump him and rough him up with a few slaps and threaten him with the knife and bat. If need be they would tie him up and beat him until he disclosed the combination for the safe which Alfie knew Symington had in his bedroom.

Fifthly, they would need transport to do this job and they would have to ensure the transport couldn't be traced back to them. Alfie said he had already thought about this and had arranged for Jacko Quinn, another ned, who lived in North Shields, who he and Lochans both knew, to go to a van auction market in Newcastle and purchase a white van, using a false name and false identity. He told Lochans they wouldn't tell Jacko what they needed the van for and he wouldn't ask. Eastly confirmed Jacko didn't have a police record and it would be hard for the cops to identify him as the purchaser of the van, if in fact the van could ever be tied back to the job.

He said they wouldn't take any chances with the van being connected to them and arrangements would be made to put it through a crusher when they were finished with it. Then there would be no chance of any forensic evidence being recovered.

Lochans just nodded in agreement with everything said by

Alfie. To be honest he could hardly take all this in but Ea.. was still in full flow and carried on describing his plan.

He told Lochans they would need £500 to buy a van but he had that covered as well. Mary would give him the cash from her savings, after he made up a story about needing the money for funeral costs for his recently deceased uncle in South Shields.

Lochans was totally impressed, in fact he was in awe of Alfie. He said he was keen to get involved and get his hands on the cash, which Eastly said they would split 50-50, after a retainer had been paid to Jacko.

Eastly then returned to Glenrigg in the knowledge he now had a suitable, if somewhat naïve accomplice who would become expendable if Alfie's liberty was at stake...

Two days later he got the cash from Mary. Shortly thereafter a phone call from Jacko confirmed he had bought an ex council, white coloured, Ford van, for £450 using 'duff' identity. In reality he had got it for £400 but he was sure Alfie, as he called Eastly, wouldn't twig he had skimmed the extra £50 for himself...

Eastly, was nothing if not thorough and when he next met with Lochans he explained he also had a Plan 'B'...

If the safe contained nothing of value or if Symington refused to open it, then they needed an alternative plan.

This was his plan 'B'...

He said Symington must have money somewhere if he owned a

...sion like The Laurels, a Mercedes and four sports cars. He probably wouldn't want to give his money over easily. If it took longer than they thought to get the cash from him or he refused to open his safe, they might have to get him away from the house to 'work' on him.

Alfie said if this was the case, even after they had beaten him, they would tie him up and gag him. Then they would put him in the boot of his own Merc and take him, and his up market car, away from The Laurels to a hidden location, where they could work on him.

Alfie told his accomplice with Symington being a bit of a recluse nobody would notice he was missing for a while. If he and his car disappeared at the same time who would think anything untoward had happened to him?

Eastly confirmed he had already identified an ideal cottage for rent in Hillgate, a rural village thirty miles from Stratshall and they could take Symington there.

He had found the cottage when checking the local papers. When he went for a look around he saw it was secluded and had a barn beside it, big enough to conceal Symington's Merc, a van and at least another car. He told Lochans once they got Syminton inside the cottage, if necessary they could work on him, if need be drug him, and pressurise him into telling them where all his money was kept.

Lochans was bowled over with Alfie's attention to detail and told him he couldn't wait to get on the 'job'. Alfie reined in his enthusiasm by telling him nothing would happen till they carried out a 'recce' at The Laurels to confirm what Sheila said about the mansion and Symington...

Now they needed to rent the cottage in Hillgate but Alfie said he had this in hand.

Eastly told Lochans he had spoken to Joe Blyth from Jarrow, a guy he trusted to keep his mouth shut. He was getting the van from Jacko and would drive it north to a service station twenty-five miles from Newholm. Joe would ask no questions and would just be happy to get the £200 Alfie had 'borrowed' from Mary. After it was delivered he told Lochans he would go and get it at the service station and bring it to the cottage.

Lochans said "You have thought of everything" and Alfie being his cocky self said, "Probably." To further impress his acomplice he said by getting one guy to buy the van at auction with false identity and another to drive it to a service station, it would further distance the van from any connection with them. The other reassurance was once they were finished with the van it would go through a crusher. If and when the police came to investigate Symington and his money's disappearance, they would have difficulty finding anything out about the van or connect it to them.

On hearing these words of wisdom Lochans grinning from ear to ear...

He maybe would not have been grinning if Eastly had told him they might have to keep Symington for quite a while to get all his cash. If it wasn't in the house, it was most likely held in different banks and financial institutions and it would take time to get at it.

He did not disclose to Lochans, once they got Symington's cash they might have to make his disappearance permanent...

Lochan's now couldn't stop thinking about the money he could get from this job and was rubbing his hands. On Eastly's instruction, he not Alfie, met the farmer who was renting out the cottage.

After a very short conversation he paid a months rent in advance, in cash. He supplied a false name and told the farmer he didn't want disturbed when he was at the cottage. He just wanted time on his own to get away from his wife, who was seeking a divorce.

Once he had the key to the cottage he picked up the van, hid it in the barn, and moved in. He then phoned Alfie and said everything was going to plan. Alfie said, "That's great, but make sure you keep the curtains drawn and don't answer the door." Lochans confirmed he understood by saying, "OK boss."

That night Eastly went to the road workers portacabin. There was no added security at the cabin and the front door was only protected by a hasp and padlock. It was easy for him to unscrew the plate holding the hasp and padlock and get in. He had a torch with him and he soon found one cupboard, containing safety helmets, and another containing fluorescent jackets. He helped himself to two of each and made his way quickly out of the portacabin. Before leaving he screwed the retaining plate back into position so there would be little evidence a break-in had occurred.

After ten days of reconnaissance by the two neds, Alfie decided the time was right to attack Symington. Naive Sheila had confirmed on Tuesday's Mr Symington always wanted her in and out of the house as quickly as possible. He told her Tuesday was his busiest day. He needed time on his own then to conduct his business from the house, using his computer and making confidential calls from his study.

Today was Tuesday and Eastly had made sure Symington's silver Mercedes was in the driveway at the front door of the mansion, confirming what Sheila had said, Symington was at home...

Sheila completed her work at 11 am. as usual for a Tuesday. When she arrived home Eastly, who now had a key for her house, was waiting for her. Through general conversation with her he got further confirmation Symington would be at home, working for most of the day. He then told her he would be out of the village for a few days attending to his uncle's funeral in the north east of England and Sheila accepted this without question.

At 12.30.pm. he borrowed Mary's car, drove to the cottage at Hillgate and picked up Lochans. They got the van out of the barn, put Mary's car in it and covered it with a tarpaulin.

Both then set off for Symington's mansion...

Before entering the driveway they put on their fluorescent jackets, pulled their stocking masks on top of their heads, under their safety helmets, and drove the van towards the house. At the top of the driveway they veered left and parked the van against the converted stable, housing Symington's sports cars. Prior to leaving the van Eastly got a knife from under the drivers seat and Lochans got his baseball bat from under the passenger seat. They concealed their weapons under their jackets and put some rope, tape and a blindfold, they brought with them, in their jacket pockets. After checking that nothing was showing beneath their jackets, they pulled the skips of their hats down over their eyes and made their way to the front door of the mansion...

Eastly rang the old fashioned bell attached to the large mahogany front door frame, and after some time they could hear Symington approaching the door from the inside. Before opening the door he shouted out asking who was there. Eastly said they were employees of the road construction firm working in the area. They wanted to inform him about some work they would be completing near to the entrance to The Laurels which may cause some inconvenience.

Symington looked through his spyhole in the door and seeing the hats, and the fluorescent jackets with the company logo, thought no more about it. He began to open the door and by this time Eastly and Lochans had pulled down the stocking masks they had on top of their heads.

When the door was fully opened, Lochans punched Symington full in the face, knocking him to the ground. Then Eastly, kicked him on the head and told him to "fucking shut up." They then dragged him behind the front door and closed it.

Lochans tied Symington's hands behind his back and rapped him over the legs with the baseball bat. He and Eastly then dragged their victim away from the door, in the process knocking over a vase which was on a small table, and asked him where his money was. He said nothing and received another crack, this time along the ribs from Lochan's baseball bat and another punch from Eastly, which produced a spray of blood from his nose.

Eastly then produced his sharp knife and held it against Symington's throat and asked him if he had a safe. This time their victim saw little point in non-compliance and told them he had a wall safe in his bedroom on the first floor. Limping badly, he led the way and showed them where the wall mounted combination safe was. Eastly then demanded the combination and Symington, regaining some bravery, told them to, "Fuck Off." This brought a quick response from his two assailants. Eastly punched him in the face again, breaking his nose and Lochans cracked him across the legs again with the baseball bat.

Symington now in a lot of pain, decided he would disclose the combination and Eastly was quick to open the safe. Inside were some business papers and approximately £1000 in cash. Symington said that was all the money he had in the house and all his other money was invested.

Eastly then took the £1000 and asked Symington where the keys for his Mercedes were and he replied they were in his trouser pocket. Eastly, retrieved the key and instructed Lochans to gag their victim using the tape they had and to tie his legs together above and below the knees. Once Symington was bound, gagged and blindfolded, Eastly left the mansion with the car keys and brought the Mercedes right opposite the front door. He then got the van and parked it next to the Mercedes.

They then carried Symington out of the mansion and put him into the back of the van. Eastly drove the Mercedes followed by Lochans in the van and in convoy they made their way to the cottage at Hillgate. On arrival at this remote location they quickly carried Symington out of the van and into the cottage. Lochans then hid the van and the Mercedes adjacent to Mary's Ford Escort in the barn, under some polythene silage wrapping that had been left there.

Eastly told his accomplice Mary's escort would need to be well hidden. He had informed her he was only using it to go to a funeral in South Shields and would be back in two or three days. Lochans confirmed the escort was now well covered, and he would take the van back to the same service station it had been left at by Joe Blyth, when Eastly was returning Mary' car. Alfie nodded and told him Blyth had already been paid to return and pick up the van and he would put it through the crusher in either Sunderland or Newcastle..

Once the cottage was secured from the inside and the curtains drawn they began threatening and beating Symington again, demanding he tell them where his cash was.

By now this poor man feared for his life...

If he needed any further encouragement to disclose these details, it came when Eastly ran the knife along his throat, causing a superficial cut but also a loss of blood which led to significant staining to Symington's shirt.

On feeling the blood seeping through his shirt their victim told them he had £100,000 in an account in a named bank in Stratshall but all his other money was tied up in investments.

This was music to their ears and it earned Symington a couple of sandwiches and a cup of tea laced with temazepam...

The next day the two neds got Symington rallied round. After slapping him about a bit and threatening him with the knife again, they told him he was going to phone the manager of his bank in Stratshall. When Symington asked what he was to say, he was instructed to tell the manager he needed £50,000 in cash to buy a race horse, and he wanted the money transferred to the Leeds branch of the bank.

When he phoned the manager, Mr Cowan asked Symington how he was and what could he do for him. A somewhat nervous Symington said, as he had been instructed, he needed £50,000 urgently to buy a racehorse. In keeping with the story Eastly had devised for him, he told Cowan he knew a trainer who was planning to sell a horse at the yearling sales in Doncaster. This trainer had agreed not to put the horse through the sale ring if he got cash for it. A meeting had now been arranged with him at a hotel near Doncaster to hand over the cash.

Unknown to Eastly and Lochans the bank manager was a close friend of Symington's. When he took the call from him asking for the money to be transferred he knew there was something not quite right. Symington had often told him about his revulsion at what he saw as the cruelty of horse racing.

Cowan knew there was no way he would ever contemplate buying a racehorse...

As a result of his suspicions he tried to keep Symington talking, without success. He did manage to tell him it would take at least two days to get this sum of money transferred. He asked him to phone back at 10 am the next morning and he would up date him on what he needed to show to the Leeds bank staff to identify himself, and when the money would be ready for collection.

After the call ended Eastly slapped Symington on the head and said "Well done, for now."

Cowan, was also Jimmy's bank manager and a good contact of his. He decided to phone him. He then told McBurnie he was really suspicious about Symington's request for this amount of money, especially when Symington said he needed it to buy a racehorse. McBurnie didn't waste any time getting to the bank and was briefed on Joseph Symington's telephone conversation by Cowan. By now he shared the same suspicion as the bank manager.

Something wasn't right...

Jimmy being Jimmy decided to travel to Glenrigg and The Laurels. After getting no reply at the mansion he called at the local shop and asked the shopkeeper what he knew about Joseph Symington, and asked if he had seen him recently. The shopkeeper confirmed the owner of The Laurels kept himself to himself. The only real contact he had with people in Glenrigg was with his house keeper, Sheila Campbell.

Not long after leaving the shop, Jimmy was at Sheila's house following directions from the shop keeper...

Sheila was shocked when McBurnie produced his warrant card and told her he wanted to ask her questions about her employer Mr Joseph Symington.

She asked him to come in and he didn't waste any time telling her he had real concerns over her boss' well being. She was surprised to hear this but she confirmed she had attended at The

Laurels that morning and got no reply. She told Jimmy she didn't normally have a key for the mansion but if Mr Symington was going to be away for any length of time he would leave a key with her. On this occasion he hadn't left a key and she found this a wee bit strange.

She told McBurnie she had seen her boss the day before and as normal on a Tuesday she had to have her work completed by 11 am. When she had called round this morning at 8 am she got no response and noticed Mr Symington's silver Mercedes car was missing. Her boss hadn't told her he planned to be away anywhere on the Wednesday but she just thought it must have slipped his mind. She said she felt everything would be all right and Mr Symington would contact her during the remainder of the day, but he hadn't so far.

The D.I.s really suspicious now and he telephoned Cowan and told him he would be at the bank, with him, first thing in the morning.

He now needed a closer look at Symington's mansion...

Fortunately there was a porch window to the side of the front door. Jimmy climbed onto the window sill and looked through the window. He could see what looked like blood splattered on the floor behind the front door, a broken vase which had been sitting on a small table, and a trail of what looked like blood leading away from the rear of the door. There was no doubt in McBurnie's mind there had been a struggle there.

He telephoned D.C.I. Johnston, told him what he had seen and asked him to join him at The Laurels. When he arrived they agreed they would need to get access to the house urgently. There was little doubt in either of their minds, Symington was the victim of something sinister. The apparent blood splattering behind the door, the broken vase, the trail of what looked like blood, were all signs of a struggle. They needed to get into the mansion in case Mr Symington was lying dead or injured.

Johnston decided to get a Crime Scene Manager and a Scenes of Crime Officer to attend.

Before forcing entry by a side door, they got suited up into protective clothing, to avoid cross contamination and to keep the house sterile, prior to a full forensic examination. They then went through the house, room by room, following the advice and guidance of the trained Crime Scene Manager. There was a trail of blood leading from the rear of the front door all the way up the stairs to a large bedroom where there was a large combination wall safe, which was secure.

The house was then fully searched but there was no sign of Mr Symington.

Jimmy's boss then decided they would secure the house now they were sure Joseph Symington wasn't there. Trained officers would keep it under surveillance in case anyone, including Mr Symington, turned up and before the house could be fully forensically examined.

Once back in the office Jimmy told his boss he planned to be at the bank the next morning before Symington phoned. He would stay with the manager when Symington called and brief Mr Cowan on what to say.

Johnston said meanwhile he would have a team carry out enquiries in Glenrigg to find out all they could about Joseph Symington, and if anyone had seen him or heard from him.

Johnston could see his D.I. was excited and so was he. Johnston stressed to him to keep him up to date with what happened at the bank.

Jimmy left the office in a hurry and headed to the control room where he completed a missing person form, officially registering Joseph Symington as a missing person. He spoke to the sergeant in charge of the control room, passed the details of Symington's Mercedes to him, and instructed him to log it on the Police National Computer (P.N.C.). McBurnie told the sergeant to put a 'Flag' against the entry, ensuring any sightings of the vehicle would be notified to him.

It was late when McBurnie got home that night.

He was very worried now about what had become of Joseph Symington and convinced he would soon be investigating another serious crime...

During his conversation with Doris all he could think about was Joseph Symington's disappearance. He never used to say much about his investigations to her. This time she could see his mind was in overdrive and she couldn't get his attention. She gave up and went to bed early. When he went to bed he tossed and turned, going over and over in his mind all the possibilities to account for Symington's disappearance and how he would address them.

He couldn't wait for daylight to come and when the bank

opened at 9am he was the first member of the public in the door. He was ushered straight through to Cowan's office. Now he had plenty time to brief the bank manager on how to respond to Symington's call at 10.am.

His strategy was to write out a series of 'Q' cards with pertinent questions for Cowan to put to Symington. These questions were aimed at gathering as much information as possible about Symington, without alerting him or anyone listening to the call, about their suspicions. The questions were constructed to make sure Jimmy would know, in advance, exactly when Symington was due to arrive in Leeds. They would also confirm Symington wanted the money transferred for the purchase of a 'race horse'.

A very nervous Cowan was almost shaking with excitement when, at bang on 10 am Symington phoned. Jimmy immediately started showing Cowan the Q cards they had previously discussed, with their individual questions. Cowan reiterated word for word what was said on the cards to Symington.

On one of the cards Jimmy had completed, Cowan was asked to stress to Symington he would have to appear at the bank in Leeds, in person and provide proof of his identity. This factor was of paramount consideration for McBurnie as he knew if Symington had to appear at Leeds then he would have to be alive!

By the end of the conversation Jimmy knew Symington had confirmed the money he wanted transferred was to buy a race horse. He also knew Symington would be in Leeds the following day, travelling in his silver Mercedes and attending at the bank at 2pm. to collect the £50,000.

Cowan had followed Jimmy's instruction and questions on the

cards, to the letter and Cowan, following Jimmy's instruction, told Symington when he arrived at the bank in Leeds to ask for Mr Harley the bank manager. He was the person who would ensure the transfer of the cash and he would check Symington's identity.

Jimmy thanked Cowan for his assistance and swore him to secrecy but with a promise he would keep him updated on progress. By the time McBurnie left the office, Cowan was mentally exhausted but felt he was now a quasi detective. He was now experiencing the same adrenalin rush Jimmy and other detectives were so used to.

McBurnie raced back to the office and briefed Johnston.

The new D.C.I. was getting as excited as his D.I. Both were convinced Joseph Symington had been abducted and his abductor(s) were now trying to extort money from him.

Johnston said he would contact the Police in Leeds and have the bank put under surveillance, backed up by firearms and hostage negotiation teams. He told McBurnie he might need some clout to get the Yorkshire cops' assistance, because at this stage they had no real proof about the abduction, only very strong suspicion.

He left his D.I.and briefed D.C.C. Cobble. The Deputy was all ears and after he was briefed was as excited as his two detectives and shared their suspicion. He contacted an old friend, A.C.C. Harrower, in Leeds and explained the situation in detail to him. Being an old detective, as he always put it, he stressed to the A.C.C. how he feared, not just for the safety of Symington, but if their suspicions were founded, there could be a real threat to the public from dangerous criminals.

The A.C.C. was only too willing to help his old friend and confirmed his firearms, surveillance and hostage negotiation teams would be duly authorised and in place, once he had written confirmation of what Cobble had just told him.

Cobble assured him he would have it within the hour.

Harrower was now getting a 'rush' as well and before their conversation finished he asked Cobble when the officers leading the investigation would be in Leeds to brief his teams.

Cobble confirmed both the D.C.I. and D.I. would be there later in the day and would provide a full and comprehensive briefing. The D.C.C. then phoned Johnston and told him to get to Leeds post haste and to ensure McBurnie went with him.

Jimmy had just time to get home to Doris, collect some fresh clothes and tell her he would be away for a few days on the 'Symington' investigation. Doris was used to Jimmy disappearing at short notice and as always, had an overnight bag and fresh suit waiting for him.

The two Scottish detectives headed south, arriving in Leeds at 11.pm. at a hotel their English colleagues had booked for them. After another sleepless night and an 'adrenaline' charged breakfast, both were in the main police station in Leeds at 8am briefing the A.C.C. the firearms, surveillance and hostage negotiation teams.

The bank was now going to be totally surrounded and all it needed was Symington and whoever was with him to turn up...

While they were waiting McBurnie and Johnston kept in touch with their troops in Scotland by telephone for any updates at their end.

Green did phone confirming his team had carried out all their enquiries in Glenrigg which corroborated what Jimmy already knew. Symington was a loner and his only local contact appeared to be Sheila Campbell.

The D.S. being the thorough individual he was, told McBurnie he had found Campbell liked a drink and attended the only pub in Glenrigg on a fairly regular basis. Once she had a few drinks she started taunting the locals about how wealthy her new boss was, telling them all he was at least a multi millionaire. With this information, Green, using his own initiative, had interviewed Sheila again and sheepishly she confirmed this story.

He was also able to get out of her she had a semi-regular boyfriend called Alfred Eastly, who had recently moved into the area and who she had met in The Maze pub.

Green said he had checked Eastly on the police computer with the limited details that Sheila could provide, but all the checks came came back 'no trace' showing Eastly appeared to have no previous convictions.

Jimmy then told Green to get a search warrant authorised for The Laurels. McBurnie knew time was of the essence. He didn't want to lose any opportunity to carry out a detailed scenes of crime examination of the property but under the auspices of a warrant.

He told Green everything was in place in Leeds and the

Yorkshire firearms, surveillance and negotiator teams were set to go.

This all changed at 12.30.pm when Jimmy got another call from Green...

The D.S. could hardly speak, he was so excited by what he had to tell Jimmy. McBurnie could sense his excitement and said "Calm down, speak slowly." Green relayed the following story;

Symington's Mercedes had been sighted a short time ago in Newholm but it wasn't Symington behind the wheel. It turned out the driver was a guy with a 'Geordie' accent. He tried to run two cops down before he was stopped by a cop with a panda car, which he rammed, but which still managed to block the road. Five cops were quick on the scene but they had to smash the drivers window to get this guy out and he put up a real struggle before he was batoned, handcuffed and arrested. Two of the cops were now in hospital, one with a broken nose the other with two broken ribs.

Jimmy was taken aback but even more frustrated he hadn't been in Newholm at the time.

He became even more so when Green told him when the cops tried to stop the Mercedes, an old Ford Escort, which appeared to have been in convoy with it, drove off at speed and managed to get away. It was a man who was driving the Escort and he appeared to be on his own. The car number had been noted and put on the P.N.C. and cops throughout the country were looking for it.

Green said the owner of the Escort was shown on the computer as Mary Armstrong, from an address in Glenrigg, and Green said he already had a team of officers heading to that address...

Jimmy then asked if Symington was in the Mercedes but Green said it was only the guy with the Geordie accent. He was now refusing to provide any details about his identity or who was driving the other car. He had been arrested on charges of attempting to murder two cops and taken to Newholm Police Station.

To say Jimmy was agitated would be an understatement. All the action was in Newholm and he and Johnston were stuck in Leeds!

Once he came off the phone he briefed Johnston, who thought for a minute and then said they would still wait in Leeds and see if Symington turned up at the bank.

McBurnie was now pacing up and down the floor of the observation point they were in. Totally mad he was missing the action.

About an hour later Green phoned him again and provided him with a truly astonishing account of what had taken place since his last call...

A local P.C. named Jake Millar, had seen Mary Armstrong's Ford Escort heading south about ten miles from the village of Hillgate and had chased it in his panda car. He had put on his blue lights and signalled for it to pull over but the driver of the escort ignored him and drove off at speed.

Jake was a no nonsense cop, not used to non compliance, and pursued it. After a chase of about five miles, at high speed, the escort was driven up a single track farm road. Jake apparently knew the layout of the farm and the farmer. He was well aware the only way out of the farm by vehicle was down the one track road which he had blocked with his panda car.

Millar had then contacted the control room to let them know he had the escort boxed in and asked them to send assistance.

Before other cops could arrive, Jake saw the farmers Volvo heading towards him from the farm. He got out of the car and stood in the middle of the road. The driver of the Volvo, who wasn't the farmer, got out of it, walked round to the passenger door and pulled out a man who had been in the foot-well. He was blindfolded, had his hands tied behind his back and his mouth was taped over.

Once the driver had hold of this man he went into his pocket and brought out a needle and syringe and shouted to Jake to move the panda. If he didn't then he told Jake his passenger was getting 'fucking' injected with poison from the syringe.

Jake, like Jimmy, was a product of the shipyards and was built like a tank. He had a well deserved reputation in his local community as a cop not to be messed with. He told the guy with the syringe to drop it and release the blindfolded guy or he would baton the 'fucking' life out of him.

There was a stand-off for a while, with insults and threats being thrown backwards and forwards. Then the bad guy, seeing Jake with his baton drawn and walking towards him, knew this cop was serious. His bottle crashed he dropped the syringe and released his captive.

Jake then got hold of the abductor by the neck, pushed him face down on the ground and told him not to 'fucking' move. He then put his foot on his back, produced his handcuffs and cuffed him with his hands behind the back.

Millar then untied the victim and removed the tape that was covering his mouth. His first words were, "Thank God! You have saved my life, he was going to kill me."

Jake asked him his name and he said Joseph Symington then he burst into tears and started shaking uncontrollably.

Millar then apparently turned to his custody and said "What's your name arsehole?" and got no reply.

If the cavalry in the form of police back up, hadn't appeared at this time then Green was sure this guy would be telling Jake his name and his life history. Instead he was arrested and taken to Newholm Police Station, while his victim was removed to the local hospital.

On hearing this information Jimmy told Green to detain both Mary Armstrong and Sheila Campbell and take them to Newholm Police Station.

He then told Johnston their suspicions had been right all along, Symington had been abducted. He relayed the story Green had told him and after hearing this Johnston phoned Green. He instructed him, no one was to interview the two men who had been in convoy and had abducted Symington until he and Jimmy returned from Leeds. Once they got to Newholm he said they would conduct the interviews with these bastards.

Jimmy heard Johnston's instruction to Green and put another mental tick in his 'friend' box...

Johnston then briefed A.C.C. Harrower and his teams and told them their assistance would no longer be required. They were disappointed there was to be no action on their patch but understood why. Johnston thanked them for all their support and professionalism.

Harrower then offered the services of a high speed traffic car and driver to take them back to Newholm and this was gladly accepted.

Before long Johnston and Jimmy were heading north at 137 mph, with Jimmy telling the driver to put his foot down!

When they arrived at Newholm, McBurnie and Johnston made their way rapidly to the C.I.D. office, without taking time to thank the English driver who risked his life to get them there a.s.a.p.

D.S. Green was waiting for them and Johnston ushered him and Jimmy into his office. Johnston asked Green for a quick but detailed update on the current position...

The D.S. was able to confirm both men, had now given their names as Alfred Eastly and Dale Lochans and were in two separate cells downstairs. Sheila Campbell and Mary Armstrong were also detained and in separate cells.

Joseph Symington had been seen by a doctor at the hospital who said he was in no state to be interviewed at this time. He was now being treated for shock, two broken ribs, a broken nose and facial bruising. Green said he had arranged for a trained victim liaison police officer to stay with him. Victim Support had also been notified, but told they would have to wait some time for clearance from the Police, before they could speak to Mr Symington.

Green as expected had used his guile and made sure that both Sheila Campbell and Mary Armstrong knew they had been 'used' by Eastly.

The D.C.I. was as impressed with Green's thoroughness as Jimmy. He told him to get his team of interviewers together, interview both women under caution and impress upon them, just how difficult a position they were in, and they could be charged with conspiracy.

Green headed for the cells leaving the D.C.I. and D.I. alone.

Johnston wasn't daft and knew this was going to be a high profile and High Court case. The result of any slip-ups in the investigation could end up at his and Jimmy's doors.

Consequently, he told Jimmy to interview Eastly who had threatened Symington with the needle and syringe, while he interviewed Lochans who had been driving Symington's Mercedes.

Jimmy relished the opportunity, but as with all serious crimes he dealt with, he always wondered what type of bastards commit these crimes. Being the sceptic he was he hadn't much faith in criminal profilers and didn't believe these neds fitted any stereotype. For him they were all different and many outwardly, appeared perfectly normal...

Before he went to interview Eastly he reflected on his last High Court case, which was the trial of his tout Tommy Stevenson (Hasty Lad) for the murder of Mr Jim Cahill. This was the first time he was the reporting officer when the murderer was one of his touts...

Initially he had mixed emotions about giving evidence which would put his tout away for a long time, but these didn't last too long. The more he thought about how violently Stevenson had murdered this old gentlemen, then there was no doubt he deserved to be put away for life. When he was younger, Jim Cahill had been a well built, 6'2" tall, heavy weight boxer who had represented Scotland as an amateur. Jimmy knew Stevenson wouldn't have attacked him then but it was a different story when he was eighty two years of age and very frail.

Stevenson looked a normal guy. In fact being the product of a Scottish mother and Scandinavian father, he was quite handsome, and with his blue eyes and blond hair a lot of women found him attractive.

McBurnie now knew these features masked what was a truly violent individual, who even when he had been arrested and remanded in custody had continued to use extreme violence.

While in prison another inmate, learning of Stevenson's victim age, decided to teach him a lesson by throwing a cup of boiling water over him. This did result in a nasty scald mark along Stevenson's face but the inmate who inflicted the injury had no idea what awaited him.

A prison officer who Jimmy knew, told him, about two weeks

after this incident, the inmate who inflicted this injury was now in a worse condition than Stevenson, after he was attacked by him. He suffered two broken cheeks, the loss of an eye, a broken nose and five teeth were knocked out. Stevenson had hit him repeatedly across the face with a sock containing two pool balls which he had stolen from the recreation area within the jail.

Neither Stevenson or the other inmate made any complaint of either assault to the prison staff or the police.

McBurnie had thought he knew quite a bit about his tout before this and would never have predicted he would commit such a brutal murder. The closer he analysed his behaviour and what he knew of Eastly's, he had to admit there were indeed some common denominators...

Both had targeted weak and vulnerable individuals.

Both had planned their crimes in great detail.

Both used extreme violence.

With these thoughts in his mind he headed for the cells to get Eastly. On the way there he asked himself, "Why the hell is it me whose dealing with these arseholes and why am I getting such a buzz from it?"

Then he thought perhaps he wasn't normal either?

Wisely, he didn't dwell on this, but put his mind to identifying a suitable corroborating officer to interview Eastly with him.

At the time of the Stevenson investigation Jimmy had vowed to all the investigation team at the start of the enquiry they would get the 'bastards' responsible. Nobody bought into this more than D.C. Starkey. As a result Jimmy used him as his corroborating officer when he interviewed Stevenson.

The case had been as watertight as it could be. Starkey had learned a lot from Jimmy about case preparation and doing all your homework before you go to trial.

During the trial both Jimmy and Starkey received a torrid time from the Q.C. representing Tommy Stevenson.

Initially Starkey had been blasé about appearing in the High Court but after five hours in the witness box being cross examined, this cockiness left him. It was then he was thankful he had followed Jimmy's advice and accompanied him on their 'homework' meetings before the trial.

All in all Jimmy felt Starkey had stood up to his ordeal quite well. Like Jimmy he was relieved when Stevenson was found guilty of murder and sentenced to eighteen years imprisonment.

Jimmy now acknowledged he was a suitable 'apprentice' and he would corroborate the interview with Eastly...

Starkey was pleased when Jimmy told him to accompany him to the cells, and even more pleased when he was told he would be Jimmy's corroborating officer. He was sure not to be cocky this time because he knew now what to expect. The stories Jimmy had told him about the witness box being the loneliest place in the world, the sweat that would run down your back during interrogation by a smart arse Q.C. and how you would never be constipated, before, and during the trial, were all true.

Jimmy made his way to the cell area with his young colleague, identified himself and brought Eastly out of his cell.

Eastly certainly did not fit any stereotype. In McBurnie's mind he just looked 'normal, but then again so did Stevenson. He was reasonably well dressed, almost 6' in height with a slim build and he had a neat haircut. McBurnie thought if he had been wearing a suit you could almost have taken him for a respectable businessman. On the way to the interview room Eastly started calling Jimmy, 'Sir' and walked behind him in a subservient manner, followed by Starkey.

To McBurnie, Eastly's actions and language were of a guy who had spent some time in prison. This did not correspond to the details he had supplied to Green and recorded on his arrest sheet, showing he had no previous convictions.

Before starting the taped interview Jimmy went through these details with Eastly. He asked him if they were correct because he didn't believe they were.

Eastly looked Jimmy in the eye and after a pause asked to speak to him on his own. This was a bit unethical but Jimmy knew sometimes rules have to be bent, so he asked Starkey to leave the interview room.

After he had gone Eastly said before the interview began Jimmy should phone a Peter Black, a senior investigator in Customs and Excise. When Jimmy asked why, Eastly said everything would become clearer after the phone call and provided the telephone number for Black.

Jimmy summoned Starkey and a custody officer into the tape recording room and told them to stay with Eastly but not to engage in conversation with him.

After checking the number given to him by Eastly and confirming it did belong to Customs and Excise he phoned and asked to speak to Peter Black.

Black was eventually located and Jimmy told him he had a guy called Alfred Eastly in custody, charged with abduction, attempted extortion and serious assault.

There was a sharp intake of breath from Black, and after a considerable pause, he asked Jimmy to go to a secure line, then phone him back with the number, and he in turn would phone Jimmy.

McBurnie did as requested and when he spoke to Black this time the Customs' man asked him what the strength of the evidence was against Eastly. McBurnie didn't go into detail but told him Eastly would be going 'away' for a while.

There was another long pause...

Black then said Eastly, as Jimmy had suspected, was not the man's real name. He was in fact Reginald (Reggie)Corberry and Black provided his real date of birth...

Black then stated, what he said next was a bit embarrassing, but Jimmy needed to hear it and it should go no further. Jimmy told him to carry on. He said...

Corberry had fairly recently completed two years of an eight year sentence in Spain after being convicted of drugs importation. As McBurnie had suspected he did have a long list of convictions for violence, dishonesty and drugs.

While in prison in Spain, he shared a cell in a wing occupied by British prisoners, who were also there convicted of drugs offences. Security at the prison was so poor they were still conducting their drug business from inside.

Corberry had no difficulty being accepted by these inmates because, like most of them he was locked up for drug importation. Being in police parlance a 'percentage man' he was looking for something to negotiate his way out of jail. Consequently, he started noting everything said on the wing, and built up quite an 'intelligence' portfolio on his other inmates activities. When he was ready to trade, he requested a meeting with the prison governor. At the meeting he asked to be put in contact with British Customs and Excise and their Spanish counterparts.

Reluctantly the governor agreed, and it wasn't long before Corberry was supplying details from his intelligence portfolio, in return for a guaranteed early release and a new identity

The information he supplied was top grade and a whole network of drug distribution between Morocco, Spain and Britain was unearthed. The main dealers on the 'inside' and the 'outside' were arrested. His information resulted in further hefty sentences for some of Corberry's fellow inmates and their associates.

The inmates conducted their own internal investigation to find out who the 'grass' was. They were not long unearthing Corberry as the snout, but before they could get their hands on him he was moved to another jail. That didn't stop them putting a 'contract' on his life, which meant he would always be looking over his shoulder.

Customs kept their side of the bargain as did the Spanish and Corberry was released after two years of his eight year sentence. Before he was released not only was he transferred to another prison but because of the threats, he was kept in solitary confinement.

On his release Customs supplied him with the identity of Alfred Eastly and all the necessary documentation to go with it...

Black asked Jimmy what would happen now and Jimmy said he would be interviewed and charged under his own name. The crimes he had committed were too serious to ignore and he would have to take his chances in court. However, if Customs wanted to approach the Crown to get some leniency for him, then that was a matter for them.

McBurnie promised he would keep Black updated on the investigation and what happened to Corberry at court. He confirmed Corberry's involvement with Customs would not be disclosed. Furthermore, there would be no charge libelled against Corberry for providing false identity, and Jimmy would ensure this as he would appoint the reporting officer.

After he finished the phone call and was making his way back to the tape recording interview room Jimmy thought to himself,

Corberry's a 'TOUT'...

He was not one of his stable and there was nothing he could do for him here. He would have to take a significant 'fall'. After his release however, if he stayed on Jimmy's patch, he was sure to be recruited by 'The Trainer'. Providing of course he wasn't bumped off first!

Jimmy updated Johnston on this major development before returning to Starkey in the interview room. He never disclosed to his colleague the details of his conversation with Peter Black. He just told Starkey that Eastly had provided a false name and false details.

While McBurnie and Starkey interviewed Corberry, Johnston and D.S. Patricia Allan, a twenty six year old, 5'3", blond, who was slightly overweight, very mouthy, and with a fiery temper, interviewed Lochans.

Both neds knew the game was up and it didn't take long for them to provide full admissions of their crimes involving Symington. Not surprisingly during the interview, Corberry tried to portray Lochans as a fearsome criminal and the 'brains' behind the abduction. He tried to put most of the blame on him, stating it was him who rented the cottage in Hillgate, he who purchased the van they used, and it was all his idea. Corberry claimed he was afraid to say no to Lochans as he knew how violent he was and what would happen if he didn't go along with his plan!

Anyone who met Lochans would not take long to establish he didn't have the intellect or guile to plan these crimes. After both interviews were complete McBurnie and Johnston shared details of what each ned had said. When McBurnie told Johnston and Allan about Corberry's claim, Lochans was the brains behind the abduction they both burst out laughing. Johnston said emphatically "I don't think so, I don't even think he could fill in a coupon, let alone plan an abduction and extortion."

Both were charged with abduction, theft, attempted extortion and serious assaults and kept in custody.

Allan was totally surprised, but delighted, when she was told she would report the case. However she was puzzled when McBurnie, without any explanation, told her not to libel any charges against Corberry for providing false details.

She didn't know her D.I. and D.C.I had a private meeting, where they decided neither should be the reporting officer. Both men now knew about Corberry's identity and involvement with Customs and Excise and they didn't want that coming out before or during court proceedings.

Sometimes ignorance is bliss...

Johnston briefed D.C.C. Cobble on how Jimmy and he had managed to detect the case and about the 'identity' situation with Corberry. (Eastly).

Cobble was delighted with the result and pleased Jimmy had still shown he had the thirst for crime fighting. Having been a detective himself, he knew there would be plenty of loose ends to tie up before this enquiry was complete. He told Johnston, Corberry's involvement with Customs and Excise should be dealt with at a higher level. He would now liaise with them and neither him nor Jimmy, should have any further contact with them, before clearing it with him.

Symington was released from hospital after treatment for his broken nose, ribs and numerous bruises. The media pursued him constantly to get his account of what it was like to be the victim of such a horrendous crime. Being the private individual he was he managed to retain his privacy, by moving to another property he owned in Tuscany, until the case was over.

With abduction and attempted extortion being so rare the media were desperate to get the inside story. Now with Symington saying nothing and not being contactable they resorted to what McBurnie saw as their usual M.O., invention and speculation. Not surprisingly, when Corberry and Lochan's appeared for their first court appearance there were plenty of press photographers in attendance.

McBurnie made sure when the accused entered the court building from a rear door, their heads were covered with blankets. He always tried to protect the identity of his own charges. With a contract being out on Corberry's life, he wasn't going to be the person responsible for him being identified by the media, and possibly being eliminated.

The story of the abduction became front page in the newspapers and on both local and national TV, but no photographs were shown of the two accused.

As expected both men were remanded in custody to the local prison.

D.S. Allan was now a busy girl, getting all the available evidence against Corberry and Lochans. It didn't take her long to recover the van they had used. It had never reached a crusher and was still at the cottage they rented at Hillgate and still under cover.

The van and the cottage were subjected to full Scenes of Crime examinations and plenty evidence via DNA and fingerprints was recovered. This tied both men into the van, into Symington's Mercedes which had already been seized and the cottage.

Importantly, this evidence confirmed their physical contact with their victim and was further supplemented with the forensic evidence the scenes of crime teams had managed to recover from The Laurels.

Mary Armstrong's Escort had been seized and fully examined. It too contained fingerprints and other samples identified as belonging to Corberry, Lochans and their victim Symington.

Mary and Sheila, were now both well aware they had been 'used' by Corberry and both provided full witness statements, which fully incriminated him. They hoped, beyond hope, there would be no trial, where their naivety would be disclosed, and their reputations left in tatters if they appeared as witnesses.

Symington was interviewed in depth by D.S. Green who had been tasked with liaising with him

His abduction and treatment was something that would live with him for the rest of his life. He supplied Green with a very comprehensive statement containing all the graphic details of his horrendous experience.

Green was sure Symington would make an excellent witness but wasn't so sure about the two women. As he was saying goodbye, Symington asked him to do him a favour and Green replied, "Certainly, what is it?" Symington said," Tell Sheila, to start looking for another job."

Green then interviewed Mr Cowan the bank manager. He would also be a good witness and Green could see he was still experiencing the "high" of being a 'part-time' detective.

By the time Allan and Green had finished their enquiries they had more than enough evidence against both men. Jimmy thought, only fleetingly, if there was ever a 'stonewall' case against two real 'baddies' then this was it.

Johnston and Jimmy prepared their witness statements ensuring Corberry's previous dealings with Customs and Excise would not come out in court. From the discussions they had, Jimmy knew Johnston was certainly a 'detective' and 'maybe' could even be trusted.

Another tick in the 'friend' box...

Two weeks before the trial was due to start the Procurator Fiscal received notification from Corberry and Lochans defence solicitors. They were pleading guilty to all charges and there would be no trial. Corberry had still tried to claim Lochans was the main man but the Crown weren't having it.

When Jimmy told Starkey this news, there was a big sigh of relief, and both men just smiled. D.S. Allan on the other hand was disappointed when she heard. She had put a lot of work into this case and was now going to be deprived of her day (s) in court. Starkey told her just to be thankful because he knew, through experience, just what she would be missing...

When Corberry and Lochans appeared in court McBurnie put precautions in place again to ensure they were never photographed entering or leaving the court building. He was making sure that Corberry, in particular, knew he was protecting his identity and him. McBurnie could be guaranteed to remind him of this, when, after what was sure to be a lengthy sentence was completed, he was recruited to his 'yard'.

The presiding judge, Lord McCarty, was not known for his leniency. When he heard the details of the crimes the men had committed and then their guilty pleas he sentenced Corberry, who he classed as the brains of the crime, to fifteen years imprisonment and Lochans to twelve.

Ex D.S. Rory Martin had been following the case in the media and he wanted to get the 'inside line' on the investigation. He knew abduction and extortion was a rare crime in Scotland. There had been less than eight such cases in the last twenty years. He was desperate to find out how Jimmy had got on to these neds and left a message for him to contact him.

When Jimmy got the message he decided he would visit him and give him an abridged version of his investigation.

He called at Martin's home and his wife said he was out, but would be home shortly. She told Jimmy he wouldn't believe her husband had now taken up jogging at the age of sixty five.

Jimmy had tea with Mrs Martin and shortly thereafter was greeted with the sight of her 6'1", ginger haired, Highland born husband, collapsing on the settee in a state of exhaustion. Jimmy had to look twice at Martin, who was wearing a track suit and tammy, before he actually believed it was him.

After, 'the runner' got his breath back, Jimmy relayed his version of events, minus any information about Corberry's identity or involvement as a tout. Martin was delighted to have been kept 'in the loop' and really chuffed the fight against the neds was still going strong.

Without prompting, he told Jimmy his reasons for taking up jogging were to get himself fitter and also raise money for a local cystic fibrosis charity. In three months time he was scheduled to complete a 10 K sponsored run for this charity and told Jimmy he would be sponsoring him. Jimmy never argued the point but agreed to donate £20 before he left.

His next port of call was to Mr Cowan, the bank manager, whose quick actions and assistance had first put Jimmy on to the trail of the two criminals.

He had tea again and before leaving he deposited a nice bottle of malt whisky, in gratitude for Cowan's quick actions and assistance.

After leaving the bank manager he headed back to the C.I.D. office and met up with the D.C.I. This time Johnston suggested they go for a drink to a pub he was frequenting near Stratshall.

Jimmy didn't need to be asked twice and before long they were enjoying a good few pints and reminiscing over the details of this very unusual case.

Johnston thanked Jimmy for being loyal to him and for his support. As the night progressed they became noisy, quite drunk and engaged in 'war stories'.

The next day Jimmy came into the office, a bit under the weather, and when he clapped eyes on Johnston, he noticed he too was suffering. After numerous cups of coffee and some laughter they got on with the day's work.

At lunch time Johnston summoned Jimmy into his office, and although they were both suffering from a hangover, they had a good laugh about the previous nights drinking. After the hilarity died down Johnston said he had a proposal to put to Jimmy, and one which he should think seriously about.

Jimmy told him to go ahead, he was all ears...

Johnston said a few Inspector's in the force had undergone Hostage Negotiator training at the Scottish Police College. There was an expectation among the hierarchy all Inspectors should 'volunteer' for this course, which was quite demanding.

Jimmy said he had heard about it but he wasn't volunteering for anything. He was more interested in sticking to his core role of getting the bad people off the street. The D.C.I. told him he should think about his career. By becoming a licensed hostage negotiator it would add another string to his bow and could help in the promotion stakes.

When McBurnie heard this he laughed out loud and told his boss they both knew any further promotion for him was out of the question, as long as Chief Superintendent Scott and A.C.C. Ramsden were still in post.

Johnston stressed to him to look beyond the present. Scott in particular was ultra ambitious, very young to be a Chief Superintendent and would likely move to another force to get promoted again. Ramsden meanwhile had only two years left before he retired. Johnston told Jimmy he had completed the Hostage Negotiation course when he was a uniform inspector and it was very worthwhile. It broadened your outlook when you were one of the persons who could, through negotiation, save somebody's life...

McBurnie being both the sceptic and cynic he was, told the D.C.I. it was all very well if things panned out OK during the negotiations. It would be a different matter when things went pear shaped. Then you would be on the spot and if the hostages were hurt or killed, then your arse was on the line. He told Johnston his arse was already there without the added complication of being a Hostage Negotiator.

Johnston was nothing if not persistent and asked his D.I. to think seriously about it as it could turn out to be a good career move. McBurnie said before he came to any decision he would discuss it with Doris when he went home. He was promising nothing, all he would do was 'think about it'. He owed the force nothing, he was just the 'fall guy' when things went wrong, and somebody whose successes in the crime fighting stakes were purloined, by those who had never seen an angry man or investigated a crime.

As he was leaving the office his boss gave him a knowing look and said, "Think seriously about it."

When Jimmy got home and once the evening meal was finished, the school homework complete, and the kids in bed, he spoke to Doris about the proposal put to him by Johnston.

She asked how long the course would last and he said it was fully two weeks, and unlike other courses at the college, this one started on a Sunday afternoon not a Monday morning. Jimmy said some guys who he had spoken to, who had been on the course, told him it was hard work, stressful, and totally different to normal police work.

Not everyone passed the course, which you had to, before you were licensed. If you were successful then apparently you came back from the college with another string to your bow. If Johnston was to be believed you also came back with your horizons broadened.

Jimmy conceded he could see some merit in it, especially now in light of the case involving Symington and his two abductors. If they hadn't been captured the way they were, then it could have ended up in a hostage situation in Leeds or elsewhere. Obviously negotiators would have been a necessity in trying to bring events to a peaceful and successful conclusion.

After hearing this she told her husband she thought it was worthwhile but ultimately the decision was his. At least if he was home at the weekends and not at work, this would be a pleasant change, and if this course took his mind away from Scott and Ramsden, then this would be an addad bonus.

The next morning Jimmy told D.C.I. Johnston he could put his name down for the course. Johnston was pleased and said it was a wise decision but Jimmy wasn't so sure. He replied, "Maybe, I'll suck it and see."

HOSTAGE NEGOTIATION

When he received the joining instructions, which included a requirement to bring some old weatherproof clothes with him, he was informed, as he had expected, the course started at 4 pm the following Sunday afternoon.

At 1 pm. on the Sunday he said his goodbyes to Doris and the kids and promised to phone home every night. Doris believed Jimmy was now looking forward to attending this course and his kids were delighted when he told them he would bring them a present on his Friday return. It may have looked like he was happy to Doris, but in reality he hated attending the college with its strict quasi military regime and discipline code.

Since his probation day's he had completed many specialist courses and made many friends and contacts throughout Scotland. However, he couldn't accept what he saw as a manufactured environment where young probationers were instructed to call anyone they met in the college corridors, 'Sir' or 'Mam'.

He remembered this stage of his own career only too well.

He had been a week into his initial probationer training before he realised he had been calling cleaners and maintenance men 'Sir' and 'Mam' when he met them...

He was well past the probationer stage now but still hated having to spend time there, away from his family and his addiction to crime fighting. The only benefits of being at the college as a detective, were you didn't have to wear a uniform, and you could drink in one of the better bars, away from the probationers and those who trained them. He thought this segregation was a deliberate policy on the part of the college staff, especially when you saw some of the states the detectives were in at the end of a night's drinking session.

As he drove through the college gates he still had that sinking feeling at the bottom of his stomach...

After he parked his car he went to the reception area for course attendees and was met by Detective Superintendent Hosie. The Detective Superintendent, was in charge of all aspects of detective training which also included hostage negotiation.

Twenty Inspectors, some uniform, some C.I.D. and other police departments from all over Scotland were on the course. Jimmy had met two of them before on other courses, so it was nice to recognise some friendly faces.

Once they had been allocated a room they were instructed to meet in one of the lecture rooms at 4 pm. prompt.

When they were all seated, in walked a cop who had been a hostage in a siege. He spent three hours explaining what it felt like to be a hostage and how thankful he was to the negotiators who negotiated his and the other hostages release.

This presentation was followed by another from two men who had also been hostages on an aircraft. Terrorists had been passengers on the plane and had seized control of it at gunpoint forcing the pilot to land it in a far eastern country. From there they made specific demands from the government of that country to release some of their terrorist group held in prison there. If their demands weren't met they threatened to kill some of the passengers and in fact they did kill some passengers and threw them from the plane.

The two lecturers explained they were next in line to be killed and only with the help of negotiators and the military were they alive. The negotiators had kept the hostage takers talking, agreeing to some requests by them, until the military could storm the plane and overcome the hostage takers. Unfortunately, not everyone escaped and some hostages and all the hostage takers were killed.

By the time these presentations were completed it was 10.30 in the evening and Hosie and his team told the course members breakfast started at 7.30 am. He said if they were quick the next morning, perhaps they would manage a bacon roll before the course started again. Hosie then looked at his watch and informed the students they had time for one drink at the bar, but to make sure they were back in the same lecture room at 8.am. the next morning.

Detectives never miss any opportunity for a drink and the detectives on the course were the first in the bar ordering two or three drinks before it closed.

Jimmy's mind like every one else's on the course was now in overdrive. Everybody realised what they had let themselves in for by 'volunteering' for this course.

The next morning twenty weary looking students, only two of whom had managed any breakfast, were seated in the lecture room wondering what happened now.

Detective Superintendent Hosie told the course each day of their training would last somewhere between 8.am. and 11.pm. He stressed if they were fortunate they could catch a sandwich at lunch time, if not then that was too bad.

The detectives on the course weren't thinking about food. Their main concern was the bars in the Police College which all closed at 11.pm. meaning there would be no drinking on this course.

To everyone's relief Hosie said if they all paid in £10 to a kitty his staff would buy some drinks for the 11.pm. finish. Then they could have a 'few' while everyone was de briefed on the day's events.

Every student including McBurnie gladly handed over their £10...

. The group were then split into teams of two and four and given a scenario to follow and roles to play. No one would escape scrutiny on this course and each person was subject to constant observation and assessment in each role by trained hostage negotiators from all over the U.K. These trained negotiators would play the roles of hostages and hostage takers throughout the course's two weeks duration.

Day one dealt with hostage situations more on a domestic as against a terrorist level. The hostage takers and hostages played their roles realistically, as was evidenced by the sweat running down the faces and backs of the trainee negotiators.

Before the first week ended the trainees had faced situations, where a woman had been held hostage by a former partner, in a field, and another where both women and children were being held hostage, and yet another where the hostage taker was holding two women hostage with a handgun.

Each scenario held its own logistical problems and the students had to work in conjunction with firearms teams, public order teams, psychologists, and incident commanders.

Every member of the course took it in turns to perform all the roles in the negotiator framework. Each was exposed to the different pressures of these roles, the administration required of specific roles, and most importantly how to work as part of a team.

As a hostage negotiator it had been instilled in them on day one, their role was crucial to the safety and well being of hostages. It was constantly reinforced that operational decisions were not theirs to make, but were solely the remit of the incident commanders.

For Jimmy who was used to being 'hands on' and leading from the front, this was difficult. Nevertheless, after getting a few verbal reprimands from some of the assessors, he soon learnt the error of his ways. They stressed the importance of team work and following instructions and advice from those who had been through this training.

When he arrived home on the Friday evening with the first half of the course completed he felt exhausted. As promised he brought the kids two huge bags of sweets and Doris some flowers, and collapsed into his favourite living room chair. There was no doubting he was really glad to be home...

The weekend didn't seem to last long and before he knew it he was back at the Scottish Police College with his trainee hostage negotiators, getting a grilling, and their ego's kicked about all over the place.

This second week was even more difficult than the first. In one scenario the students had to negotiate with a hostage taker who had taken a young woman hostage in her own home. The scenario was as real as the ones the previous week. This time Jimmy was the first negotiator on the scene. As he arrived at what was a top flat in a three storey building, he was briefed by a uniform cop. He was told a young woman was being held in the flat by her estranged husband and it appeared her husband had cut her ear off. He was now threatening to cut her throat if she didn't agree to him coming home to live with her and their one year old child. The child was still in the flat.

Jimmy could hear shouts and screaming coming from the flat, the woman begging for help and the child crying...

All the time, as it had been in every previous scenario, the assessor was standing with a clip board, waiting to take notes. These would include; how Jimmy received the briefing from the cop, how he responded to what he was told, what questions he asked and what notes he took in relation to the flat, the woman, her husband, and the child. This was further supplemented to include whether or not he noted his time of arrival, what demands the hostage taker had made or was making, deadlines which had been set, and how long the woman had been held against her will.

If it was not bad enough trying to take all this in, when he tried to talk to the hostage taker from the third floor landing, he was responded to in a different language.

Nobody had briefed him about this...

Jimmy didn't recognise the language the people in the flat were using, but things became clearer when he was joined at the scene by an Urdu speaker. The problem now was for Jimmy to control the dialogue between him and the hostage taker, without letting the Urdu interpreter, put his own questions to the hostage taker, or display his own feelings towards him.

McBurnie resorted back to being the D.I and left the interpreter in no doubt he was in charge of the negotiation. He told his Urdu speaker to translate, word for word, what he said and under no circumstances to raise any questions of his own. He gave this guy a very knowing look and asked if he understood, and sheepishly the interpreter nodded. Jimmy could see the assessor giving him a grin and a tick in the 'good' box for standing his ground and being explicit with the interpreter.

Eventually after instruction from the incident commander and with some back up from his fellow trainee negotiators, the hostage taker in this scenario agreed to give himself up. The hostage and her child were released unharmed.

That night at the 11 pm. debrief, Jimmy was critiqued like his peers, and many ego's, including his, were deflated. He had to take it on the chin which was never easy for him, but in the trained negotiators, who were the actors on the course, he had people he respected. Subsequently, he held no grudges and engaged in some banter with the role players who had acted out their roles so well.

By now he realised, like them, just how serious the role of the negotiator was...

If he thought this scenario involving the interpreter was stressful the following day would prove to be even more so. This time he was part of a negotiator unit, negotiating with a man who had escaped from a mental institution and had taken an old woman hostage. Only through telephone contact with this man did the negotiators learn he hated both women and the police, with equal vengeance.

According to the scenario they were briefed on, and now involved in, the hostage taker had beaten this woman and threatened to cut her hand off and send it to the police. Each time the negotiators contacted him by telephone they could recognise his West of Scotland, gruff accent. Despite their best efforts none of them could calm him down. Each time they phoned him, before putting the phone down he would call them 'police bastards' 'fucking bastards' and 'wankers' and tell them he was going to cut the woman up bad if they didn't get off the 'fucking' phone.

If this wasn't bad enough while he was cursing and swearing each negotiator in the unit could hear the woman who had been taken hostage, in the background, screaming and begging for help.

Crucially, to keep this woman from further harm the lead negotiator had to keep the hostage taker talking. This meant phoning him back immediately he put the phone down, and getting called everything under the sun, without raising their voices or disclosing how they really felt.

Paramount consideration of the negotiator's unit was always the woman's safety. To achieve this they had to negotiate time deadlines and demands made by the hostage taker. Each negotiator now knew, verbal abuse should not interfere with these priorities.

As a negotiator trying to save lives you took whatever abuse came your way.

After eight phone calls, where the hostage taker was consistent in his verbal abuse of the lead negotiator, and the woman hostage was screaming and pleading for help, Jimmy was given the lead position.

All of his unit, including Jimmy, knew what had gone beforehand and he was expecting dogs abuse like his peers, who had already performed the lead role.

You can imagine his surprise when he phoned the hostage taker and was met with a short period of silence. Jimmy could still hear the woman sobbing in the background and in the distance he could hear Elvis Presley's music being played. He knew he was on the designated direct line to the hostage taker and wondered what was happening.

Following the advice he had been given when performing the lead negotiator role, Jimmy tried starting the dialogue with the hostage taker by saying, "Hello my name is Jimmy and I am here to help." He was expecting to be told to 'Fuck Off' or be called a 'Police Bastard' but this time he was responded to, by what appeared to be a male, American voice.

"Hi," said the voice, followed thereafter by "Are you a fan of mine?"

Jimmy was puzzled but nevertheless replied, "Yes."

"Well that's nice, you sound as if you are phoning from far away" said the hostage taker.

"I am. I'm phoning from Scotland" said Jimmy, to which the other guy replied, "That's great, all the way from Scotland," and then he asked Jimmy if he had any favourite songs of his.

By now it had dawned on Jimmy this guy thought he was Elvis Presley, hence the reason for the music in the background and the American accent. Jimmy knew when they were briefed it was confirmed the only people in the victim's house were her and the hostage taker. Consequently, it must be the hostage taker who now thought he was Elvis.

Jimmy was thinking this guy must have a split personality but there was nothing in the briefing about this at the start of this scenario.

As he was contemplating what to do next the hostage taker asked him what was his favourite song. Quickly Jimmy thought of Elvis songs that he knew and came up, appropriately, with "Suspicious Minds."

When he told 'Elvis' it was his favourite he replied that it was his too.

Then all of a sudden he said to Jimmy, "Hey Jimmy why don't we sing it together, that should be fun."

Well now was a dilemma for Jimmy, but he knew as a hostage negotiator you did what you must if it could save someone's life.

The assessor's, the other members of Jimmy's unit and those members of the course staff who were monitoring the unit remotely, could hardly keep a straight face. Here was McBurnie and the quasi Elvis, singing "Suspicious Minds", in harmony, down the line...

After Jimmy had been in 'good voice' another trainee took over the lead role.

It was another long day where each trainee was exposed to the demands of all the roles in the unit. The hostage taker was eventually overpowered while still on the phone and the hostage was released without further injury.

At the 11pm de brief, McBurnie took some ribbing from the college staff and his other trainees about his singing. However, he knew his peers were just relieved they were not chosen to be the singer.

That night Jimmy met 'Elvis' but there was no singing this time. It was good humoured banter but ended when Jimmy pointed at him, shook his fist, laughed and said, "Your next song will be jail house rock."

The next three days were spent on a large scale hostage terrorist scenario which tested everybody to the limit. Not just the negotiators, but also the incident commanders, the communications, interpreters, firearms and public order teams.

Jimmy felt he was lucky to have passed the course and become a licensed Hostage Negotiator. Before attending this course he never anticipated there would be much of a requirement for negotiators in his police force. Now having completed the course and thinking back to the case involving Joseph Symington, he was convinced otherwise.

That week end with Doris, he explained what the course involved and about his meeting with 'Elvis'. They both had a good laugh but Jimmy said he had learned about negotiation on the course but also quite a bit about himself.

She was pleased he had undertaken this training not just from a career development or professional point of view. His mood on the two week-ends he had been home was great. Never during those week-ends did he ever mention Scott or his work. She thought perhaps this was a new beginning for him and they could be a truly united 'normal' family. Jimmy appeared, at last, capable of leaving his work in his workplace.

If she thought this was going to last she should have known bet

AWAY FROM 'THE TRACK'.

When he got back to work Jimmy told Johnston the course was definitely worthwhile and he had learned plenty. He had to admit, hostage negotiation was as stressful as he had been told by his boss and others who had completed the course.

What he didn't tell Johnston was he had found out something about himself on this course. In particular he had unearthed emotions he thought he never had and he now acknowledged how important it was to be part of a team.

Having his ego deflated on a regular basis had left him in no doubt, there is no room for pride when you are part of a negotiator's unit or for that matter, at any other time. He even found he had a sympathetic and forgiving side, but he didn't know if this extended to Scott...

Now it was getting close to the time for the summer holidays and Doris was hoping Jimmy would be able to forget about work and concentrate on the family.

Derek and Stephanie kept pestering their dad about how long it would be before they were headed to Lanzarote for two weeks in the sun. Every day they got out the holiday brochures and asked Jimmy what size was the pool at their apartments, would they go to the beach, get plenty of ice cream, and play games in the water?

Jimmy too was looking forward to the break and hopefully being able to switch off from his obsession of getting revenge on Scott, but even at a great distance, still manage his stable of touts.

It was a happy family that landed at Arrecife Airport in Lanzarote in July, 1987, and welcomed by a temperature of 35 centigrade. Doris had booked the holiday and their accommodation consisted of a semi detached mini bungalow surrounding a large communal pool.

On their first morning at the complex the kids were straight into the pool, followed by both mum and dad. Some great fun and quality time was enjoyed by them all. After lunch they did some sightseeing before Doris made the evening meal, which they ate outside their semi bungalow. When the kids had gone to bed, exhausted by the days activities, Doris and Jimmy shared a bottle of wine, and both agreed this is what family life should be like.

However, Jimmy being Jimmy, a twenty four hour a day detective had not fully switched off from his work...

He had noticed and old guy, maybe approaching seventy, wearing the equivalent to a gold dog chain round his neck and tattooed up both arms and hands. One tattoo in particular on his right forearm caught his attention...

It displayed the words 'Cop Hater' in large letters...

This guy had only one full leg the other was amputated below the knee. He just sat round the swimming pool for most of the day reading a newspaper. Immediately Jimmy heard him talking, to what he took to be his wife, his antenna was up. He knew they were not only neds but Scottish neds.

The next morning Jimmy was up early and out to the pool before the kids or Doris had their breakfast. He grabbed a sun bed close to where the old ned had been lying the day before, put his towel on it and lay down.

It wasn't long before the old Scottish guy appeared from his semi bungalow in the complex, and with the aid of a walking stick limped to a sun bed near Jimmy. Being the only two people at the pool Jimmy said, "Morning," and the old man on hearing Jimmy's Scottish accent, asked him where he came from in Scotland and what he did for a living.

Jimmy told him he came from near Stranraer in the south west of the country, but before that he had worked in a Clydeside shipyard in his trade as a blacksmith. With the shipyards closing he had managed to get work in a wee smiddy in Stranraer.

This story was a 'legend' which was believable and one which Jimmy had the knowledge and experience to carry off. It also was helpful that Jimmy had a friend in Stranraer who he sometimes visited. This equipped him with some knowledge of the place, even though it was one hundred and fifty miles from Newholm and well outside his own force area.

Jimmy's countryman confirmed he was from the east end of Glasgow and had previously worked as a scaffolder before he fell, damaging his leg beyond repair. The accident was the reason for him now having only one leg.

McBurnie knew, even early in the conversation, this guy with his tattoos and his huge gold chain round his neck was an 'old soldier' on the crime front. If he could gain his confidence Jimmy was sure he had many 'war stories' from the 'other side' to tell him.

From his time in the Clydeside shipyard and through other cops he met on C.I.D. courses, Jimmy knew about a few neds with big reputations in Glasgow's east end, and started to 'name drop'. He soon learned his new 'friend' knew every name he mentioned and he was now giving Jimmy and his legend some credibility.

McBurnie always thought he had a 'listening ear' but his 'hearing' had improved on the negotiators course. Now he was going to put it to best effect and encourage his new 'buddy' to start talking.

Before long the old fellow was quite openly telling him about how he had been a safe blower in his younger days, and of crimes he had committed when he was a younger man, some of which he said were in Stranraer, Aberdeen, Inverness and the Scottish Borders.

Jimmy was now all ears and making a mental note of everything he was told so he could pass it on to detectives in Dumfries and Galloway Police and elsewhere.

Just as the conversation was becoming even more interesting they were joined by the old ned's wife, his single, forty-five year old daughter and her two sons who were both in their early twenties.

Jimmy thought even a blind cop could see this was a family of neds. The two women were covered in heavy gold jewellery and the sons both wore heavy gold identity necklaces and had tattoos all over their arms. In Jimmy's mind, and from what the father had told him, there was little doubt the jewellery had all been stolen.

Doris and the kids then showed up at the pool and Jimmy hurriedly got them sun beds but positioned them far enough away from the ned family. He didn't want the neds getting into conversation with Doris and the kids and finding out through them he was a cop.

He made his apologies to the five Glaswegians then joined his own family. He briefed Doris, under no circumstances should she or the kids mention he was in the police.

To say Doris was angry when she heard this would have been an understatement and she wasn't slow telling Jimmy he should have left his work in Scotland and not bring it on holiday. They were in Lanzarote as a family to enjoy themselves, not to act on behalf of the police.

Jimmy whispered an apology but stressed to Doris this ned family were heavily involved in crime. How would she feel if any of her family had been their victims and nothing had been done about it. He told her if he kept his ear to the ground then these baddies would get what they were due and maybe some of their associates as well. Then their victims might get some satisfaction and closure by seeing them locked up.

Doris was only too well aware of Jimmy's addiction to crime fighting and although she would never admit it, some of it had rubbed off on her. For the remainder of the holiday Jimmy found Doris was desperate to find out about his conversations with the neds. He ended up having to debrief her each night in the privacy of their semi bungalow, on what he had learned during the day, before he put it on paper.

The grandfather had been taken in by Jimmy's legend and told his grandsons they could trust Jimmy. By speaking to them he learned they had robbed two banks in Glasgow.

The younger grandson told McBurnie how he had been the man on the 'inside' with the demand note and gun when they went on a third bank robbery. On this occasion he said he was hung over from a heavy drinking session the night before and nerves had got the better of him. When he entered the bank he had a bad feeling, his knees and hands started shaking and he ran out before presenting the demand note or the gun. Once outside, he noticed his brother and another of his buddies, who was in the getaway car, had left him. He had to do a 'runner' in the true sense of the word, and told Jimmy he was lucky to get away, no thanks to that 'bastard' of a brother.

When he got home he said he had attacked his brother with a hammer but his grandfather had got between them and broke it up.

It had taken a while, but they had now made up and could laugh about it.

Jimmy joined in the laughter when they were reminiscing over this crime and other crimes they had committed and gotten away with. The more time he spent with them the more they trusted him.

Somehow he managed to juggle this information gathering and spending time with Doris and the kids. Thankfully, he was successful in keeping his true identity secret. He only managed this by keeping his family and the neds family apart for the duration of the holiday and by telling the grandfather, his wife didn't really know what line of dodgy 'work' he (Jimmy) was involved in.

The old guy swallowed this story and said experience had shown him it was a good idea to keep it that way. The last thing you wanted was your wife or kids 'bursting' to the polis.

On return to Scotland McBurnie was straight on to the intelligence section in Glasgow and other detectives throughout Scotland, passing on all the information he had gleaned. The Glasgow cops in particular were astounded at the amount of information he had managed to obtain. Once they had carried out checks on the family, the intelligence section informed Jimmy just what a list of previous convictions these neds had between them. The list included both the grandfather, the granny, their daughter and the grandson's.

Not long after this Jimmy was contacted by Detective Superintendent Melrose, the head of one of the surveillance units in Glasgow. He said he had scrutinised the information Jimmy had submitted and he would be putting a team on both grandsons before they arrested them for the bank jobs Jimmy had told them about.

With the tip off from Jimmy they had tasked one of their own touts from the east end, to infiltrate the team. He was able to confirm what Jimmy had learned that they had another bank job lined up for that week.

This suited McBurnie fine. If the neds were caught 'hands on' they wouldn't suspect the information came from him. He was desperate to ensure his wife and family were well removed from this 'police matter' and raised his concerns with Melrose.

The Detective Superintendent said he would ensure his involvement would never be known. To reassure McBurnie further, he said they now had enough info from other sources, backed up with some CCTV evidence, to jail the brothers without them committing another job. However, as Jimmy knew it was always nice to catch them red handed and this is what Melrose was aiming for.

After he finished his call with Melrose, Jimmy thought to himself he had moved from being a trainer of touts, to becoming one himself. After some reflection, he scratched his head and asked himself, why anyone would want to be a tout with the risks and precautions you had to take...

Two weeks later Melrose called him to say the brothers had been caught on a bank job after their tout provided specific information about the bank they were targeting, and when the job was coming down. When the grandsons turned up at the bank with a gun and machete they got the shock of their life. They were surrounded by a police firearms team who had been waiting for them. One of them had actually wet himself while being told by one of the firearms officers, who was pointing a gun at him, to kneel on the pavement with his hands behind his head.

Searches of their home also recovered property stolen from five other locations and now the father and mother were also in custody. Other detectives from out with Glasgow were now travelling to the city to interview the family. Melrose thanked Jimmy for all his input and confirmed he would be writing to the Chief Constable of Jimmy's force, suggesting Jimmy receive a commendation.

McBurnie thanked him but told him he preferred to keep his input 'secret'. Anyway he knew the likelihood of him ever receiving a commendation was remote and he didn't supply the information to get a commendation. He just wanted to help get the baddies off the street.

That night when he went home he told Doris about developments in Glasgow and how their holiday 'friends' had all been arrested. She said that was all well and good but the next time the family went on holiday, in keeping with his fondness for horse racing terms, she was taking 'blinkers' and ear plugs for him, so he would hear and see nothing to do with crime.

Jimmy, with a smile on his face, apologised for putting the family in an awkward position and assured Doris it wouldn't happen again. She didn't believe him for a minute...

NEGOTIATION WITHOUT A HOSTAGE OR HOSTAGE TAKERS.

Once back in Force McBurnie looked up all the members of his stable and confirmed things were 'galloping' along smoothly. He got his usual tips on crime happening in Stratshall, Newholm and the surrounding areas and none of his charges were causing him too much of a problem.

It wasn't long after his holiday when he got a visit from D.C.C. Cobble. As usual when the Deputy visited McBurnie he told him to put the kettle on, and after he had made a brew they both adjourned to Jimmy's office.

Cobble asked how the negotiators course had gone and Jimmy said he didn't expect to enjoy it but he did. He told Cobble it had pushed him hard and gave him another perspective on policing.

Initially he hadn't thought there would be much use for hostage negotiators in his part of the world, but the Symington case could have taken a different turn and Symington could have ended up a hostage. He said he was happy now to be one of the four trained negotiators in the Force, even if it meant taking on another remit with 'call'.

The 'on call' was nothing new for Jimmy.

He was almost on full time call, between his C.I.D. supervisor call out and being at the beck and call of his stable, especially when 'tips' were coming in. This extra 'call' would mean he spent even less time at home with his family but he wasn't going to tell Doris that.

Cobble still relished the thought of being a detective and told Jimmy to give him the 'low down' on the Symington case. Once he had finished, Jimmy was left feeling his D.C.C. was almost addicted to crime as much as he himself was...

After three weeks back in the Force he was sent on a local training course about a new communication system being introduced at Police H.Q. It was the middle of December and the temperature was minus 3 degrees, so Jimmy was glad at least the training would be indoors. Not that he wasn't used to the cold. When he was working in the shipyard there had been some really cold days when he was at the mercy of the elements and it didn't really bother him.

He thought he must be getting soft now...

Halfway through the first day his Negotiator's bleeper was activated. He answered the call by contacting the force control room to get some details...

Sergeant Hunter was in charge of the control room and he told the D.I. there was an ongoing incident at an old derelict factory building, in an industrial estate on the outskirts of Stratshall. It involved a nineteen year old man, called David Newberry. He was a paranoid schizophrenic, who had been reported as a missing person some two days earlier.

He was now standing on a 3' wide window ledge on the third floor of an old factory, threatening to jump. Above his head was an 'H' shaped girder set into the a concrete lintel and protruding some 5' out from the window.

Hunter told him Newberry had tied an orange nylon rope tightly round the girder and had made a noose with the other end of the rope.

This was round his neck...

How he had managed to get to this position was a mystery to everyone at the scene. Most of the internal floors and staircases had been demolished. All that was left of the building was the external walls, part of the roof, and a remnant of flooring behind the window ledge he was standing on.

Sergeant Hunter said Newberry had been there for two hours in this very cold weather and he was not wearing a hat, overcoat or gloves.

Jimmy asked who was at the scene and was told the local Inspector was there with two cops and Doctor McVee, the man's G.P., was also in attendance.

Hunter then expanded on his briefing...

From what the doctor had told the police, Newberry was a confirmed paranoid schizophrenic who had stopped taking his medication. Prior to this incident, the local police had been called three times to the home he shared with his mother. Each time they attended he was on the roof of the house talking to himself and threatening to jump. On each occasion Doctor McVee had attended and managed to talk him down and get him back on track with his medication.

This time his mother had again contacted the doctor and told him he hadn't been home for two days. She thought he had been taking his medication, but on checking her kitchen cupboard she found it was all intact and had never been opened. She was worried sick about him and had reported him to the police as a missing person.

The sergeant, who was monitoring radio communications between the officers at the scene then said one of Jimmy's fellow negotiators, Inspector Kathleen Porter was now in attendance.

Jimmy knew Kathleen Porter, she was a good looking twenty nine year old, single woman, who was very career orientated. He had never worked with her before, but any reports he had about her were favourable. She seemed a go ahead, no nonsense, type of person not prone to 'waffle', which suited Jimmy just fine.

Jimmy had some dealings with schizophrenics before and knew just how unpredictable it was when talking to one person with two personalities...

When he was a young uniform cop he had been called to an incident, where a man suffering from this illness, had wrecked his own home with an axe and a hammer, causing his wife and family to flee. When Jimmy and a colleague arrived at the house they tried to talk the man into putting down the weapons. He did put them down but then lifted a small bottle of liquid from the kitchen table and drank it in front of Jimmy and his colleague, before they could over power him.

Sadly, what the man had drunk was a strong weed killer and two days later he died in hospital. This had quite a traumatic effect on Jimmy and his fellow officer at the time.

He wondered what lay ahead here?

If only he knew then he would have wished he was somewhere else and it was not his turn to answer the call...

McBurnie had been well briefed by Sergeant Hunter and quickly made his way to his car. After twenty five minutes he was at the scene. The uniform cops had cordoned off the area. A fire engine and crew who had recently arrived, were concealed at the designated rendezvous point, (R.V.) behind an adjacent factory wall, and out of sight of the potential jumper. The Incident Commander was Inspector Muir who was stationed at Stratshall. He was short of experience with only eight years police service, but nevertheless destined to advance quickly through the ranks.

He was delighted to see Jimmy because he felt the pressure was now off him, and either Inspector Porter or McBurnie would now take control of this incident. Before he could begin to brief them, Jimmy informed him that as Incident Commander he would have to make all the operational decisions. Quoting what he had learned on the negotiators course he told Muir, "Negotiators 'negotiate' while Incident Commanders' command."

To reinforce his message he said, "That means you will have to make the operational decisions."

A nervy Muir then began his briefing after pointing to where Newberry was standing, with the noose round his neck, and Doctor McVee standing below him, shouting up to him.

He told Jimmy and his fellow negotiator, David Newberry had been reported as a missing person by his mother. Muir said he knew Newberry's history and wasn't surprised when he learned he had been found that morning by a man walking his dog through the industrial estate. That was some three hours ago now.

At this time Newberry was already on the third floor window ledge some 25' from the ground, with a nylon rope tied to an 'H' shaped girder above his head. The other end of the rope formed a noose which he had round his neck. When the man walking his dog asked him what he was doing up there, initially he got no response or eye contact.

After repeating the same question Newberry did eventually make a comment, not to the questioner, but to himself, and shouted, "Jump ya bastard."

This stunned guy then contacted the police and Muir said he and two uniform cops soon arrived at the old factory, after contacting Doctor McVee and asking him to join them. Once there, they cordoned off the scene and set up the R.V.

Muir said he had contacted the fire service, and following the advice of the doctor, asked them to attend, but conceal their fire engine behind the adjacent building, where Newberry could not see it or them. If Newberry did see it then Doctor McVee was of the opinion this would spook him and he might jump out of the window ledge and hang himself.

Muir confirmed the fire engine was equipped with a turntable ladder and a heavy ladder which could be carried and put into position manually. However, it would be impossible to introduce either of them without Newberry seeing them approach, from the position he was in.

After hearing, what was a good briefing, McBurnie contacted the leading fireman, George Sim. He confirmed the hand held ladder would be the only way to get to the window ledge without giving David Newberry too much notice of its arrival. Sim said there was no other way of getting up to it. He confirmed, with the perilous state of the building he was at a loss to establish how Newberry had managed to get onto the window ledge in the first place.

Inspector Porter said she had arrived half an hour before and between Doctor McVee and her they had tried talking to Newberry with no success. He just stood dangerously close to the edge of the window sill, staring into space. Any conversation they tried to have with him was just met with him staring into space or him talking to himself saying, "Jump ya scared bastard."

Once she returned to relieve Doctor McVee, Jimmy asked the doctor what his thoughts were on the likelihood of David Newberry jumping. He said the intervals between his mood swings were shortening, and in his view, there was every chance he would jump. There was even a risk with the weather being as it was, Newberry could fall from the window ledge and hang himself.

Jimmy then asked Sim how long it would take to get the ladder to Newberry. He said from where they were positioned, some one-hundred yards from the window ledge, it would take three firemen at least four or five minutes to carry the ladder to the location. It would take time to climb it, plus they didn't know what difficulties they could face when trying to get Newberry down.

By asking these questions Jimmy had contradicted what he had told Inspector Muir. Here he was now taking stock of operational matters when they shouldn't be a matter for him, but he couldn't help himself...

It was obvious no one could accurately predict when Newberry would jump nor how, or if, they would get him down safely. The longer he remained on the window ledge with the noose round his neck the more likely he was going to jump or even fall. Jimmy knew the only method of getting him down would be if he agreed to come and that was extremely unlikely. To get this agreement they would have to negotiate with him. This would be difficult enough with any person contemplating suicide, let alone a paranoid schizophrenic.

He thought to himself, "They don't teach you how to deal with situations like this at the college." All negotiator training then had been 'hostage' negotiation training, with the aim of getting hostage takers to negotiate and eventually surrender, leaving the hostages unharmed.

This was a different matter altogether!

Now was time to ask the man above for help, so Jimmy said a silent prayer...

After another very brief conversation with Inspector Muir, Jimmy and Doctor McVee joined Porter who was standing directly under the window where David Newberry was.

Porter and the doctor both introduced Jimmy by his first name and explained to Newberry they were all there to help. They then took it in turns to ask him to come down and reassured him they would get help to get him down safely.

They got no response from him and all he did was stare into space...

Both Porter and Jimmy then took it in turns trying to constantly engage him in conversation, and offer him food and drink, which they said they would throw up to him. After fifteen minutes they got the same response his doctor had been getting before their arrival. He looked into space and shouted "Jump ya bastard are you scared?"

Doctor McVee left to grab a cup of tea with the firemen and Inspector Muir, leaving Newberry with the two negotiators. He hadn't finished his drink when he heard Newberry shouting and swearing at himself again. He left his tea and joined the negotiators. The only response they were getting was Newberry telling himself to "fucking jump."

The situation got more precarious when Newberry leaned out of the window, holding onto the nylon rope with one hand above his head, and leaving just one foot on the window ledge. He kept shouting to himself, "Jump ya bastard."

This created a real panic amongst the doctor and the two negotiators and together they started shouting over and over again, "David, get back."

It took a good five minutes of verbal badgering before Newberry stopped shouting at himself. He looked totally confused, started looking about, put both feet back on the window ledge, and sat down with his legs dangling over the side. It was obvious he was not aware of what was happening.

It was now getting really cold and this poor man was shaking from his head to his toes.

Porter asked him if he would like to come down and get a hot drink and some food. Surprisingly this time he understood what she said and nodded his head, but made no indication he was coming down.

Doctor McVee got a can of coke from one of the firemen and Jimmy put it in a bag, along with two chocolate bars some of the other firemen had given him. After five attempts at throwing it up to Newberry, he managed to catch hold of it.

He then sat on the window ledge again with his feet hanging, dangerously over the side, and began eating the chocolate. When he opened the can of coke he had difficulty holding it because he was shaking so much. He did manage a couple of sips before it fell from his grasp.

McBurnie and his two colleagues were just relieved he was seated and at least eating something, but they all knew this was only a short term success...
They too were now feeling the cold and decided they would take it in turns to try and grab some tea and something to eat at the R.V.

Jimmy had arranged through Inspector Muir to get some hot food and some flasks for everyone at the scene and some warm clothing for David Newberry.

He told Porter to take the first break to go and get a drink and a bite, leaving him and Doctor McVee talking to Newberry.

Some clothing arrived shortly thereafter and Jimmy offered Newberry an anorak and some gloves. The only response he got to this offer was a mouthful of incomprehensible language and a vacant look.

Doctor McVee also offered him food and clothing but the only response he got from Newberry was "Fuck off" followed by another vacant look.

After five hours in freezing temperatures the situation was worsening. The doctor told the negotiators, with Newberry's mood swings changing rapidly he was in no doubt he was going to jump soon.

Jimmy went to Inspector Muir and relayed what Doctor McVee had said and asked him as the Incident Commander what action he wanted to take.

Muir, understandably, didn't know what to say and Jimmy had some sympathy for him. This was not an easy decision and he had already run through all the options in his own head.

There were no good ones...

If he decided to introduce a ladder to the scene then it would take three firemen four or five minutes to carry it to Newberry's location.

From his elevated position Newberry had a clear view of his surroundings and he could see the ladder coming and decide to jump.

If they were lucky enough to get the ladder into position without him jumping, what resistance could the firemen meet when trying to bring Newberry down?

What were the risks not just to Newberry but also to the firemen in trying to bring him down? Would he put up a struggle and knock a fireman to his death?

If Muir decided the negotiators should keep trying to talk Newberry into coming down, and he still jumped or fell, then he could still be heavily criticised. If this poor guy died it might end in a fatal accident enquiry where everybody's actions at the scene would be open to public scrutiny...

For McBurnie it didn't matter which way you looked at it there was every likelihood that Newberry was going to jump and hang himself.

Muir obviously didn't want to have to make the decision and all he could suggest was for the negotiators to keep trying to talk Newberry down. Jimmy did stress to him that Doctor McVee was in no doubt that Newberry would jump, but Inspector Muir still asked Jimmy and his fellow negotiator to keep trying to talk him down.

Jimmy noted his response in his notebook, timed it and asked a reluctant Muir to sign it. He then had Inspector Porter countersign it.

McBurnie knew if it did end in a fatal accident enquiry there could be fingers of blame being pointed at the police, irrespective of how well intentioned everyone had been. Being the sceptic he was he was just ensuring they could not be pointed solely at him or his fellow negotiator.

One hour later and Doctor McVee confirmed to both Jimmy and Porter with Newberry's mood swings now occurring approximately every five minutes, there was no doubt in his mind that he was going to jump very soon.

Leading Fireman Sim had been watching the scenario unfold through a set of binoculars. He told the negotiators and the doctor he had seen Newberry hanging onto the rope with one hand and with only one foot on the window ledge on five separate occasions. He said it was credit to them they had managed to talk him back and he didn't know how they had achieved it.

Jimmy knew, it was only with help from above, had they been able to talk him back into the window ledge and get him to sit down.

They had now been talking to this poor guy for seven hours. Over the last three hours he had been cursing and swearing almost non stop to himself, calling 'his other half' a "coward" and a "scared bastard."

His mood swings were now nearly every two minutes and he was leaning out the window ledge holding onto the rope with one finger of one hand and standing on the toes of his right foot. His other foot was hanging outside the window opening and all the time he was shouting to himself "jump ya scared bastard."

Jimmy returned to Inspector Muir and asked what course of action he wanted to adopt now. It as was obvious that David Newberry was going to jump. Muir said he had summoned an ambulance and it was on its way. All he could suggest was to keep talking to Newberry in the hope they could talk him down safely.

Doctor McVee was privy to the conversation and told Muir this was not going to happen and Newberry was going to jump and very soon.

When the ambulance crew arrived at the R.V. point they were briefed by Doctor McVee and Inspector Muir. Inspector Porter had taken the opportunity to grab a hot cup of tea and listened in to the briefing.

This left Jimmy on his own talking to David Newberry who was sitting on the window ledge staring into space. Jimmy was trying everything he knew to keep Newberry seated but with little effect. After less than a minute he stood up, still with the noose round his neck and started shouting and swearing, telling himself he was a "scared bastard."

Jimmy, relying on his faith, told him God wouldn't want him to hurt himself, and pleaded with him to sit down. There was a pause and then Newberry leaned out over the window ledge again, holding the rope above him with one hand and one foot on the ledge.

Jimmy wondered if God was listening to him because Newberry almost fell out the window and was still shouting at himself, "jump ya scared bastard."

McBurnie was joined then by Inspector Porter and Doctor McVee and this time, even with a team effort, they couldn't talk Newberry back. He was getting angrier and angrier with himself and shouting, "Do it now ya scared bastard."

Doctor McVee said,"He will jump any time know."

Jimmy then stepped out of the role of negotiator and ran back to the R.V. He told Inspector Muir, time was up, soon they were going to have a fatality on their hands.

Muir didn't say anything when Jimmy told Leading Fireman Sim to bring the hand held ladder to where Newberry was situated.

Three firemen picked up the ladder, but before they set off Jimmy asked if they had a sharp knife in their kit and Sim retrieved a 5'' bladed knife and gave it to Jimmy, who put it up his sleeve and joined Porter and Doctor McVee.

As the firemen set off with the ladder Jimmy was almost counting the footsteps they were taking in getting to Newberry's position. Every step without Newberry, who was now leaning out the window ledge repeatedly shouting to himself "Jump now", without him jumping was a bonus. It was an extremely relieved Jimmy when they got the ladder directly below the window ledge.

His relief was only temporary, because when the ladder reached the window ledge and a fireman put his foot on the first wrung, Newberry did jump out of the window...

For Jimmy and the others it was now a horrific scene...

Newberry was swinging from side to side at the end of the noose. His neck was contorted, his feet were kicking out in all directions, blood was gushing from his mouth, he was making a gurgling noise and his eyes were bulging out of his head. Shortly after this his arms were hanging limp at his side and he appeared to be dead.

Jimmy immediately retrieved the knife from his sleeve and gave it to the fireman who had his foot on the ladder. The fireman then climbed the ladder as quickly as he could, and after what seemed like an eternity, he managed to cut the nylon rope.

Doctor McVee, Inspector Porter and Jimmy were waiting below the window ledge and managed to catch what they thought was the body of David Newberry.

The doctor was then joined by two ambulance staff and between them they managed to locate a very weak pulse, cut the noose and clear his airway. The ambulance crew then supplied him with oxygen and he was transferred to the ambulance and rushed to Newholm Hospital.

Everybody was traumatised and Jimmy asked Doctor McVee what were Newberry's chances of survival and he said virtually nil...

McBurnie thanked the doctor and then told Kathleen Porter to join him near the R.V. point. When they met up, away from everyone else, he asked her if she was O.K. After a short pause she said she thought she was, but she never wanted to experience anything like this again

Jimmy was a hardened detective and had attended many suicides where people had hung themselves, taken poison, lain down in front of trains, shot themselves and jumped from buildings. He had also cut people down after they had hanged themselves. He knew the images of these scenes remained with you and sometimes woke you up in the middle of the night in a cold sweat.

The incident with the murderer Craig Norton was one which came back to him regularly, not just during the night, but every time he heard Mike and The Mechanics sing 'The Living Years'.

The effect of this incident would be even more horrific...

McBurnie knew with help 'from above' he would cope, and situations involving death were part and parcel of a detective's life. He also was toughened by the hard life experiences of being brought up in a mining community and working in a ship yard.

In the 1950s and 60s there had been a number of pit disasters. This is when the miners' sense of community really came to the fore. It was also a time where men in particular didn't readily show their emotions. They just got on with helping each other while internally they must have been torn apart.

Jimmy, coming from a mining background where such disasters were experienced and with his own work experiences, had, metaphorically speaking, been at the 'coal face' of life for a while. He would cope but how would Inspector Porter cope?

Only she knew the answer...

Before leaving her he told her if she needed to speak about what they had just witnessed here, then she should not delay contacting him and they would share their thoughts and fears.

She said nothing but just nodded...

McBurnie then spoke to Inspector Muir. He had sympathy for him because this was a no win situation and as a result he just patted him on the shoulder and said, "He is not dead and with a bit of help from above maybe he will pull through", though even McBurnie himself had some doubts about it.

Muir's head was down and Jimmy hoped for his and everyone else's sake Newberry did pull through, albeit Doctor McVee had said this was unlikely.

When he got back to the office Jimmy telephoned the hospital and asked if there was any news on David Newberry. He was told it was too early to say, but his prospects of survival looked bleak.

He went home and on seeing Doris he told her "I think we lost a young guy today." She didn't know what he was talking about, but after he had composed himself, he explained what he had witnessed without going in to all the horrific detail.

That night he prayed to God asking for a miracle in the form of David Newberry's survival.

The next morning immediately after he arrived in the C.I.D. office, he phoned the hospital again. He was told Newberry had survived albeit he had damaged his voice box permanently.

It was now time to say a private 'thanks' to the man above for answering his prayer...

He telephoned Kathleen Porter and told her the good news but was surprised she wasn't as ecstatic about this news as he was. She just thanked him very much and put the phone down.

He followed this with a call to Inspector Muir and he could hear the huge sigh of relief coming from him before he thanked Jimmy for his help and support. He like Jimmy knew now there would be no Fatal Accident Inquiry because there was, thank God, no fatality.

In the following five weeks visions of Newberry swinging at the end of the orange rope from the window ledge would periodically come into Jimmy's mind. Thankfully he only had one night of prolonged disturbed sleep with this vision.

He suspected others must be suffering and of his own back he arranged a debrief at Newholm Police Station. Everyone who was at the scene including Doctor McVee, Inspector Porter, Inspector Muir and his two cops, the ambulance crew and all the firemen attended the debrief.

Jimmy thanked everyone for coming and then went round the table asking each one individually, how they felt and what impact this hanging had on them.

It was only then they all learned just what effect the incident had on the whole group. Everyone took comfort from learning they were not alone with their thoughts and nightmares.

At the conclusion of the meeting they all agreed this coming together had been very worthwhile and each person's contact details were exchanged. Doctor McVee offered counselling support to anyone who needed it.

Jimmy felt better after this but he knew he would still get flash backs, but that went with the job.

He not only had a stable of touts to worry about now. His experiences had 'saddled' him with a mind full of horrific memories, which as a trainer he would need to manage. This would mean balancing the dichotomy of being sharp enough to actively recruit and control informants whilst hoping there was no increase in the number of such memories he had to cope with.

He was just glad he had a faith!

COMEUPPANCE

After the incident with David Newberry, Jimmy had become a bit subdued. So much so D.C.I. Johnston, who was well aware of the hanging incident, asked him if he needed some counselling or professional help. McBurnie was too macho to accept this and told Johnston he would cope as he always had done.

Johnston wasn't so sure and made a commitment to himself to keep an eye on his D.I.

Even at home Jimmy was a bit quiet and the kids had to keep pestering him to get him to play with them or help them with their school home work. Doris knew the signs, but she was also the product of a mining community where women quietly supported their men no matter what the difficulties were. Experience had taught her there were such occasions when her support would not be clearly visible, but was certainly required. This was such an occasion, and she tried to make family life appear as normal as possible. She would always to be there for Jimmy if he wanted to talk through his troubles but knew this was unlikely to happen, unless he had a few drinks.

One night after work, D.S. Martin Green, who could see his boss was quite morose, asked Jimmy if he fancied going for a pint. Reluctantly Jimmy agreed, albeit drink made him more communicative, when it wore off, he could become depressed.

They ended up in Green's local where one pint led to two and two led to three. Some three hours later, Green was quite well under the influence but Jimmy appeared to still be sober. This was remarkable, considering he had now drunk five pints and two whiskies.

Green then suggested they try a new pub in town called 'The Rigger' which was set in its own grounds in a quiet residential area. It was an old Victorian building which had recently been modernised by the new owner. Green thought it would be a good venue for himself and Jimmy to have a quiet chat.

It wasn't really Jimmy's scene...

He would liked to have gone to his local which was classed by his young detectives as 'an old man's pub' but he said he would go, if only to appease Green.

As they walked the half mile to The Rigger, Green kept trying to gee up Jimmy. To a certain extent, with the help of the drink they had swallowed, and Green's non stop chatter, it seemed to be working. At least McBurnie was now becoming involved in the conversation and they started exchanging 'war stories'.

To get to the pub you had to walk up a long driveway before you reached its well lit front door. There was also a side door and a separate footpath leading to it, but this area was poorly lit.

It was a really dark night and as Jimmy and Green got near the top of the driveway they could hear the sound of cursing and swearing, coming from the area of the side door. It sounded like someone was on the receiving end of a beating and a woman was screaming nearby.

McBurnie and Green ran to the side door only to see a male figure and the woman disappear, into the darkness at the back of the hotel, and then out of sight. Green ran after the man and woman, but before long he returned to the hotel and told Jimmy there were about six streets at the back, and they had managed to get away.

While Green had been pursuing this couple, Jimmy attended to the man who was lying face down on the gravel, near the side door of the hotel. He could hear him groaning and he could see he was in considerable pain.

Very carefully he managed to turn this guy over onto his back. It was then he thought he recognised this man even through his face was heavily blood stained.

He couldn't be sure, because the lighting was so poor, but as he got him to his feet, nearer the light at the side door, he was left in no doubt who he was.

It was Chief Superintendent Scott!

Jimmy told him he would help him into the hotel and then telephone the local uniform police.

To McBurnie's amazement Scott refused to go anywhere near the hotel, and strenuously emphasised he did not want the police contacted. Jimmy asked him why and he said it was a private matter and he would sort it out himself.

Green had a look of amazement on his face when he recognised who the victim was and what he had said.

McBurnie asked Scott if they could get a taxi to take him to hospital to have his injuries treated, but again Scott declined. He told Jimmy he would be all right and said his car was parked at the rear of the hotel. He would manage to drive it home without any help.

Jimmy again offered him assistance but he said he required none. Before heading for his car he asked both Jimmy and Green if they would keep the details of this incident to themselves.

Both officers nodded and Scott limped to the back of the hotel car park, which was very poorly lit, holding his ribs, and eventually drove away in his red coloured Alpha Romeo Sports car.

Well, Jimmy's conversation was not stilted when he entered the hotel with Green. He asked the barman what had happened and the barman just shrugged his shoulders and told them he didn't know what they were talking about. He did confirm, not long before they arrived, a couple had been sitting in a quiet area of the lounge bar and had left after two drinks. He had heard raised voices coming from outside the hotel not long afterwards, but thought nothing of it.

Jimmy and Green then engaged in speculation about what was going on with Scott. To Green's amazement Jimmy stressed they would not talk about the incident to anyone but wait and see what developed.

They had three drinks in The Rigger and kept quizzing the barman, but he could not or would not, add anything further to what he had told them initially. Both off duty cops then headed home, still completely puzzled why Scott had been attacked and why he did not want the police involved or any treatment at the hospital.

It was to be two weeks before Jimmy learned the true story...

During this time both McBurnie and Green kept their 'ear's to the ground' but never disclosed that they had witnessed the incident with Scott. When they first got back to work, Newholm Police station was buzzing about the Chief Superintendent who had returned to work the day after the attack, sporting a black eye, severe bruising to his face and holding his ribs. When asked by his staff officer and the support staff how he came about these injuries, Scott stated he fell off a ladder in his garage while mending a fuse.

One of Jimmy's sources in the personnel department had been keeping him up to date with Scott's activities and his comings and goings since Jimmy's last failed attempt at promotion. There was nothing this guy had told him so far which McBurnie could use to plot Scott's downfall...

The only useful piece of information he had, which came from more than one source, was that Scott had an eye for the ladies. Apparently, he used his rank to impress good looking young police women and civilian staff.

Jimmy knew, Scott had applied for three promoted positions outside the Force after the incident with his old boss D.C.I. Chambers. He had been unsuccessful on each occasion and Jimmy was now wondering if Scott was getting 'knock backs' because his reputation was tarnished after the internal investigation. Alternatively, was there another reason he didn't know about?

Many cops in Newholm Police Station knew about the fraught

relationship between the D.I. and Scott. Not surprisingly Jimmy was now repeatedly asked by them if he knew how Scott came to be injured. McBurnie was sure there was suspicion among them that he had inflicted these injuries, but when he was asked he just shrugged his shoulders and said, "Maybe he was telling the truth and he did fall?"

Neither Jimmy nor Green ever uttered a word about what they had witnessed...

McBurnie didn't owe Scott and favours but he still operated under the miners code of not shopping work colleagues to the bosses, provided it didn't include dishonesty. This code now extended to Scott.

After about two weeks one of Jimmy's other internal sources, who was friendly with the publican of 'The Signet' bar in Stratshall, came to Jimmy. He said the publican, Norrie McIntyre, told him there had been an altercation in his pub involving Scott about three weeks before.

McIntyre knew Scott to see but had no idea he was a senior police officer. He knew he came from Newholm and had seen him with some good looking women in his lounge bar from time to time. The last time he had been in the pub he was in the company of a beautiful young woman.

The couple hadn't been in the pub long before what looked like this woman's husband or boyfriend came in, marched straight over to where the couple were seated, and told the woman she was leaving. He then went face to face with Scott. McIntyre could see this guy left Scott in no doubt what would happen if he ever went near his woman again.

According to the publican this guy (Scott) almost 'crapped' himself, never uttered a word, and just nodded.

Jimmy's source then told him Wilma McKinnon, a stunning twenty-three year-old, married woman, had joined the service some four months before. The source who worked in the training department, had interviewed her and her husband Bert, who was a well known amateur boxer, after she passed the police entrance exam and fitness test.

He felt they were both pretty naïve about what police work entailed. He knew they hadn't considered the unsocial hours, being away from home for long spells, losing friends and only mixing with cops. These factors he told them would all put a strain on their marriage. Knowing the cops as he did, he thought to himself, with her looks she would become a target for the attentions of some male cops.

Neither the woman nor her husband could not be deterred and as there was no good reason reason to refuse her application, and there was a shortage of applicants, Wilma McKinnon became a probationer constable.

Once she finished her first stage basic training at the Police College, according to Jimmy's source, when she returned to force she was a bit starry eyed and in awe of cops with rank. It appeared the higher the rank the more she looked up to them.

Jimmy's informant knew her husband had difficulty with her being away at college and this difficulty was compounded by the amount of shifts she was working when she returned to force. She wasn't at home much and even when she wasn't on shift she was out socialising and drinking with her fellow cops.

This wasn't like her and joining the police had turned her life around, much to Bert's angst.

In fact he had recently spoken to the informant, hoping in turn, he would speak to Wilma and talk some sense to her. He knew now the advice they had received from him after her interview, was sound, but they had been too stupid and too naive to listen.

He said before his wife joined the police they had been a very close couple who spent most of their free time together. She took a keen interest in his boxing and regularly went with him to bouts. He in turn pampered her at every opportunity. He couldn't believe he had landed such a beautiful wife and he was as much in awe of her, as she was now of the police.

Things had changed dramatically since she became a cop. She never showed any interest in his sport or him. She was totally absorbed with the police and all she could talk about was the 'job'.

He told Jimmy's informant he could see they were growing apart and this was the last thing he wanted. In fact he had tried reasoning with her and suggested maybe it was time to start a family, but his words fell on deaf ears. She told him she now had a career, doing the job she loved, and at this stage a family was not on her agenda.

Bert said increasingly, she didn't return home at the end of her shift and he was suspicious she was seeing someone. The thought of losing her or her being with another man was eating him up.

He didn't reveal, the situation had become so bad he was concealing his car in a busy car park near the Police Station and watching who she left with when she finished work. Mostly she left with a group of cops and headed to the pub across the road from Newholm Police Station. She wasn't there long before Bert joined her and her cop buddies. He hated being in company with cops who all they could speak about was neds, people they had locked up, and promotion hopes.

However, if this is what it took to keep his wife he would suffer it.

Three nights before Jimmy and Green came across Scott, was the time Norrie McIntyre was referring to about the incident in The Signet.

McBurnie's source said he had now spoken to McIntyre again and he was able to add more detail to what he saw and heard that night. It was clear from McIntyre's description the woman with Scott was Wilma. McIntyre had seen her arriving at The Signet in a red coloured Alpha Romeo car driven by her male friend.

The two of them were only in the bar for ten minutes when Bert marched in and started shouting at her. He said he had gone to her local in Newholm but she wasn't there and none of her colleagues knew where she was. He then said he had seen her getting into the Alpha Romeo and followed them to The Signet.

He told Wilma to get her coat as she was leaving with him 'now'.

From the look of fear on Wilma's face Norrie knew you could only go so far with Bert. By the colour of his face and his vicious expression she knew she better leave before there was a real scene in the pub.

Before they left Bert told the guy who had been with Wilma, if he saw him with his wife again he would need his face reconstructed. The male, who McIntyre knew now was Scott, started shaking, and just nodded when Bert asked him if he understood...

Jimmy's informant was delighted to be passing on this piece of gossip, as he also had no time for Scott, who he saw as supercilious and a chancer. To his amazement Jimmy just said, "All very interesting, but it might have no connection to how Scott came about his injuries."

When he left his 'stunned' internal tout, he contacted Green and asked him to have a pint and a quiet word with some of Wilma's shift colleagues. Especially ones who had been on duty the night of the incident in The Signet and the night of the incident at The Rigger.

The D.S. was a very gregarious person and well respected by many uniform cops. He had no difficulty getting the 'inside line' on Wilma. After a few pints he learned some guys on her shift really fancied her but any time they tried chatting her up her husband would appear. They knew he was an accomplished boxer and they didn't fancy being on the receiving end of a beating, so they ended up giving her a wide berth.

Wilma in her naivety had been openly telling her colleagues

Chief Superintendent Scott was taking a personal interest in her and was going to give her advice on how to progress her career. She said he had already told her, even at this early stage in her service she was showing positive signs she could achieve high rank.

Scott's involvement and Wilma's husbands reputation meant for her male shift colleagues, she was definitely out of bounds.

Green learned, three nights before the incident with Scott at The Rigger, she told her shift she hadn't time to go for a drink after work as she had an urgent appointment. The cops who told Green this said it was strange because on the same night her husband never came into the pub looking for her so they assumed she was with him.

Green being the quality detective he was, found on the night Jimmy and him had come across Scott at The Rigger, again she hadn't gone for a drink with her shift mates. When they asked why she wasn't joining them this time she said she had a prior engagement, which again they thought must have something to do with her husband.

Strangely, none of the cops Green spoke to admitted to linking Wilma's husband to Scott's injuries and Wilma had never said anything about her husband's or her two meetings with Scott.

Jimmy now had something tangible about Scott but there was no way he was going to use it. That is not to say he didn't think about it, but whenever he did the words of his old minister, Sandy Morrison, came back to him.

While engulfed with rage and planning on how to get even with Scott, Morrison told him to forget about revenge and leave it to God, who had a plan for him. He said seeking revenge would be like a cancer which would totally consume him and turn him into a bitter and twisted man. It might even destroy his family life and if he was wise he would leave matters like this to the 'man above'.

Jimmy could see now just how wise and prophetic his words had been...

Three weeks after the incident at The Rigger Jimmy's informant in the training department contacted him again. He told him, completely out of the blue, Wilma McKinnon had tendered her resignation and she was now leaving the force. He had interviewed her to get a handle on why she had decided to resign but all she would say was it was for personal reasons.

McBurnie thought it was just as well she was leaving...

He knew from personal experience, the pressures police work could put on a marriage even without the involvement of characters like Scott. He sympathised with both her and her husband and hoped her resignation might save her marriage and at least give them the chance of a 'normal' family life.

Throughout this period Jimmy had bumped into Scott on two separate occasions at Newholm Police Station.

For the first time since he was assaulted by Jimmy's ex D.C.I. Chambers, Scott acknowledged Jimmy, and asked him how things were in the C.I.D. world.

Jimmy was courteous because he knew to acknowledge him, Scott would have had to swallow his pride and his loathing for him. Now because of the incidents with Wilma McKinnon, which neither Jimmy nor Green had disclosed, Scott must have felt he was in their debt.

Initially, Jimmy felt quite smug about this but after some thought he let his ego deflate and harked back to Sandy Morrison's advice to leave it to the man above.

He just got on with his work but now he had a bounce in his step.

TEMPESTUOUS LAD.

Jimmy never did receive a commendation but did get a memo from the Chief who said how pleased he was that Jimmy had helped solve some serious crimes in other forces. He attached a copy of the letter he received from Detective Superintendent Melrose and asked Jimmy to sign both the letter and the memo and return them to him. It would then be placed in his personal file.

Jimmy wondered to himself what else was in his file?

Before returning the documents he showed both to Johnston and asked him what he thought now about him having any chance of further promotion. Before he could reply, Jimmy, being a bit big headed, said if any other cop had unearthed what he had, and while off duty, there would be no doubt they would be commended. He told Johnston it didn't matter how well he performed, what crimes he cleared, some senior officers, including that old bugger Ramsden, would ensure he never received the acknowledgement he was due.

He almost mentioned the incident with Scott and Bert McKinnon but something 'pulled him up' and he kept it to himself.

Johnston couldn't say much, other than tell McBurnie not to let the bosses get him down, he would continue to support him at every turn.

Through all this scepticism Jimmy still harboured hopes, maybe he was wrong and had 'tholed his assize' over the earlier incident with Scott. However, this didn't seem to be the case and he was certain, in his heart of hearts, he would never beat the system or be forgiven for not being a witness against ex D.C.I. Chambers.

All that was left for him now was to continue to get a buzz through motivating his team of detectives and in training his stable of touts and exploiting opportunities to recruit new ones...

He had recently 'signed up' a new tout who he had named 'Tempestuous Lad' due to his volatile nature.

Tempestuous was twenty-one years old and one of five brothers who had all been involved with the police at some stage in their lives. He had a babyish face and had long brown hair which almost reached his waist. He wore 'John Lennon' style, round glasses, and on first appearance he looked a bit like an easy going hippy. Below this exterior lay a very angry young man who often got into fights, especially when people tried to tease him over the length of his hair and/or his babyish appearance.

He had a few convictions for assault and minor thefts but he was not someone Jimmy had come across.

That was until he assaulted an off duty cop one night in a trendy pub in Newholm. The cop had too much to drink and when he saw this guy with the long hair standing at the bar, chatting up a good looking girl, who had already given him the knock back, he became mouthy. He asked the girl what was wrong with him and what was she doing with this hippy arsehole. The words were no sooner out of his mouth when he was punched, only once, full in the face by Tempestuous, and rendered unconscious.

Had the cop known that Tempestuous was a black belt in karate maybe he would have been more careful with his words. Anyway, the police were called and Tempestuous was locked up. That night his aunt called at the police station asking to see her nephew and was told by the custody officer no visits were allowed.

Fortunately Jimmy had been in the reception area of the station at the time and knew the aunt.

She was 'Delicate Girl' and she was in a bit of a state...

She looked like a walking skeleton, her hair was unwashed and she wore the same clothes she always wore. She obviously didn't use the vouchers Jimmy had given her.

Nevertheless, Jimmy was only too happy to see her, at least she was still alive...

The D.I. told the custody sergeant he would supervise the visit and he ushered Delicate through to the waiting room in the cell area. He then took her nephew from his cell and told him to accompany him as he had a visitor.

McBurnie stayed in the waiting room throughout the visit and during their conversations. He agreed, before she left, Delicate could put cigarettes and fresh clothing into her relative's property bag, after it had been checked with the custody sergeant.

Delicate was then returned to the reception area and Jimmy asked her to wait a minute while he handed the property over to the custody officer. When he returned she thanked him for the visit and he said, "It's nothing." He then took her to another waiting room and before she left he told her to look after herself and confirmed if she needed help he was always available.

He then took Tempestuous back to his cell and engaged him in conversation.

He thanked the D.I. for the visit and said it was the first time out of the five previous lock ups he had been allowed a visitor. He told Jimmy he owed him a favour and Jimmy thought to himself, "You do and I will soon be calling it in."

Tempestuous appeared at court the next day and was bailed.

One week later, Jimmy bumped into him as he was walking home alone from a local pub, in the pouring rain. As he had done with Chocolate Treat when he recruited him, he offered the guy a lift home in the unmarked C.I.D. car. Seeing it was Jimmy who was driving he'd accepted.

During the journey of three miles Jimmy 'tested the water' and soon learned Tempestuous was short of cash and would be willing to take the 'King's Shilling' for supplying information.

It wasn't long before he earned that shilling with information which cleared a break in at a Newholm Amusement Arcade.

Tempestuous was now a member of Jimmy's stable and the trainer thought, here was another charge with potential to be a classic contender.

Just how true this was would soon became obvious...

On a Tuesday afternoon McBurnie was just about to leave for home when he got a call in the office from Tempestuous. The tout said he needed to meet with him, soon, as he had some info about a guy trying to take over 'everything' in Newholm. The guy was an Irishman called Seamus with some 'heavy' friends in London, Manchester and Newcastle and he was giving drugs away in Newholm for nothing!

Jimmy arranged the meet at a derelict warehouse on the outskirts of the town and when Tempestuous arrived he said the guy he was talking about was a 'one off'. Jimmy asked his tout to explain what he meant. Tempestuous said the guy had turned up in a nearly-new Porsche, at the ground floor flat of his girlfriend. Apparently Seamus had met the touts, girlfriends brother, Callum, who now lived with his sister, while both he and Callum were serving a prison sentence in the same jail.

Tempestuous had heard Callum talking about him saying when they were in prison together just how 'off the wall' he was. He had frequently heard him boasting about his links with paramilitaries in Northern Ireland, the crimes he was involved in, including drug running, high value thefts, 'ringing' and exporting performance cars, passing counterfeit money and break-ins at high class stores. At 6' 2'', built like a wrestler and with terrorist connections, no one ever challenged him about his claims and he never got any trouble from anyone on the 'inside'

Out of the blue Seamus had turned up at Callum's sisters flat on his release, in the Porsche. Immediately he was in the flat Tempestuous said he started swaggering about how smart he was and how he had decided he would move up to Newholm and take over 'business' in the town.

The next night he turned up at the flat again, this time with a pocket full of L.S.D. paper squares, forty wraps of speed and twenty wraps of smack. He 'instructed' Callum to give the drugs away to some local users for free and this would get this side of the business started.

Callum being too afraid of the Irishman's reputation and contacts, agreed, and distributed the drugs to users he knew in town. As expected they couldn't believe you got drugs for nothing, but they weren't going to look a gift horse in the mouth.

The next night Seamus turned up again and said he was moving out of the top hotel in the town he was staying in and he had rented a five bedroom house on the outskirts, known as 'Woodend'. Callum and Tempestuous both knew this house and had a rough idea of how much it would be to rent and it wouldn't be cheap.

What was different this time was he didn't appear in the Porsche but in a top of the range Audi Quattro. Yet again he had a supply of free drugs and told Callum to give them out again to the same punters for nothing, which he did.

Jimmy was all ears now...

The lack of a commendation, his thoughts on Scott and Ramsden and all the negatives in his life, were put on hold for the time being. His addiction to fighting crime had kicked in again. Now he was on the trail of what appeared to be a real 'nasty', but nevertheless a professional criminal. This was a challenge, as all active criminals were for Jimmy. The 'heavier' the ned the more he relished the challenge. He decided, in keeping with his use of horse racing terms, this guy was taking a 'fall'.

He paid Tempestuous £100 up front from the tout fund and supplied him with the code name 'Chalky'. McBurnie told him to use this code name if and when he ever had to phone the C.I.D. office when he couldn't get hold of Jimmy. The D.I. would make sure the detectives in the C.I.D. would all know, if Chalky phoned, Jimmy should be contacted immediately.

Back at the office Jimmy told all the detectives including his boss if a man named 'Chalky' called asking for him, they had to contact him, no matter what time, day or night.

Tempestuous had provided a good description of Seamus and McBurnie set his best intelligence officer, Andrew Thomason, the task of positively identifying him and finding as much as he could about his background and associates.

Thomason could be relied upon to be thorough and after a few days he came up trumps. Seamus was Seamus McGarrigle a thirty five year old native of Lisburn, Northern Ireland. He had previous convictions for serious assaults, fraud, embezzlement and had links to paramilitaries in Northern Ireland.

His last sentence was for five years and served in England after he was found guilty of distributing almost £500,000 of counterfeit, Bank of England, £20 notes. It was whilst in this prison he had befriended Callum.

Thomason told Jimmy this was only the start of his intelligence gathering. He had ongoing liaison with the English and Northern Irish Police, Prison Service, the military and specifically with four

English forces where McGarrigle was known to have addresses.

Jimmy thanked him and knew, like him, he wouldn't rest until he had found out all he could about Seamus.

Two nights later at 2.30a.m., Jimmy got a call at home from one of the night shift C.I.D. detectives, saying 'Chalky' had phoned and asked the D.I. to contact him urgently.

Doris by now knew if the phone rang in the middle of the night there was every likelihood her husband would be going back to work. When it rang this time she just turned over and went back to sleep.

McBurnie told D.C. Calder, the caller, he would make contact with 'Chalky' and thanked him for the call. After he phoned Tempestuous he changed quickly and got into his car. In no time he was at the location he had previously agreed with him and he couldn't wait to hear what the tout had to say.

Tempestuous told him the Irishman hadn't stopped 'blowing his own trumpet' since he arrived in Newholm. He was now bragging to Callum telling him to wait and see what car he turned up in tomorrow.

Tempestuous thought this information might be of interest to Jimmy. It would certainly give him the opportunity to see what Seamus looked like and what car he arrived in. Unfortunately he couldn't say at what time Seamus would turn up because he told Jimmy he had appeared in the middle of the night before.

Jimmy thanked his tout dropped him a 'King's Shilling' and

told him to keep in touch as there was plenty more where that came from.

Both men then left their meeting place.

Tempestuous went home while McBurnie went into the C.I.D. office arriving there at 3.30.am. He told the three D.C.s in the office, they were going with him and to look out the surveillance equipment. When they asked what they would be doing McBurnie said, "You are coming onto a plot in Newholm." He didn't tell them where it was but just told them to follow him.

Within the hour they were plotted up in an old van with a fictitious plasterer's details on the side. They sometimes used this van and another old van for surveillance jobs, changing the details on the side of them, to blend into the area where they were doing the surveillance work.

At 8a.m. a nearly new, top of the range BMW sports car, drew up at the flat and a guy fitting the description of Seamus, got out. He walked straight into Tempestuous' girlfriend's flat, without knocking or using a key. Those inside must have been expecting him.

Jimmy's cops managed to photograph him and the car, and they quickly relayed the number of the B.M.W. to the force control room and asked for it to be checked on the Police National Computer (P.N.C).

The check came back quickly, confirming the car was not stolen, and the registered keeper was a man in Chester. Jimmy noted the details and he and his team remained in the van for the next five hours, before Seamus left in the B.M.W.

Once back in the office McBurnie briefed Johnston, who was sitting at his desk, almost completely hidden behind a mountain of paper.

Johnston as usual was bowled over by Jimmy's enthusiasm whenever he got any tip about active neds. In fact he had never seen a guy so 'switched on', or so determined to catch criminals and lock them up. The ned Jimmy had the information about this time seemed from what McBurnie was saying, to be a real nasty bastard with a lot of guile and bottle.

Jimmy, as was his habit, when talking about neds nearly always resorted to horse racing terminology. He told his boss Seamus would be taking a serious 'fall' and 'put out to pasture for a long time'.

Johnston never doubted it. He knew just how driven his D.I. was but he also felt sorry for him. The bosses, other than Cobble, couldn't, or refused to see, what a commitment he was making to the force and the community.

Jimmy shot out the office after the briefing and tasked D.S. Green with doing a follow-up enquiry with the police in Chester, to see if the keeper of the B.M.W. as shown on P.N.C. still owned it.

Later in the afternoon Green came back to him and said the owner of the B.M.W. had sold it two days before for £20,000 to a man fitting Seamus' description, who gave the name Rory McNiven. The guy paid £20,000 for it by means of a bank draft.

Not long after this Tempestuous phoned Jimmy again. He said

the reason Seamus had been at the flat that morning was to tell Callum to round up all the druggies he had supplied with freebies, and tell them to be in 'The Barnacle' pub at 6 o'clock that night.

The tout said this was the first opportunity he had to contact Jimmy and it was now 8pm.. McBurnie had missed the chance to spot Seamus' customers but Tempestuous told him he had been at the meeting and knew who they were.

Tempestuous said, as usual, that Seamus had been strutting up and down the pub, leaving the druggies in no doubt they now owed him for the drugs. He said didn't want cash as payment but they would do what he wanted when he called upon them. Just to reinforce the message he passed round photographs of both men and women with horrendous facial injuries. He then smiled and said they would look like the people in the photographs if they didn't comply.

A right nasty bastard thought Jimmy!

The following day the extent of the Irishman's activities became a little clearer. D.S. Green came into McBurnie's office and said the cops from Chester had been in touch. The bank draft used to buy the B.M.W. had been one of a batch of thirty blank bank drafts stolen during a break-in at a building society in Manchester some ten days earlier. The car had been advertised for sale in a national motoring magazine.

Green, on his own initiative was carrying out enquiries with the issuing bank to ascertain what had happened, if anything, with the remaining twenty nine drafts.

Jimmy now had to admit he had some sort of warped

admiration for McGarrigle with the diversity of his crimes. Having said this he was still in no doubt as he had told Johnston, McGarrigle was being permanently 'pulled up'.

Green toiled away and soon found that the owner of a Porsche in Chelsea had also been duped into handing over his car after being presented with one of the same batch of bank drafts. The same thing happened to the owner of an Audi Quattro in Southport. Both car owners had advertised their cars for sale in the same motoring magazine as had the owner of the B.M.W. from Chester.

Green told his D.I. the issuing bank were totally embarrassed about these thefts and their subsequent fraudulent uses. He had to be persistent with them before they supplied some details of where and what they had been used for. It wasn't just cars that were bought. In fact, one draft had been accepted in Bristol as payment for a speedboat for a sum of £250,000!

McBurnie instructed Green to keep digging away until he had identified where they had all been used, and for what purchases. Then, he said, they would know just how widespread the Irishman's tentacles extended.

Tempestuous was on the phone again the next day and said something had spooked Seamus, who had told him he was lying low for a while and moving out of Newholm to England. He didn't say whereabouts in England, nor how he got spooked.

On hearing this Jimmy became frustrated and angry, thinking he was at a stage where he could nab this Irish 'entrepreneur' but now he had disappeared.

All was not totally lost, because his tout said he had forgotten to mention at the meeting Seamus had in The Barnacle, he had singled out a druggie couple who Callum had been supplying with a lot of freebies.

He told the couple, who Tempestuous knew as Sarah Bryant and Walter Coogan, they owed him for a considerable amount of kit and he wanted paid. He confirmed, as he had done with the rest of the druggies, it wasn't cash he wanted. He instructed the couple to go to Aberdeen Airport and hire a top specification Mercedes from a rental company for three days. How they hired it was a matter for them, but once they had the car they were to drive to Lancaster to a named service station on the M6, park up the car, and leave the key under the drivers seat. Before the three day hire period elapsed they were to report the car as being stolen to cops in Lancashire.

How they got home was a matter for them...

As he was leaving the pub the Irishman placed a photograph of a young woman whose face had been beaten to a pulp, on Bryant's lap and told her and her boyfriend not to fail. If they did she would end up looking like the woman in the photograph.

Tempestuous told Jimmy the couple had now gone to Aberdeen by train. He was sure they would do as Seamus had instructed because they were terrified. He had heard them say they would have to hire the car using the girl's licence because Coogan was disqualified from driving, and his licence had been revoked.

Jimmy thanked his tout for the info, promising to square him up shortly and telling him to keep his ear to the ground.

Once McBurnie had finished his call with his tout he made calls to all the car hire firms at Aberdeen Airport. Sure enough a Sarah Bryant from Newholm had hired a top of the range Mercedes from one of the companies, twelve hours before, for a period of three days.

He was in no doubt Seamus, or some of his cohorts, would change the identity of the car and some unsuspecting punter would end up buying a 'rung' vehicle.

He obtained a full description of the car, including its registration number, from the receptionist at the car hire firm and put a 'flag' against it on the P.N.C. He asked the receptionist if they had CCTV coverage in their office and she confirmed they had. He told her to remove the tape and keep it secure until a local cop contacted her.

It was time for Jimmy to reflect on what exactly he was dealing with in relation to Seamus and what evidence he had at this stage to 'put him away'...

He could now confirm Seamus had fraudulently used four blank bank drafts which were part of a batch of thirty stolen from a building society in Manchester. This was the only concrete evidence at this stage and it all related to crimes south of the border. Jimmy didn't mind helping other forces but Seamus was on his patch and if any one was going to 'bring him down' that was going to be him.

The Mercedes hired at Aberdeen Airport would not fall into the category of a completed crime, until it was reported stolen during the three day hire period.

Locally, he had intelligence about Seamus supplying drugs and boasting about other crimes he had committed but this was hardly evidence, and only based on info from Tempestuous.

As usual Jimmy received some help from above...

D.S Green called into his boss' office and said he had now found out where all the stolen bank drafts had been used. Importantly, one of them had been accepted in Stratshall two days earlier for the purchase of a high specification Lexus for £18000. The 'purchaser' this time gave the name, Robert Wooller. Like all the other vehicles Seamus had obtained, it too had been advertised as a private sale in the same motoring magazine.

Jimmy said a private 'thanks'...

He told Green to join him and they would interview the Lexus owner. During the interview of the owner and his wife, McBurnie showed them a selection of photographs and they both picked out Seamus McGarrigle. He now had enough evidence to arrest McGarrigle for fraud and at least reset (receiving) of the stolen bank draft.

Now thought Jimmy,"I am going to nail this bastard."

When they got back into the office he telephoned one of the local Procurators Fiscal, Tom O'Brien, and described the case he had against the Irishman. O'Brien said to give him a brief report and if the evidence was as good as Jimmy said then he would issue a warrant to arrest him.

Jimmy was quite adept at two finger typing so he by passed the typing pool and within two hours the fiscal was reading Jimmy's report and request for an arrest warrant, which was granted without delay.

McBurnie, with the arrest warrant had now made himself the 'front runner' in the race to get McGarrigle.

To make sure all the other police forces and customs officers knew this, he placed an entry on the P.N.C. confirming he held the warrant. If and when he was picked up, anywhere in the country, they had to contact Jimmy immediately. He then spoke to a contact he had in Customs and Excise, in case they already held a warrant, which they didn't.

To reconfirm the fact his force held the only arrest warrant for McGarrigle, and find out the full extent of his criminality, McBurnie decided to hold a meeting. He invited detectives from each area where one of the stolen bank drafts had been used, and his contact in Customs and Excise, to Newholm.

Twenty six detectives and a Customs and Excise officer attended. McBurnie hosted it, assisted by a more than enthusiastic Thomason. On opening, Jimmy wasn't slow to reiterate again he had an arrest warrant for McGarrigle.

He then disclosed some of the information Thomason had compiled on his behalf about this criminal 'entrepreneur'. Thereafter he asked each one of the attendees to disclose details of the crimes McGarrigle had committed in their areas, and what information or evidence they held concerning him.

This was very revealing and by the time everybody had declared their interest, it was clear, in keeping with Jimmy's race horse analogy, McGarrigle was no 'novice' but a 'classic thoroughbred' ned.

The thirty bank drafts that were stolen had been used to obtain high performance and four wheel drive vehicles, boats, horse boxes and trailers with a combined total value of £700000!

In addition some of the other forces had other crimes which fitted with McGarrigle's diverse criminal activities. For Jimmy these were matters for another day. For now he was focused solely on arresting him and getting him off the street before he could cause more mayhem...

It was no surprise when Sarah Bryant reported the Mercedes she had hired from Aberdeen Airport as being stolen in Manchester, on the third day of the hire. Immediately on learning of this 'alleged' theft the receptionist at the car hire company telephoned McBurnie.

He in turn contacted the cop in Manchester who received the false theft claim, hoping Bryant and Coogan were still with the police. Unfortunately, the cop said after making the report Bryant and her boyfriend had been keen to leave Manchester and were taking the train home to Newholm.

McBurnie then again contacted Aberdeen C.I.D. and told the D.S. he had been liaising with and who had the CCTV from the hire company, the Mercedes had now been reported as stolen.

He confirmed with both these English and Scottish officers he would detain the two druggies when they got back to his patch. By detaining and later arresting this couple, Jimmy would get the inside line on Seamus and evidence of his drug distribution in Newholm. Hopefully this would be enough for him to add charges of drug dealing to the Irishman's growing list of charges. Jimmy always seeing himself as the tout trainer, was also thinking this might be an opportunity to recruit two new charges to his stable?

He contacted D.S.Green and D.S. Allan and they went to Newholm Railway Station and detained Bryant and her partner Coogan. When they arrived at Newholm Police Station McBurnie was waiting for them and left them in no doubt he knew who had put them up to hiring the Mercedes and falsely reporting it as stolen. He took it in turns to look both of them in the eye and said, "The reason you did this was to pay Seamus McGarrigle for drugs. That's right, isn't it?."

The couple looked scared, and puzzled how McBurnie knew about Seamus and their drug involvement with him. They were even more worried when the D.I. told them he also knew about the threats and photographs used by the Irishman to frighten them.

Both were left wondering how this cop knew this much about McGarrigle and his 'arrangement' with them. Before they could contemplate this further, Jimmy said he already had enough on Seamus to ensure he would be going away for a while without their help.

If however they opened up about their involvement with him then he would guarantee no harm came to them and would make their assistance known to the prosecuting authorities. This would obviously help them when they appeared at court charged with theft of the Mercedes and falsely reporting it as stolen.

After a few minutes in hushed conversation they both stated they would tell the whole story, including where they had left the Mercedes, on Seamus' instruction, at a service station on the M6 at Lancaster.

Jimmy called Allan into the interview room and carried out a tape recorded interview, firstly with Bryant and then Coogan. They both disclosed details of their dealings with McGarrigle and what they had done with the Mercedes.

Once the taped interviews were finished McBurnie told both druggies,"You both have much more to tell."

After a short period of reflection they told Jimmy and Allan about the amount of drugs Callum had given them and named twelve other locals who he had also supplied, with both heroin and L.S.D.

McBurnie said he would release them to be reported for the theft and possible drugs offences at a later date. However before they left the building he made sure they understood they owed him 'big style'.

Both nodded confirming they did...

After they had gone Jimmy was on a high. He sensed Seamus McGarrigle's days were numbered. He had completely forgotten now about the lack of a commendation or about Scott and Ramsden. He could think of nothing except McGarrigle.

There was no doubt now in Jimmy's mind, McGarrigle was definitely going to take a significant 'fall'. He had more than enough evidence against him to charge him with a number of crimes. In addition he had recruited a new filly and perhaps, being naughty, he told himself, maybe a gelding as well, to his stable.

The joys of a trainer...

Icing on the cake would be when McGarrigle was arrested and Jimmy couldn't wait to meet him face to face.

The following week McBurnie arranged for D.S. Green and D.S. Allan and their teams to detain all the druggies named by Callum, Bryant, Coogan, and also to detain Callum himself.

To protect Tempestuous from being identified as the tout they were told to pick up Callum last. By doing this all the druggies he had supplied with gear would already have been interviewed. None of them would know who had 'spoken' to the police. McBurnie wanted to be doubly sure Callum didn't suspect Tempestuous, so decided he would interview Callum.

Things went according to plan and each druggie detained gave statements about getting drugs from Callum and being threatened by Seamus.

Callum wasn't detained.

By the time all the statements of the drug users had been obtained there was more than enough evidence to arrest him.
On Jimmy's instruction Callum was arrested and charged with supplying controlled drugs, which really put the frighteners on

him. When he was placed in a cell McBurnie visited him and told him if he didn't come across about his involvement with McGarrigle, then he was sure to be going away for a long time.

Callum was many things but not stupid. He opened up to McBurnie but only after the D.I. promised him protection. Jimmy then got the whole story about Callum meeting the Irishman in prison and how he had turned up at Newholm after he was released.

McBurnie sat with this guy for three hours during which he told him all about McGarrigle's pedigree. When he was finished, he had a comprehensive picture of the Irishman and his criminal capabilities. As well as distributing drugs, using stolen blank bank drafts to purchase cars, 'ringing cars' and threatening other neds he know knew McGarrigle had exchanging counterfeit American dollars with a face value of £250000 in Aberdeen, Birmingham, Liverpool and London.

To keep Callum on side after getting all this information McBurnie told him he would release him to be reported to the Fiscal at a later date.

This guy was delighted at this news but McBurnie tempered it by saying he now owed him, and the only way to repay the debt was by supplying more information.

Callum knew he had no option...

McBurnie was left thinking if his stable continued to grow at this rate he may have to contemplate taking on another apprentice trainer...

Green by this time had been in touch with the Police in Lancaster about the stolen Mercedes but when the cops got to the service station named by Bryant, the vehicle was gone.

The following week McBurnie got a call from a D.S. from Liverpool who had been at his meeting in Newholm. The D.S. said he had information Seamus was at an address in St Helens. He asked Jimmy if he wanted the arrest warrant executed and he confirmed straight away, he did. He told the D.S. he would send down D.S. Green and D.C. Starkey with the warrant A.S.A.P.

Later, Green phoned from St Helen's to say they had their man and described him as being as 'wide as the ocean'. He told Jimmy after repeatedly knocking the door of the flat the Irishman was in, and getting no reply, they kicked the door in and found him frantically shredding documents through an industrial shredder, located in the hallway. Before they could caution him and read over the terms of the warrant, he told the two Scottish detectives and their English colleagues they were all going to be subject to a complaint of harassment, and demanded all their shoulder numbers.

Green said he just went about his business, cautioned him and read over the terms of the arrest warrant.

McBurnie was well aware his D.S. never took any nonsense from neds and Green told him he soon had McGarrigle handcuffed, taken to the waiting Police car and transported to St Helens Police Station. Once the necessary documentation was completed Green told Jimmy they would be heading back across the border.

Jimmy couldn't wait for their arrival...

At 8pm McBurnie was in the C.I.D. office, pacing up and down, when Green came in and said McGarrigle was in an interview room downstairs, in the cell area, with D.C Starkey and a custody officer.

The D.S. said on the journey north, the Irishman had never uttered a sound. Before, when he was taken to St Helen's Police Station, again he never said a word and even refused to disclose who he was at the custody processing area. The same happened on his arrival in Newholm Police Station.

McBurnie just smiled and told Green to accompany him to the interview room. Green grabbed the sleeve on Jimmy's jacket. He said before they interviewed him Jimmy needed to look at a document McGarrigle hadn't managed to shred before he was arrested. There was a whole bag of documents they had seized before McGarrigle could destroy them and they would take time to go through but this one merited some scrutiny now.

It was something different...

Green handed the document to McBurnie, and when he examined it he found it was a yearly contract between a company in Hull and an Eastern European country, for the supply of 200 Range Rover cars per year.

What next thought Jimmy!

On entering the tape recording room Jimmy introduced himself and said to McGarrigle he was delighted to meet him at last. The Irishman just grinned...

McBurnie then commenced the interview by asking McGarrigle his name, date of birth and address, but got no reply. Undeterred he then proceeded to go over all the evidence he had against him but again this brought no response. The interview lasted four hours and many documents were placed before McGarrigle and he was asked to comment on them. He just kept looking at the floor or smiling at McBurnie.

The D.I. then charged him with the break in and thefts of the bank drafts from Manchester. Again the only response he got was a smile. Jimmy smiled back and charged him with their fraudulent use at numerous locations, the supply of controlled drugs, threats, and passing counterfeit currency.

To leave McGarrigle in no doubt who was boss, he told him other charges were likely to follow once his enquiries were complete.

Again McGarrigle said nothing and McBurnie switched off the tape. As he got up to leave the room, after telling Green to lock up the Irishman, McGarrigle spoke for the first time, and asked to speak to the D.I. on his own.

Perhaps unwisely McBurnie told Green to leave the room but winked at him, which Green understood he was meant to listen at the door.

McGarrigle said then, "What's the deal?" and Jimmy said for him, with the serious and numerous crimes he had committed, there would never be a deal. McGarrigle replied "There is always a deal."

McBurnie told him not to waste his time but the Irishman said he could put him onto something really big which had an international dimension to it.

Jimmy said he would think about it and left the room and returned to his office in the C.I.D.

Green joined him after incarcerating McGarrigle in a cell.

McBurnie asked his D.S. if he heard what McGarrigle had offered, which Green acknowledged he had. Jimmy then said, "We will let him sweat for a couple of hours and then bring him into my office and see exactly what he is talking about."

Two hours later on the D.I.s instruction Green removed McGarrigle from his cell and took him to his boss' office.

Again the Irishman asked to speak to Jimmy on his own but McBurnie told him Green was staying. If he wanted to say anything he would say it when both Green and him were there.

The Irishman nodded and said if he disclosed what he knew he wanted some 'assistance' when he appeared in court. McBurnie told him he was promising nothing. If what he was about to disclose was a crime of an international nature and the culprits were detected then he would let the Procurator Fiscal know he had assisted.

Perhaps that would reduce the length of sentence he would receive but McBurnie reiterated he was promising nothing. In truth he was wary of saying anything to McGarrigle, and was even more so, when he saw him making what appeared to be, mental notes of the surroundings of his office.

After a short pause McGarrigle said he knew of a scheme where a team from the south were involved in importing gold bullion from South Africa into Britain. Jimmy asked what value of gold was involved and he said about £6m a trip. Jimmy said this was not really a matter for him but if McGarrigle was agreeable then he would contact Customs and Excise and put them in touch with him.

It wasn't often Jimmy passed up the chance to recruit a tout but on this occasion he knew McGarrigle would be going 'away' for a while. Anyway, he felt he was so 'off the wall' he couldn't be trained or disciplined.

McGarrigle agreed to Jimmy's proposal but before being returned to his cell he shouted back to Jimmy. "There is always deal."

McBurnie just laughed because he knew on this occasion he was right not to recruit this loose cannon.

As expected McGarrigle got remanded in custody at the local prison while awaiting trial. During this time, Jimmy and Green sent reports to all the Forces involved with the Irishman, confirming he had been arrested and was being held at Newholm prison.

It wasn't long before the prison was being visited by cops from all over Britain, all wanting to interview Seamus McGarrigle.
From the feedback Jimmy got the Irishman did as he had with him at interview and didn't say a word!

As promised McBurnie did contact Customs and Excise in the

form of D.I. Black whom he had come across in the Eastly case. Black was very interested in what McGarrigle had to offer but Jimmy suggested Black meet with him first, before he visited McGarrigle.

When they did meet Jimmy told the Customs man everything he knew about this dangerous ned and warned him to be on his mettle, and definitely watch what he said to him.

Black took on the advice but still met with McGarrigle in prison. Two months later he phoned McBurnie to tell him, thanks to the Irishman, one of the Customs and Excise enforcement teams in Dover had recovered £4m of gold bullion hidden in the bumpers of two Range Rover cars. It was believed the bullion originated from South Africa where the V.A.T. rate was significantly less than in the U.K. meaning the smugglers could make a profit when it was sold on.

Jimmy didn't think it prudent to ask who the Range Rovers belonged to...

He had already passed on details of the export contract his team had recovered from McGarrigle, to a D.S. he knew in the Stolen Vehicle Squad in Humberside. The D.S. had made enquiries and found the company named on the contract did not exist. The supposed company premises were in fact a run down industrial unit near Hull Docks. He made enquiries at other premises in the area and confirmed approximately once a month six or seven Range Rovers were driven into the unit and shipped out to the continent two days later. The rest of the time the unit lay empty. The D.S. had now passed the enquiry onto his Fraud Squad and the Customs and Excise.

McBurnie thought to himself "What the hell is McGarrigle not involved in?" He knew with this scam having an international aspect it would end up being a protracted enquiry and knowing McGarrigle it would be hard to tie anything back to him.

One thing for sure, McGarrigle wasn't going to admit it...

The week the Irishman's trial was due to start his defence Q.C. raised many objections, all of which delayed the legal process before it had even begun. In fact McGarrigle while in the prison library, had unearthed a piece of legislation which apparently allowed him out of prison to view the productions (exhibits) in his case. McGarrigle had one 'away day' from prison.

When the trial eventually did start the owner of the Lexus and his wife, were subjected to rigorous questioning over the identity of McGarrigle as the man who purchased their car using one of the stolen bank drafts. They had already picked him out when McBurnie showed them a selection of photographs and both identified him in court. However, McGarrigle's Q.C. got them to admit they were really only 80% certain it was him, creating the first doubt in the minds of the jury.

All the druggies were subjected to similar questioning and only two of them identified McGarrigle in court again creating further doubt in the jury's mind.

As expected, all the police witnesses were given a torrid time by the Irishman's Q.C.

When it came to Jimmy's turn, he was accused of offering the Q.C.s client a 'deal' and to give this claim some credibility, the Q.C. described Jimmy's office in the C.I.D. in exact detail where this supposed 'deal' took place.

This location, said the Q.C., was where D.I. McBurnie had offered her innocent client a chance of his freedom if he 'shopped' the local drug dealers in Newholm. She described details of photographs Jimmy had on his walls, certificates he had displayed there and asked Jimmy to confirm his office was furnished as she had stated.

McBurnie had no choice but to agree and this brought a smirk to McGarrigle's face as he sat in the dock...

Jimmy could see some members of the jury wondering why McGarrigle was in his office in the first place. He knew through previous court experience it didn't take much to discredit a witness in the eyes of the jury and this female Q.C. was doing her best to achieve this.

As a witness in court he knew he shouldn't be asking questions other than to clear up ambiguity but he responded to the Q.C.s claims by saying it would be prudent for her to ask her client, why he was in his office, and at whose request.

This brought a reprimand from the judge but Jimmy knew the jury needed to hear his question to the Q.C. and importantly her response. She was temporarily taken aback, but totally ignored McBurnie's comment, which brought some inquisitive looks from the jurors. She felt she had achieved her objective in raising more doubts about the Police's case. McBurnie however, was sure he had also raised doubts with them after she refused to answer his question.

After three weeks, and by a slim majority, McGarrigle was found guilty of most of the charges. Before passing sentence the judge was approached by the Head of Customs and Excise U.K. and told how the accused had helped them dismantle a major smuggling network

Instead of being sentenced to ten years the Irishman received a four year sentence...

Jimmy was just glad to see the back of him but there was no doubt he was a 'classic' ned but one who could never be trained.

Johnston had been kept up to date about the investigation and trial by his D.I. He would have liked to have been 'hands on' in dealing with such a criminal 'entrepreneur' as McGarrigle, but in his present role he was almost office bound and rarely got such opportunities.

When Jimmy asked him to sanction the payment of £600, which was £100 over the limit a D.I. could authorise, to Tempestuous Lad, his boss had no hesitation in handing over the cash, telling him it was "V.F.M."

For Jimmy this was another tick in the friend box...

The tout was well pleased with his reward and a happy Jimmy had managed to protect his identity. He knew only too well if he had been unearthed as the tout then he could have ended up dead.

McBurnie was an astute trainer and by detaining so many people and involving so many police forces it was anyone's guess where the information about McGarrigle came from. The other bonus for him was he now had another three charges in his stable, in the form of Callum, Bryant and Coogan. He needed to supply them with stable names but that would not be too onerous a task.

He thought of their mannerisms and attitudes and sticking with his his fondness for horse racing, he named Callum 'Cucumber Cool', Bryant became 'Bashful Girl' and Coogan was named 'Sloppy Joe'.

BASHFUL GIRL

Once McGarrigle had been sentenced Jimmy made individual calls to his three new charges. This was to remind each of them they were in his debt and to keep contact with him with any 'tips' they had about crimes. As an experienced tout trainer Jimmy knew, dealing with more than one tout at a time could be a recipe for disaster. He hadn't been comfortable meeting Bashful and Sloppy at the same time.

His first bosses in the C.I.D. had told him you could never trust a tout and certainly you shouldn't discuss 'business' with two at the same time or meet them on your own. One or both could set you up or they could have a fall out with each other and one could shop the other as a tout, to other neds.

McBurnie realised this was sound advice and yet, in the past, he had ignored the part about not meeting them on your own. Now thinking about it he had put his future as a cop, a detective and the future of his whole stable at risk.

He wasn't taking any more risks and arranged a meeting with Bashful, told her to tell no one about it, and to come on her own. To further 'cover his back' when meeting her, he decided to take D.S. Allan with him for corroboration.

When they met, Bashful expressed her thanks for getting McGarrigle away from her and her boyfriend, Coogan. Before Jimmy responded, he asked her if she had told Coogan she was meeting him. She said she hadn't but said she was worried about D.S. Allan being present. McBurnie told her not to worry about it,

Allan was trustworthy.

Bashful was cagey and all she would say was she was working on something which might be of interest to him but she didn't have all the details yet. She asked Jimmy if he could meet her on his own the next night at an old church graveyard, between Stratshall and Newholm, when she would have further information. This set alarm bells ringing in his head. He was convinced he was being set up but he didn't show the tout this concern. As they were leaving Bashful, he turned to D.S. Allan and told her she would be coming to this meeting, and any further meetings he had with Bashful or his other female touts.

In the past he regularly had one to one meetings with the other 'fillies' in his stable but he was never comfortable with this arrangement. He was a bit wiser and guarded now, especially after the accusations in the trial of McGarrigle and he had lost part of his gallus 'gung ho' approach. He was now ensuring if things went 'pear shaped' at least he would have some corroboration.

Allan was pleased and excited to have been invited to the first meeting. Now she was looking forward to seeing Bashful again the next night and finding out what she had to tell the D.I.

Up to this point Jimmy had never mentioned to her who his touts were. Only D.S. Green had met with some of them and he never mentioned being there to any of his colleagues. Allan wasn't aware of this and she felt her D.I. who she had the utmost respect for, really trusted her now.

To a certain degree she was right but in reality McBurnie trusted nobody...

He had seen how Allan performed in court and in rough situations with neds. She always stood her ground and more importantly, never spoke out of turn. He knew she had a hot temper and had seen her put some of her colleagues and some big reputation neds in their place, with some strong language and by going face to face with them.

Thinking to himself, and with no little humour, he knew if she had been a tout he would have named her 'Feisty Lady'.

Although she didn't know it, meeting touts with him was an important part of her, as it had been with D.S. Green's, 'apprenticeship' as a future trainer, as it had been with D.S.Green's 'apprenticeship'. If she said nothing to anyone about these two meetings with his tout it would prove she was listening to what he said. It would also provide a good indication of her reliability.

That still wouldn't mean he trusted her...

Before they arrived for the meeting McBurnie told Allan to watch what she was saying, in case Bashful was 'wired up' with a concealed microphone.

When they met, Bashful said she was worried that Jimmy had not come alone. Allan was about to respond when Jimmy looked at her sternly, turned to Bashful, and said, "It's 'company policy' now to have a woman with me when I am meeting another woman." He told Bashful he trusted his colleague to keep her mouth shut and whatever Bashful told him would remain secret, as would her identity. Bashful should have no concerns.

The tout was still reluctant but eventually agreed to talk.

McBurnie was very wary and watching carefully what he and Allan said. He decided to let the tout do most of the talking...

She asked Jimmy if he knew 'The Cuckoo's Nest' pub in Newholm and Jimmy said he, and probably every cop in Newholm knew it, because of the amount of drug users who 'supposedly' used it. She then said everybody in the town got their supply of acid (L.S.D.) and smack (heroin) there. Jimmy said he had heard this but getting information about what was happening within the pub was what was required. He told Bashful, no drug user wants to cut off their own supply. Then he let her continue without interrupting.

Bashful said a couple of years ago it had been 'cool' in the pub because everybody knew everybody else. The guys who supplied the kit were not out to make a huge profit, they were all users the same as their customers.

Things had changed now and the regular suppliers had been beaten up and warned to stay away. The drug business had been taken over by some real nasty bastards, who she named. Allan noted the names, every one known to McBurnie who said nothing...

He was well aware, what Bashful was saying was right. He had personal experience of it. In the 1980s he had seen the drug dealing paradigm change dramatically...

It used to be mostly recreational use and sharing among friends and associates. Now it was mostly a highly lucrative business controlled by criminal 'heavies' who were making huge profits. Many of these neds had been housebreakers, robbers, serious assault merchants and fraudsters who McBurnie had locked up. They were quick to see opportunities to make huge profits as long as they controlled the distribution network.

They didn't want recreational users. They wanted addicts who had no option but to buy from them alone. The younger the addicts the better. They had no scruples about selling drugs to school kids just to get them hooked and have them as life time customers.

Jimmy knew power struggles were erupting regularly between the different dealers. Some locals were sporting facial scars, while others had left Newholm under threat, but nothing was being reported to the police.

The limited intelligence the police held suggested the drugs kingpin was Frankie Hawkins, a forty year old acquaintance of 'Capo', one of Jimmy's thoroughbred informants. At any of McBurnie's meetings with 'Capo' no mention was made of Frankie, but Jimmy suspected behind the scenes Capo was Frankie's controlling figure in the local drug scene. Knowing his tout as he did he was sure, if things got too hot for Capo, who would never be 'hands on', Frankie would become dispensable and would take the 'fall' not him.

For now there was nothing like enough info or intelligence to nab Frankie. Perhaps, thought McBurnie, Bashful was now going to provide enough information to do just that.

McBurnie was delighted then when Bashful named Frankie as the main supplier to the pub. She went on to tell him how and when he delivered to The Cuckoos Nest, with his girlfriend Isla Nielson, and a seventeen stone, power lifting minder named Gary

McIlroy.

The tout said it was always the girlfriend's car they used and Neilson was always the driver. When a delivery was being made Frankie phoned the barman, Jamie, in the pub, to tell him when he would be there with the gear. Jamie in turn contacted all the regular users, including Bashful, and told them at what time they should be in the pub to collect their gear.

Immediately Frankie was leaving whatever safe house he had stored the drugs in, he would telephone Jamie and say he was on his way. Once this call was received, Jamie then sent two of his sidekicks, who Bashful named and who were known to Jimmy, outside the pub to act as 'scouts'. One would stand outside the front door of the pub and the other at the main road junction Nielson's car had to cross before arriving there. Both scouts had white hankies and if they saw any sign of the cops near The Cuckoos Nest they would wave the hankies to each other and Frankie. This was a signal to Frankie and Isla not to stop but to drive on by. Once the scouts returned to the pub when there had been a drive by, Jamie, who never took his eye off the door scout, let the punters in the pub know the cops were about.

If the coast was clear then Nielson would drive as close to the front door of the pub as possible. Frankie and his minder would enter the pub quickly with the gear, which was handed to Jamie to put behind the bar. Thereafter anyone purchasing the drugs had to get the nod from Jamie before they went to the outside toilet where Frankie met them and the deal was done.

According to Bashful the pub owner knew what was happening in his premises but was too afraid to object, knowing the reputation Frankie and his minder had for violence.

Bashful confirmed the type and colour of Nielson's car and where she lived.

By now D.S. Allan was unable to control herself and before McBurnie could stop her she blurted out she knew Nielson, and had dealt with her before for petty theft and possession of speed,(amphetamine). She said she knew where to find her and the car and what she looked like.

McBurnie just gave her a scowl...

Bashful said the next drop was due in three days time and she would be in the pub with her boyfriend to collect the gear, normally about 8 pm.

Jimmy told her, he and his team would cover the pub watching for the delivery. He then instructed her to be sure to be in the pub and be alert because he had a job for her...

Once Jamie confirmed to the potential 'customers' the gear was on its way, she would walk out the front door of the pub without wearing her bright red coloured floppy hat. She always wore it, but instead if the gear was on its way, she should carry the hat in her right hand. If she was wearing the hat it would mean there was no delivery.

Jimmy said he would be watching the pub and he would see if she had the hat in her hand or was wearing it.

McBurnie now like Allan had a wee adrenaline rush on but was saying nothing more...

He thanked Bashful and said he would be in touch with the reward, if and after, the job came down.

As they left he told Allan not to be so keen, or tell any tout what you knew. He said, "Let them do the talking. You just listen and don't show them you are excited about what they tell you."

Allan said she was sorry and it wouldn't happen again. McBurnie told her to forget it, she would still be involved in the 'hit', but because it was a drugs job it would be passed to D.S. Jones and the Drugs Squad to report. Any non drug information received after the hit would be acted upon by her, after consultation with Jimmy.

Jimmy then returned to the office and briefed Johnston on the job and the need for extra staff to ensure they captured Frankie and his team. The D.C.I. was as enthusiastic as his D.I. and Jimmy could see that Johnston would have loved to have been involved but he was almost completely office bound.

He felt sorry for him...

McBurnie told his boss, for them to cover all the bases would take both the six officer Drugs Squad and four D.C.s from the C.I.D. Allan who knew Neilson, would carry out observations on Neilson's house and car, and give the team the 'off' when Neilson entered her car. Allan would also be responsible for detaining Frankie's girlfriend and making sure she didn't escape or dump drugs. Jimmy said Jones would be in charge of the operation and reporting the case, but he would oversee it.

The D.C.I. gave it the go ahead but told Jimmy to try and keep overtime to a minimum...

McBurnie just smiled before wasting no time in briefing D.S Jones who was delighted to receive the information. Frankie had been on his radar for a while but he was getting little in the way of specific information about him.

Everything was in place on the day...

Allan confirmed the registration number, make, model, and colour of Neilson's car, and that it was parked outside her front door.

The D.S. was now in a position where she could watch the car and give the heads up to the others when the car left, and confirm who was in it.

McBurnie and Jones were hidden within an old van in a car park fifty yards from the pub but with a good view of the front door.

The remaining D.C.s from the Drug Squad and C.I.D. were in unmarked cars in close proximity to the pub.

McBurnie had asked for two uniform cops and was supplied with two rugby playing officers, both built like gorillas. These two guys were roughly dressed and sitting on a public bench, only thirty yards from the front door of the premises. To any onlookers they appeared to be quite drunk and were surrounded by empty lager cans.

Excitement was growing among the team and it wasn't long before Allan radioed her D.I. to let him know Neilson had left her house and driven off in her car in the direction of where Frankie lived, some two miles away.

Shortly after this Bashful came out of the pub door, not wearing her hat which was now in her right hand.

Jimmy radioed to all the team and said, "Game on."

After Bashful re-entered the pub the two scouts left it. One remained near the front door, where he could be seen from the window at the side of the bar, by Jamie the barman. The other walked to the main junction leading to the street where The Cuckoos Nest was situated.

D.S. Allan had now left her observation point and covertly joined Jimmy in the van. To keep the adrenaline running he told her, "You are responsible for detaining Neilson and making sure she doesn't ditch anything. Have you got that?." Allan told her boss he needn't worry, she would take care of 'business'. McBurnie was in no doubt she would, and if Neilson didn't co-operate with her, then she was in for a nasty surprise from his go ahead female D.S.

When Neilson's car, with Frankie as the front seat passenger, and McIlroy his minder, seated behind him, approached the turn off for the pub, the scout had his hands at his sides and just smiled.

Frankie gave him the 'thumbs up' sign and a big grin.

Shortly thereafter the second scout at the door of the pub

turned round and gave the bar man, Jamie, the thumbs up sign.

Neilson then drove the car to the front door of the pub and just as she stopped she got the shock of her life. The van Jimmy had been in pulled across the front of her car and another unmarked car driven by a Drug Squad, D.C. pulled in tight behind it and the cops surrounded it.

The two cops on the public bench were now at the front door of the pub with the scout. Thanks to them he was now lying face down on the pavement with his hands handcuffed behind his back. Two other D.C.s had captured the scout at the junction. He too was on the pavement, face down and his hands handcuffed behind him.

McBurnie shouted to Neilson to open the car doors but she just kept her head down and refused to look at him. He was about to smash the drivers window, but before he could do this he heard the glass shattering. Allan was definitely on an adrenaline rush and as 'high as a kite'. Without any delay she had used her wee police issue baton to smash the drivers window. She then reached in, opened the door and dragged Neilson out of the car, forced her to the ground and handcuffed her hands behind her back.

Jones, McBurnie and the rest of the team weren't long in getting a startled Frankie and his minder, McIlroy, out of Neilson's car. Frankie didn't say a word while McIlroy started yapping until Jimmy showed him the error of his ways, sweeping the feet from this seventeen stone bear, kneeling on his back and telling him to be a good boy and remain quiet. He was then handcuffed with his hands behind his back.

Frankie, didn't put up any struggle and he was handcuffed by Jones in a similar manner to his minder. The three occupants of the car were told by Jones they were all being detained under the terms of the Misuse of Drugs Act. They would be taken to Newholm Police Station, with their car, to be searched and interviewed. The two scouts were detained by the two rugby playing cops.

McBurnie then entered the pub which was full of panicking customers waiting for 'goodies' they wouldn't be getting. Before anyone could say anything Jimmy grabbed a scared Jamie and told him he was being detained.

Being the character he was McBurnie couldn't leave without making an announcement to all the punters in the pub. He said, "Sorry to disappoint, but no delivery tonight." Initially, nobody said a word until he grinned and waved as he was leaving, to shouts then of 'you bastard' and other derogatory terms.

On the way out he told the other barman on duty to tell the pub owner he would be hearing from him soon about how he ran his pub.

The detainees were taken to Newholm Police Station, all except Frankie, who said nothing, protesting their innocence.
When they got to the station they were all strip searched.

Neilson had no drugs on her. Jamie was found in possession of four tenner bags of speed(Amphetamine)but no other drugs. Frankie had £800 folded in what was known as dealer folds of £100, where four twenty pound notes were held together by another twenty pound note, folded over them at right angles.

This money was seized by Jones' team and then he and Jimmy went out to the police pound with a Scenes of Crime officer and searched and photographed Neilson's car.

Under the front passenger seat, where Frankie had been sitting was a chunky, metal tin and contained within the tin were 300 'eye patch' patterned acid (L.S.D.) tabs, 25 wraps of what looked like speed (Amphetamine) and 30 wraps of what appeared to be Smack (Heroin).

Jones team carried out field tests on the drugs in the metal tin, which confirmed the wraps recovered contained amphetamine and heroin. Then, him and D.S. Allen, and he carried out interviews with the male detainees, with the exception of Frankie. They turned out to be in Jimmy's terms 'prisoners of war' all refusing to answer any questions.

McBurnie and Green interviewed Hawkins...

Green showed him the tin containing the drugs and said it had been found under the seat he had been sitting on in Neilson's car. Frankie said, "It's not mine, somebody must have pushed it under my seat from the back." When McBurnie told him only McIlroy was in the back of the car, Frankie just shrugged his shoulders and said he had never seen the tin before. Frankie made no further comment.

After the interview McBurnie and Green returned to the car and examined the floor.

They noticed there was a metal ridge, which was an integral part of the floor, which ran horizontally, under the full width of the passenger seat. Jimmy took measurements of the interior of the car, in particular the dimensions of the floor and the height of the metal ridge. Between the top of the metal ridge and the underside of the front passenger seat there was less than 1 inch of clearance.

This meant it would have been impossible to push the tin, which had a minimum depth of 2 inches from the rear passenger foot well, to where it was recovered, on the floor in the front foot-well, where Hawkins was seated.

He instructed the Scenes of Crime Officer to photograph the floor in detail and show the clearance mentioned.

D.S. Allan almost got an admission from Neilson during her interview but she said if she spoke up she would be killed by Frankie's friends and the 'family'.

Jamie was arrested and charged with being found in possession of amphetamine. He was released because he only had a small amount of speed on him. The two scouts who had been detained were released at the same time and all three were told they might yet be charged with being concerned in the supply of controlled drugs.

With the items in the tin confirmed as heroin, amphetamine and L.S.D. the three occupants of Neilson's car were arrested and charged with being concerned in the supply of controlled drugs. They were kept in custody as they were obviously the 'main players' in the supply network. Neilson's car was retained as a production (exhibit) as was Frankie's cash and the drugs in the tin.

McBurnie made arrangements to have all their houses searched under warrant, but he wasn't surprised when no drugs or anything else of evidential value was recovered. The D.I. knew, in Frankie and his team, he was not dealing with mugs. If anything of evidential value had been found then he would have been delighted but more than surprised.

Jones was happy. He felt he had a good case against all three, especially when they were refused bail at court the next day and remanded in custody.

McBurnie wasn't as sure but he knew with a bit of help 'from above', Frankie and his buddies would take a 'fall'. In the meantime, along with a still hyper, Allan, he contacted Bashful and gave her a 'King's Shilling' reward of £300.

No one in the pub, including her boyfriend Coogan, suspected Bashful had been the informant and Jimmy confirmed her involvement would always remain secret. This reassured her, and she told him she would keep in touch. McBurnie just said, "I am sure you will."

He knew now he had recruited another 'pedigree' filly but one who would need constant 'schooling'.

Jamie the barman and the two scouts, because they were released and didn't appear in court right away, were now eyed with extreme suspicion by the 'customers'.

McBurnie always suspected Capo was the head of this drug dealing network. If this was the case then Jamie and his buddies would not only be classed as the 'grasses' by the drug fraternity, but were sure to be subject to a serious interrogation and beating by Capo's underlings.

Two weeks into the remand period Jimmy received an anonymous telephone call, which when he heard the content, he suspected came from one of Capo's troops.

The caller stated McIlroy was the main dealer and Frankie and his girl friend were both innocent parties. To confirm this, the caller told Jimmy he should search McIlroy's garage at his home, especially the vent above the up and over door as he hid his drugs there.

The caller then rang off...

McBurnie was suspicious because the information was too specific, but still contacted Jones and instructed him to organise a warrant for McIlroy's house and garage which had been searched previously.

Sure enough in the vent above the garage door they recovered fifty acid tabs with the same 'eye patch' pattern recovered from Neilson's car.

When Jones returned with the tabs Jimmy asked him if the garage had been searched thoroughly on his previous visit and he confirmed, to the best of his knowledge it had. He couldn't state categorically, the vent above the up and over door had been looked at but he had spoken to the cops who did the initial search. They confirmed the first search was thorough. Whether this was to protect themselves from flak for missing the drugs, or they were telling the truth, Jones couldn't say, but he told McBurnie he had no reason not to believe them.

McBurnie knew what he believed...

He told Jones he was convinced this was a set up. However, he never told the D.S. he suspected it was orchestrated by Capo, to get Frankie off the hook and put the blame onto McIlroy. In his own mind he had little doubt Capo had instructed one of his foot soldiers to 'plant' the acid in the garage and then phone him.

For McBurnie this deviousness indicated how well Frankie was regarded in Capo's organisation, and how expendable his minder, McIlroy, was.

The following day after a briefing by McBurnie, D.S Jones and D.S. Allan went to the prison with the acid recovered from the minder's garage. They interviewed McIlroy under caution and showed him the drugs recovered from his garage. He started cursing, swearing and banging his fist on the table. He told both cops, "I have been fucking set up by Frankie and his fucking pals."

D.S. Jones said, "Well now you can get them back. Just tell us about Frankie's dealing and how the drugs are his and not yours?" The minder said, "I can't, Hawkins is too well connected."

Allan told him to think carefully about this as he could be facing eight to ten years in prison, while Frankie and his girlfriend walked free. While he was thinking about what to do, Allan charged him with another charge of being concerned in the supply of L.S.D.

McIlroy said nothing in response to the charge but as he was being returned to his cell he shouted to Allan and Jones, "Its not finished yet, the bastards"

Two days later Jimmy received a call from McIlroy's solicitor, Glynn Wainwright, asking if he could meet with him.

Wainwright was one of the few local solicitors Jimmy liked. He had cases before where Glynn had represented the people he had arrested. After he had interviewed these clients and they admitted they were responsible for the crime(s)Jimmy had charged them with, Glynn would refuse to tender a not guilty plea or represent them further. He was one of the few solicitors who Jimmy knew who adhered to the ethical code they took on qualifying as solicitors.

McBurnie and Wainwright met in Jimmy's office that afternoon and the D.I. told him straight away he suspected McIlroy had been set up. However, with his client refusing to speak up, his officers had been left with no option but to charge him with the offence relating to the acid recovered from the garage.

When it came to court, McIlroy would now be facing this additional charge, which related to the same type and pattern of L.S.D. recovered from Neilson's car. It would be hard then for any solicitor representing McIlroy, to convince a jury he was not the main supplier.

Wainwright said he accepted what Jimmy said and he agreed with his conclusion.

He told McBurnie, after McIlroy had been charged in prison, he had met with him and explained the dire situation he was in and what his options were. He could either take the blame for something that was not his and admit to owning the L.S.D. found in his garage. This would be crazy and it would ensure he would be facing a really heavy sentence. On the other hand he could do the sensible thing and give evidence against Hawkins and Neilson.

This would bring its own dangers but it might also get any sentence handed to him, reduced.

Wainwright said McIlroy had thought carefully about the options and decided he would give evidence against his boss and his girlfriend, provided the police would protect him.

The ball was back in McBurnie's court now...

It was a strange request from a seventeen stone 'bear' of a man, but it highlighted just how much 'clout' Frankie had. In Jimmy's mind it also showed, if his suspicions were correct, how much McIlroy feared Capo and his connections.

McBurnie said he would need to speak to the Procurator Fiscal(P.F.) first and put the proposal to her. If she agreed then he could get McIlroy on the witness protection programme, if, and after he had been dealt with at court. Wainwright thanked him and before he left Jimmy reiterated he would meet with the P.F. soon and get back to him.

He met Miss Helen Scobie the next day and explained the situation with McIlroy and his meeting with Wainwright. He confirmed to her he was in no doubt Frankie was the main dealer and McIlroy had been set up by friends of Frankie's. He made no mention of Capo.

He described in detail where the drugs tin had been found in Neilson's car and showed her photographs and measurements of the floor of the vehicle, under the front passenger seat. He supplemented this with a full intelligence picture relating to Frankie. Scobie was now in no doubt Hawkins was the main drug dealer and Neilson and McIlroy were his driver and minder.

She asked for a detailed written report. If it confirmed what Jimmy had told her verbally, and if the evidence backed up his theory, she may even drop all the charges against McIlroy and use him as a witness.

McBurnie completed the report late into the night. In it he emphasised where the drugs had been found in Neilson's car i.e. under Frankie's seat and how Frankie had claimed the tin had been pushed from the back footwell. He included further photographs and measurements of the floor layout of the car, showing how it would have been impossible for anyone to push the tin containing the drugs, from the rear foot-well to underneath the front passenger seat.

In his report he confirmed if this evidence could be supported by a statement from McIlroy about Frankie being the main dealer, then Hawkins true role would be clearly identified.

Once Miss Scobie had read the report, she phoned Jimmy and asked him to have McIlroy interviewed under caution, in the presence of his solicitor, Mr Wainwright. Jimmy thanked her for her support and made arrangements for D.S Allen and a D.C to interview McIlroy.

When his two officers returned they said McIlroy had provided a detailed statement confirming Frankie was the owner of the drugs in the car and he had been supplying regulars in The Cuckoos Nest for about a year. McIlroy made no mention of Capo which didn't surprise McBurnie. He knew if he had incriminated Capo who knows what would become of him.

McIlroy had then signed his statement and the P.F. confirmed she was going to use him as a witness against Frankie and his girlfriend.

Now Jimmy had to get him on the witness protection programme, out of Newholm, and away from Frankie, Capo, and their 'cohorts.

He didn't think it would be a problem...

McIlroy was released from prison on the instructions of the Fiscal and kept in a secure location eighty miles from Newholm, with all the necessary police back up he needed until the trial.

When the trial, presided over by Lord Lochdale, started, Jimmy noticed none other than Capo, with a team of four well known neds round about him, sitting in public benches of the court. As usual, both McBurnie and his tout avoided eye contact, but Jimmy could hear Capo playing his role well, telling his underlings to, "Watch out for McBurnie, he is one devious bastard?."

He also saw Hawkins and Neilson arriving at the rear entrance to the court in a prison van. When they left the van escorted by two prison officers, Jimmy could see they were both dressed immaculately. Hawkins was wearing a very expensive suit, a white shirt and matching tie and looked like someone you would see on church duty on a Sunday. Hawkins was dressed modestly, wearing a two piece suit, court shoes, and with her hair tied above her head. Jimmy thought she looked more like a businessman's secretary than a drug dealer's moll.

Jimmy knew they were following their solicitor's advice. By their dress they would look to the jury like respectable, 'butter wouldn't melt in their mouth' people, and not the neds they really were. He was sure the solicitors would also have coached them on how to behave in the dock in front of the jury, to further convince them, these two couldn't possibly be involved in drug dealing.

The curtain had gone up and the theatre of the court was just about to begin...

McBurnie was ready for it, sure he and his colleagues would be the ones portrayed on the courtroom stage, as the villains, by the theatrical performances of the two defence Q.C.s representing Hawkins and Neilson.

The first witness to be called was Jimmy. The Prosecuting Advocate, Miss Fairweather, used him to set the scene for the jury after he had identified both Hawkins and Neilson...

Jimmy explained how he had received confidential information confirming drugs were being sold at The Cuckoo's Nest pub. The informant had told him the drugs were being delivered by car and the car belonged to Isla Neilson. He then said the informant claimed Frankie Hawkins, who was Neilson's boyfriend, would be in possession of the drugs and claimed Hawkins took these drugs to sell to his customers, who were also patrons of the pub.

Jimmy then provided details of how he had received further information confirming when a drugs drop would take place at The Cuckoo's Nest. As a result of this information he mounted an authorised surveillance operation on Neilson's home address and the pub, using both C.I.D. uniform and Drugs Squad officers.

He then gave details of how Neilson's car, with Neilson

driving, had been seen picking up Hawkins and a man called Gary McIlroy, from Hawkin's home address and heading to The Cuckoos Nest.

He described how they had stopped the car at the front door of the pub with Hawkins the front seat passenger and McIlroy seated behind him. Then, how when they searched Neilson's car they recovered wraps of amphetamine, L.S.D. with an 'eye patch' pattern, and wraps of heroin in a tin under the front passenger seat, where Hawkins had been sitting.

Miss Fairweather asked Jimmy to describe the layout of the car's floor, underneath the front passenger seat, using photographs which had been taken of the vehicle. She asked the jury to look at copies of these photographs.

Jimmy described in great detail about the metal ridge that ran under the seat which only had a clearance of 1" between the top of this ridge and the bottom of the seat.

She asked him if it would be possible, as Hawkins had claimed at his interview, to push the tin from the floor of the rear seat, under the front passenger seat, and into the front seat foot-well, where it had been recovered.

McBurnie said he had tried but it was physically impossible, which brought some knowing looks from the jury.

Lastly, before she finished leading Jimmy through his evidence and was just about to sit down, she turned round to him and asked what occupation Hawkins claimed he had when he was detained. Jimmy said Hawkins stated he was unemployed and in receipt of unemployment benefit.

She then asked him how much money Hawkins had on him when he was arrested. McBurnie said £800, and some jurors gave him another knowing look...

Miss Fairweather then handed him this money and he confirmed it was the same money seized from Hawkins and that he had signed the production label(exhibit) confirming this identification. She then asked him if there was anything special about the way it was folded.

The D.I. responded stating four £20 notes secured by folding another £20 note over them at right angles, indicated to him this money was in 'dealers' folds, and the £800 was made up of eight such folds.

She thanked Jimmy and sat down, knowing by the look on some of the jury members faces, she had inflicted serious damage to Hawkins' defence.

Jimmy had thought Fairweather would ask him to describe the layout of the vehicle in more detail but she didn't. Perhaps he thought, she had covered this point satisfactorily or maybe she would refer to it again when she was summing up before the jury considered their verdict?

After Fairweather had finished leading Jimmy through his evidence both Q.C.s took it in turns to give him a torrid time. They accused him repeatedly of telling lies and claiming he had struck a deal with McIlroy so he could convict their innocent clients.

Jimmy refuted these allegations, but they kept bringing them back up and asking him why McIlroy was not in the dock instead of their clients. Jimmy stated this decision was a matter for the Procurator Fiscal not him. He just oversaw the case while D.S Jones reported it. Thereafter, the Fiscal was supplied with a report containing all the available evidence.

Both Q.C.s then took it in turns to ask him if either of their clients had been found with drugs on them when they were stopped and searched. Jimmy replied they hadn't and confirmed the only drugs recovered were those found under the front passenger seat, where Frankie Hawkins was seated.

While cross examining Jimmy, Ogilvie who was representing Hawkins, took every opportunity to claim his client was a public spirited individual who would help anyone. As such, the last thing he would do, knowingly, was give a lift or get his girlfriend to give a lift, to someone who was carrying drugs.

He suggested to McBurnie that on the night in question, his client and his girlfriend, Isla Neilson, had volunteered to give McIlroy a lift to the pub, while having no knowledge McIlroy was carrying drugs. Jimmy said this could be possible, but if it was the case why did Neilson pick up both Hawkins' and McIlroy at Hawkins' house and why did his client not mention this at interview?

This set the Q.C. temporarily back on his heels...

After he had composed himself he put it to the D.I. the lift could have been pre-arranged and Hawkins could have offered McIlroy shelter in his home until his girlfriend arrived in her car.

Needless to say Ogilvie made no mention of his client failing to mention this at interview.

Jimmy responded by saying, tongue in cheek, "Anything is possible when using your imagination." This comment brought him a reprimand from the judge, who told him just to answer questions put to him, in a civil manner, and refrain from putting forward his opinion, unless asked for it.

Jimmy apologised, but at the same time he saw a smile on Fairweather's face. She knew he had taken the wind out of Ogilvie's sails.

Then Ogilvie asked him if he had received information about drugs being in McIlroy's garage, and had he or his team searched the garage. Jimmy confirmed it was he who received this anonymous information about drugs being hidden in McIlroy's garage. He also confirmed he had arranged for the garage to be searched under warrant by some of his officers.

The Q.C. then asked him if anything was found in the garage and Jimmy confirmed L.S.D. was recovered there, and D.S Jones and his officers would confirm, in detail, exactly where these drugs were found, when it was their turn to give evidence.

Ogilvie then asked if he had seen these drugs once they were recovered, and he said he had. He then instructed the court officer to hand over a bag containing fifty L.S.D. tabs to McBurnie and asked Jimmy to describe them. Jimmy said they were fifty L.S.D. paper squares. Ogilvie was nothing if not persistent, and asked Jimmy what pattern was on these paper squares. Jimmy said they all displayed the 'eye patch' pattern.

Seeing an opportunity to score some more 'brownie points' with the jury and create some doubt in their minds, he asked Jimmy what was the pattern on the L.S.D. paper squares recovered from Neilson's car.

Jimmy confirmed they too displayed the same 'eye patch' pattern.

Ogilvie was in full flow now. Looking at the jury but with his back to Jimmy, he asked him if they could have come from the same batch.

Jimmy said that was a possibility.

Lastly, still with his back to Jimmy, he asked him to tell the jury again where these fifty paper squares were recovered from. Jimmy said they came from McIlroy's garage and the Q.C. then asked him if McIlroy was an accused person or a witness and Jimmy said, "A witness."..

Ogilvie looked at every member of the jury and before turning away from them he repeatedly shook his head and muttered, "A witness", which he followed with a more than theatrical sigh.

Meechan, representing Isla Neilson, followed a similar line of impeachment, blaming McIlroy, and confirming his client would never have given McIlroy a lift that fateful night, had she known he was carrying drugs.

He too kept asking Jimmy why McIlroy was not in the dock, especially when fifty L.S.D. paper squares, with the same pattern as those which had been recovered from his client's car, were found in McIlroy's garage.

Jimmy gave the same response he had given to Ogilvie. He said he just oversaw the case. D.S. Jones compiled a report which he countersigned and it contained all the available evidence. This was forwarded to the Procurator Fiscal. She decided who to prosecute, not him.

D.S. Jones was the next witness and went through his evidence smoothly with Miss Fairweather. Once he had finished with the prosecution, like his colleagues he received a torrid time from the two defence Q.C.s. Both accused him of getting McIlroy to set up their clients. He like McBurnie was asked, more than once, if McIlroy was an accused person or a witness. Jones confirmed he was a witness, which brought more theatrical antics from both lawyers who were well experienced in playing to the jury.

Jones had often heard McBurnie say some lawyers and Q.C.s should have equity cards and these two certainly should have.

He was asked in detail by them where in McIlroy's garage the drugs were found, and what pattern was on them. He confirmed it was in the vent above the garage door and the drugs recovered had an eye patch design.

He then, like McBurnie, confirmed this was the same design found on the L.S.D. tabs, recovered from Neilson's car.

When the defence teams were finished cross examining him Miss Fairweather got to her feet again and said she had only one further question for him...

Had his team searched McIlroy's garage on the night of his arrest and were any drugs recovered then? Jones confirmed they had searched the garage then but no drugs were recovered.

Ogilvie got to his feet again and asked him if they could have been missed during the search and Jones replied, "I doubt it." Ogilvie then pushed further and asked if was 'possible' they could have been missed.

Jones replied, "Possible but highly unlikely."

When McIlroy appeared in the courtroom and you could hear a needle drop. As he entered the witness box he tried to look only at the judge and Miss Fairweather. However, from the corner of his eye he could see he was being given dirty looks and stares by Capo, and his buddies, seated in the public benches.

Miss Fairweather asked him if he could identify Hawkins and Neilson and he pointed to them, both seated in the dock.

She then led him through his evidence.

He said Frankie Hawkins was the main drug dealer in Newholm. His girlfriend, Isla Neilson, knew Frankie was the dealer because she regularly used her car to take him to his drop off points with drugs. One of his regular drop points was 'The Cuckoos Nest'.

Fairweather asked McIlroy what his role was in this set up and he said he was Frankie's minder. His job was to ensure nobody stole drugs from Frankie and those who purchased the drugs 'paid up' promptly.

Miss Fairweather then asked why he was in Hawkins home when Neilson came to pick him up on the night they were arrested.

McIlroy said this was always the way it worked. He went to Frankie's house and they both waited for Neilson to turn up with her car to take them to the relevant drops. Frankie always packaged the drugs on his own before he arrived at his house and only Frankie knew what was in the tin he kept the drugs in.

Miss Fairweather then showed him the tin recovered from Neilson's vehicle and McIlroy confirmed it wasn't his but it looked identical to the tin Frankie used to carry his drugs.

Fairweather then asked him to explain, in some detail, how the drugs were delivered and McIlroy replied...

Frankie always insisted in occupying the front passenger seat and he always sat directly behind him. This was so Frankie could get out of the car, which Neilson always stopped at the front door of the pub, and get into the pub in a hurry with the gear.

Neilson was always the driver and it was usually her car they used for 'deliveries'.

On visits to The Cuckoos Nest, Frankie would phone the pub and confirm with a barman there, the gear was on its way.

The barman who received the call would notify the punters and have 'spotters' positioned near the pub, ensuring there were no cops about before Frankie arrived with the gear. These spotters would signal to Frankie when he was on his way to the pub if the coast was clear or not. If it was, which it nearly always was, Frankie would instruct Neilson to stop the car as near to the front door as possible. Then he would rush inside carrying the gear in the tin and McIlroy said he would follow him in.

Fairweather asked McIlroy why Frankie kept the tin containing the drugs, under the front passenger seat. He confirmed, if there was any indication they were going to be stopped by the police, Frankie could easily empty the contents of the tin out of the passenger window. If there was no time for that, he could throw the tin out. He was never going to be found in possession of drugs.

She then asked him if he knew who the barman and the spotters were, but he denied knowing them. This was obviously a lie, but McIlroy was now of the opinion it wasn't them who had tried to drop him in the shit. It was Frankie and he would get what was coming to him, even if McIlroy would now be known as a 'grass' and have to leave Newholm for good.

Fairweather thanked him for being so candid and brave and then sat down.

Now it was time for Ogilvie and later Meechan to cross examine McIlroy. Both immediately accused him of being the drug dealer and trying to divert attention away from himself by blaming Hawkin's and Neilson. Ogilvie even suggested he was helping the police to set up his client and his girlfriend, who had no knowledge of drugs. He accused him of planting the drugs under the front passenger seat of Neilson's car when he first entered the vehicle, in the knowledge the police were waiting to pounce on the car, and would find the drugs under Hawkins' seat.

McIlroy said all these accusations were nonsense. Frankie Hawkins was the main drug dealer in Newholm and everyone in the local drug world knew it. He never struck a deal with the police or agreed to set up Hawkins. The only set up was carried out at Hawkins instruction, when he had drugs planted in his garage, while he was on remand in prison.

Ogilvie, when it was his turn to cross examine McIlroy again asked him how the same type of L.S.D. ended up in his garage as was found in Neilson's car. He responded, pointing to Hawkins and Neilson, both seated in the dock, "They planted them on me."

When he replied in this manner, he was asked by Ogilvie how it was possible for his client, or his girlfriend to plant drugs in his garage, when they were remanded in custody, like him, at the time.

McIlroy, still trying not to look at Capo, stated, "They had connections on the outside." When asked who these 'connections' were, he said it was a matter for him and he would be saying nothing further.

Ogilvie then sat down slightly exasperated but thinking he had raised serious questions in the jury's mind over McIlroy's credibility and status as a witness.

When it was Meechan's turn to cross examine McIlroy again he suggested to him, his client, Isla Neilson, was only a pawn in this game. All she had done was to give him and Hawkins a lift to The Cuckoos Nest pub.

McIlroy again stood his ground and said Neilson was well aware of Hawkins' drug dealing. It was her, using her own car, who dropped him off at different locations with drugs. He told Meechan the night they all got arrested, Neilson was taking

Frankie and him to do a delivery at The Cuckoos Nest. She knew what was going on.

Meechan didn't have much left to come back at McIlroy with, other than raising the same question as Ogilvie about how L.S.D., with the same pattern as that recovered in Neilson's vehicle, came to be found in his garage. McIlroy replied, as he had done with Ogilvie, the drugs had been planted in his garage by some of Hawkins' connections.

Meechan finished his cross examination by accusing McIlroy of being a liar and of him being the only 'plant' in this scenario. He told McIlroy he should come clean and admit he had been the police 'plant' and was used at their behest, to set up both Hawkins and his client.

McIlroy responded, "Absolute rubbish!"

Before the prosecution and defence addressed the jury Miss Fairweather asked for Jimmy to be recalled as a witness.

When he appeared for a second time, she said she had a few questions which required clarity from him, which had been raised by the defence.

She then asked him the following questions:

Did either Hawkins or Neilson mention they were just giving McIlroy a lift on the night in question, when they were interviewed at Newholm Police Station? Jimmy said they didn't and in fact Neilson made no reply throughout her interview.

Did the information concerning the drugs found in McIlroy's garage come from an anonymous source? Jimmy confirmed it did.

Was this information specific about the location of these drugs in McIlroy's garage? Jimmy replied it was, and the anonymous informant told him the drugs were in a vent above the up and over garage door.

She then suggested to him, information of such accuracy was unusual. Jimmy said in his experience it was and even more so when it came from an anonymous source.

She asked if he had any thoughts on how these drugs came to be in the garage at the precise location given, especially when it had been searched before. McBurnie was quick off the mark and before the defence Q.C.s could stop him he said, "They could have been planted."

Lord Lochdale told the jury to ignore this comment as it was merely supposition and reprimanded Jimmy. However, both Jimmy and Fairweather knew the damage had been inflicted on the defence case when the jurors heard his response.

When she addressed the jury, Fairweather put on an impressive display. In summing up she asked them to accept McIlroy's testimony as credible. The police held no intelligence he was a drug dealer and what had he to gain from giving evidence against Hawkins and Neilson. In fact by doing so he had put his life at risk and made himself a fugitive.

She referred the jurors to Jimmy's evidence and the photographs of the floor of Neilson's car. She asked the members of the jury to look again at the photographs of the car floor that they had in front of them.

Once she had their attention and each member was looking at the photographs she highlighted the impossibility of pushing the tin containing the drugs, from the rear foot-well, where McIlroy was seated, to the front passenger foot-well, below where Hawkins was seated. This was what Hawkins had claimed at his interview but she told the jurors they could now see this was not only a lie but an impossibility. The only conclusion one could draw was Hawkins had put the tin there so if he was being stopped by the police he was in a position to dispose of the tin and/or its contents quickly. This fact was supported by the evidence of McIlroy.

Again making reference to Jimmy's evidence she asked the jury to consider the specific detail of the anonymous information he had received. Surely, she suggested, this information was far too specific. Both Jimmy and D.S. Jones had confirmed it was very unusual to receive such detailed information, especially from an anonymous source. She told the jury they had heard McIlroy's garage had been searched thoroughly on the night they were arrested and no drugs were recovered. Was it not strange then, when fifty L.S.D. tabs, with the same pattern of L.S.D. recovered from Neilson's car, were found during a second search of the garage. She asked the jurors to ask themselves, how this could have happened, especially when the garage had been searched before and no drugs found?

She said of the three people in Neilson's car, only Hawkins had any substantial amount of money on him when they were arrested. McIlroy had £8 in his possession, hardly the amount of money a drug dealer would carry with him. Hawkins, who claimed to be unemployed, had £800 in his possession and this money was in 'dealer folds'.

Miss Fairweather then suggested taking all these factors into account there was little doubt about who the drug dealer was. If they needed further confirmation they should ask themselves the following questions:

Why Neilson refused to make any comment at interview unless she had something to hide.

Why did neither Hawkins or Neilson mention giving McIlroy a lift, until the trial began.

She finished her summing up by stating there was more than enough evidence to convict both Hawkins and Neilson, beyond reasonable doubt, of being concerned in the supply of controlled drugs.

Ogilvie and Meechan's summing up was confined to blaming McIlroy for being a police 'plant' used to set up their innocent clients. He was the drug dealer, not their clients. Both Q.C.s placed heavy emphasis on the recovery of the same type of L.S.D. found in Neilson's car and in McIlroy's garage to put doubt into the minds of the jury.

Lord Lochdale then asked the jury to retire and consider their verdict, which he said must be based on whether or not they believed the Crown(prosecution) had proved their case beyond all reasonable doubt.

After two hours the jury returned. Their foreman, when asked by the judge if they had reached a verdict, stated they had. He said they had found Hawkins guilty by a majority verdict of being concerned in the supply of controlled drugs. In relation to Neilson they had found the case against her 'Not Proven'

Lord Lochdale then told a very relieved Neilson she was free to leave the court.

He was then handed a list of convictions which related to Hawkins. These included convictions for robbery, serious assault and drugs possession. When the jury members heard this, there were some gasps because now they knew Hawkins wasn't the innocent, clean living guy, Ogilvie wanted them to believe. He was in fact a drug dealing ned who was about to get what he deserved.

Ogilvie then stood up and attempted to give a plea in mitigation but really there was little he could say to help his client, other than ask the judge to be lenient.

It didn't take Lord Lochdale long to ask Hawkins to stand up.

Hawkins had forgotten all about his previous exemplary behaviour in the dock and his coaching from Ogilvie. He started to sneer as the judge addressed him.

Lochdale told him he had been found guilty of a very serious charge. It was obvious he was a threat to society and he needed to be removed from it for a considerable time.

He then told him he would be sentenced to nine years imprisonment and instructed the police officers guarding him to take him away.

McBurnie was pleased when he heard the result, because at least one 'nasty' would be off the street for a considerable period.

His suspicion's over Capo's involvement with Hawkins was more than confirmed, when he had seen him sitting in the public benches on five days of the eight day trial!

Capo left the court with his 'hangers on' immediately after Hawkins was sentenced and McBurnie knew it wouldn't be too long before he had appointed a new 'lieutenant' to replace Frankie.

McBurnie returned to the office and told Johnston all the cops in the case had coped well with the trial, and the other good news was Hawkins was out of commission for nine years.

The local press had a field day and Frankie Hawkins photograph was on the front page of each newspaper, together with photographs of The Cuckoos Nest, labelled ' Newholm's Drugs Den'. There were full page articles about how the cops had detected Hawkins and there was even a photograph of the Chief Constable and a statement from him telling the 'good news'

When McBurnie saw the newspapers, with the statements and photographs of the Chief, being the cynic he was, he asked Johnston, "Was the Chief on this job because I don't remember seeing him?" Johnston laughed, and using Jimmy's liking for race horse terms replied, "That's because you are blinkered." Jimmy just laughed.

McBurnie had no sooner finished with this case, when he went looking for Cucumber Cool, who owed him a big favour after the situation with McGarrigle...

Together with D.S. Green, he made contact with him and reminded him about the favour he owed him. He told him to keep his ear to the ground and let him know when Capo's new dealer was on the scene. Meanwhile, D.S. Allan was tasked with keeping regular contact with McIlroy and with the cops in the witness protection scheme, to ensure he was safe.

Jimmy then located Bashful and while accompanied by Allan he gave her the 'King's Shilling' amounting to £500. Jimmy asked her if there was much talk about the arrest of Hawkins in the local drug scene. She confirmed it was the talk of the 'steamie' and everybody was convinced McIlroy and maybe Jamie were the touts. She was pleased her involvement was kept secret, but felt sorry for McIlroy, who she knew would now be looking over his shoulder for the rest of his life.

McBurnie said this might not be the case. Details of the set-up had come out in court and been reported in the newspapers. Once the drug community had the time to digest this they would perhaps have a different opinion of McIlroy.

Bashful then confirmed Jamie the barman had been sacked after appearing at court and fined £1000. The owner of The Cuckoo's Nest was now trying to sell the pub, fearing he would lose his licence. Jimmy had a role in this because he had visited him and given him a severe warning. He told him losing his licence was a distinct possibility and if he was wise he would sell the pub as soon as possible.

Bashful then said the regular drug punters who used the pub, were now desperately trying to find another watering hole, and more importantly a new source of supply. She had heard something about a guy called Meeko, who Jimmy knew worked for Capo and had been in the court with him. Meeko was telling some of her friends, supplies would soon be available and everything would be back to normal within a week.

McBurnie asked her to keep her eyes and ears open and get back to him when she heard who would be supplying the gear and when it would take place. She confirmed she would as long as he guaranteed her involvement would never be known. McBurnie reassured her it would not be a problem but at the back of his mind he still had concerns about this tout's motivation.

As he and Allan left, his mind was working overtime, not just thinking about Bashful, but wondering what he was going to do about the problem with one of his own stable, Capo?

In his own mind he knew Capo was behind the drug dealing in Newholm, but no one would speak up against him, confirming he was the drugs kingpin in the town.

He decided Capo needed some serious 'schooling' and put away for a while, it looked like he was the only one who could do this. Capo was breaking all the rules of his 'trainer' and Jimmy wasn't having it.

He had to take a 'fall'...

This would be easier said than done. Capo was street wise and he and his family were feared in Newholm.

Undeterred, Jimmy started making plans for his tout's downfall. He had already tasked Bashful to find out all she could about Meeko and how and when the drugs supply would continue. He hoped she would come back to him with some info, especially when she had received a substantial 'King's Shilling' for helping him put Frankie Hawkins away.

He knew even if she did get info about Capo he would still be difficult to 'bring down'. He needed a two pronged approach and would supplement the tasking of Bashful, with tasking another of his new charges.

CUCUMBER COOL

With Frankie off the scene Jimmy had initially thought there was going to be a short term 'drought' in the availability of drugs. Now after what Bashful had told him it appeared the drought wasn't going to last too long. He knew, if, as he suspected, Capo was behind it, Bashful's info would be correct. Drug dealing was a profitable business and Jimmy knew Capo was the last person to miss out on such a profit.

Three weeks after Frankie was sentenced Jimmy contacted Cucumber. He tasked him with finding out about both Meeko and Capo and a couple of days later he called asking for a meeting with McBurnie.

The D.I. was making doubly sure he always had some back up, especially now when he was targeting one of his main tout's. D.S.Green would supply the back up...

Cucumber, like Bashful, had reservations about Jimmy not turning up on his own but Jimmy said Green could be trusted. The tout then told them according to his information, Meeko appeared to be only a minion in the network being run by Capo.

In fact its new lieutenant was a woman, Capo's sister Brenda who was well known to Jimmy...

Brenda was thirty seven years old, quite a bit overweight with red hair and a freckled complexion. The fact she was only 5' tall with an angelic face, didn't curtail what came out of her mouth. Every second word she spoke was a swear word.

In her younger days McBurnie had come across her when she was part of a shop lifting team and when she was committing catalogue and other frauds. She had been locked up many times and every 'brave' man she ever got involved with was a ned.

Cucumber told Jimmy the local drugs scene had changed considerably since Frankie was locked up. There had been almost an inquisition to find out who had shopped him. Everybody initially thought McIlroy was the tout but this didn't seem to satisfy the guys who worked for Capo. Meeko and his buddies had given several of the pub regulars, especially Jamie, a going over but the tout was never unearthed.

On hearing this Jimmy just smiled to himself and thought "Thank God."

Jamie as well as getting beaten up, had been sacked and the pub owner was now crapping himself. The publican told Cucumber just what McBurnie had told him. His licence would be revoked at the next Licensing Board meeting after the police raised objections based on the drugs operation. He had now put the pub up for sale...

Consequently, The Cuckoos Nest was no longer the drug pub in Newholm and just as Jimmy had predicted there had been an initial shortage of supply.

All this information confirmed more or less what Bashful had told him but the information about Brenda and Meeko was new. Jimmy thought his two pronged approach of tasking more than one tout with a specific remit, was now paying dividends.

Cucumber said since Brenda had taken over the drug deliveries if anyone wanted drugs they had to phone her, at her mothers address, where she and Capo still lived. The drug drops were now at locations specified by Brenda in and around Newholm. She kept changing these and she could turn up in any one of five different cars. Sometimes she even used different taxi firms.

McBurnie knew Capo would be the brains behind this diversity of tactics. He would ensure the mistakes he made with Frankie by not changing cars or drivers, and not having enough different drop off points, would not happen again.

McBurnie expected nothing less from his charge and knew it would be difficult to nab Brenda, but not impossible. He also knew if he did get her then there would be real pressure on Capo.

Capo's 'family' in true Mafia style were sacrosanct and if Brenda was arrested this would cause him no end of angst. It would also put pressure on his relationship with Jimmy, but Jimmy was never going to condone crime. If Capo could be nailed then so be it...

The only caveat would be that he would pass on the info and evidence to another cop, and hopefully, still keep the trainer/trained relationship with Capo.

If the information kept coming in, McBurnie felt it would just be a matter of time before his tout would be locked up, and as he predicted, 'put out to pasture'. Jimmy knew sometimes trainers have to accept the loss of a 'thoroughbred' but he still had new and quality intelligence coming from the rest of his stable.

He asked Cucumber if he had bought anything from Brenda. Sheepishly, he said just a bit of 'personal' (Cannabis) but she was able to supply Smack, Coke, Acid, Speed and Hash. He then asked who else had purchased from her and Cucumber gave the names of nine punters.

McBurnie now needed a plan to arrest Brenda in possession of a dealers supply of drugs, whilst ensuring Cucumber's involvement, like Bashful's remained secret. He was aware he would also require a back up plan to ensure Capo was taken out, but not by him.

He tasked Cucumber with finding out if Brenda ever dropped off drugs to a group of people at the same time, or just one individual, acting independently or on behalf of the group.

A week later Cucumber got back in touch and said Nigel Banks the eighteen year old son of a publican who owned four pubs, two in Newholm and two in Stratshall was a regular customer of Brenda's for Coke.

Cucumber described Nigel as a spoiled boy who liked to show off in front of his pals. His parents owned and lived in a huge converted mill three miles from Stratshall. He had a wing of this building, complete with living room and two bedrooms to himself.

The parents spent much of their time looking after their pubs or taking regular holidays abroad, leaving Nigel with more or less, the run of the place. Cucumber said Banks regularly had parties where there could be upwards of thirty people present and he distributed the coke freely.

He told Jimmy, this incoming Saturday, Bryant (Bashful), Coogan, (Sloppy Joe) and he were among the invited guests. Bank's mother and father were away to Tenerife so he had the run of the place. The tout said he was sure coke would be delivered there by Brenda, but when or how it was delivered, he couldn't tell.

McBurnie thanked him and arranged to meet with D.S. Jones to formulate his plan. In relation to any back up plan, because it involved one of his main charges, he would construct and manage this himself. Only he would know about it...

Along with D.S. Allen he located Bashful and asked her if she had any plans for the week end, he should know about. She had a startled look on her face when he mentioned this and after a pause she said she was just about to phone him. McBurnie knew she was still using and his suspicion's over her motivation for 'touting' were real. There would be no doubt she would be hoping to get some gear at Nigel's party.

He asked her what she was going to tell him, and when, before he instigated the meeting. Quietly, she said she was going to a party, at a guy named Nigel Banks' house on the incoming Saturday. She was sure there would be drugs at the party because she had been to Banks' parties before and he always had plenty of 'kit'.

McBurnie gave her a stern look and told her to keep him updated about the party. She assured him she would.

He thanked her and as he and Allan were leaving he made a mental note to ensure she received some 'schooling', once Capo and his team were out of commission.

When they returned from the meeting with Bashful he went to see Johnston and briefed him on his first plan and asked for a budget to carry out surveillance on Capo's mother's house. This was quickly agreed, as was his request for surveillance trained troops to tail whichever vehicle(s) Brenda used on the day. He said further troops would be required to 'turn' (search) Capo's house under warrant and he would need the use of one of the force's sniffer dogs. The D.C.I. jokingly said, "Is that all?" and Jimmy replied, "Aye for now."

There was a good rapport between the two detectives and Jimmy knew Johnston would have loved to have been on the 'turn'.

Rapport was one thing but McBurnie never mentioned his connection with Capo or his second plan. He only confirmed Drug Squad officers would search Capo's mother's house with the dog. If any drugs were found it would be the Drug Squad who would detain and arrest Capo, and anyone else in the house, including Capo's divorced mother.

She had a list of previous convictions for thefts and frauds going back thirty-five years. Word was she always got her share of the profits of any crimes her kids committed, and she always supplied alibi's for them when the police came calling.

McBurnie disliked her immensely. He suspected even Capo and Brenda, if they had a different mother, might never have become involved in crime, but it was too late for that now.

Jimmy's second plan was still actively under consideration but he had already formulated part of it...

He knew if Capo's mother's house was searched and quantities of drugs found, Capo would not let her go to jail. It was his gear and he would end up taking the rap for her. When, and if, this happened, it would give McBurnie, with no obvious 'hands on' role in this operation, an opportunity to distance himself from, what Capo would see as the 'bad guys', the drugs detectives. He could even end up being seen as the 'good guy' if he could get Capo's mother off the hook.

Capo would still have to be arrested but Jimmy had resigned himself to this loss. His tout was dealing drugs and there was no way he would ever condone it. He deserved to be put away and indirectly, the trainer would see to it he was.

As usual he asked help from the 'man above' and waited to see how things turned out.

On the Saturday the surveillance trained cop's plotted up a good distance from the family house, using a variety of van's and hire cars.

At 7.30.pm Brenda was seen leaving the house on her own in a taxi and the surveillance cops tailed it. D.S. Jones and four of his officers, with the drugs dog and its handler, remained in the vicinity of the house, armed with a search warrant.

McBurnie stayed well away from the 'hits', remaining in the C.I.D. office listening to the radio communications between Jones and his teams.

It wasn't long before Brenda's taxi was heading for Nigel's address. Jones had another two officers and D.S Allan, hidden behind an old stable block some fifty yards from the front door of the house.

When the taxi stopped at the front door Allan ran straight over to it just as Brenda opened the door. She dragged Brenda out of the vehicle, pushed her face down to the ground, and told her she was being detained under the terms of the Misuse of Drugs legislation.

Before Brenda could say anything, Allan had her handcuffed behind her back and transferred to one of the surveillance vehicles which had been following the taxi.

Nigel's party crowd had heard the commotion outside and Banks came out of the house to remonstrate with the cops, calling them 'bastards', 'arse holes' and 'shit bags'. His show of bravado quickly came to an end when he was promptly arrested for a breach of the peace.

On hearing Brenda had been detained, Jones and his team made their way to the house. They did away with the niceties of knocking the door and just kicked it in...

No sooner were they in the house than they were subject to abuse by Capo and his mother. Jones stood no nonsense and soon mother and son were arrested for threatening police officers.

The dog and its handler began their house search and after half an hour the dog sat and looked at a light socket in one of the bedrooms, refusing to move. This was a good indication drugs were concealed in that vicinity.

Jones unscrewed the socket and found two plastic bags. One containing twenty wraps of white powder, the other held twenty wraps of brown powder and within it, a separate, smaller bag were fifty 'eye patch' design L.S.D. paper squares (tabs).

Capo and his mother were taken to Newholm Police Station along with the wraps and tabs which would be field tested there and later confirmed to contain cocaine, heroin and L.S.D.

On the journey to the station all the cops had their parentage questioned by both Capo and his equally foul mouthed mother! Mother and son were locked up after being strip searched.

Capo's mother, because she was the householder was also charged with being in possession with intent to supply controlled drugs.

Brenda too was strip searched when she arrived at Newholm Police Station and initially nothing was found. That is till Allan saw a sliver of polythene protruding from her vagina. When it was retrieved it was found to contain thirty wraps of what turned out to be cocaine.

She too was locked up as well and charged with being in possession of controlled drugs with intent to supply.

All the cops on duty at Newholm Police Station had previous dealings with Capo and his family. At one time or another all had been subject to abuse by them.

Now they were confronted with a scene they never thought they would witness. Capo, his mother, and his sister all locked up for serious crimes.

Needless to say there wasn't any sympathy for them and there was much hilarity among the cops in the station, at their expense.

Time now for McBurnie's second plan...

After Capo had calmed down he asked the custody officer if D.I. McBurnie was on duty. This officer had been 'primed' by McBurnie and said the D.I. was on duty but he was out on a job, and wouldn't be back in the office for an hour.

Capo asked the officer to contact him when he came back and have him come to his cell. The custody officer nodded and walked away smiling.

Jimmy was in fact in his office and the officer phoned him and said he had complied with his instruction to say he was away for an hour.

McBurnie thanked him and thought to himself this plan had got off to a good start. He then met with Jones and Allan and got all the details of the recoveries and arrests.

After about an hour he went to Capo's cell and took him to an interview room.

Jimmy played dumb, while Capo said he and his family had been set up by other neds, who had planted drugs in his house. He told Jimmy he must know he never dealt in drugs. A wee bit petty crime here and there but drugs were off limits.

Jimmy made no comment...

He then asked McBurnie what he could do to help him and

Jimmy said all he could do was speak to D.S. Jones of the Drugs Squad. He was the officer in charge of their cases and Jimmy said he would find out from him how strong the evidence was against the family members.

He took Capo back to his cell and had another discussion with Jones. There was plenty evidence against Brenda and her mother in relation to the drugs they recovered, even without admissions.

There wasn't much against Capo yet everyone knew he was the 'main man'. McBurnie told Jones they would wait and see what the neds said at interview before deciding about Capo. In the meantime he went back to Capo and told him Brenda had been caught with a large amount of drugs and there was no way out for her. His mother being the householder where other drugs were found was also looking at a heavy sentence. The only one of the family who might 'walk' would be him.

Capo asked Jimmy to leave him for a wee while but wondered if in the meantime he could see his mother and sister. McBurnie said such a meeting couldn't be allowed.

He then left Capo with his thoughts...

Nigel Banks meanwhile had been interrogated by Drugs Squad officers and had lost all his bottle. Soon he was telling Jones' team about how often he got drugs from Brenda. Little did he know that by putting her in deeper shit he would become a witness, not just against her but also 'the family'.

Not a good position to be in...

When Jimmy went back to see Capo, the tout said he had thought long and hard about the position he was in. There was no way he was allowing his mother to be locked up for years. He told Jimmy he would admit to ownership of the drugs found in his mother's house provided she was released without charge.

Jimmy, keeping his true thoughts to himself, told Capo he shouldn't be admitting to crimes he hadn't committed, but Capo said he knew where he stood. He wasn't going to admit to something he hadn't done, he had in fact been caught cold, it was his rap. McBurnie said it was up to him and Jones and his team would be interviewing the family soon.

Capo was later interviewed by Jones and his colleague and admitted ownership of the drugs recovered in the house.

Brenda was interviewed next and all she did was curse and swear at the cops interviewing her. They were unperturbed because they had heard it all before. Strangely she had no answer to how the drugs taken from her got to such an intimate place without her knowledge...

Capo's mother was interviewed last.

She had lost all her mouthiness but still denied any knowledge of the drugs found in her house, saying they must have been planted there by the police.

When the interviews were complete Jones updated McBurnie who decided it was time to phone Helen Scobie one of the Procurators Fiscal. He explained the situation to her...

Capo's sister Brenda had been followed and detained at Nigel Banks' house before she could deliver drugs she was carrying internally. Initially when she was searched no drugs were found but after a detailed strip search drugs were recovered from her vagina. This prompted a giggle from the fiscal before she said "Well she will be staying in custody."

The family house had been searched after Brenda was detained and both mother and son had threatened the cops searching the house. As a result they were both arrested. The search continued and the drugs sniffer dog gave a positive indication near a light socket in a bedroom. Within the socket they found twenty wraps of white powder (cocaine) twenty wraps of brown powder(heroin) and fifty 'eye patch' L.S.D. tabs.

Capo had been interviewed and admitted ownership of all the drugs recovered in his mother's house.

His mother, when interviewed denied the drugs were anything to do with her. She alleged they had been 'planted' there by the police.

Nigel Banks had made a statement admitting he was supplied regularly with drugs by Brenda.

Scobie listened intently and then asked McBurnie if there was any merit, or suficient evidence, sufficient to keep the mother in custody. McBurnie confirmed in his view there wasn't anything at this time other than the threats she had made to some officers. The P.F. told him it wasn't worth keeping her in a cell just because she had been abusive to cops. She could be released, but she wasn't ruling out having her arrested at a later date, if further evidence was gleaned against her in relation to the drugs. This decision was all Jimmy needed to complete his Plan 'B'

Scobie said she was delighted Jimmy and his team had made such recoveries and looked forward to seeing Capo and his sister in court on the Monday.

Jones told Capo's mother the good news, she was being released but she may be subject of a further report to the Fiscal at a later date. She was relieved when she heard the news, but then asked "What is happening to my son and daughter?"

All Jones said was they were staying in custody and would appear at court on the following Monday. She asked for a visit with them but this was refused...

After his mother had gone Jimmy visited Capo in his cell and told him his mother had been released. McBurnie asked him if he thought he had done the right thing and Capo nodded and said "Family is all important" and Jimmy nodded agreement. Trainer and tout then spent a good half hour reminiscing about the 'good old days' with McBurnie knowing it would be a good few years before this charge took up occupancy of his stall again.

Before he left Capo asked him if he would keep an eye out for his mother, who might come under pressure from some locals, now he was going away for a while. Jimmy confirmed he would.

Once he left he thought now it would be wise to carry out a review of his stable, including some of its new intake...

Capo and Brenda later appeared at the High Court in Edinburgh and both pled guilty to being in possession of controlled drugs with intent to supply. Capo received a seven year sentence while Brenda was sentenced to five years. Fortunately, because both had pled guilty, Banks did not have to appear in court as a witness. He wasn't off the hook because Capo's defence team had interviewed all the witnesses and both Capo and Brenda were now aware of what he had said to the police.

Wisely, Banks left the country to live with his aunt in the U.S.A....

STABLE REVIEW

Hasty Lad was not seen as a loss by McBurnie. He had definitely crossed the line and his eighteen year sentence for murder meant he would be out the loop for a long time. In fact Jimmy had made up his mind he would never have Hasty in his yard again and hoped he had to serve his whole sentence before release. With his uncontrollable and extreme violence it was unlikely he would ever get parole. Even after his release, whenever that would be, he would remain on licence for the rest of his life and be subject to constant scrutiny by the authorities.

His 'racing days' were over...

With the imprisonment of Capo and Wise Archie, Jimmy had lost another two thoroughbred touts, who would be hard to replace. In the case of Wise Archie he was more than half way through his sentence for supplying controlled drugs, so it wouldn't be too long before he took up his stall again.

As his trainer Jimmy wondered if Archie's time spent 'out to pasture' would make any difference to their relationship but he was convinced it wouldn't. He was also sure Archie would soon be back involved in criminality, and only when it suited him, supplying information. Jimmy was in no doubt, as he was with all his charges, if Archie crossed his criminality line again he would have to take another fall.

If he was behind this fall, as he had been this time and with Capo, then so be it...

McBurnie knew Capo was going to be the biggest loss with him receiving a seven year sentence but was in no doubt he too got what he deserved. Like with Archie, Jimmy was sure Capo didn't suspect he had anything to do with his capture, and his stall too would be available for him when he was released.

The D.I. knew neds like Capo and Archie would always be involved in criminality, when out of prison, and maybe even when in prison. He was also in no doubt whilst Capo was inside, his mother would be carrying on the 'family business' on the outside...

Welsh Rarebit was now the main thoroughbred in his stable and according to Jimmy he was ' ultra wide'. He kept infrequent contact with the D.I. but when he did it was always with good quality info.

Recently he had provided information which enabled Jimmy to lock up a man and woman who had moved into Newholm from Cardiff.

Their speciality was passing counterfeit money and they had flooded the town and surrounding area with Bank of England, forged £20 notes, which they had sourced in Wales. In addition they had a supply of poor quality forged £1 coins which had been turning up all over the place in fruit machines, pool tables and cigarette vending machines.

Thanks to Welsh Rarebit, they had been captured in possession of counterfeit notes with a face value of £10000, while a search of their flat after their arrest, recovered counterfeit coins with a face value of nearly £5000.

Jimmy knew Rarebit's info was always 'on the money' but as

with all his other touts McBurnie constantly tried to get the 'inside line' on what criminality he was involved in.

He knew Welsh Rarebit needed close monitoring and he kept tasking some of his other touts to get information about Rarebit's' activities. Never was there much forthcoming about him, which in Jimmy's mind reinforced this tout's thoroughbred status and confirmed his view of him being worth the watching...

Chocolate Treat was now married with two daughters and according to some of Jimmy's other sources he now had a sixteen year old girlfriend, who he had got pregnant. His morality was certainly questionable but the quality of his information was not. He was regularly in contact with Jimmy supplying info and getting the 'King's Shilling' as his reward.

Jimmy suspected, as always, he was involved in some petty crime but this couldn't be paying, because any time Chocolate contacted him with info, he was always needing cash urgently. It was no surprise to McBurnie when he thought about the chaotic lifestyle this tout was leading.

Like Capo and Archie or any of his other touts, if Jimmy heard about crimes Chocolate had committed, he was sure to pass them on to colleagues, making sure his input remained anonymous. If he lost Chocolate as a tout because he had hit the 'hurdle' of crime detection, he knew it would only be for a short time, because of the low level crimes he committed...

Nervous Boy was his usual quiet self and in keeping with the name Jimmy had given him, he was always very nervous when he felt Jimmy might have heard something about crimes he knew about. On such occasions he would contact McBurnie to get him off his back.

He was even more nervous when Jimmy contacted him. Recently Nervous had heard about a team of local shoplifters who were very well organised and professional in their approach.

The team consisted of four men and one woman who didn't operate on their own turf, where they were well known. They travelled the length and breadth of the U.K. shoplifting high value items, mostly to order.

Nervous told Jimmy they were actively shoplifting at least five days a week and some days they would be in Aberdeen, others in Newcastle, Birmingham, Glasgow or Leeds. They had access to a variety of cheap cars which were not registered to them and which they kept hidden in lock ups rented by other neds. The composition of the team changed depending what store(s) they were targeting and what goods they were after.

The female member of the team, who Nervous named as Charlotte McKenna, was well known to Jimmy. He had first come across her as a cheeky thirteen year old, who was a bit of a rough and ready tomboy. She lived with her mother and four brothers in a really deprived area of Newholm where most of Jimmy's 'clients' lived. Often she saw McBurnie there arresting many of her neighbours, which for her was just a normal event.

When he was taking some of of the miscreants to the Police Station she always seemed to be in the street. Like the rest of the onlookers, she called Jimmy and his colleagues all sorts of foul names but at the same time she winked at him. Jimmy suspected, in reality she had a grudging respect for him and perhaps saw him as a bit of a male role model, which she did not have at home.

Whenever he was passing through her scheme and he saw her he would always stop and engage in banter with her, and before he left he would tell her to behave herself. If she didn't, he told her he would hear about it and she would end up in the 'pokey'. As normal, she stuck her tongue out, gave him the 'V' sign and then laughed and winked.

Jimmy had seen a lot of kids like Charlotte McKenna and he knew they weren't bad kids. All they needed was some decent parenting, stability in their home life, someone to show an interest in them and keep them on the straight and narrow.

McBurnie knew this was easy to say but almost impossible to achieve in such an an area of social deprivation, where dysfunctional families were the 'norm'.

Sadly, two years later when she became fifteen he found out Charlotte was using hash and amphetamine. Most of her friends were still boys but now boys who were all abusing drugs.

Jimmy increasingly was hearing about her from his sources and every time he met her he tried to talk some sense to her. By now she was a lost cause, and through lack of parental control or interest, she succumbed to peer pressure and behaved like the boys on the street she ran with.

McBurnie knew she was on the slippy slope to addiction and a wasted life...

Some of his touts were telling him she wasn't just involved in drugs, she was game for anything. They said she even went with some of the male neds she was friendly with on break-ins. Her speciality was entering premises from their roofs.

Jimmy had one tout who told him because of her diminutive size she was always the one who was lowered into commercial premises on the end of a rope. Once inside she opened them up to allow her buddies in to raid the place.

She was fearless...

Needless to say, just as Jimmy thought would happen, she didn't stick with hash and speed for long.

Soon she was addicted to heroin and at the age of sixteen she had lost her innocence and had both a baby and a habit to feed

She was a sad case and by seventeen she had an extensive criminal record, having been arrested four times for possession of heroin and another five for shoplifting.

She was now twenty, although looked to be at least thirty, with two children but no permanent partner. As her need for cash grew to feed her children so too did her need for money to feed her habit. According to Nervous her habit was so bad now she needed at least a £100 a day just to finance it never mind feed her kids.

Jimmy was sure these were the reasons she was now part of this travelling team of shoplifters, who on a good day could steal goods with a face value upwards of £5000. When they were sold on to punters who didn't question where they came from, or who had placed an 'order', the team would net at least a grand, which they split five ways.

Charlotte's share like her cohorts always went on smack...

Nervous supplied Jimmy with details of two cars the team used, and the location of the two council lock-ups where they were hidden.

Jimmy as usual paid him the 'King's Shilling' and passed the information to D.S. Allan. He told her to arrange for observations to be kept on these lock-ups. Once the shoplifting team had picked up the cars, then Allan should ensure they were followed to whichever city they were targeting, and the local cops notified of their arrival.

Within two days the neds had been 'clocked' picking up the cars. Allan contacted Jimmy, and then she and her team, tailed them from Newholm to Newcastle. Once they had parked their vehicles in a multi-storey car park in the city centre she contacted the local police. They then joined her police team in the car park and took over the surveillance on the two cars and their occupants.

For two hours the neds, including McKenna, who was sporting a blond wig covering her mousy brown hair, were seen to return regularly to their cars and deposit numerous items into the boots. Each time they returned they changed their coats and jackets from a supply of clothing they kept in the boot of one of the cars.

McKenna even changed her blond wig for a ginger one...

When they had stolen everything they wanted they got into the cars and attempted to drive out of the car park, only to be stopped by the local cops.

The game was up...

Designer clothes, cashmere jerseys, perfume, three suits and jewellery were all recovered. The goods had a value of £6500 and five Newholm neds, including Charlotte, were now looking at a night in the cells in Newcastle. With their convictions, also the likelihood of a long custodial sentence in an English prison.

Well that's how it appeared...

D.S. Allan contacted Jimmy and relayed the news of their arrests. The D.I. congratulated her on getting a 'result' and said he hoped she would get recognition from Northumbria Police for their capture. He told her she might even get what he couldn't, a commendation, and they both laughed...

McBurnie and Allan couldn't believe it when they heard the next day their shoplifters had been bailed from court with a trial date set some four months hence.

Jimmy being Jimmy, told Allan to locate Charlotte and bring her into the station for a quiet word. He wondered if there was anything he could do to get her on the straight and narrow but thought to himself, the state she is in now, its unlikely.

Nevertheless, it was still worth a try.

She was easily picked up as she had overdosed on heroin on her return to Newholm and had been taken to the local hospital, where thankfully she recovered.

Allan brought her to the station after her release from hospital and when Jimmy met her he was sorry to see just how far she had slipped into the mire of addiction. She was in a terrible state, her eyes were sunk into her head, she was lucky if she weighed six stone and she appeared to be on another planet.

Jimmy had a lump in his throat when he asked her how her kids were doing, and she said social services had taken them from her, after finding her 'out of her face' during a visit to her home. They were now in care but she said she desperately wanted them back.

Allan being a bit too enthusiastic to follow her boss' example of recruiting touts, offered Charlotte an alternative to thieving. She told McKenna if she supplied reliable information then she would receive cash and her identity would remain anonymous. The D.S. said she would also try and help her get her kids back.

McBurnie understood Allan's enthusiasm, but experience had shown him just how problematic and soul searching it was to manage touts such as Charlotte.

He interrupted his D.S. before she got into full flow. He stressed to Charlotte, his and Allan's first priority was not getting her to supply information, but for her to get off the drugs and away from the dealers who were supplying her. Once she was clean, then there was a chance she would get her kids back and then he would help her as much as he could, but the onus was on her. She would have to prove to the authorities, herself and him, she wanted to be drug free.

Jimmy had never been able to overcome the ethical and moral

problem of paying touts who had drug habits, with cash. He knew the cash nearly always ended up being spent on drugs. Even when he had replaced the cash with vouchers, as he had done with Delicate Girl, she exchanged them with other druggies, either for cash or drugs.

The last thing he wanted was for Charlotte who had been a cheeky, but likeable thirteen year old, to end up like Delicate, dead from an overdose of heroin...

McBurnie had been really upset when he found Delicate had died. He wondered what else he could have done to help this young woman with the addiction and chaotic lifestyle. Probably he could have done nothing more than he did, but that didn't make her death any easier to handle.

As a result, he told both Charlotte, and by now a subdued D.S. Allan, if Charlotte did supply information, which he stressed was not his first concern, then any reward would not be cash. Nor would it be in the form of vouchers. It would be in the form of groceries, clothing and supplies for her kids. Any cash left over would be used to help make her house acceptable as a family home when visited by social services.

In no uncertain terms he told her she was under no obligation to supply info. The most important thing was for her to get 'clean' and free from drugs. If she made the effort Jimmy said he would put a word in with the police in Newcastle. This might help her avoid a custodial sentence and give her a better chance of getting her kids.

As he was leaving D.S. Allan with Charlotte, he told this sad young woman to stay in touch. He confirmed he would be liaising with social services on a regular basis and hoping to get good news from them.

As he left the room his thoughts strayed back again to Delicate Girl...

She had helped Jimmy in the past to put Wise Archie away and had supplied good information about Capo's activities and other neds. Now she had ended up dead and alone in her flat after a drug overdose. When he first read this information on a 24 hour report his heart had sunk. He left the main C.I.D. office he was in then and went to his own office and said a silent prayer for this tragic young woman.

He had always been in the dichotomous position of being her handler and tout trainer while wondering what she was doing, if anything, to kick her drug habit. He had tried to help her on many occasions but all without success.

Times like this made him question if he was in the right job and made him ask the man above for guidance. To be honest he couldn't reconcile the two...

Now there were two young girls who would never know or meet their maternal mother or learn how much she yearned for them. Jimmy knew if life had taken a different turn for Delicate, then her two daughters would have had a very proud and caring parent who would have doted on them.

Once he had found out where and when her funeral was he had sent a wreath and a card addressed to 'A Delicate Lady' from a

'True Friend' which finished with the words 'God Bless'.

The last thing he wanted was for Charlotte McKenna to end up like Delicate...

However, it was not all doom and gloom with his female touts...

Tarnished Beauty had managed to stay clean of drugs. She had her kids back and had been allocated a house in the rural village of Kirkloaning, located between Stratshall and Newholm, and away from her drug dealer and fellow users.

Jimmy was really pleased she had kicked the habit and was now showing just what a good mother she was. She was no longer a tout, but this didn't stop him from keeping up with her and he visited her and her kids occasionally.

Every time he visited, he was delighted to see just how happy she was with her new life and her children. She proved lives can be changed, and for Jimmy these visits helped him ameliorate his distress over what happened to Delicate.

After the meeting with Charlotte McKenna, Jimmy took D.S. Allan to meet Tarnished Beauty in the hope she could see there was a 'human' side to touts. It wasn't all about getting information from them and paying them. Some of them, even heroin addicts, could, if given the right support and encouragement, turn their lives around.

When they met Tarnished in her well kept house, Jimmy asked her if any of her previous contacts had been putting pressure on her. She said no one seemed to know where she lived and she was really happy now in her own home with her children.

She made Jimmy and his D.S. tea and she and Jimmy engaged in some light hearted banter about the area she used to live in, and some of the nasties she was involved with.

Allan had never seen this caring side of her D.I. before and she was touched when she saw him playing with Tarnished's kids. As they were leaving, as he always did, he told Tarnished to keep in touch if she received any unwanted contact and he would 'sort it'.

On the way back to the station Jimmy told Allan if she had seen Tarnished a few years ago then she would never have believed things could have turned out as they did.

Privately, he hoped by meeting with his ex tout, Allan would take on board, touts are human beings like the rest of us. They become touts for a variety of reasons, be it revenge, getting rid of criminal opposition or for money. Whatever the reason, they were still somebody's sons and daughters, and deserved respect, some more than others.

He told Allan, Tarnished only provided info because she needed cash which he believed she spent mostly on drugs. Handling touts like her always caused him both a moral and ethical dilemma. If Allan was going to recruit touts with an addiction she could face this same dilemma. She would find then the more you dealt with them, the more difficult it became to keep the relationship of tout and handler.

Drug addicts as well as having to feed their habits, all brought their own emotional baggage. Many had children and other dependants, which meant you were not just dealing with them but sometimes their families too.

Allan appeared to be listening intently to her boss but he wasn't sure she was taking it in. He hoped she didn't have to learn the hard way in situations like the tragic death of Delicate Girl.

He decided he would watch closely how she dealt with Charlotte McKenna, if Charlotte decided to become a tout...

NOVICE FORM

Cucumber Cool and Bashful Girl were the most recent additions to Jimmy's stable and classed by him as 'novices.' He had high hopes for them thinking, one, if not both of them, may end up being 'classic' contender(s) in the tout stakes.

Bashful had been responsible for the arrest of Frankie Hawkins and also provided an opportunity for Jimmy to task Cucumber. This in turn resulted in the arrest of one of Jimmy's thoroughbred touts, Capo.

As always Jimmy was sorry to lose touts but when they crossed the boundaries he had set for them, then there was no choice. Capo had been playing both ends against the middle for a while, and as a result his trainer (Jimmy) had to 'school' him and put him out to pasture.

Sloppy Joe as yet was untested but he was sure to receive a visit soon and some tasking from McBurnie...

As usual after he met with his touts he reminded each of them if they committed crime they were on their own. In truth he knew nearly every one of them was involved in some form of criminality. If evidence of that criminality came his way, he would pass it on to colleagues, even if it meant reducing the size of his stable, as had been the case with Wise Archie and Capo.

The Viking, who Jimmy still classed as a novice tout, had been very quiet after his involvement with the gypsies, who specialised in tie-up robberies and the enforcer who had shown them the error of their ways. McBurnie was wondering what was causing the drought in the information he supplied and decided to visit him...

Like a few of his other touts, Viking knew when McBurnie visited he could have information about his criminal activities. If this was the case it was better to give him a 'tip' to keep him off your back.

When they met, Viking said he was meaning to contact Jimmy but it wasn't necessary now he was here. He said he had heard about an out of town, Scottish team, who had gypsy connections, across the border in England. The team specialised in daytime housebreakings and they toured Scotland and the north of England taking every opportunity to break into secluded rural houses.

McBurnie was well aware there had been a significant rise in the number of daytime break-ins in his force and in other areas of the country. The C.I.D. in many Forces, including his, were 'getting it in the ear' from their bosses to get these crimes cleared. It was no surprise then his antenna was up when Viking mentioned these crimes.

McBurnie had already tasked Thomason, his main intelligence officer, with doing some research into these break-ins to see what common factors there were. He found they all had similarities especially their Modus Operandi (M.O.)...

All the houses broken into were situated near a public road.

Each had a large hedge or fence obscuring it from the road.

The break-ins always occurred during day light hours.

Entry was gained by forcing either a side door or side/rear window.

The houses were ransacked indicating the thieves spent as little time as possible in them searching for 'goodies'.

The property stolen usually included jewellery, cash, drink and ornaments.

Pillow cases were taken from the houses and used to carry away the booty.

Interestingly, within the team must be someone with specialist knowledge about jewellery, because when some of the pillow cases were recovered nearby, they were found to contain fashion jewellery and articles of little value. Only items which had a reasonable value were retained by the thieves.

There was no fingerprint evidence at any of the crime scenes and there was little intelligence or information identifying who the culprits were.

The value of the property stolen in this five month rampage now exceeded £1,000,000...

Jimmy, being both a sceptic and a cynic, thought the pressure from the bosses to clear these crimes was not solely because of the high value of the thefts. The owners of some of the violated houses were wealthy and had influence with their respective Forces. Some victims were lawyers, politicians, doctors and members of the police authority.

McBurnie was used to getting this sort of pressure but for some reason there was none coming his way from Chief Superintendent Scott, but plenty still coming from his other adversary A.C.C. Ramsden...

During the meeting with The Viking he learned the team responsible for these break-ins were from the central belt of Scotland and usually comprised five males, one who was named by Viking as Tom O'Rourke, who was part gypsy.

Viking said the formation of the team changed regularly, depending on who was sober, but it was not unheard for them to complete 1200 miles in one day and break into an excess of forty houses.

He told Jimmy they usually bought an old banger car using false identity, at a variety of car markets. They kept these cars for up to a week without notifying D.V.L.A. of any change in ownership. When they were finished with them they set them alight, or drove them into flooded quarries, destroying any chance of forensic evidence being recovered...

On leaving his tout the D.I. had an adrenaline rush on. He immediately contacted the C.I.D. at O'Rourke's home town and found out this ned was well known to them. They supplied McBurnie with an extensive list of his convictions and details of his associates. Between them they had hundreds of convictions, mostly for dishonesty but also some had convictions for armed robbery, attempt murder and serious assault.

McBurnie, on scrutinising these convictions, thought it was lucky no householder had disturbed them while they were breaking in. If they had they would no doubt have been badly beaten up or worse...

Being as shrewd as he was he 'clocked' the local cops hadn't been able to get much current information about O'Rourke or his pals. The intelligence they did hold was very limited and out of date. He suspected this would be because they were not committing these type of crimes on their home turf.

Nevertheless, he asked for everything they had to be passed to him. When it was received he went through it with D.S.s Green and Allan and Thomason.

The daytime housebreaking's continued with the same M.O. present at each crime. Then A.C.C. Ramsden's house was one of the houses broken into and the balloon went up...

Ramsden lived in the country some five miles from Stratshall. His house was a five bedroom villa which was located adjacent to a main road. It was surrounded by 15' high conifer trees, which meant once you had entered the driveway, either on foot or in a car, you could not be seen from the road. It was a housebreaker's dream...

Ramsden's house like many of the other houses violated was when he was at work. It like many of the rest had been entered by forcing a side door. The house was ransacked and the thieves stole a small safe, containing approximately £2000, some jewellery, including a gold and emerald necklace and a Rolex watch with his father's name inscribed on the rear.

Apparently, Ramsden's father had been killed in the 2nd World War, while Ramsden was still a baby and the watch was of huge sentimental value to him. It was not surprising then, with this item in particular being stolen, the A.C.C. was more than annoyed.

Immediately after being notified about the break in by a neighbour, not the police, Ramsden headed for his house. He found the place turned upside down and the safe and the other property missing.

He was irate when he left the scene and made straight for D.C.I. Johnston's office...

Johnston was discussing an operational order with one of his support staff when Ramsden stormed in and told the young lady to 'get out'. She was shocked and scurried out the door.

Everyone in the main C.I.D. office could then hear Ramsden bawling and shouting at Johnston. He kept telling the D.C.I. how incompetent he and his detectives were. He also threatened him with demotion if he didn't get his crime cleared, and get his money and property back, without delay.

Johnston was astute enough to let Ramsden rabbit on without interrupting him or getting into an argument with him.

When the A.C.C. had finished ranting, Johnston told him the C.I.D. held some intelligence on who might be responsible and were working diligently with neighbouring forces on ways of detecting them. He also pointed out to him, it was only the C.I.D. and D.I. McBurnie in particular, who had come up with any intelligence so far about this team of housebreakers.

He informed the A.C.C. the lack of intelligence in the Force about these neds was surprising, as each house broken into was next to a main road and the crooks were using cars. Surely cops on mobile patrols must be stopping and checking cars and their occupants, but as far as he was aware, there was no intelligence suggesting this was the case.

He then, tongue in cheek, suggested to Ramsden maybe uniform and traffic department officers could start passing on the details of their vehicle stops to the C.I.D. Then they would have a fuller picture and might be able to identify some of the vehicles used by the housebreakers. If they did this then Thomason, who he said was already collating information on potential suspects, would be tasked with collating all the intelligence, including that submitted by traffic officers. He could then share and compare it with data held by other Forces and C.I.D. teams throughout the country. Everyone would then be in a better position to identify these active crooks.

These comments by Johnston stuck in Ramsden's throat. He had spent most of his service in general policing and in the Traffic Department which he believed to be the force's premier department. He had little time for the C.I.D. who he saw as not much better than crooks themselves.

To further annoy Ramsden, Johnston told him that he was sure with the 'team' effort the neds would be caught!

To say Ramsden was mad would have been an understatement. His face was red with rage as he stormed out and headed for the traffic department and Chief Inspector McCann, who was head of the department.

McCann although a stereotypical traffic officer, was a friend of both Johnston and Jimmy. Occasionally he joined them for a pint after work and they had some great banter. He was taken aback when Ramsden, who was one of his biggest supporters, stormed into his office and subjected him to abuse.

Through his ranting and raving the A.C.C. left McCann in no doubt where his future lay. If he didn't get his finger out and get his officers to stop every bloody vehicle with likely looking neds in it, and pass the details of these stops to the C.I.D. he would be on the move.

Before leaving he shouted to McCann to make it happen soon and to get his arse out of his chair and go and speak to D.C.I. Johnston. McCann was shell shocked and within two minutes he was in Johnston's office in a panic and at a loss to understand why Ramsden was so angry. He had never seen him like this before.

Ramsden in his rage never told him his house was one of the houses that had been broken into...

Johnston could see McCann was in a panic. He told him to calm down, saying the A.C.C. had been in the C.I.D. ranting and raving before heading for the traffic department. Normally, as McCann knew, Ramsden had no time for the C.I.D. and nobody was more surprised to see him in the department than Johnston. The D.C.I. told his colleague, Ramsden had been the victim of a housebreaking and he hadn't even heard about it first from the police but from a neighbour. That was one reason why he had stormed into his office and ranted and raged.

He then told McCann what he had told Ramsden about the

lack of intelligence from out with the C.I.D. and how Ramsden, on hearing this, had stormed out his office and obviously headed for McCann.

Johnston was totally frank and said in all honesty little intelligence was coming from the traffic and uniform departments. For that reason he wasn't going to let Ramsden try to pin the blame solely on his department for failure to catch these housebreakers.

McCann was honest. He said he would have done the same if the boot was on the other foot. He confirmed the cops were already doing regular stop checks, but he didn't know why the details were not being fed into the intelligence system. He stressed this would happen now and suggested they meet daily to ensure his officers' intelligence was being submitted and received by the C.I.D.

Johnston said if everybody contributed to the intelligence picture maybe they would get the housebreakers. Then both of them could get that old bugger Ramsden off their backs.

McCann then said another reason why his troops would appear not be submitting enough intelligence was, Ramsden kept putting pressure on them to meet targets. These were for speeding and other road traffic offences, or 'ticks in boxes' as he called them. He was used to getting it in the neck from Ramsden about not meeting these targets, but this was different.

Before leaving Johnston's office McCann assured the D.C.I. he would be getting more intelligence from traffic cops than he could handle.

After he left, Jimmy came into Johnston's office and asked him what was up with Ramsden. Johnston explained the situation and how, reluctantly, he had put the ball back into Ramsden's favourite department, the traffic department's court.

He said when he had told the A.C.C. the traffic and uniform cops were contributing little in the way of intelligence about this travelling team of housebreakers and how crime detection was a 'team' effort, Ramsden had blown a fuse, stormed out of his office and made for McCann.

Jimmy just smiled and put another mental tick in Johnston's 'friend' box.

The D.C.I. told Jimmy to get a hold of Thomason and tell him he would now be a busy guy collating intelligence from both the C.I.D, other Forces, uniform cops and now traffic cops. McBurnie just smiled and said Thomason would love it. The more intelligence he received the better.

McBurnie then contacted Thomason, gave him the good news and said they would meet twice weekly, go through what intelligence they had and see if there were any leads or common denominators...

Jimmy's next port of call was with The Viking again to see if he had heard any more about this team. Unfortunately he hadn't but promised to contact him immediately he heard anything.

On D.I. McBurnie's next meeting with Thomason, who as expected had completed some sterling work, they had found a Vauxhall car with four occupants had been seen in suspicious circumstances at a remote house near the village of Rigloan, thirty miles from Stratshall.

The intelligence report containing this information had come in from a community cop. From reading it Jimmy and Thomason found this car had been driven to the rear door of a detached sandstone house named 'Troutbank'. The house, like many of the houses which had been broken into, had a high perimeter fence and sat in its own grounds near a main road.

One of the occupants of the car had knocked on the rear door of the house, and according to the house owner, a sprightly eighty year old woman, this guy got the fright of his life when she actually answered the door.

He began stuttering and stammering before asking her for directions to Stratshall.

She was wise enough to give him the directions he wanted, and suspicious enough to note the car number when it was driven away.

It wasn't just that she didn't like the look of the man who knocked on her door which made her suspicious. More importantly, she was wondering why he would ask her for directions to Stratshall. There was the equivalent to a motorway sign on the road immediately outside her driveway showing directions to Stratshall!

"Game on!" thought McBurnie and without delay he headed for McCann's office. Once there he told the Chief Inspector about the sighting of the suspect car. He said he had put a 'marker' against it on the P.N.C. for it to be stopped if seen, the occupants details obtained and for him to be contacted.

McCann, pleased at hearing about this possible break through confirmed with Jimmy every shift of traffic officers would now be looking for this car.

As he left the office, heading for Johnston's office to brief him on developments, McBurnie could feel the adrenaline starting to kick in again, but experience had taught him not to count your chickens until they hatched. He knew the car would need to be sighted soon. Viking had confirmed the neds only kept the cars they used for these break-ins for a maximum of a week before disposing of them...

After briefing Johnston with the good news he told D.S. Green they were heading to Rigloan. Once there he tasked Green with interviewing the community cop who submitted the intelligence report and noting a statement from him. Meanwhile, he would interview the old lady who had contacted this cop and take a detailed statement from her.

Jimmy spent two hours with this genteel old woman, who, between supplying him with cups of tea and shortbread, was able to describe in detail the suspect car. She also gave a good description of the person who had been knocking her door.

Once back in Newholm all Jimmy could do now was sit and wait, in the hope that a cop somewhere would sight the vehicle and notify him.

Two days later he knew he had help from above...

Two traffic cops from his own Force who were patrolling the main road between Stratshall and Newholm had come across the suspect car. It was being driven by non other than Tom O'Rourke and had three neds as passengers.

O'Rourke could not produce a licence, insurance or log book for the vehicle which he said he had just bought at a car market in Glasgow. He and his passengers and their car were taken to Newholm to be checked out. In keeping with the 'marker' on the P.N.C. Jimmy was notified about their arrival and he contacted D.S.s Green and Allan. He told them they would be required to interview these neds after the traffic cops had finished with them.

McBurnie then spoke to the traffic cops who had stopped the car. He asked them to search it thoroughly before the interviews began and to check again what previous convictions all the neds had.

During the search they recovered two crowbars, three stocking masks, four pairs of gloves, a length of rope and three hammers. A second check of their convictions revealed they had one hundred and twenty-three amongst them, ranging from attempt murder, serious assault, robbery, thefts by housebreaking and numerous other dishonesty convictions.

McBurnie told the traffic cops, with these finds and the neds previous convictions, there was enough evidence to arrest them all and charge them with going equipped to commit crime and the other road traffic offences.

The traffic cops completed the initial interviews and charged them as suggested by Jimmy. They then locked them up to appear at court the next day.

Now they were under arrest and not going anywhere soon...

This meant Jimmy and his team wouldn't be curtailed by the maximum six hour detention period, allowed in Scots Law, for detainees. Their status was changed after being arrested. McBurnie and his detectives could now spend as long as they wanted interviewing them before they went to court, about the daytime break-ins, including of course, the break-in at A.C.C. Ramsden's house.

Jimmy told Green and Allan he would interview O'Rourke together with D.C Starkey, while they interviewed the passengers. After all the interviews were complete they would liaise with each other and he would decide what happened next.

The interviews with the four neds, including O'Rourke, went as expected, with, as they had done with the traffic cops, none of them answering any questions. In Jimmy's parlance they were 'dog tag' men, who when captured only supplied there names and addresses.

During his interview with O'Rourke it was obvious this criminal detested the police. He did nothing but sneer at Jimmy and Starkey and repeatedly give them the 'V' sign. The D.I. was well used to this and just carried on with the interview, knowing the less O'Rourke said, the more the fiscal at any forthcoming trial, could comment on his refusal to respond.

Help was coming from above again and at McBurnie's meeting with Green and Allan, Green said one of the passengers he had interviewed, Aidan McBride, a twenty eight year old from Glasgow now had the shakes and was craving alcohol. He had asked Green if he could speak to his boss.

The D.I. decided McBride could wait, while he decided what he would do next...

After mulling over the situation he instructed Green to collect the crowbars and the hammers found in the boot of the neds car. Once he had them, he told them to preserve them, label them and then send them to the forensic laboratory for comparison against any marks found at any of their break-ins. Even if they didn't match any of the marks found at any of the points of entry in Jimmy's Force area, they should be retained and compared to similar marks found at points of entry at other break-ins across Scotland and Northern England.

He then phoned the cops in the neds home town about the arrest and gave them enough information to allow them to get warrants to search each of their addresses.

While waiting for the searches to be completed he took McBride out of his cell and into an interview room. This ned was obviously an alcoholic, he was shaking like a leaf. Even after Jimmy got him a cup of tea he couldn't hold the cup without the contents spilling all over the floor.

McBurnie asked him what he wanted from him and McBride wondered if there was any way he could get the charges dropped. He said he was only a passenger in the car and nothing found in it belonged to him.

McBurnie just gave him a wry look and asked him if he

thought his head buttoned up the back. McBride who up to this point thought he had been dealing with a 'country cousin' type cop, gave the D.I. a knowing smile.

Jimmy told him he had checked his convictions. He had twenty for housebreaking, one for robbery and ten for other dishonesties. There was no doubt he wasn't a 'tourist' and he and his buddies had been breaking into houses all over Scotland and the north of England.

Jimmy said it was time for him to come clean...

While he was engaging in this verbal 'joust' with McBride McBurnie's mind was already focused on what would happen when these neds appeared at court. He was sure after he had a word with the Procurator Fiscal, and their previous convictions highlighted, McBride like his pals might be remanded in custody. If this was the case it would help him and his cops to get enough evidence to put them away for a while.

Returning to McBride...

He was relatively young in years but Jimmy classed him as an 'old soldier' on the crime front, and one who knew the score. He was shrewd enough to acknowledge, when Jimmy said he could be looking at between six and eight years inside, he wasn't bluffing.

He then offered Jimmy a deal...

If he named the person receiving the stolen property would McBurnie put a word in with the local P.F. on his behalf? Provided of course, none of his co accused knew anything about his 'assistance'. McBride said if they, and in particular O'Rourke, found out he had 'shopped them' he would end up a dead man.

Jimmy had already scrutinised O'Rourke's convictions which included attempt murder, firearms and serious assault and knew McBride's fears were not unfounded.

He assured McBride he would speak to the Fiscal, providing the information was as accurate as he said it was and the stolen property was recovered.

McBride then asked how he would know Jimmy had kept up his side of the bargain and was told, "It's a matter of trust."

McBride had no option but agree...

He then supplied the name John Carroll, a pawn broker and antique dealer with a business in Huddersfield, as the receiver (resetter) of most of the stolen property. McBride said Carroll was O'Rourke's contact and any business with Carroll was only carried out by O'Rourke. The rest of the team got their cash once O'Rourke had sold the stolen gear to the pawn broker.

He went on to say Carroll had been a pawn broker in Glasgow before moving to Huddersfield ten years earlier. While in Glasgow he reset stolen property on a regular basis but had never been caught by the cops. McBride claimed Carroll must have been paying the cops off, because he was never even turned over by them.

Jimmy just shrugged his shoulders. All he could think of now was clearing up these break-ins and maybe adding another stall for this new member of his stable, albeit it wouldn't be for a while and after he had 'dried out'.

After returning McBride to his cell he spoke to Johnston and told him about Carroll and the ongoing investigation. He confirmed he told this ned he would speak to the Fiscal, but only if the stolen property was recovered, and whatever happened thereafter was a matter for the Fiscal.

D.C.I. Johnston said he was delighted and in the meantime he would speak to Chief Inspector McCann and thank him for his staff's assistance. He would also let Ramsden know how helpful the traffic department had been. This should take some of the heat of them and also off the C.I.D. Lastly, he said he would ensure Ramsden knew what role Jimmy had played in this investigation.

After leaving Johnston's office Jimmy telephoned the Fiscal. He told her about the seriousness of the crimes they were investigating and the likelihood this team were responsible for housebreakings all over Scotland and Northern England. He also mentioned about his meeting with McBride.

She understood the impact these crimes were having on the public and confirmed she would ask for the foursome to be remanded in custody, but stressed, as Jimmy knew, there were no guarantees. It all depended on the Sheriff...

McBurnie sat in his office till the early hours of the morning waiting for the results of the house searches at the neds home addresses. Needless to say he wasn't surprised when nothing of value was recovered. Neds as active as this team were unlikely to keep any stolen property, but convert it to cash as soon after they committed the crimes. In their case use the cash for drink.

It was all down to the accuracy of McBride's information now.

He went home and after only two hours sleep he returned to work. When the neds appeared at court they were all remanded in custody for a week and this took a bit of pressure off him.

Jimmy felt it prudent now to visit the Procurator Fiscal's office and speak again to Miss Scobie.

He explained to her the house searches at the neds home addresses were all negative, which is what he expected. He confirmed, McBride, had told him who had purchased the stolen gear and asked if he would let his 'assistance' be known to the Procurator Fiscal. He was doing that again now, and making plans to search the home and business of the resetter, John Carroll.

Without McBride's input, he said the only evidence they would have had, related to the lesser charges of going equipped to commit crime and the road traffic offences.

Miss Scobie said she fully understood and told McBurnie to progress the Carroll side of the investigation. She confirmed she would liaise with her counterparts in the Crown Prosecution Service in England and make arrangements for McBurnie and his team to search the pawn brokers premises and house, under a Magistrates warrant.

Her decision on McBride would be made once the results of the search at the pawnbrokers were learned. Having said this, she was in little doubt McBride was part and parcel of this active team of house breakers. His actions could not be condoned or forgotten about. Jimmy said he accepted that and agreed with her.

After a pause she confirmed if McBride's information was accurate and the stolen property recovered, she would make his involvement known to the judge.

Cheekily she then asked McBurnie, "What are you waiting for, I am looking forward to seeing Mr Carroll appearing in court?.."
McBurnie could take a hint and soon he had a team organised to visit Huddersfield the following day and carry out the searches under warrant.

He arranged for Green, Allan and Thomason to join him on the trip, where they would accompany local cops on the search of Carroll's business and home addresses.

The next day they were in Huddersfield by 9am and with some local cops, confronting a shocked pawn broker with a search warrant. The pawn broker would become more shocked as the day progressed...

The shop was an Aladdin's cave and a significant amount of stolen property, contained in the lists Thomason had compiled from the daytime break-ins, was recovered.

More stolen property was found in Carroll's mansion and he was now in deep shit. Jimmy cautioned him and told him he was being detained and would be taken back with the property seized, to Newholm.

At McBurnie's request the local cops secured both Carroll's shop and house, seized the CCTV systems from both locations and gave them to Jimmy. Jimmy told the Yorkshire cops he was taking all the property they had seized, back to Newholm, along with

Carroll. Once back he would be contacingt other police Forces
whcre the housebreaking team had been active. They may send
officers south to see if they could identify any property stolen from
their respective areas.

By the time they got to Newholm, Carroll was singing like a
canary, fully justifying the comment, there is no honour among
thieves.

He told McBurnie he had bought all the 'stuff' they had seized,
from Tom O'Rourke, but he was worried about naming him in a
witness statement or at court. If O'Rourke found out he had
'talked' he would end up a dead man.

Jimmy, with some humour, thought to himself, "Now where
have I heard this before?"

A scared Carroll then told McBurnie he knew of other guys
who had crossed O'Rourke and then disappeared. Others had been
badly beaten up because O' Rourke suspected them of 'grassing.'

Jimmy then looked closely at Carroll and said, "Are you telling
me O'Rourke's a bit of a hero?"

Carroll just raised his eyebrows and nodded...

Jimmy and Green then completed in-depth interviews with
Carroll and asked him to comment on every item they had seized
from him. He was fully compliant and admitted all the items
shown to him had been purchased from O'Rourke. He said
because he knew the items were stolen he hadn't put them through
his books, just gave them a value and passed the money to

O'Rourke.

He was now physically shaking at the thought of meeting up again with O'Rourke, but McBurnie wasn't finished with him yet. He wanted to ascertain if it was only O'Rourke he bought the stolen gear from. Carroll did confirm this, and stated he had been buying jewellery and other items from him for over a year.

The CCTV seized from his shop was shown to Carroll during the tape recorded interview and he was asked to comment and identify people shown in it. One of his regular customers was none other than O'Rourke, who he identified by name. He could be seen handing over jewellery and other items and receiving payment.

The D.I. then asked him if there was any routine to O'Rourke's visits but Carroll said there wasn't, O'Rourke just turned up. If other customers were in his shop at the time when O'Rourke arrived, he just waited his turn, acting like a normal punter. Once his turn came O'Rourke handed over the jewellery and other stolen items and he and Carroll agreed a price.

Carroll wasn't stupid. He wanted all the transactions covered on the shop's CCTV system. Then if the shit hit the fan, as it had done now, he would have the insurance of the cameras to show he had bought the gear, not stolen it. He deliberately treated O'Rourke in the same manner as all his customers, so as to avoid suspicion and to make sure O'Rourke never got behind the counter.

He told the D. I. if O'Rourke had gotten behind the counter he was sure he would be robbed by him.

When asked by Jimmy again to confirm the person he had identified from the CCTV was O'Rourke he did so, but reluctantly.

McBurnie then asked him if O'Rourke ever brought stolen gear to his house and the pawnbroker replied that O'Rourke's fearsome reputation went before him. The last thing he wanted was for O'Rourke to find out where he lived. No deals had ever been carried out at his home, any stolen gear recovered from his house had been taken home by him, after purchase in his shop from O'Rourke.

By the time McBurnie had collated all the evidence he had, he was in no doubt, there would be more than enough to charge the four housebreakers, particularly that smug prat O'Rourke, with at least forty housebreakings. Of course this was provided the property recovered from Carroll could be positively identified by its owners as stolen property, and Carroll also identified O'Rourke in court.

Nothing was ever straightforward, thought Jimmy. He would need to visit Miss Scobie again and explain the pressure Carroll would be under not to identify or speak up against O'Rourke in court.

When they met, Scobie fully understood and said she would deal with Carroll first, then use him as a witness against O'Rourke and the other three. It would be up to Jimmy to arrange to get Carroll safely to court and suitably protected, before, during, and after the trial.

Jimmy confirmed he had this in hand with assistance of his

Yorkshire colleagues.

He then made plans to put the goods recovered from Carroll on display in the police station. With the help of the media he invited individual victims of the housebreakings in the area to attend and hopefully identify their property.

Before this, he needed to get at least some property positively identified, in order that he could arrest Carroll and charge him with reset (receiving). He was in no doubt two items in particular could be readily identified.

Armed with them he headed to A.C.C. Ramsden's office...

Once outside his office he asked his secretary, who had a small office adjacent to her boss, if he could speak to the A.C.C. She knocked the door, went into Ramsden's room and returned shortly thereafter saying Jimmy should just go in.

While he had been waiting for her to return he had heard Ramsden saying to his secretary, "What does that idiot want?"

When he entered Jimmy wasn't acknowledged and was left standing in front of Ramsden who remained seated at his desk, apparently scrutinising some paper work. After two or three minutes Ramsden lifted his head and shouted at Jimmy, "What do you want McBurnie?"

Jimmy said nothing but just handed over an inscribed Rolex watch and a gold and emerald necklace...

Ramsden's face lit up as he gazed at these items, which he

thought he would never see again. It took a few seconds before he again spoke, and then in a much more civil manner asked Jimmy where he got them.

Jimmy explained in detail how the investigation had progressed so far and asked his A.C.C. if he could identify these articles, as being part of the property stolen from his house. Ramsden said nothing but nodded confirming they were his. Jimmy then asked him to sign a label attached to each, positively identifying them, and Ramsden duly complied.

The A.C.C. asked if any of his money had been recovered and Jimmy said there was no chance of this happening.

He then thanked Ramsden and made his way to the door.

Before he got there the A.C.C stood up and after stammering, and struggling to get the words out, he thanked Jimmy, and instructed him to keep him informed about the ongoing investigation.

McBurnie treated the A.C.C. in the same manner he had been treated initially, just nodded and left without saying anything...

As he was walking along the corridor from Ramsden's office he thought to himself perhaps Ramsden's opinion of both him and the C.I.D. had changed now. However, he knew better than to dwell, on what was likely to be an impossibility and just went to his D.C.I. and updated him.

D.C.I. Johnston asked how he got on with the A.C.C. and McBurnie just smiled and said, "Not too bad taking everything into account." Johnston looked bemused but McBurnie made him none the wiser and left.

McBurnie and Green then arrested and charged Carroll with reset of A.C.C Ramsden's necklace and watch. Carroll admitted he had bought these items from O'Rourke and he suspected they were stolen when he bought them.

Jimmy then took him back to his cell to lock him up.

As he was shutting the cell door Carroll pleaded with the D.I. to be released. If he went to court and got remanded to the local prison, he told Jimmy he would end up inside along with O'Rourke.

McBurnie said, "Have a little trust."

Jimmy said he had already spoken to Miss Scobie who knew the importance of keeping him away from O'Rourke. If he decided to plead guilty to the charges libelled against him the following day, he would be dealt with in relation to the reset of only the two items belonging to Ramsden. It was very unlikely, although not impossible, he would be imprisoned for this crime, as he had no previous convictions.

McBurnie told Carroll the Fiscal had confirmed once the public viewing of the property recovered from him was complete, he would have to appear in court again, to answer what was likely to be, numerous charges of reset. She would ensure these charges were brought before the court urgently and before O'Rourke appeared.

Jimmy, being totally honest, informed the pawnbroker he could receive a prison sentence then. If this was the case the Fiscal had told him, she would make it known to the judge what threat he was under and what assistance he had given. It would be left to the judge then if he would take cognisance of this when sentencing him.

Carroll was still scared but he had little choice other than put his trust in Jimmy and maybe later, the witness protection scheme. He knew if O'Rourke could get to him he was a goner.

The last thing Jimmy wanted was for O'Rourke to 'walk' from court through Carroll being too scared to identify him or speak up, so he said he would be in court when he appeared.

The next day Carroll was brought to court and decided to plead guilty to the two charges of reset. He was fined £1000. Jimmy wasn't slow to remind him things had gone according to plan and he would be hearing from him soon. A much relieved Carroll nodded but couldn't wait to get away from both Jimmy and Newholm.

Carroll knew he would be back at court in Newholm soon and the D.I. was well aware he was not looking forward to the possible outcome. He certainly did not relish becoming a witness against O'Rourke and facing him in court.

Wisely, McBurnie contacted the Yorkshire Police at Huddersfield and made them aware of developments and the possible threat to Carroll. He then contacted detectives in the neighbouring forces, updated them on developments, and left it to them to carry out their own investigations with Carroll, once he was back in Huddersfield....

After personal invitations to the victims of these housebreakings, supplemented by press releases and articles on radio and TV, the stolen items were put on display at Newholm Police Station. Nearly all the property Jimmy seized in Huddersfield was identified, and as a result, forty five housebreakings were detected.

This was a good news story and Johnston rightly let Jimmy take the lead with the media. This earned him another tick in Jimmy's friend box and a bit of exposure for the D.I. both locally and nationally.

One month later Carroll appeared at court and again decided to plead guilty to some of the charges of reset. His plea was accepted by the Crown and Miss Scobie approached the judge. Before he sentenced Carroll she informed him of the assistance he had been to the police and the threat he was now under. The judge sentenced him to one year in prison which he ended up serving in an English prison.

The four housebreakers, including McBride, were kept in custody at the local prison and a date was set for their trial on the initial charge of going equipped to commit crime. After trial all four were found guilty and each sentenced to six months imprisonment.

O'Rourke as usual was smug when he got the sentence, knowing in a few weeks he would be released because of the time he had already spent on remand.

His smugness didn't last too long when D.I. Jimmy McBurnie and D.S. Martin Green appeared at the custody room at the court. McBurnie told him he would not be going back to prison right away but would be taken to Newholm Police Station for a tape recorded interview in relation to numerous break-ins.

On the short trip there O'Rourke seemed a bit bemused and neither Jimmy or Green made him any the wiser...

When they entered the tape recording room, O'Rourke, for the first time, saw the cops had recovered some of the property he and his buddies had stolen and which he had sold to Carroll. This was a shock to his system but being the professional criminal he was he showed no emotion and said nothing.

McBurnie cautioned him and during the interview showed him all the items taken from Carroll, which had now been identified by their rightful owners. He asked O'Rourke to comment when he showed him these items but all he got in response was a glare.

Before the interview concluded Jimmy charged O'Rourke with forty five charges of theft by housebreaking. O'Rourke said nothing, but gave Jimmy an evil stare, which Jimmy responded too with a huge smile.

The officers then took O'Rourke to a holding cell to await his transfer back to prison. As Jimmy was locking the cell door O'Rourke shouted to him, "You will prove fuck all against me, you have no evidence." Jimmy replied, "Wait and see"

Five weeks later O'Rourke appeared at the High Court for trial, on his own. The fiscal did not think there was enough incriminating evidence to charge his co-accused, including

McBride, and she did not proceed with charges against them. They had now completed the remainder of their six month sentences and were released.

Carroll was the main witness against O'Rourke...

He was brought from an English prison to the High Court and after identifying O'Rourke, reluctantly gave very shaky evidence against him. Only after being threatened with being charged with prevarication did he confirm he had bought all the stolen property from him. He somehow withstood a torrid time from the Q.C. representing O'Rourke who claimed he (Carroll), had stolen all the property and not his client.

During the cross examination the Q.C. asked him to confirm if he was a convicted prisoner and did his conviction relate to the same property. Carroll confirmed he was and the conviction did relate to the property displayed in the court. The Q.C. then made great play of this to the jury, claiming Carroll, already convicted with regard to this property, had worked a deal with the Crown to accept reduced pleas and put the blame on O'Rourke, an innocent man, and protect himself.

Carroll was cross examined for two days and managed to avoid eye contact with O'Rourke for most of the time.

During breaks for lunch, O'Rourke, once outside the courtroom and being transferred to a custody holding area, away from the eyes of the judge and jury, looked round. On seeing Carroll being transferred to another holding cell he gave him the cut throat sign...

The prosecutor had little difficulty in corroborating Carroll's rocky evidence after McBurnie, when giving his evidence, referred to the CCTV in Carroll's shop. When the CCTV was shown to the jury they could clearly see O'Rourke handing over jewellery and other property to Carroll and getting money in return.

However, because of the poor quality of the camera, no items handed to Carroll by O'Rourke could be positively identified. It was Carroll who provided the physical identification of each item and confirming he bought these particular items from O'Rourke. This left a gap in the evidence trail and possibly some doubt in the jurors minds. O'Rourke's Q.C. wasn't slow to exploit this and asked McBurnie more than once if any of the stolen items could be seen on the CCTV. McBurnie had no option other than concede they didn't, which placed further onus on the identification of Carroll.

It was no coincidence then when O'Rourke's Q.C. explained why his client was shown on the CCTV in the first place. His explanation was Carroll had been an old friend of his from Glasgow who he visited occasionally and sometimes he did pawn articles that were of little use to him.

However, he didn't expand on how O'Rourke was featured on the CCTV system in the Pawn Broker's in Huddersfield on over 35 occasions in a year...

His defence was Carroll, not his client, who had been found in possession of all the identified stolen property. He was the thief not his client. He reaffirmed to the jury it was Carroll who was found with the property not O'Rourke. In addition Carroll was a convicted felon. He had obviously worked a deal with the prosecution to get some charges dropped and convict his innocent client...

It didn't take long for the jury to return with a guilty verdict and nor did it take long for the judge to sentence O'Rourke to six years in prison.

After sentence O'Rourke lost his calm and started shouting at Jimmy who was seated in the public benches, "You are fucking getting it," followed by a cut throat sign.

McBurnie just smiled in response...

Once outside the court the D.I. spoke to Green and said by the time the other forces had accrued all the evidence they had against O'Rourke, he could end up doing a fifteen to twenty year sentence. This would be of some relief to Carroll who had already told the witness protection team he would not be needing them on his release. He was moving to France.

Green just smiled, happy to be involved in taking another dangerous ned off the street.

Jimmy now had stable business to attend to...

He looked up his new charge, McBride. The tout was thankful he hadn't received too heavy a sentence on the initial charge but was still worried about returning to his home town in the central belt. He was afraid O'Rourke maybe suspected it was him who 'fingered' him and because of possible repercussions he had decided to stay in Newholm.

This suited Jimmy just fine but as with all his charges he knew

McBride would bring his own baggage. With him coming from the central belt of Scotland, his lifestyle and connections were also a bit of an unknown quantity.

Jimmy did know with his 'pedigree' on the crime front this tout would have no difficulty becoming accepted by the local neds. Once accepted he could task him with getting information about them and their criminality. Provided of course, he could get him off the drink, which might be easier said than done!

McBurnie wondered what stable name he would give him and decided on 'Red Beak' which appeared apt, considering the discolouration of his nose caused by his heavy drinking.

His next visit was to The Viking and McBurnie paid him £500 from the tout fund for the information which saw O'Rourke, Carroll and the team of housebreakers being 'pulled up'. For Jimmy paying this amount of cash to a tout, especially with the results he achieved, was in keeping with the bosses terminology of value for money - V.F.M. He knew very few of them would ever have experience of using it, or thought of it being used, in this context, which brought a smile to his face...

All in all McBurnie was quite pleased with himself. Not only had he taken these nasty criminals off the street, he had recovered Ramsden's jewellery and hopefully become accepted by him. He had also recruited another tout with some potential. However, he knew from experience, never to take anything for granted and as far as crime detection went, you were only as good as your last case.

When the next serious or high profile crime was reported both the D.C.I and him would be getting it in the neck, from bosses with no experience of detecting crime, to get a result and quickly.

He spent the week-end having quality time with his family and even managed a visit to his old retired minister, Mr Morrison, to thank him again for his advice and words of wisdom.

BAD HAIR DAY

On the following Monday he wasn't long back at work before he got a call from Wise Archie, who had just recently been released from prison.

Archie said he was a bit stuck for cash and asked if Jimmy could help him out. McBurnie told him he knew the rules, to get cash he would need to supply some info and if the info was right, then he would be paid.

Archie then said he had only been out of prison for ten days but had learned about a break in at a hotel in Perchfield, some sixty miles from Newholm. According to what the culprits told him, they had been disturbed during the break-in. While they were forcing open a money cabinet, gaming and pool machines, the hotel owner came upon them.

Archie said he doubted if it would have been included by the owner when he reported the crime, but the neds responsible for the break-in told him the owner was a nut case. One of them said when he was levering open the pool table he heard something whizzing past his ear, followed shortly thereafter by something ricocheting of the pool table. This was followed by the owner shouting to him, "Stay where you are you bastard or I will blow your fucking head off."

The ned said he nearly shit himself before him and his buddy jumped through a window they had forced to get in, with the sound of bullets shattering the glass in the window.

Archie named the two neds as John Forrest and Jamie Kilmartin, two guys he had met in prison and who had struck up a friendship with him. They were released before him but kept in touch. Archie said housebreaking was their game, especially at pubs and hotels. They had been bragging to him while 'inside' about the amount of break-ins they were responsible for throughout Scotland.

He told McBurnie they came from Fife and had phoned him the night after the break-in telling him just how crazy the owner of the hotel had been, and laughing, said there was no way they would be back there.

Archie described them as being a bit dim and not having a lot of bottle...

Jimmy noted the details and being as suspicious as he was he was wondering if Archie had actually set this job up. He knew Archie had a sister who worked in a hotel in Perchfield. It would be no surprise to him if she worked at the same hotel Archie was talking about and had given him info about the hotel, which he had passed on, for a 'cut' of the proceeds. Now if the info was right he would be in line for a payment from McBurnie!

McBurnie said he would get onto it and as usual, if the information was right Archie would receive some cash.

McBurnie returned to Newholm Police Station and asked D.S. Allan to look out the crime report for the hotel in Perchfield. It didn't take her long to return with it and sure enough The Pheasant Hotel had been broken into on the date Archie said. Two intruders had been disturbed by the owner before making their getaway.

There was no mention of a gun being discharged...

Jimmy told Allan to get a car and while she was doing this he checked with the firearms department. The owner of the hotel, Malcolm Wearing, held both a shotgun and firearms certificate.

They headed to Perchfield and The Pheasant Hotel. When they got there Wearing was just closing the bar. Jimmy introduced both he and Allan to the publican, who offered them both a drink, which they declined.

Wearing asked Jimmy why a D.I. from Newholm had travelled all the way to Perchfield to investigate the crime at his pub. As far as he was aware the local uniform cop was dealing with it. The scenes of crime people had been but told him they found no fingerprints. Wearing said he didn't have much faith in the local cop and didn't hold out much hope about the culprits ever being detected. Now with a D.I. on the job perhaps they would get these guys.

McBurnie explained he had a possible lead on who the culprits might be, but before he could pursue this he needed some clarification from Wearing.

The publican looked puzzled, wondering what else he could add, to what he had already told the Police. Jimmy asked him to go over in detail, what happened the night of the break-in...

Wearing confirmed he closed the bar at 11.30.pm as usual and went to bed with his wife in his private accommodation on the first floor of the hotel. This would be about 12.30.am after clearing and up having drunk a couple of brandies.

Their bedroom is directly above the function and pool rooms of the hotel. Around 1.45.am he heard a noise coming from the pool area and got out of bed, picked up a torch he kept in a bedside cabinet, and went to see what was causing it.

He said he tried to be as quiet as possible and didn't put on any lights or the torch. Slowly he entered the staircase leading to the function room and he could just make out a figure leaning over the pool table, with what appeared to be a crowbar in his hand. He could also make out another figure standing in the shadows beside the main window of the room.

The window was wide open and the curtains were blowing in the wind.
He knew immediately these characters had forced this window because he had secured it as normal before he went to bed.

He then said he shone his torch in the direction of the figure at the pool table and shouted to him to stay where he was. This obviously spooked the two intruders who had no intention of remaining in the hotel and both escaped through the open window.

McBurnie noted what the publican said and nonchalantly asked him if he owned any firearms. Wearing confirmed he owned a.22 rifle and a shotgun and had up to date certificates for both weapons.

McBurnie then looked him in the eye and asked if he had any of these weapons with him when he disturbed the intruders.

After a long pause Wearing admitted he had a .22 rifle with him. The D.I. then asked if he had used it and again after a considerable pause, he said he fired a couple of warning shots at the intruders before they fled.

Wearing wondered if he was in trouble now and Jimmy said he would have to report the matter to the Procurator Fiscal for that decision. He could possibly be prosecuted for reckless discharge of a firearm. On the other hand if one or both of the intruders came forward, which was highly unlikely, he may even be charged with attempted murder!

This took the publican's breath away and his eyes almost popped out of his head. He stressed to Jimmy he was the victim here and only protecting his property. He never meant to cause the housebreakers any harm, just scare them.

Jimmy stated it was a matter of proportionality but again it was a decision for the Fiscal.

He then cautioned the publican in the presence of D.S. Allan about his use of the rifle. A stunned publican shook his head in disbelief, but made a frank admission about his use of the rifle, claiming he had a right to protect his wife and his property. He said the guys who broke-in could have killed both him and his wife and he was taking no chances. His use of the rifle was for legitimate reasons.

McBurnie had some sympathy for him, if he had used the rifle just to 'scare off' the intruders. However, from what Archie was telling him, he was intent on doing more than that...

Wearing was distraught now and asked McBurnie and Allan why he, the victim, was being persecuted for protecting his wife and property. Jimmy said he accepted he was a victim, but he, like everyone else, had to comply with the law. He assured him he would do his utmost to detect the culprits, but Wearing had now lost all interest in them.

McBurnie wondered what he would have done in similar circumstances. He certainly wouldn't have used a firearm but he may have used something else like a shovel or a brush shank...

The D.I. then contacted the local cop and told him to seize Wearing's weapons, pending the result of the Fiscal's decision on prosecution. He had already told the publican if the Fiscal decided not to prosecute, the Chief Constable could still revoke both his firearm and shotgun certificates.

Both detectives left the hotel and once in their car Jimmy told his D.S. the information he had received must be sound. Before Wearing had admitted using a rifle only the intruders and his informant, whose identity Allan was not privy to, knew about its use.

With Wearing admitting to using his rifle and in effect corroborating his tout, Jimmy said they were now on the intruder's trail...

Once back in the office he phoned the C.I.D. in Glenrothes, in Fife, and supplied them with the names and addresses of the two neds named by Archie. He asked the Detective Sergeant he spoke to, to detain them both on his behalf, in relation to the break-in at The Pheasant. Once they were detained Jimmy confirmed he would travel to Glenrothes with a colleague and interview them.

The next morning he got a call from his colleagues in Fife stating both men had been detained and were in a cell awaiting his arrival.

McBurnie contacted Allan and they set off on their journey.

When they arrived at Glenrothes Police Station the detective who had detained the men, D.C. Clarke, informed Jimmy, from his experience, these guys would say nothing and only provide their names and addresses. They had forty previous convictions between them for housebreakings, robbery and assault and they were certainly 'Old Soldiers' as far as crime was concerned.

Clarke said he had interviewed them many times before. They weren't the brightest, but would admit to nothing. You had to have all your evidence at hand before you detained and arrested them.

McBurnie just looked at Allan and in Clarke's presence said, "Never say never."

He then asked for one of the neds to be brought to the tape recording interview room.

John Forrest was the first to be interviewed and Jimmy introduced himself and Allan to him. The ned asked him what they wanted him for and out of the blue Jimmy said, "Are you the guy with the centre parting in your hair?"

Forrest couldn't keep a straight face and burst out laughing before stating, "That bastard is crazy, there is no way he should be running a pub, he nearly killed me."

McBurnie and Allan then engaged in a bit of banter with Forrest before completing a tape recorded interview with him in which he admitted breaking into the hotel, but said he was there on his own. He was then arrested and charged with the break-in and returned to his cell.

While waiting for Kilmartin to be brought in Allan asked her boss how he thought about introducing the line about the centre parting at the start of the interview. Jimmy responded by saying he had never known housebreakers to be shot at by the victim. He had a vision in his mind, almost cartoon like, of the culprit with a centre parting in his hair, caused by a bullet passing through it.

Forrest must have shared this vision.

Allan burst out laughing when she thought about Jimmy's description...

Kilmartin entered the room and Jimmy went through the same procedure with him, again introducing the comment about the centre parting. Like Forrest he too couldn't keep a straight face, burst out laughing and then said, "That guy in the hotel is one fucking lunatic."

Like with Forrest, Jimmy struck up a rapport with Kilmartin and during the tape recorded interview he too admitted breaking into the hotel in Perchfield, on his own.

McBurnie then arrested and charged him with the break in and had him returned to his cell.

The two Newholm detectives then went to the C.I.D. office and McBurnie told D.C. Clarke he had arrested both men who were now admitting this crime. He and Allan would now be taking them back to Newholm.

Clarke was taken aback and wondered how Jimmy had managed to get them to admit to this crime.

Jimmy leaned over to him and said "It's all about hair styling"

Clarke was puzzled and Jimmy left him that way...

Before long, he and Allan were en route to Newholm with Forrest and Kilmartin. On the journey the neds said that the publican, Wearing, should be locked up and kept in solitary.

It never crossed their minds they shouldn't be breaking into hotels, pubs and houses and Jimmy knew this was because they saw breaking in as their occupation. Cops were one hazard of the job, but being shot at was one they never ever anticipated...

Forrest and Kilmartin appeared at court in Newholm the next day and plead guilty to the break-in at The Pheasant. Both were sentenced to six months imprisonment.

Jimmy then met up with Archie and handed over £300 from the tout fund. Archie was expecting more but McBurnie reminded him he had been a bad boy and jokingly asked him if he was aware of the economic recession and the need for prudence. These comments left Archie somewhat bemused and before he could reply, Jimmy said now he was out of prison he would need to keep his nose clean.

He knew Archie would already be involved in some sort of crime but was still glad to have this bemused thoroughbred, but problematic tout, back in his yard.

The D.I. then met with the Fiscal and discussed the position of Wearing. She decided she wouldn't prosecute him but would send him a warning letter. She recommended the Chief Constable revoke his firearms and shotgun certificates and destroy the weapons.

The Chief did revoke the certificates and after some careful thought Wearing did not appeal the decision and the weapons were destroyed.

For the next two weeks, McBurnie, when he saw Allan in the C.I.D. office, would walk over to one of her fellow detectives seated in the office, and examine his or her hair. This brought howls of laughter from her and looks of bemusement from their colleagues, who were totally in the dark about what Allan and their boss found so funny...

THOLED HIS ASSIZ

Moments of humour which Jimmy had in the case involving Forrest and Kilmartin, brought some relief from the trauma of Delicate's death and the moral and ethical complexities of having drug addicts as touts.

Perhaps, he told himself, he was in the right job after all?

He was enjoying his work again and 'outwardly' seemed to be pleased with the support D.C.I. Johnston was giving him. Johnston knew his worth and they had a good working relationship...

McBurnie hadn't seen D.C.C. Cobble for a while because he was busy representing the Force, and the Chief, in many forums where the topic of terrorism was high on the agenda.

One Saturday morning when things were fairly quiet, who walked into the C.I.D. office, none other than Cobble. He made for Jimmy's office and as he had been in the habit of doing, he told Jimmy to put the kettle on.

McBurnie was glad to see him and it wasn't long before they were having a brew. During the conversation Jimmy learned Cobble had been keeping up to date on his investigations. He knew about the cases involving Eastly/Corberry, Hawkin's, McGarrigle and O'Rourke and as usual wanted the 'inside line' on all these crimes.

Jimmy trusted Cobble but this didn't stop him giving him sanitised versions. The Deputy was worldly wise and he knew what he was getting wasn't the whole story but he also knew if their roles had been reversed he would have been equally circumspect.

The D.I. did tell him, in some detail, about the break-in at The Pheasant and how he had opened up his interviews with Forrest and Kilmartin with the comment about their middle hair partings.

This brought howls of laughter from Cobble who being as he described himself 'an old detective' could relate to the detective style of humour.

Before leaving McBurnie's office he said had seen a difference in Ramsden's attitude to the C.I.D. especially after his house had been broken into. In fact he had heard Ramsden speak highly of Jimmy, and even Scott now never uttered a bad word against him and in fact praised him for his good work.

He told Jimmy he could understand why A.C.C. Ramsden's view of the C.I.D. and Jimmy in particular, had changed, but he was at a loss to provide any explanation about the change in attitude by Chief Superintendent Scott although he welcomed it.

Jimmy being loyal to the miners code of not shopping fellow workers, said he couldn't put his finger on it but he was glad things had changed. To quickly end the conversation about Scott, McBurnie suggested maybe the Chief Superintendent had mellowed, after, like him, unsuccessful attempts to get further promotion. This brought a grin from Cobble and a warning, also tongue in cheek, not to be so flippant.

As he was leaving, Cobble told Jimmy he would be retiring in ten weeks time and he didn't know who would be replacing him. It could be Ramsden, but the D.C.C.s post would have to be advertised out with the force, and it was sure to draw applicants from across the U.K.

Jimmy said he would be sorry to see him go and 'The Dep' confirmed he would be sorry to leave but told Jimmy, when your time was up, it was up. Anyway his retirement would give him the opportunity to reflect on his best time in the Force, as a detective...

The D.C.C. left and Jimmy immediately started to think about his future again. Cobble was his biggest supporter among the Force's senior officers. With him gone any remote chance of promotion would also be gone. He hoped he had turned things around with both Ramsden and Scott but was still convinced they wouldn't be supporting him if a vacancy came up for a Chief Inspector.

A week after Cobble's visit Johnston asked Jimmy to come into his office for a quiet chat. Once inside Johnston said he had been tasked with carrying out an internal enquiry into the neighbouring Force. It related to an allegation of corruption between a uniform inspector and a local councillor. The nature of this allegation meant it would become a protracted investigation.

On hearing this Jimmy's mind went back to the time he spent in Stratshall as uniform inspector, and councillor Allan Gemmill, who was a Police Committee member, a publican and a friend of some of his police bosses.

Jimmy hadn't been in Stratshall long before Gemmill tried to gain his confidence, offering to take him and Doris for meals and inviting them to his holiday home on the coast.

McBurnie was street wise and knew Gemmill had an ulterior motive in trying to befriend him. This became apparent when the councillor asked him if he ever bent the rules. At the time Jimmy thought, Gemmill must think his head zipped up the back if he believed he was going to disclose the tactics he used when investigating crimes. He suspected Gemmill was being used as a 'plant' for some of the police bosses, most likely Scott.

As a result he decided to reverse the roles and put Gemmill under the spotlight. He used his touts to find out about Gemmill's business interests. It didn't take long to learn he was the money man behind a pub in Stratshall where drug dealing regularly took place.

When he then suggested to Gemmill he had information about drug dealing in this pub, and claiming with Gemmill's help, they could arrest the dealers, get the pub closed, and the licence withdrawn, Gemmill was shocked.

It wasn't long after this Jimmy, without any good explanation, was returned as a D.I. to Newholm....

He wondered now what would have been the outcome if there had been an internal investigation into Gemmill's dealings with the police bosses?

His thoughts then returned to what his boss was saying...
Johnston said he would be leading the investigation and he would be taking D.S. Allan and two shop floor detectives, who were good statement takers, with him.

McBurnie told him he didn't envy him because there was nothing worse than investigating one of your own.(He could speak from personal experience after being interviewed and interrogated as a witness against his old boss, D.C.I. Chambers and refusing to incriminate him. He was still paying the price for that decision when it came to consideration for promotion.)

Nonetheless, if the allegations were true then Jimmy said the Inspector didn't deserve to be in the job and Johnston nodded in agreement.

Jimmy and his boss then discussed internal investigations.

Both agreed the public didn't expect or believe police internal investigations were thorough, or impartial. As they both were well aware, 'internals' were open to public scrutiny and independent review. Any cop then appointed as investigating officer would have to make sure his or her investigation would withstand both internal and external scrutiny. Every line of enquiry would need to be pursued as far as it could be taken and as a result internal reports were of the highest standard. The last thing the appointed investigating officer wanted was criticism from both within and outwith the Force, or a reinvestigation instigated by the Chief Inspector of Constabulary.

Johnston said only cops knew this and forces should do more to highlight the high standard of internal investigations. Anyway, he told McBurnie he would be as thorough as possible in this investigation which he knew would take considerable time.

He then told McBurnie this wasn't his only piece of news...

Jimmy was going to be appointed Acting D.C.I. and D.S. Green appointed Acting D.I. for the period of his absence, which Johnston estimated, could be anything up to a year.

The D.C.I. looked at Jimmy, who instead of being pleased, now had a scowl on his face. Johnston warned him he should accept this temporary promotion and not to stick his 'sceptic's' head in the sand.

McBurnie was quiet before he asked him how he knew he was getting the Acting rank. Johnston said D.C.C. Cobble had appointed him as the lead internal investigating officer and also told him to tell McBurnie and Green about their acting positions and report back to him, promptly. Paperwork confirming these appointments would follow soon.

Jimmy thought then it was no coincidence when he got a visit the previous week from Cobble. He was probably checking him out.

He told Johnston he had completed the Acting D.C.I. role before and by all accounts quite successfully. Where did it get him when it came to a full time promotion? Nowhere!

Why should he do it now?

His boss told him to get his thinking head on. He was now on better terms with Ramsden and Scott, who he classed as his two biggest 'hurdles' for promotion. If he performed well as D.C.I. which Johnston said he had every confidence he would, he would be the clear 'favourite ' for the next Chief Inspector's position that became vacant.

Jimmy relied, "Aye right."

Johnston then summoned Green into his office and told him he was being appointed Acting Detective Inspector. Green was over the moon at this news but after the initial excitement had passed he asked the D.C.I. what was happening to Jimmy.

The D.C.I. looked at Jimmy for a response and got none.

Jimmy then looked at Green who he could see was delighted at getting the chance to be a D.I. and in Jimmy's mind it was a well deserved opportunity.

After a pause he told Green he too was taking up an Acting position as D.C.I., while D.C.I. Johnston was out of force leading an internal investigation.

Both Johnston and Green smiled and they all shook hands.

After they left the D.C.I.'s office it was almost finishing time and McBurnie and Green went for a pint, at Green's instigation. Green couldn't contain his delight and kept telling Jimmy the neds were in for a shock with both of them on their tails.

Jimmy didn't share Green's enthusiasm and was quite subdued.

After two pints he told Green he was returning to his office and when he got there he shut the door.

He couldn't get it out of his head he was being 'used' again when it suited the bosses and he hated being in this position. He would never accept this, but he was in the dichotomous situation of having to admit to himself he wanted to be a D.C.I.

He began to briefly analyse his position...

He accepted what Johnston had said about Ramsden and Scott and this time they had not tried to block this temporary appointment.

He knew Cobble was his biggest supporter and was hoping to get him (Jimmy) firmly on the promotion ladder before he retired...

After some thought and a few measures of whisky from the bottle he kept in his drawer, he decided to, suck it and see.

When he arrived home he discussed the acting position with Doris and she said, "We have been here before." Jimmy just nodded...

After the kids were in bed he told her something she already knew, he was being 'used' again. She agreed but told him he wanted to become a D.C.I. and have a department full of real detectives, not just cops there to get their card stamped on the way up the promotion ladder. He said "Aye that's right, but I am still being used." At 11.30. pm a very frustrated Doris said she had had enough of his moaning and headed for bed.

At work the next day the C.I.D. shop floor talk was all about Johnston leaving to head up the 'internal' and about Jimmy's and Green's acting positions. As was normal whenever there was mention of an internal investigation the gossip factory got to work. This time the investigation was in another Force. It still didn't stop the 'inquisitive' cops trying to carry out their own investigations, to find out what it was about, and who was the subject of the investigation.

Once Jimmy heard the rumour mill in full flow he held an informal briefing. In no uncertain terms he told his officers to keep their thoughts to themselves. All they needed to know was D.C.I.

Johnston was carrying out an internal investigation in another Force. If their inquisitiveness persisted and the media got hold of it then the investigation could be prejudiced. There could also be another aspect which they should think carefully about. If any leaks to the media originated from the C.I.D. then he would make sure the person who leaked it would be the subject of the next 'internal'...

All Jimmy's cops knew he wasn't to be messed with and he meant what he said. Consequently, it was no surprise when no one uttered a sound as he delivered these words of warning.

D.S. Allan came to see him for a private word after the briefing and asked him why she wasn't considered for the acting position Green was taking up. Jimmy said it had nothing to do with him and he had a lot of time for both officers. He did stress to her Green had more service and experience than she had and her chance would come in time. Furthermore, being second in charge of a high profile and political internal investigation would also be great experience and would help her advance in the future.

She wasn't convinced and Jimmy had some sympathy for her, but he knew if it had been down to him, Green would have been his choice, for the reasons he had given her. He was sure she would be promoted again because she was a determined detective who was now, like him, treating crime as a 'personal' matter...

Johnston was now out of force and Acting Detective Chief Inspector Jimmy McBurnie had taken up his office and inherited what he dreaded, a mountain of paperwork, most of which he regarded as irrelevant.

It still had to be responded to and for his first week in post Jimmy ploughed through the correspondence. The more he looked at it, the more he recognised the police were now involved in matters that weren't their remit. They were taking the lead in many multi agency forums, including, social housing, drug and alcohol committees and other meetings, which in Jimmy's mind, were mostly the responsibility of the Social Work Department.

Some officers obviously found their niche in such environments and some got promoted through their involvement in them. Jimmy being a cynic, and the hard nosed detective he was, thought for these guys, it was a way of avoiding, what he saw as the police core role, catching the baddies and reducing crime by taking them off the street.

He felt sorry for Johnston now he was filling his post and lumbered with the same bureaucratic and administrative nonsense. The difference was he wasn't going to be desk bound at any cost...

To avoid this he took a substantial amount of paperwork home each night and completed what was required there, even if it meant him working till 11pm. During his shifts he spent as much time as possible with his troops, motivating, encouraging and directing them till they saw crime, like him, as something not to be tolerated.

His stable of touts was still supplying him with information but increasingly he was passing it on to hand picked 'soldiers' in the C.I.D. to deal with, under his monitoring. Detections increased under his command and it wasn't long before he had a team he was proud off, and in Green a D.I. who he could trust and who led from the front.

After four weeks he was well in control of his workload, albeit he was working fifteen hours a day. He had no slackers on the shop floor and he was pleased things were going according to plan. His home life was suffering because of the amount of time he was dedicating to 'police' matters but he selfishly put this to the back of his mind.

DARK HORSE

At the start of his fifth week as D.C.I. he was in the office when Green received a call from a uniform sergeant stating one of the four sub Post Office's in Newholm had been robbed at gun point. Fortunately no one had been hurt but the robbers had made off with approximately £10,000.

The balloon was up now and there was no way Jimmy would be confined to the office while there were armed robbers at large. He told Green to round up his troops and get them and him to the post office that had been robbed a.s.a.p.

When they arrived ten minutes later, his uniform colleagues had the Post Office cordoned off. Wisely the sergeant who contacted Green initially, had kept all the customers who were inside at the time of the robbery, within the premises until they could be interviewed and the scene examined.

Jimmy tasked Green with being the Senior Investigating Officer (S.I.O.) but stated he would oversee the investigation. If truth be known, he found it difficult to take a step back, but knew in his present role he couldn't become too 'hands on'. He told himself by stepping back he would be in a better position to ensure no stone was left unturned by the investigation team, till these dangerous guys were caught. Well that was the theory anyway...

He wasn't long in contradicting his pledge of not becoming too hands on.

After appointing Green as S.I.O. he told him with all

confidence, once these neds were picked up, Green would be interviewing them. This however would be together with him and these neds would be left in no doubt they didn't commit crimes like this on their patch.

Green knew Jimmy couldn't take a step back but was still pleased to have his full support, if not a free rein.

The Acting D.I. couldn't wait to get the investigation under way and soon Scenes of Crime officers, door to door teams, enquiry officers and a Major Crime Administration Team had all been assembled and tasked.

The two women counter staff who had been held up and handed over the cash were interviewed at length. This was a difficult process as both were severely traumatised after having a gun presented to them and forced to hand over money.

With the right amount of tact the detectives were able to get reasonable descriptions of the two robbers who had walked into the Post Office wearing gloves and stocking masks. Their descriptions were confirmed when Green's team examined the CCTV systems in the Post Office and on the street outside the front door.

The detectives now knew they were looking for two men aged between twenty and twenty-five years, one was approximately 5'9'' in height and another over 6'. Both were of slim build and both wore dark coloured shell suits.

Importantly, one of the counter assistants had noticed the taller of the two men had a tattoo on his right wrist which was visible above his gloved hand. She wasn't sure what it depicted but it looked like one circle inside another.

The description of the tattoo struck a cord with McBurnie but he couldn't explain why...

She said this guy also had a slight stutter but maybe that was because he was as nervous as her at the time.

McBurnie and Green viewed the CCTV closely to see if they could identify the robbers, or any other specific detail about them the Post Office staff or customers had missed. On the street CCTV camera the two neds could be seen with their backs to the camera and pulling something over their faces just before they entered the Post Office. One of them appeared to have long hair.

The cameras both within and outside the Post Office showed both men were wearing gloves. Much to the cops frustration the street CCTV cameras were of such poor quality you could not make out any distinct features of the robbers.

The internal CCTV system in the Post Office wasn't much better but it did corroborate most of what the staff were saying and what the robbers did inside the premises...

Once inside the Post Office the smaller of the two robbers could be seen closing the front door and removing a revolver from inside his shell suit. He then grabbed one of the customers in the post office, stuck the gun to her head and pointed to her to lie on the floor and she complied. The other seven customers could be seen getting face down on the floor as well.

All eight customers, when interviewed, confirmed this gunman pointed the gun at them all and told them to get face down onto the floor. He told them if they didn't do what he asked he said he would 'blow their fucking heads off.'

His taller accomplice could be seen running to the counter also armed with a revolver which he had concealed under his shell suit. He climbed onto the counter and held onto the glass security screen. There was a small gap between the top of the screen and the ceiling, enough for him to put his hand through. With the gun in this hand he pointed it downwards at the two women assistants and told them to fill a well known supermarket's carrier bag he had with him, with cash.

The two counter assistants had confirmed these actions in their statements and said he'd told them, through his stutter, if they didn't do as he said he put a bullet in each of their heads.

The two terrified woman said initially they couldn't move because of fear and this caused the nervous gunman to threaten to blow their heads 'completely off' if they didn't get a move on. In a panic they filled the bag with notes and slid it through the serving hatch under the security screen.

The robbers, as shown on CCTV were in the premises for a total of three minutes and twenty seconds.

When they ran out of the Post Office, the customers and staff confirmed in their statements, they shouted for everybody to stay where they were, and not to call the cops till they were gone.

Once outside, the street CCTV showed them leaving on foot

by the side of the Post Office, into a street not covered by CCTV.

McBurnie said to Green, "Real nasty bastards" and whilst deep in thought he got a message on his radio asking him to contact D.C.C. Cobble.

He left Green at the scene and made his way back to Newholm Police Station and the D.C.C.s office.

Once inside, Cobble shouted, "What the hell is going on, guys robbing a Post Office with guns, in Newholm!." Jimmy just said,"Aye that's right" and before being prompted, briefed Cobble about the robbery and how he was going to investigate it. He said he had appointed Green as S.I.O. but he would oversee it. Cobble asked if he had confidence in Green getting a result in a serious crime like this. McBurnie confirmed he had no doubt Green was the man for the job. He was sure the C.I.D. would pull out all the stops to get these two arseholes.

He told the Deputy he would need a decent budget for this investigation because it looked like it was likely to be protracted and incur overtime. He would also need some uniform cops right away for door to door enquiries.

Cobble said not to worry about the budget as he would ensure the money was there. Jimmy then asked if D.C. Starkey could be appointed Acting Detective Sergeant and left to deal with the other 'domestic' crimes the C.I.D. had or received. The D.C.C. said he would speak to the Chief but there was no reason Starkey could not take up this position.

He later confirmed Starkey in this role.

Cobble was satisfied with what he had been told but mad because neds thought they could rob a Post Office in one of his towns and think they could get away with it. He instructed Jimmy to get a move on and contact Chief Superintendent Scott about the uniform and any other troops he needed.

The Acting D.C.I. didn't hang because he knew the time immediately after a crime has been committed was crucial, known by some cops as, 'The Golden Hour'. He went immediately to the Chief Superintendent's office.

Jimmy had little contact with Scott after the incident at The Rigger and didn't know what kind of reception he would get from him. In the past when he went to him for uniform troops he only got a limited number, well below what he required, and was told to have them returned to their 'more important' duties without delay.

At the time he had wondered what was a more important duty than investigating serious crimes like murders, but because of the difference in rank he had to keep his thoughts to himself. However, this attitude by Scott had filtered down to other uniform supervisors creating animosity between them and the C.I.D.

Even after one day, dedicated to a serious crime investigation, Jimmy was being inundated by requests from them to get their cops back, to complete these 'important' duties. McBurnie knew Scott was the catalyst behind these requests and was trying to make life as difficult as possible for him. That was bad enough, but he was also creating a barrier between uniform and C.I.D. cops, and Jimmy was sure with this friction, the public were not being best served.

He wondered what Scott's attitude would be this time when he asked him for extra cops...

Scott answered McBurnie's knock on his door and told Jimmy to come in and take a seat. This was a first for Jimmy, he had never been offered a seat in Scott's office before but always left standing and unacknowledged.

Once seated he told Scott there had been an armed robbery at the sub Post Office. Before he could explain further Scott interrupted and said he had heard details of the robbery being passed across the radio.

He told a surprised McBurnie he suspected he would need some uniform cops in a hurry, to help with door to door and other enquiries. Jimmy said that was the reason for his visit. Scott then told him to give him details of how many he wanted and he would ensure he got them without delay.

He than almost took Jimmy's breath away by stating, if any of these cop's bosses demanded their officers return before the enquiry was completed then Jimmy should contact him. No officer would be returned to their normal duties until Jimmy was sure they were no longer required for his investigation.

McBurnie nearly fell off the seat and had to compose himself before thanking Scott and making his way, hurriedly, to the C.I.D. office.

When he got to his office he thought to himself how powerful a wee bit 'inside' information was...

He was joined shortly thereafter by Green. McBurnie told him Chief Superintendent Scott had agreed to supply as many troops as they needed. Green asked Jimmy if he had heard him correctly and McBurnie just said,"You heard right." The C.I.D. and the initial cops who had attended the scene now had that area controlled and were soon supplemented by ten uniform colleagues who were tasked with door to door enquiries and being a visible presence for the public.

Once they were in place McBurnie and Green, discussed their priorities, strategy and tactics and went over what had already been put in place;

Green was able to confirm an Incident Caravan had been located outside the post office to draw the public's attention to the crime, and hopefully trace people who had been in or around the vicinity at the time of the robbery. The extra cops would be a great help with this.

Everyone who had been in the Post Office at the time of the robbery had been interviewed in depth and statements noted. Each witness had been offered counselling.

The media had been given a briefing and promised regular briefings during the course of the investigation.

Post Office Headquarters had agreed to put forward a substantial reward. This had been passed to the media to circulate along with the location of the Incident Caravan and contact telephone numbers for the public.

The CCTV coverage from the Post Office and the street had

been seized. It would be sent to a specialist unit which dealt with video enhancement to see if they could get more detail about the robbers.

The scene was still protected while scenes of crime examination was ongoing.

Two cops had been tasked with making enquiries with the supermarket whose carrier bag the robbers had used to take away their booty.

Thomason the intelligence officer had been tasked with drawing up a list of local 'potential' suspects. In particular any with a circle within a circle tattoo and/or previous convictions for robbery. He would also scrutinise all current intelligence and liaise with other forces to see if they had any similar type crimes in their area, or if they held intelligence on potential suspects.

Door to door teams had began carrying out enquiries within a one mile mile radius of the Post office and if this was unsuccessful it would be extended to two miles.

Each officer on the door to door team had been asked to complete a Personal Descriptive Form (P.D.F.)including details of any tattoos the people they spoke to had, and whether or not they had long hair and/or a stutter. This would hopefully identify people fitting the descriptions of the robbers, who may be holed up or living close to the Post Office.

Checks were being made with the Post Office to establish if they could provide any serial numbers or batch numbers of the notes that were stolen. If they could then these would be circulated nationwide...

McBurnie knew Green had completed all the basics and was impressed with his thoroughness. Nonetheless, he told him to task a couple of D.C.s to work alongside Thomason and also carry out detailed checks on the two counter staff and the eight customers who were in the Post Office at the time. Maybe there was something in their or their family's backgrounds to indicate an 'inside' job.

He then instructed Green to get the Fraud and Financial Investigation Unit to liaise with the Post Office Fraud Unit and find what intelligence they held relating to the Sub Post Office or any of the staff there. For example had money gone missing from there before, were any of the staff in debt, were there any internal investigations ongoing into the running of the Sub Post Office?

Green noted everything Jimmy said and was about to leave when his boss told him to brief all the troops. Tell them to task their touts with finding out about the robbery and make particular mention of the substantial reward being offered by the Post Office.

Green and Jimmy then signed and dated the Policy Book which they would use throughout the investigation to record their decisions and justification for them.

McBurnie suspected it was time now for the hard slog. Scott had been as good as his word and all the cops he needed were now part of the enquiry team.

Green and him would now be under a considerable amount of pressure from both the police bosses and the media to get a result...

Jimmy had every confidence in Green but still made a mental note to, in police parlance, 'cover the back door' for him. This would ensure those people who were putting the pressure on him either internally, or externally, would have to speak to Jimmy first.

The Acting D.C.I. then set about contacting all his stable of touts...

None of them could shed any light on who was responsible for the robbery. After three days there was very little coming in which the investigation team could work on.

Door to door teams had drawn a blank even after their area had been extended to two miles. Jimmy told Green to have the P.D.F.s gone through again to see the cops completing the door to door had asked the right questions and completed full descriptions of everyone they spoke to, satisfactorily.

The enquiry at the supermarket revealed there were thousands of the same carrier bags used by the robbers in circulation across the country, so this line of enquiry was a dead end.

Scenes of Crime had turned up nothing evidentially.

The Post Office had no record of the serial numbers of the stolen notes.

The CCTV had been enhanced but the quality was still poor.

Thomason and the two detectives working with him had found two teams, one from the central belt of Scotland and one from the North East of England. They were robbing Post Offices, but no members of these teams fitted the description of the Newholm robbers and their M.O. was completely different. Nevertheless, McBurnie instructed the two detectives to still look into these teams and update the enquiry team...

Green was beginning to show he was under pressure which McBurnie could see and relate to only too well. The acting D.C.I. reassured him by telling him they would definitely get these clowns but it would take time.

The longer the investigation continued the more the media were hounding McBurnie for progress reports. He was being inundated by calls from both local and national reporters. He didn't complain as he felt he was taking the heat off a stressed, Martin Green.

One week later the situation got worse. McBurnie and Green were reviewing the investigation when they received a call from another uniform sergeant in Newholm confirming a second sub post office in the town had been robbed by two gunmen...

The two detectives could hardly take it in. After the first robbery the Post Office management had assured them they had increased the security at all their branches.

The detectives immediately made their way there. As with the previous robbery the uniform cops had sealed off the locus and made sure everyone who had been in the sub post office when it was robbed was still there.

It appeared from what the witnesses were saying this robbery had the same M.O. as the previous one. Namely;

The two robbers were of similar build to the two at the other Post Office. There was no CCTV on the street outside this time but it was likely these guys donned the stocking masks they were wearing before entering the post office.

Both had guns but this time the guns were not revolvers, which had been used in the first robbery. From the descriptions of the witnesses these were semi automatic hand guns.

One robber threatened the five customers in the post office with the gun he had and ordered them to lie face down on the floor, which they did.

The taller of the two ran to the counter and presented the gun at the one member of staff, a sixty five year old lady. This witness and another customer in the Post Office, said this robber seemed to have long hair under his stocking mask.

The robber gave her a plain carrier bag and told her to fill it or she would get her head blown off.

The terrified woman filled the bag with £8500 in notes and slid the bag underneath the counter to the robber.

Both robbers made good their getaway after telling everyone to stay face down on the floor and not to call the police till they had left.

McBurnie said it looked like they were after the same two who had robbed the other Sub Post Office, but told Green they would keep an open mind. At this stage they didn't know how many neds could be involved in these robberies. He asked Green if he was happy enough to run as S.I.O. with both enquiries and Green confirmed he was.

Jimmy then left him and went to answer a call summoning him to attend at D.C.C. Cobble's office immediately. On the way there he was being inundated with messages to contact journalists, who through their sources, had already heard about the second robbery.

His meeting with Cobble got off to a bad start after the D.C.C. told him he better get a result and quick. He said the Chief was now getting it in the ear from the media and he didn't like it one bit.

McBurnie was about to go into detail about what they had in place when Cobble said, "You will need extra troops, I know that, so get along and see Chief Superintendent Scott." Jimmy felt he was being given 'the bum's rush' but as he was leaving Cobble's office the D.C.C. shouted to him "Don't panic you will get these bastards." Before leaving Jimmy said he had told Green the same thing, then grinned at the D.C.C. and left.

He headed for Scott's office and didn't have to wait long before he was invited in and offered a seat again. Jimmy told the Chief Superintendent he expected he knew why he was there and Scott said he had heard all the communications on the radio about the second robbery. He asked Jimmy how many uniform cops he needed this time and the Acting D.C.I. of the top of his head, gave him a slightly exaggerated figure. Scott agreed to release this number without question, but told Jimmy not to keep them any longer than necessary.

Jimmy confirmed they would be returned to their normal duties at the earliest opportunity. Scott nodded and wished him and his team good luck.

While heading back to the C.I.D. Jimmy could hardly take in the change in attitude by Scott but he was too busy to dwell on this. He just shook his head in amazement...

He had arranged a media briefing for that afternoon and decided he would take any flak directed at the force.

Green had used what troops he had left to kick off the investigation. This time it was going to be even more difficult to detect. There was no CCTV coverage on any street leading to the sub post office. The CCTV system inside the post office was again of very poor quality but was good enough to show the robbers with what looked like semi automatic hand guns.

The Acting D.I. had viewed the internal CCTV system, which at least allowed him to follow the actions of the robbers, confirming they were almost identical to those in the first robbery. The taller of the two did as he had done in the first robbery. He jumped on the counter, presented a gun to the one member of staff behind the counter and ordered her to give him the money. His smaller accomplice forced the customers in the post office at gunpoint to lie on the floor while he kept guard at the front door.

He was fortunate in having an M.C.A. team already up and running from the first robbery. This would save setting up time and they could administer this investigation as well, with the robberies appearing to be linked.

In Green's mind the C.I.D. would have very little capability to deal with any other crimes now. It would take nearly every cop they had, including the extra cops Scott could supply, to investigate these two serious crimes.

It would also put extra pressure on Starkey because Green was now taking two of the four detectives he had been utilising to deal with 'domestic' crimes.

Green knew he would have to get the robbers sooner rather than later. God forbid, if there was a third robbery it was unlikely they could deal with it without utilising officers from right across the force or even from other forces. If this happened then not just his and McBurnie's reputations would take a hit so too would the force's and Green was sure no Chief Constable wanted that.

The pressure was really on...

Green was a bit morose and dwelling on all these facts when McBurnie returned. His boss could see he was under real pressure and said, "We will get them, don't worry." Then as they had done before they went over what evidence they had and talked through the details of this second crime.

They adopted the same strategy as in the previous robbery but Green said to cover all the bases he would need more cops for door to door and some good statement takers. McBurnie gave him a knowing look and said 'helpful' Chief Superintendent Scott had sanctioned the release of the uniform cops Jimmy told him he needed, provided they were returned to their stations at the earliest opportunity. These cops were on their way now.

Green was delighted but like his boss could hardly believe it.

After the priorities, strategy and tactics had been agreed they signed and dated the Policy Book. Then prompted by McBurnie they adopting a very unscientific approach and held a brainstorming session, bouncing ideas off each other and each taking turns to play 'Devil's Advocate'. They even tried to place themselves in the mindset of the robbers and what they would be doing now.

The brainstorming session was maybe not scientific but it did highlight how they had a similar take on these crimes. Both detectives had been thinking maybe, just maybe, the culprits were out of towner's. Perhaps that was why there was no info or intelligence coming in about them, even with the offer of a substantial reward.

McBurnie however said he still believed they were local. He had a 'gut feeling' about it. There was something about one of them having a circle within a circle tattoo and long hair which was ringing a distant bell with him. He knew it was wrong to put any credence on gut feelings or instinct, but the tattoo was something and he couldn't get out of his mind.

He told Green the two crimes were almost identical but there was one point of difference which merited further investigation...

Both robbers had now what appeared to the witnesses and from CCTV to be semi automatic handguns, while in the first robbery they had two revolvers. This was an extra cause for concern when neds, as dangerous as these guys, had access to different firearms. Where they got these firearms and where they were now was of paramount concern and a priority action.

Having said this, two witnesses in this most recent robbery had confirmed the tallest of the robbers had what appeared to be long dark coloured hair. They could see his hair pulled back behind his face under his stocking mask. This looked like it was the same guy on both jobs.

Jimmy told Green to get a hold of Thomason and have him research what firearms had been stolen in the region and with neighbouring forces. Then get one of his D.C.s to circulate details of both robberies nationally.

McBurnie then instructed his understudy to get two detectives to reinterview all the witnesses from the first robbery. See if any of them could provide more details of the robbers descriptions and in particular, if any of them could confirm if one or both had long hair or a tattoo...

By now the police were getting numerous requests from the media for updates. Some of the national press were resorting to sensationalism, portraying Newholm like the Wild West with gun men on the loose. Thankfully, the local journalists were not being so irresponsible and were helping the police by repeatedly making reference to the reward and appealing for witnesses to come forward.

There was no doubt now, with all the media coverage there was a climate of fear in the town and Green's team needed to get a result quickly.

McBurnie was doing his best to protect his Acting D.I. from the press which was no easy job. He fronted the media briefings controlling what information went out and sanitising press releases. He took the decision to make no mention of one of the suspects possibly having long hair or a tattoo as he felt it was too specific information to give out at this time.

At the back of his mind and he really couldn't explain why, these two facets of identification kept coming back to him.

Like all senior investigating officers he knew it was always necessary to keep the media on side or in police parlance 'feed the beast', but you had to control them, not the other way around. For that reason he ensured they were updated on a regular basis but again only with the information he felt should be released.

He had told the witnesses from both Sub Post Offices not to speak to the media...

The last thing he or Green wanted was the 'specialist' knowledge of the tattoo, the long hair, the stutter, and the language used by the robbers entering the public domain before these guys were picked up. These were things only known to the witnesses and the robbers. If they appeared in the media the neds could change their appearance and if this specialist information became public knowledge it would prejudice any forthcoming interview or trial.

He knew the journalists would still seek out their own information and much against his will they would try and identify and interview the witnesses. However, if they interfered with the investigation and did prejudice the enquiry he hoped the Procurator Fiscal would take appropriate action.

This would be of little comfort, as by then the damage would have been done and it might result in two nasty bastard's getting off with these crimes.

McBurnie wasn't having it. He told himself nothing was going to prevent him giving these neds what they deserved, a long time spent 'inside."

Thomason reported back he had checked both locally and with neighbouring forces. Some forces had firearms stolen but with the scant description of the weapons used by the two robbers there was little to confirm they were using any of these stolen weapons.

Out of the blue, Green said there was a bit of good news...

One of the witnesses in the first robbery when re interviewed, thought the tallest of the two robbers had long hair under his stocking mask. This further corroborated other witnesses accounts in the second robbery and it was likely now that at least one of these neds was responsible for both crimes.

While Green and McBurnie were going over the evidence they were joined in the Major Incident Room by D.C.C. Cobble. As normal he made straight for McBurnie and asked him if they were making any progress.

The Acting D.C.I. said progress was slow but confirmed the part about one of the robbers at both post offices having long hair and about the tattoo and the stutter.

Cobble then went through his mental 'tick' list of investigative strands which thankfully Jimmy was able to confirm Green and him had already completed.

On occasions like this McBurnie always felt under pressure from the D.C.C. but knew his 'cross examination' was worthwhile. It not only reassured him he was doing the right things, but kept both him and his team on their toes. Cobble was an old detective in the true sense of the word. Accordingly, any suggestions or instructions he put forward were always based on experience.

The D.C.C. then asked him what his stable of touts were saying and McBurnie had to admit, at this time none of his charges knew anything about the robberies. McBurnie was beginning to get a bit frustrated with this mini interrogation but told himself at least the D.C.C. visited the Major Incident Room.

No one else in senior management did...

Cobble was satisfied with Jimmy's responses but before he left he told him the Chief was getting flak from the new chair of the Police Authority and from some sections of the media. Cobble said Jimmy should take account of this, because if there was another armed robbery then both his and Green's positions would be under threat.

Jimmy thought to himself "So what's new, does the Chief actually believe guys like these robbers fall out of trees and surrender with there hands in the air?"

After Cobble left Green and McBurnie went over the evidence and intelligence again. It looked like they were in for a long hard slog. At the back of their minds they knew. Like Cobble said, there could be another robbery at any time and people could get hurt.

The joys of being a detective...

In situations like this Jimmy knew there was one place he could be assured of getting assistance. So he said a wee prayer to the man above.

Sure enough two days later he received a telephone call, for the first time by one of his new touts, Sloppy Joe, who was a process worker in a canning factory in Newholm.

Sloppy told McBurnie he had been following news of the robberies with the press and had heard something about the robbers carrying different guns on each crime. Jimmy was hoping mad when he heard the media had somehow got hold of this information and released it. Nevertheless, he told sloppy to continue.

The tout said it may be nothing, but he was aware that a guy who worked in the small workshop at the canning factory had a fascination for guns. He had even heard through the grapevine this guy could convert replica guns into weapons capable of firing and had been converting these weapons, using the lathes, drills, milling and shaping machines in the factory workshop.

McBurnie was really interested now and asked Sloppy who this guy was and where he lived.

The tout said he was called Paul Shephard, a guy about twenty five years of age, who lived with his girlfriend in a remote cottage at Highforth, six miles from Newholm. He confirmed Shephard had only been with company for seven months and before that he had worked in an engineering factory near Coatbridge. He also confirmed Shephard owned a Harley Davidson motor cycle which he used to get to work.

Jimmy thanked his new charge, told him to keep his ear to the ground and arranged a further meeting with him for three days hence.

Once off the phone, he tasked Thomason with doing background checks on Shephard and he told Green to apply for a warrant to search Shephard's house for firearms.

Thomason wasn't long coming back. He said he had checked with the cops in Coatbridge and they held some intelligence on a Paul Shephard who was twenty seven years old but had no previous convictions. The intelligence they did hold came from an anonymous source who alleged Shephard was converting replica hand guns and selling them to local 'gangsters' for £200 each.

This was the only piece of intelligence in the system and the local cops didn't seem to have done much about it.

Thankfully Green was able to get a search warrant mainly because there had been the two armed robberies in Newholm and the threat to the public the armed robbers posed.

That afternoon McBurnie, Green, and two detectives from the shop floor, were plotted up around the exit gate to the canning factory. They had confirmed Shephard's Harley Davidson bike was in the factory car park. It wasn't long before the bike with its unique roar, and its rider, left the factory and headed for Highforth.

Unknown to the rider he was closely followed by McBurnie and his team.

Sure enough the 'follow' ended at an old farm cottage just outside the village. Shephard had no sooner got off his bike before he was grabbed by McBurnie and Green. Initially, he was going to put up a struggle but once the two officers showed him their warrant cards and the search warrant, he calmed down.

Green cautioned him and read over the terms of the warrant before they entered his house. Once inside Jimmy kept a hold of him and asked him if he had any firearms. A very subdued Shephard said he fooled about with replica weapons but it was only a bit of fun and harmed no one.

He then took McBurnie and Green into the bedroom and on the floor was a replica A.K. 47 assault rifle, in pieces. Underneath the bed were two replica hand guns which appeared to have new barrels fitted to them and a box of empty shell casings with ball bearings super glued to them.

McBurnie informed Shephard he was being detained and him and his weapons would be taken to Newholm Police Station after a thorough search of his house.

The search recovered custom made firing pins, different types of ammunition, gun barrels and literature relating to the conversion of firearms.

A worried Shephard was now handcuffed and transferred to one of the C.I.D. cars. While in the car McBurnie asked him if he had a locker at his workplace and he confirmed he had. McBurnie then said, if need be he would get a warrant to search the locker, or alternatively Shephard could give permission for the search and hand over the locker key.

Shephard was compliant and told Jimmy to take the key from the belt he was wearing.

On arrival at the station Jimmy took Shephard to one of the interview rooms and told Green to go to the canning factory and with the permission of the management note details of all the machinery Shephard had access to in the machine shop. After he had done this, again with the permission of the management, search Shephard's locker.

Once Green had gone McBurnie left his custody in no doubt he was in serious trouble especially when Newholm was in the grip of fear, caused by two robbers with guns. If he was charged with converting replica weapons, how did he think that would go down with the judge and the public?

Shephard knew he was in deep shit and McBurnie increased the pressure on him by placing him in a cell and telling him when he returned he wanted the names of the people he had supplied with guns.

About an hour later the Acting D.I. returned with more barrels, other parts for handguns and rifles he had found in Shepard's locker. He told Jimmy the workshop had lathes, milling and shaping machines, grinders, drills and everything you needed if you had the know how to convert weapons.

Before he left the factory Shepard's bosses had confirmed Shephard would now be looking for another job!

McBurnie removed Shephard from his cell to a tape recording room and interviewed him with Green present. He was shown all the gun parts recovered from his home and workplace and asked to comment. He readily admitted ownership of all the parts and using them to convert replica weapons to ones that could fire.

At the end of the interview Jimmy knew he would have to release Shephard. Before they could proceed with charges under firearms legislation all the parts recovered and the weapons seized would have to be sent to the forensic laboratory, ballistics department and 'expert' opinion provided about there use and capability.

Of course Shephard didn't know why he was being released...

During the interview both McBurnie and Green had repeatedly asked him if he had supplied anyone with firearms and he had denied this. He was asked if he knew anything about the two robberies at the Post Offices and again he denied knowing anything about them and he didn't fit the description of any of the robbers.

Now he knew he was being released but would most likely be charged at a later date he asked both detectives if there was any way they could help his position. Jimmy said "Just tell the truth and we will see what we can do."

Shephard then told them he had to leave the Coatbridge area because of threats from gangsters who had heard he had the ability to convert guns. He had given two converted hand guns to two friends there and they all had a good laugh firing the weapons at targets he had. Somehow his skill in this field had become known to some 'heavies' who had put pressure on him to sell them guns. He had refused and they had slashed him across the chest before he could escape.

At this point he lifted his jersey and showed McBurnie and Green a 12 inch scar running diagonally across his chest.

Shephard said he thought now he had been away from Coatbridge for a while, had a job, a girlfriend and new friends he could continue with his hobby. In fact he had allowed two of his Newholm friends to use some guns he had converted, in target practice in the wood behind his house. He confirmed his friends didn't get to keep these guns and after they were used he made sure they were left, safe, protected and hidden in the wood.

McBurnie asked him what types of weapons he had allowed his friends to use and he told him, two rifles, two revolvers and two semi-automatic hand guns.

McBurnie and Green were all ears now and asked who his friends were.

Shephard said they were harmless, they just liked a laugh and they smoked a bit of dope together, now and again. Jimmy pressed him and reminded him of how serious a situation he was in.

After a pause he said one was Jocky Brownlee, who McBurnie didn't know.

The other one he did...

He was Tempestuous Lad...

Now McBurnie knew why the tattoo described by the witnesses

struck a cord with him. Tempestuous had one on his wrist which was a martial art logo showing a world within a world, or as the witnesses described it one circle inside another!

It was falling into place now, Tempestuous had long hair and was about the same build as the tallest robber. McBurnie could never have believed Tempestuous was an armed robber, but as he was well aware, you just never knew with neds.

McBurnie asked where these converted weapons were now and Shephard said he always kept them in bags in the wood behind his house. They were returned there after each target practice. He had never allowed his friends to take them away as he wanted them under his control at all times.

Jimmy then told him he would be taken home and he would hand over the guns he had converted and hidden.

To say Shephard was relieved was an understatement.

When he got home he took the two detectives to the wood behind his house and handed over the bags containing the four guns and two rifles.

McBurnie told him not to mention the recovery to his two friends. If they called again wanting some target practice, he should say he was turned over by the police and got rid off them.

Shephard readily agreed and before leaving, Jimmy told him to contact him immediately, Brownlee and his buddy made contact with him.

Green then delivered the bad news and told Shephard he

should return to work and pick up his belongings...

On their return to the office McBurnie told Green to show the hand guns from the bags to all the witnesses who were in the two post offices to see if they could identify them. Then they would be sent along with the two rifles and other items seized from Shephard's house, to the lab for fingerprinting, DNA and ballistics checks.

Not long after, the Acting D.I. returned to the C.I.D. office confirming three witnesses from the first robbery and two from the second had identified the guns as being identical to those used in the robberies.

The next day Shephard contacted Jimmy and said his friends had been in touch and had panicked when he told them he had been turned over by the police and had disposed of the guns.

McBurnie knew now, yet again, he had a tout who was involved in serious crime. He could hardly believe it with Tempestuous, but like Hasty Lad, Wise Archie and Capo before him, this tout would now have to take a 'fall'.

Checks on Jocky Brownlee, revealed he was twenty three years old, 5'7" tall, slim build, with minor convictions for shoplifting and theft.

Forensics later confirmed fingerprints relating to Shephard, Brownlee and Tempestuous had been found on three of the hand guns.

McBurnie knew there was little likelihood of the robbers committing further robberies now they had been spooked by

Shephard. However, he wasn't one to take unnecessary risks and knew it was time now to get Tempestuous and Brownlee in to custody and off the street. It was also time, to take a step back and not become involved in detaining Tempestuous.

McBurnie tasked Green with being the 'bad guy' and he was soon on their trail.

That afternoon the Acting D.I. and his team had detained both Brownlee and Tempestuous. It was no surprise to McBurnie when Tempestuous hadn't been long in the station before he was asking to see him.

Jimmy, as he had done with some of his other charges who had 'crossed the line', decided he would let him sweat. This would be as difficult for McBurnie as it was for Tempestuous. This tout was the nephew of Delicate Girl and Jimmy still felt a sense of responsibility to her even though she was dead. He knew of course he would not condone any crime Tempestuous had committed and these robberies were two really bad crimes.

Green and his team got on with interviewing the two suspects.

Once they showed them the evidence they had against them, including the guns recovered from Shephard, it didn't take them long to capitulate. Importantly they both stated Shephard was not aware they had used the guns in the robberies. After they had been target shooting in the wood behind his house, they had gone back and taken the guns and returned them after the robberies. Shephard, they stressed, had no knowledge they were using these guns and he was not involved in the crimes.

Green arrested them and charged them with the two armed robberies and various firearms offences. After the interviews he briefed Jimmy telling him they both had made full admissions. McBurnie asked him how Tempestuous had reacted when being interviewed and his Acting D.I said he got in a flap trying to answer some of his questions and began to stutter...

The internal pressure was off now and once they had been charged Jimmy telephoned Cobble. He let him know the good news, gave Green a good 'write up' and said the Chief would now be relieved.

Now it was time to speak to Tempestuous and find out why he committed these crimes.

McBurnie went to his cell and took a very subdued tout to a free interview room. Jimmy asked him what was he thinking about getting involved in armed robberies. Tempestuous had a short pause and said he needed the cash urgently, because him, his sister, Brownlee and two of their friends were in debt to a guy for gear(drugs).

McBurnie was well aware this tout could handle himself and was not an individual to back away from anyone. He asked him if the guy they owed the cash to had some clout or was well connected. Tempestuous confirmed this guy always had four heavies with him, who it was rumoured had guns and had used them. If it had been a one to one square go then he would have taken him on.

The tout said any further thought of kicking the shit out of him disappeared when these bastards kidnapped his sister and threatened to put acid on her face, destroying her good looks. They even visited Brownlee's elderly mother, smashed some of her furniture and told her to tell her son he 'owed' them.

Tempestuous said his sister was held captive by them till he and Brownlee committed the two robberies and handed the proceeds over to him, to pay off their debt. Once this was done she was released, and she was now in hiding with friends in London.

McBurnie asked him who this heavyweight was but he wouldn't say. All he would confirm was he was a scouser, not long out of prison with a fearsome reputation and dangerous 'contacts' across both Scotland and England.

The detective's mind was now in overdrive. Who, he wondered could be so feared he could intimidate someone like his tout and force him and his friend to commit these crimes?

One thing for sure. McBurnie needed to meet him and soon...

Once again he asked Tempestuous to identify this guy but he just shook his head. He told Jimmy he knew he would be going away for a while for robbing the two post offices. He asked Jimmy who was going to look after his sister or Brownlee's mother if he grassed this bastard up and left them unprotected?

Jimmy couldn't answer him because he knew the police had nothing in place to stop this guy getting at her, the old woman or even Tempestuous and Brownlee while they were 'inside'.

Jimmy offered to speak to his sister if he told him where she was living, but he refused to disclose where she was. He knew

McBurnie could eventually trace her without his help, so he pleaded with him not to go near her. He said if this guy found out she had been seen in Jimmy's company or knew she had contacted him, he would make a mess of her and maybe even kill her.

McBurnie then asked if Brownlee would say anything and Tempestuous said Brownlee was scared shitless. He didn't want to get involved in the robberies in the first place, but when he saw the state of his mother after these bastards had visited her, he felt he had no choice.

During the first robbery Tempestuous said Brownlee couldn't stop shaking. He kept telling Tempestuous they were dead men, even if they did commit the two robberies and give the guy who was holding Tempestuous' sister and threatening his mother, the money.

Tempestuous pleaded with Jimmy not to go near Brownlee, and Jimmy now understood why. He then asked McBurnie if there was anything he could do for them in relation to the robbery charges.

McBurnie sighed, and said, "The ball is in your court." He explained if they didn't tell him or the court how they were pressured into committing these crimes, how his sister had been kidnapped and Brownlee's mother threatened, then there was little he could do.

Tempestuous just shook his head...

McBurnie wanted to help, not just because of Tempestuous' link to Delicate or because of the information he had provided in the past. He hated to see any ned, let alone one of his touts, take a fall for somebody else, especially for such an evil bastard as described by Tempestuous.

It infuriated him but he couldn't think of anything he could do unless his tout spoke up. The only advice he gave was for Tempestuous and Brownlee to name this guy. If not, plead guilty and not take their case to trial. Maybe this would result in a reduced sentence. However he stressed this was a matter for them.

He told him if witnesses had to go into court and relive the experiences of the robberies, without any knowledge of what was behind them, it was sure to influence both the jury and the sentence the judge handed out.

McBurnie could see Tempestuous mulling this over but wondered what advice he would get from the solicitor representing him when he or she knew this case would be held in the High Court. Preparing a case for the High Court and representing clients in this court was a huge money earner and McBurnie was sure the solicitor's advice would be to plead 'not guilty' and take the case to trial.

As he was taking his tout back to his cell McBurnie was deep in thought. Who was now in Newholm with such power and influence and why had he not heard about him from any of his stable. Could it even be someone connected to one of his stable?

Unlikely now especially when Capo was out to pasture...

He wasn't in his office long before the press were pestering him for an update on the investigation. He decided to hold a press briefing that afternoon.

The briefing was scheduled for 2pm in Newholm Police Station and Jimmy made sure Green would be with him on the podium, telling the journalists' the 'Good News'.

He wasn't in the least surprised when an hour before the briefing was due to start, the Chief visited him and asked him to compile some notes for him about how the case was detected and when the robbers would be appearing in court. He told Jimmy he would now front the media, but if he wished, he and Green could be there to answer any specific questions he couldn't answer...

McBurnie knew that when 'Good News' was being delivered the Chief was always at the forefront. Accordingly, he did as he was told and compiled a sanitised report ensuring the Chief said nothing to prejudice the case.

He was well aware when the newspapers knew of the arrests some journalists would create articles claiming only with 'their' input was the case solved.

In fact one article by a national newspaper had really annoyed Jimmy that morning. On their front page they claimed the police in Newholm were 'stumped' and 'amateurs'. McBurnie made sure the journalist responsible for this headline received a personal invitation from him to the briefing...

The Chief opened proceedings stating how determined and committed his officers had been in this investigation and how safe a community Newholm was. He told his audience, armed robbery was almost unheard of in his force area and neither he nor his officers would tolerate it. As a result they had pulled out all the stops and quickly arrested the robbers, who were now in custody. He stuck to the 'script' Jimmy had prepared for him and when questions came from the floor looking for more detail he quickly passed them on to McBurnie and Green.

Before answering any questions Jimmy made a point of telling all the journalists, and one in particular. Contrary to hyperbole and speculation, the police had never been 'stumped' in this investigation and weren't 'amateurs'.

The journalist responsible for the damning article now knew why he had received a personal invitation to the briefing. He was reluctant to look up from his notes as he could sense McBurnie's eyes focused exclusively on him.

The briefing lasted forty-five minutes and the other journalists in the room kept probing, looking for the 'inside line' on how McBurnie and Green had managed to catch the robbers.

The two detectives were too worldly wise to provide any specifics, and the press left slightly frustrated but McBurnie knew they would use poetic licence to concoct a good story.

All Green and he conceded during the question and answer session was the public had been of great assistance. In reality this phrase included the information from Sloppy Joe but there was no way he was telling anybody about Sloppy's involvement.

After the meeting with the press McBurnie and Green went to the canteen for a coffee. They weren't there long before A.C.C. Ramsden and Chief Superintendent Scott came in. These two senior officers always had their afternoon coffee together at the same time and same table.

By having coffee in the canteen they felt they were showing, higher ranks were approachable and could mix freely with the troops on the ground.

That was their theory anyway...

They had just got their drinks from the coffee machine and were on the way to their usual seats, when they stopped at Jimmy and Green's table. Both smiled and congratulated them on their success in arresting the armed robbers.

The detectives thanked them but after they left, Green told Jimmy he had nearly choked on his scone. McBurnie just smiled and thought to himself maybe I am not public enemy number one any more. Then his suspicious nature kicked in and he told himself not to be so stupid. He would always be an outcast in the eyes of the police hierarchy, with the exception of Cobble.

The next day, along with Green, McBurnie met up with Sloppy and handed over £500 as the King's Shilling. He told him this would be supplemented by another £1000 from the Post Office as their reward, once the necessary paperwork was completed.

Needless to say Sloppy was delighted with this amount of cash and promised to keep in touch with Jimmy whenever he had any good info. McBurnie on leaving said, "I know you will son."

Green was left with the unenviable task of preparing the case for court, which Jimmy knew would have to be thorough and concise.

Omissions or errors in case preparation, as McBurnie had experienced, often resulted in detectives getting a hard time from both prosecutors and defence agents. This could easily result in the baddies getting off and damage a detective's reputation permanently.

This would be another major test for Green but Jimmy was confident he would pass the test.

It was at times like this McBurnie reflected on how only detectives get this amount of pressure. Some cops and senior officers who have never been detectives think once the bad guys have been arrested then the investigation is ended.

As McBurnie knew only too well this was just the beginning.

Preparing the case, ensuring witness safety, protecting informants and standing up to what could turn out to be days in the witness box in the High Court, all put extreme pressure on a Senior Investigating Officer. Unless you had had ever been one you had no appreciation of how stressful and difficult a role this was.

For McBurnie, being a detective wasn't just a job and for many like him, it had to be an addiction!

Shephard's converted weapons were tested at the ballistics laboratory and most were found capable of firing. The home made ammunition comprising of blank shells with ball bearings super glued to the front was also tested and found capable of penetrating quarter inch thick mild steel.

After the fiscal had the ballistics report, Shephard was summoned to appear at court. Initially he pled not guilty but before his trial he changed his plea and pled guilty to reduced charges.

The only reason the Procurator Fiscal accepted the plea to these reduced charges was because Shephard had agreed to provide evidence, confirming he converted the replica hand guns Tempestuous and Brownlee had used in the two robberies. She accepted Shephard knew nothing about Tempestuous and Brownlee taking the weapons without his knowledge and he had no knowledge of their crimes.

Shephard was defined by the presiding judge as totally irresponsible and sentenced to one year imprisonment.

Tempestuous and Brownlee were remanded in custody on their first court appearance.

When they next appeared in court, just as Jimmy had suspected, their lawyers tendered pleas of Not Guilty.

McBurnie was not surprised at these pleas. He suspected because of the strength of the evidence against both accused, it was likely they would try and come to a deal with the Procurator Fiscal, to plead guilty, with possible deletions from the charges.

This is exactly what happened...

Both were eventually sentenced to eight years in prison and the judge told them if they had not pled guilty or made witnesses relive their ordeal they would have been looking at twelve year sentences...

Jimmy had now lost a potential 'classic' winning tout from his yard in Tempestuous, but he had been through this process before. He knew he could always recruit and train another charge.

Having said this he was still wondering who the bastard was who had kidnapped his tout's sister and forced him and Brownlee into committing the two robberies.

Green had produced some sterling work and shown his worth as a D.I. Jimmy hoped he would get the substantive rank. At least he had a chance of being promoted but Jimmy still felt, in keeping to horse racing terms, the odds on him going any further were long...

On the shop floor Starkey had coped admirably with all the domestic issues and McBurnie felt he had a good team of detectives under him.

Most 'domestic' crimes allocated to C.I.D. had been dealt with in a professional manner and importantly there were many good results. Starkey had lost his cockiness and was finding out what it was like when you became a supervisor, managing the boys and girls, yet not being one of them.

Jimmy liked what he saw...

A NEW ERA

It was time for D.C.C. Cobble to retire and nobody would be sadder to see him go than McBurnie who felt he was losing his only ally in the senior management.

As was normal practice in situations like Cobble's, his position had to be advertised both internally and externally. Ramsden was due to retire soon so he was unlikely to apply and Scott's reputation in force wouldn't help his prospects. It looked like the new D.C.C. would come from another force.

A week later Jimmy learned there were six applicants, four from Scotland, one from the north of England and one from the Metropolitan Police. Scott didn't make the final list of candidates and Ramsden didn't apply.

When McBurnie found out who they were he looked up detectives he had come across over the years from the candidates home forces, to get the 'inside line' on them.

He learned of the four Scottish candidates only one had spent any time in the C.I.D. and had held the rank of D.I. The other three had almost identical career paths which included time spent in administration, personnel, training, secondments to the Police College and as project leaders.

The candidate from the North of England had spent three months in the C.I.D. as a detective constable and had never been back since.

Little was known about the candidate from London other than he was only thirty two years of age so he obviously had limited experience.

After his research Jimmy became a bit philosophical and decided it didn't matter who got the job. It wasn't going to make any difference to his 'long odds' for promotion.

He was visited by Cobble who now had only one week left before retirement. The D.C.C. told Jimmy to put the kettle on and make some tea. McBurnie duly obliged and the Deputy told him his call this time was definitely a social call.

The conversation then related to some of the cases Cobble had dealt with as a detective, how he had often had a hard time in the witness box from theatrical Q.C.s, and about some of the high profile neds he had arrested.

Jimmy loved hearing these stories and wasn't slow at throwing in some of his own. Before too long he and the Deputy were having a great laugh and any outsider would never have known there was such a difference in rank between them.

After almost an hour Cobble said he had better get back to his office. Before he left he told Jimmy he would be speaking to whoever got his job and recommending Jimmy for substantive rank.

Jimmy knew he was sincere so shook hands with him and thanked him for all his support.

Three days later everyone in force learned the successful

candidate was A.C.C. James Flemington, from Fife. He was forty-five years old with twenty-five years service and he was the candidate who had been a D.I. Jimmy was pleased when he heard the news but still felt it would make little difference to him. His card had been 'marked' over the incident with Scott and he would never go beyond the rank of D.I.

Cobble had a retirement function at a local hotel and it must have been the first one Jimmy had attended when the top brass were there. He didn't care because he knew he owed loyalty to Cobble. To show he appreciated his support, he took an 18 year old malt whisky to the hotel but left it behind the reception, where Cobble could pick it up, without Jimmy being seen giving him it.

Jimmy only had a few drinks at the bar before making his way towards his old D.C.C. wishing him well for the future and telling him where to pick up the whisky.

During their short conversation Cobble told him to expect a visitor at work the next week, but never expanded on who it would be.

Jimmy left the function early, slightly bemused but intrigued nevertheless.

The following week the new D.C.C. was scheduled to make visits to every department. Surprisingly his first visit was to the C.I.D. and to Jimmy.

McBurnie didn't know what to expect but was pleased when Flemington entered his office. As usual Jimmy stood up to show he was in the presence of a high rank and immediately Flemington told him to sit down and not be so formal. The new Deputy shook hands with him and told him to relax. He said ex D.C.C. Cobble had told him all about his Acting D.C.I. and his stable of touts.

They had a long conversation during which Flemington reminisced about crimes he had investigated and how being a detective was the best part of his career. He told Jimmy how impressed he was with what he had heard about him, his prowess as a detective, the amount of informants he had and how he was performing as D.C.I. He said he looked forward to supporting and promoting the department, including Jimmy, in the future.

When he left Jimmy could hardly take it in...

Was his old minister Mr Morrison right all along, did God have a plan for him? Things were certainly looking up and Cobble's replacement seemed to be onside.

He took stock...

Firstly, Chief Superintendent Scott had been his arch enemy, and a real obstacle to promotion. He now knew Jimmy could have caused him some embarrassment over the incident with the young, attractive, married police woman. Scott might even have become subject to a disciplinary offence but Jimmy and Green, had kept their mouths shut.

McBurnie could now only concede, Scott, if the last few serious crimes were anything to go by, seemed to be supportive of him, probably because he had said nothing about the incident at The Rigger. In fact when he had asked for uniform troops he got them without quibble or question. This was a real turnaround from what had gone before and Cobble had confirmed Scott's turnaround in attitude towards Jimmy and was puzzled by it.

Secondly, Ramsden was known to have no time for the C.I.D. or detectives in general. Cobble again confirmed Ramsden too had changed his mind about Jimmy. Cobble knew this would be because he arrested the neds responsible for breaking into Ramsden's home and recovering jewellery which was of sentimental value to him. He was now very cordial with Jimmy and he and Scott had both praised him in public for his success in catching the post office robbers.

Thirdly Cobble's replacement told him he had his full support...
All in all McBurnie felt things could not be any better. Jokingly he told himself,"Maybe I should put a bet on myself to get promoted especially when the odds are so long?"

If he hadn't been the sceptic and cynic he was, he would have believed he had a good chance of promotion. He even had a long discussion with Doris when he got home from work about the possible turnaround in his prospects. At last she could see her husband exhibit some signs of optimism.

However, she knew inwardly, no matter what he said, he would always be a sceptic...

When he returned to work the following day he put any thoughts of advancement to the back of his mind and just got on with the job. He told himself his role was to make sure those under his command in the C.I.D. always gave 100% and a steady flow of information kept coming in.

It was three months before D.C.I. Johnston was due back to his day job. Meanwhile, Jimmy was ensuring when he came back, everything was ship shape. Since he started his acting stint not only had he dealt successfully with the crimes he had investigated, but by taking paperwork home he ensured the administrative side of the department was also up to date.

The following week one of his contacts in the training department told him one of the two uniform chief inspectors in Stratshall was leaving the police. The Service had paid for him to complete a law degree, in the belief he would put his new knowledge and experience to best use within the force.

However, some other cops in the country, who had received sponsorship from their forces to study law, after the completion of their studies, had left the police to become lawyers. The Chief Inspector in Stratshall had decided to do the same.

There would now be a vacancy which would be circulated throughout the Force the following week...

Jimmy took note of what he was told and when he got home he showed his true colours and asked Doris if she thought there was any point in him applying for this post.

Doris was used to the peaks and troughs of living with Jimmy but she was in no doubt there was no one more addicted to their job than him. She told him he was applying and she would be backing him all the way.

He appreciated her support but then disclosed more of his true feelings...

He said the job that was up for grabs was a uniform job. If he got it, which was highly unlikely, then he would be leaving the C.I.D. The family might also have to move house and the kids go to a new school. Wisely, he never mentioned it would mean losing contact with some of his touts.

Doris told him not to be so stupid. If he was successful in his application, who was to say, especially with his record in crime detection, he would not be asked to return to his favourite department at a later date. That would also mean a return to Newholm and the kids were young enough to cope with a school change if they had to.

Her husband gave her a blank look and said he would think about it. She just shook her head....

The following Monday details of the post for a Chief Inspector at Stratshall were circulated force wide and suitably qualified candidates were asked to apply by the end of the week.

McBurnie left it until the last day, before, somewhat sheepishly, submitting his application form.

It was now time to wait and see what form the interview would take and who would be sitting on the selection panel. In the meantime he forgot about promotion and got on with his work...

Since Tempestuous had been locked up Jimmy couldn't stop thinking about who the individual was who forced him and Brownlee to commit the two armed robberies. Whoever it was, they couldn't have been in Newholm long because McBurnie was sure he would have heard about him. He told himself he must have some reputation in the criminal world if neds were prepared to take an eight year 'fall' without naming him.

He decided it was time for another visit to his stable. Surely with this guy's reputation for violence and drug dealing, some of his charges could shed light on his identity...

His first call was with Bashful who had given him the information to put Frankie Hawkins away and was also involved in Capo's demise.

McBurnie knew she was still 'using' and she would know about the drug dealing network in Newholm but there must be some reason she hadn't contacted him. As was normal practice now, when he met her he had somebody with him. Usually if he was meeting a female tout he took D.S. Allan, but she was now working with D.C.I. Johnston on the internal investigation.

He got hold of Starkey and told him to come with him.

Straight away when McBurnie met Bashful he asked who the scouser was who was dealing the dope in the town and why she had not contacted him about this guy. Bashful lived up to the name Jimmy had given her, and for all intents and purposes she appeared 'bashful' about saying anything, especially when McBurnie was accompanied.

In reality she was terrified and it took a bit of coaxing from McBurnie to get her to start talking. When she did she wanted every reassurance Starkey could be trusted and Jimmy would ensure her input and identity would remain secret.

McBurnie guaranteed her there was no possibility her identity and what she was going to tell him would be compromised and

Starkey could be trusted. She then said a scouser, nicknamed 'The Grip' and two other guys from Liverpool had appeared in the Cuckoos Nest pub about eight to ten weeks before, along with a small older woman. This woman was in her mid-fifties, quite a bit overweight and wearing a mini skirt. She had make up plastered all over her face and was covered from head to toe in gold jewellery. She looked a ridiculous figure but Bashful later learned she was Capo's mother...

At that time some guys in the pub had managed to get hold of small quantities of ecstasy and speed and were selling it at reasonable prices to some of the regulars. This was a risk on their part because everyone knew the 'business' was still controlled by Capo's family.

She said, immediately on entering the pub the three scousers headed for the two guys who were selling the drugs, and dragged them out to the toilets. Meanwhile, Capo's mother was struggling to stand at the bar without falling over in shoes with 5" heels.

She just smirked at the punters.

Nobody made any moves to help these two guys and the other punters soon heard screaming coming from the male toilets. After some five minutes the scousers returned to the bar and said, "If you don't obey the rules you will get what they got."

They then asked if everybody understood and everyone nodded. As they were leaving they said anyone who 'spoke' to the police better have a plot set aside in the graveyard.

After the scousers and Capo's mother had gone some of the

customers made their way to the toilet and brought back the two guys who had been taken there by the scousers. One had three teeth knocked out and a broken nose, whilst his buddy also had a broken nose, teeth missing and was holding his ribs.

Closer examination of these men revealed they had a finger nail ripped from each hand! Hence the screaming...

All the drug users in the pub, including Bashful knew the score now and that was the reason Bashful said she hadn't contacted Jimmy.

A right nasty team thought Jimmy, who told himself, in keeping with his fondness for horse racing terminology, they would be getting 'gelded'.

His next call, this time accompanied by Acting D.I. Green, was to Wise Archie who he also hadn't heard from for a while. Jimmy knew Archie must be up to something because he wasn't contacting him or looking for cash.

Initially, Archie appeared quite hesitant to talk when Jimmy asked him about the scousers and 'The Grip' in particular.

McBurnie suspected Archie must know about these guys. Nobody sold drugs in Newholm without him becoming aware of it. He was either afraid of them, which was unlikely, or he was getting a piece of the action.

Jimmy was surprised then when Archie quickly opened up...

He admitted he did know about them. They were in a different league from the usual drug dealers in Newholm but he told McBurnie nobody would be more happy than he was to see them taken out.

Jimmy knew this could be a true statement, as it was likely Archie wanted rid of the opposition, leaving the field clear for him to sell gear. What better way to remove them from the scene than get the cops to lock them up.

Archie even suggested to McBurnie he was prepared to infiltrate them, for suitable payment, provided, as always, Jimmy made sure his involvement remained secret, and he didn't turn up in court as a witness against them.

McBurnie thought this offer was strange...

At first Archie had been reluctant to talk about the scousers. Now here he was, early in the conversation, volunteering to infiltrate them. McBurnie wondered what his real motivation was for volunteering and reasoned, rightly or wrongly, Archie's 'business' was taking a hit the longer the scousers were around.

Jimmy was well aware touts gave information to the police for a variety of reasons and was convinced, this time, Archie's was to eliminate the opposition.

McBurnie told his tout he would take up his offer. If he could get inside this team, as he had done with others in the past, and report back to him, he would be well paid.

What Archie didn't know was if information came to McBurnie about his dealing activities, the 'trainer' would, as he had done previously, pass it on to his colleagues.

McBurnie never condoned crime...

Before he left, Archie disclosed, to a now deeply suspicious Acting D.C.I. he knew a bit more about these neds...

The one known as 'The Grip' was related to Capo in some way and that was why the scousers were in Newholm. The Grip apparently got his nickname because he always carried a pair of pliers with him and was 'rumoured' to have pulled out fingernails of people who crossed him. McBurnie thought to himself, "Archie is really well informed for someone who initially didn't want to say anything."

Archie then claimed, when Capo and his sister were jailed his mother had taken over running the business. Archie described her as an ugly, dopey bitch and said it wasn't long before she was getting pressure from other dealers who knew Capo was out of commission for a while.

He told McBurnie it was her who contacted The Grip and got them to come to Newholm. Once they arrived, The Grip and some of his buddies made 'examples' of those putting pressure on her and others who were dealing drugs. Archie said one guy, who Jimmy knew, had been badly beaten and slashed across the face and body. Another had also been beaten, bound and gagged and his head held under the river till he almost died. Jimmy was aware there was no records of any person making any complaint to the police about such assaults.

Archie had heard about the incident in The Cuckoo's Nest

where the two guys were beaten and supposedly had their fingernails withdrawn with pliers.

Much to Jimmy's surprise, he also confirmed the story about the abduction of Tempestuous' sister and how Tempestuous and Brownlee were forced into committing the two post office robberies.

McBurnie was now really angry, deeply suspicious and in no doubt if Archie knew all this he must be involved with the scousers. But why was he volunteering this information now?

He asked his tout when he had all this information why he hadn't contacted him about these bastard's earlier. Archie remained nonchalant and told Jimmy he was just waiting till he had enough on them to ensure Jimmy could get rid off them.

Jimmy thought to himself, "A likely story" but he had no choice, for now, but to accept what Archie told him. However being the 'terrier' of a detective he was, he interrogated Archie to establish just how much he actually did know...

During the interrogation he learned the team had been in Newholm, on and off, for three to four months. After sorting out some of the local dealers they had taken over the supply network for Capo's mother. When they were in Newholm they lived with her and she took great delight turning up at some local pubs with them and throwing her not inconsiderable amount of weight about.

It was rumoured she was involved sexually with one of The Grip's buddies but Archie said if this was true then the guy must have been blindfolded and he should get a medal.

When asked what type of gear they were selling Archie confirmed the scousers had access to all sorts of drugs in Merseyside and were able to supply heroin, cocaine, ecstasy, amphetamine and hash. Whenever they sold, they always turned up team handed. Archie suspected they had shooters, but no one had ever seen them with guns. However, he and everyone else noticed 'The Grip' always carried a pair of pliers attached to his belt, even when he was well dressed.

Archie told McBurnie he was convinced they now controlled the drugs market in Newholm and some of the gear they were selling was of higher purity than the locals were used to.

McBurnie knew this point was correct. There had been a sharp increase in the number of people overdosing, on heroin in particular, over the last few months. No intelligence had been gleaned about who was responsible for this high purity smack, but now Jimmy knew who it was.

A bit reluctantly and under further interrogation by McBurnie, the tout said the scousers had extended their business away from solely drug distribution, to protection rackets.

Two publicans in the town, one of whom was the new publican of The Cuckoo's Nest, John Beardmore, the other Betty Syme, the publican at The Black Swan, and a shopkeeper who owned one of three shops in the town, were paying them protection money. Jimmy asked Archie why would they pay and the tout said the scousers had 'visited' these business people. During the 'visits' they were told if they didn't pay up, on a weekly basis, their business premises would be burned to the ground, with them inside...

Jimmy was even more suspicious of his tout now. How did he know so much about this team unless he was involved with them.

He told himself Archie needs watching and maybe 'schooling' again but he never disclosed his suspicions and kept his body language 'normal'. Before he left he just told Archie to keep in touch.

McBurnie was in no doubt any further contact between him and Archie would only be when it suited Archie. He couldn't stop wondering just what Archie's involvement with the scousers was.

When Green and he got back to the office, he made contact with Thomason. He asked him to research the material he now had and find out all he could about The Grip and his team.

He told Green the scousers were probably the heaviest team they would ever have to deal with, but in racing terms they were still going to be 'pulled up' and 'put out to pasture'. They shouldn't think for a minute they were dealing with 'country cousin' cops...

Green, as always, laughed when Jimmy used racing terms to describe neds, but he knew his boss meant what he said.

The following day Thomason came into Jimmy's office with a folder full of paperwork. As normal he had been thorough in his research and had made enquiries not just with Merseyside Police but with other Forces, national agencies and Customs and Excise.

There was quite a file on 'The Grip' whose real name was Steven McCarthy, which included a photograph showing a small tattoo on his neck of a pair of pliers. Through his expression he showed just what an arrogant, nasty bastard he was. He was thirty years of age and had previous convictions going back to the age of thirteen. His convictions ranged from shoplifting, thefts, drug possession, G.B.H. through to armed robbery. He had spent eight years in prison, his last sentence ending two years ago.

Since his release he was suspected of running rackets, drug dealing and controlling prostitution in the Merseyside area, but there was insufficient information or intelligence to get him locked up again. It appeared people were more than reluctant to give evidence against him.

Customs told Thomason they suspected him of importing cannabis from Spain and had mounted an operation in an attempt to capture him with a consignment, but all they got were his couriers, and they didn't mention him.

Thomason then drew Jimmy's attention to a report from Humberside Police where they had investigated an allegation of a man being severely beaten over a drugs debt. The assailant was suspected of being McCarthy but the man refused to identify him. Thomason asked his boss to look at the details of the assault. As well as having his jaw and three ribs broken the victim had two fingernails ripped out with pliers...

'Just what we need", another nasty bastard', thought Jimmy. Like all the nasty bastard's who came into his patch and committed crime, Jimmy knew he would be 'sorted'.

Before Thomason left, McBurnie told him to circulate details of McCarthy and his team across the force and to keep him updated on any intelligence, however trivial, which came in. Thomason nodded and returned to his office.

McBurnie was on The Grip's trail now but needed to find out more about him and crimes he had committed or was involved in. He didn't want to rely solely on Archie for information. If he could get a victim to speak up against this scouser, he would make sure he was going to prison, and off the streets of Newholm for a long time.

He decided to visit, again with Green, one of his top touts, Welsh Rarebit...

As normal Rarebit was his usual guarded self, especially with Green present. Before speaking to Jimmy he asked Green how his ribs were, making reference to an altercation he had with him before McBurnie had recruited him as a tout. Green just smiled and said "How is your nose?" making reference to the broken nose Rarebit suffered as a result of a struggle with him.
Rarebit just smiled...

When asked by McBurnie about the Liverpool team, the Welshman said he had heard rumours about a new guy in town with some minders who were putting a lot of pressure on the local drug users.

The tout said he didn't know much about this guy other than he came from Liverpool and had spent some time 'inside' there. He did know he was living in Capo's mothers house, so he assumed Capo must have some connection with him. Apparently, the punters who were buying scouser's drugs were the same one's that Capo and his family had.

Rarebit, when asked by Jimmy, described what he classed as the 'Main Man" of the team as about thirty five years old, with a receding hairline. He told McBurnie he had only seen him once. He wore a heavy gold chain around his neck, and his two front teeth were gold. He dressed smartly and liked to swagger about the pubs and clubs with his scouse minders. He was built like a boxer and he looked a mean bastard. By all accounts he hadn't been slow to slap a few locals about and recently he heard there were a few more scousers who had been visiting him in Newholm.

Rarebit didn't know his real name but thought he was called The Grip, or Grip, by the locals and his scouse buddies. The tout said he hadn't contacted Jimmy about this guy because he didn't have much to go on and drugs weren't his scene.

As he had done with Archie and Bashful, Jimmy told Rarebit to keep in touch the moment he heard anything about The Grip or his team.

Back in the office McBurnie contacted Thomason again and told him to prepare a further circulation containing the extra details he now had about McCarthy. It should include a statement asking officers who knew anything about McCarthy or any sightings of him or his associates, to contact Newholm C.I.D. without delay. Once compiled he was to make sure it was circulated force wide and with neighbouring forces.

McBurnie's first line of enquiry now would be with John Beardmore, the new publican at The Cuckoos Nest. Archie had told him Beardmore was one of three business people paying McCarthy protection money.

Prior to attending at the pub McBurnie had completed a bit of background checking on Beardmore and the pub.

His first thoughts had been, why would any sensible business person want to take it over. The arrest of Hawkins, his cohorts, and the pub's barman for drugs offences, had all been highlighted in the media, and the pub was labelled by them as Newholm's 'Drugs Den'.

McBurnie was sure anyone taking it on after this media coverage, must be getting it for a knock down price. They would also need sufficient finance and a long-term plan for its future, and the plan would need to start with a dramatic change in clientèle. The new owner would need to accept a significant reduction in turn over before its reputation could, if ever, be restored.

A check of current intelligence and information about The Cuckoos Nest, suggested the patrons were the same drug users as before. Jimmy had also looked at the information held about this new publican, both in the Licensing File, and in the intelligence system.

His checks on Beardmore revealed the publican was thirty eight years of age, divorced, and before becoming a publican had owned a small second hand car sales business. On paper there was nothing for the police to object to him becoming the licensee. There was intelligence alleging he used a bit of hash and he was seen as a 'soft touch' by the druggies who frequented the pub.

One piece of uncorroborated intelligence suggested he even allowed his punters drink on tick and turned a blind eye to them still using drugs in the pub. A real recipe for disaster thought Jimmy.

Time for a visit...

McBurnie turned up at The Cuckoos Nest, unannounced, early the next morning. Beardmore lived with his girlfriend in a flat above the pub. He looked a weary individual when he came down the stairs to answer Jimmy's repeated banging on the flat's side door.

When Beardmore opened the door McBurnie showed him his warrant card and asked him if he could have a quiet word. Beardmore asked, "What about?" and Jimmy said he would tell him after he was in the flat. He didn't want to discuss 'delicate matters' in the street.

Beardmore told Jimmy he might as well come in then, and headed back upstairs to his flat. When they reached the living room, McBurnie was met by a good looking, twenty five year old, redhead, who was only wearing a man's shirt. She asked Beardmore who Jimmy was and he said he was a cop who wanted a 'private' word with him. Before she could say anything more Jimmy reinforced the word 'private'.

She took the hint, shrugged her shoulder's and headed for the bedroom.

To open the conversation McBurnie asked the new publican how business was and he said it was steady and ticking over. He then asked him if he was having any trouble in the pub with any of the punters. Beardmore said everything had been peaceful and his clients were normally well behaved.

This brought an immediate change in McBurnie's approach and he didn't miss Beardmore and hit the wall, when he stated, "Does that cover getting beaten up and your fingernails drawn out with pliers?."

Beardmore didn't know where to look and seemed in a bit of a daze, before Jimmy, pointedly, asked him if he wanted to keep his licence. He then started stammering and took a while before he confirmed he did want to remain the publican at The Cuckoo's Nest.

McBurnie then said, "Let's stop farting about, I know about the two guy's who were beaten up in the pub and about The Grip."

The publican now had a look of terror on his face...

McBurnie then told him he better start telling the truth or his business and him were finished.

Beardmore asked if it was O.K. if he smoked and Jimmy raised no objection. He then tried to remove a cigarette from a packet he had on a coffee table, but this proved extremely difficult with his hand shaking non stop. Jimmy told him to calm down and relax because they had quite a few things to discuss...

This certainly did not have the desired effect as far as Beardmore was concerned and he became even more nervous. He had reason to be when McBurnie said to him, "I am not going to beat about the bush, you are paying protection money to The Grip on a regular basis and you are going to tell me all about it."

Beardmore then started shouting "I can't, I can't, he will kill me if I shop him."

Jimmy said, "You have no choice, you either confide in me or you and your business are down the tube, and anyway how else are you going to get this scum off your back?."

Beardmore broke into tears and told McBurnie he was terrified and was in no doubt the scouser would make sure he disappeared permanently, if he spoke up. McBurnie said, "Leave the scouser to me, I have dealt with arseholes like him in the past and put them away. This one will be no different."

The distraught publican wasn't convinced and asked Jimmy what he could do to prevent him being beaten up, murdered or as The Grip had threatened, his pub burnt down with him in it.

McBurnie knew this was an awkward question to answer honestly, but told him he was already getting information about this scouser. How did he (McBurnie) know about Beardmore paying protection money, how did he know about the two punters getting a beating in the pub and their fingernails pulled with pliers?

Beardmore, reflected on what Jimmy said and to keep him focused the detective said there were many people in Newholm who wanted to get rid of the scousers. Why else was he getting information about them?

He could now see Beardmore was thinking seriously about speaking up. To reassure him further he told him he would supply him with a direct contact where he could get hold of him 24 hours a day.

This appeared to do the trick but only after McBurnie confirmed he didn't have to submit a written statement or appear in court as a witness against this scouser or his buddies. How, or if, this was possible to achieve was debatable but Jimmy didn't tell Beardmore that.

The publican then admitted, for months he had been paying The Grip and his henchmen £400 a week after the threats they made to him. He must have had doubts about McBurnie's confirmation he would not be appearing as a witness and stated categorically he definitely would not be supplying any written statement till Jimmy could guarantee his safety.

Jimmy then left this worried individual, and as he was going down the stairs he thought to himself, he now had confirmation, even if only verbal, about The Grip's protection racket. How he was going to keep Beardmore out of court and guarantee his safety was another matter...

He consoled himself by using the metaphor of painting...

Crime fighting was all about building up an intelligence and evidential picture. At least now he had put the first stroke on the canvas. With a little help from above he would complete the picture.

When he got back in the office he briefed Green about his

meeting with Beardmore. He stressed to Green how they needed to get more info on these buggers and soon, before somebody was killed. He then spoke to Thomason and asked him what current information and intelligence he had about the scousers.

The intelligence collator was not his usual upbeat self. In fact he was quite despondent. He said he had circulated all the details they had on The Grip and his cohorts, but there was virtually nothing coming in about them.

Merseyside police had been in contact wishing them good luck in trying to arrest McCarthy and his team. They said they had been on his tail since he was released from prison, but couldn't get close to him. Nobody wanted to speak up against him because of his, and his minder's, well earned reputation for extreme violence.

McBurnie decided then he and Green were going to the home of the shopkeeper, who he suspected was Allan Drummond, who Archie said was also paying protection money...

Allan Drummond was approaching retirement age, and lived with his wife in a four bedroom villa in an up market part of Newholm. At one time he had been the proprietor of three shops in the town, all of which sold groceries, hardware and drink. By all accounts his businesses were profitable and he was a very wealthy man.

As he was nearing retirement and had no immediate family to carry on his businesses, he sold two of his shops and kept the most profitable one, which was located in the town centre.

McBurnie had met this man on many occasions and described

him to Green as an absolute gentleman. He told Green, Drummond regularly gave to charity and at Christmas time he used to take food parcels from his store and distribute them to homeless people, alcoholics and families without very much.

He was a really decent guy...

When they got to Drummond's house Jimmy knocked the door and it was answered by Mrs Drummond. She was informed by McBurnie that they were police officers, and without checking their identity, she immediately invited them in.

Mr Drummond was seated in the living room when they entered and he got up and shook hands with both cops. He asked Jimmy what brought him to his house and laughingly, he said he hoped it was a social call. McBurnie said he had a pressing matter to discuss with him and could this be done privately?

Drummond looked puzzled but nevertheless asked his wife to leave them while he discussed a 'business' matter. She duly complied but before she left she insisted making them coffee. When it was ready it was accompanied by a fantastic selection of home baking. As they were tucking into the cakes Jimmy said, "There is no way of putting this mildly Allan. I know you are paying protection money to scousers who are threatening you."

Allan Drummond's head drooped, he got up from his chair and ensured the kitchen door where his wife was located, was closed.

He told Jimmy he knew he was stupid. He wasn't afraid for himself but he was terrified what these men would do to his wife. That was the reason he hadn't come to the police.

Jimmy asked him for some specifics...

He said he had been visited at the shop about three months before, just before closing time. This was normally when he was on his own as he liked to let his two assistants away early to catch their bus home.

Just as he was about to lock the front door three men came in and locked the door behind them. One of them had a tattoo of a pair of scissors or pliers on his neck and they all spoke with strong Merseyside accents. He took it the one with the tattoo was the ringleader as he did most of the talking. He instructed Drummond to sit down behind the counter. Once seated the scouser joined him behind the counter and started to tell him what type of car his wife drove, which hairdressers she attended and on what days she met her friends for coffee in Newholm's largest department store.

This man said she looked like a really nice woman who was in good nick for her age and with beautiful skin. He then said it would be a shame if she ended up loosing her looks after she had an 'accident' with a pair of pliers, pointing to the tattoo on his neck.

Drummond told Jimmy he was horrified by what he had heard and asked this guy what he wanted from him. The scouser said it must be obvious to him now that they knew his wife's movements, where they both lived, together with his wife's routine and habits.

Drummond said nothing because he was in a state of shock.

The ringleader then told him, if he wanted his wife to remain in 'good nick' there would be a price to pay. Remaining beautiful, as he knew, did not come cheap.

The shopkeeper was now too aware he was going to have to pay up, to save his wife becoming a victim of these thugs and being permanently disfigured. He asked how much he wanted and without delay the man with the tattoo indicated £400 per week, which he said would be roughly what his wife spent on make up. He then had the nerve to tell him, included in this cost, there was insurance against fire. A bewildered Drummond said he had fire insurance and asked him to explain. The scouser said this payment would ensure his shop, and even his house, would not be burned down with him, or he and his wife, in it. Then as a throw away remark he said "The first payment is due now."

Drummond said he then made his way to the till and retrieved £400 and handed it over to this 'animal', who smiled, said it was a pleasure doing business with him, and confirmed he would see him again next week. Before leaving the shop he told Drummond if he contacted the police his wife would end up being 'snipped' and pointed again to his tattoo...

After relaying this story to McBurnie, Drummond had trouble containing himself but for his wife's sake he managed to keep his emotions under control. The last thing he wanted was for her to find out about the 'arrangement' and threat.

Drummond, like Beardmore, refused to provide a written statement. He said he was too scared to appear in court as a witness against this evil guy and his pals, which Jimmy understood only too well.

After hearing this story McBurnie was raging inside, both of his hands were clenched and he told himself, 'What a shower of bastards'. He was in no doubt now these incomers to Newholm were going to get a big surprise and he was going to be the guy giving them it.

Before he got to the surprise, he had to think of a way, like with Beardmore, of keeping their meeting with Allan Drummond secret. He also had the problem of how he could keep from using Mr Drummond as a witness.

This was not going to be easy...

He then went to the kitchen and said goodbye to Mrs Drummond and thanked her for the coffee and cakes which he said were delicious.

As he and Green were about to leave he assured Mr Drummond he would keep their conversation confidential. If and when these neds turned up next week he was not to mention their meeting.

That is of course if they were not locked up by this time...

Once in the car he thumped the steering wheel and said to Green, "Who do these bastards think they are?" Green was as angry as McBurnie and told him, "One thing for sure, if I have anything to do with it, they are heading down a one way road to prison and for a long fucking time." Jimmy confirmed his colleagues view and said, "You fucking better believe it."

Their next call was to Betty Syme, the single, sixty seven year old publican, at the very busy 'Black Swan' pub. Betty lived in a flat above the bar. Jimmy had known her for a while and occasionally drank in her bar. She had never married and had been the publican at The Black Swan for at least twenty years. The pub and its customers had become the focus of work, home and social life for her.

Betty also had a well-deserved reputation for no nonsense and when you saw her you understood why. She was about 5'6" tall, all of sixteen stone in weight, with arms like tree trunks and a close cropped haircut. The locals who used her pub could all tell stories about how she had single handedly ejected men who were becoming unruly, and other occasions, where she had felled them with a shovel, which sat next to the coal fire in the bar.

Her cousin Sam Forsyth helped her out behind the bar on most nights.

Sam, as Jimmy knew, was a quiet wee man in his late fifties and classed as being a bit 'slow'. He wouldn't hurt a fly and was more afraid of Betty than the punters. Having said this Betty had a real soft spot for him. That is why she gave him a job in the first place and if any of the punters gave Sam a hard time she made sure they paid for it.

No one did...

She ran a very strict pub and there was no swearing allowed in the premises. It was rumoured when she banned punters they remained banned forever. One humorous story Jimmy had heard was when a local worthy, who had been banned by Betty some four years before, called at the pub just before opening time. He told Betty surely his ban was up after four years and if not, when would it be lifted? She replied, "When beer's a penny a pint and you know when that will be."

The guy knew better than argue the point and left shaking his head...

Jimmy knew she also had a softer side. She regularly contributed to local charities and often took hot meals to the homes of some of her elderly clients and elderly people who lived near The Black Swan.

She doted on children and McBurnie felt she would have made a great mother but unfortunately she had never married or been involved in any long term relationship. She could regularly be seen walking Elish, her thirty month old niece round the town and buying her sweets and other goodies, which probably this wee lassie's parents knew nothing about. Betty also really enjoyed having Elish stay overnight with her, which she did regularly, leaving Sam to run the bar. On these occasions she and her niece watched children's videos, ate crisps and sweets and had hot chocolate before bed time.

Both loved this time spent together, probably Betty more than Elish...

When Jimmy and Green entered the bar Betty was serving one of her customers but she didn't seem her usual self. Meanwhile, Sam was sitting in the corner mulling over a pint and with a severe looking black eye and bruising to his face as if he had been in the wars.

Normally when you were entering her bar you could hear Betty before you saw her. She was always cracking jokes with her clients. This time she looked sullen and withdrawn and when she saw McBurnie and Green walking in she looked away.

Jimmy suspected he knew why she was behaving like this...

He eventually got her attention and nodded, indicating to her to go to the end of the bar. When she came he asked if there was somewhere they could have a quiet word.

She summoned Sam to take over the bar and without a word raised the flap in the counter and by lifting her head, indicated to McBurnie and Green to follow her. She led the way upstairs to her flat and the two detectives followed. They entered her living room and she told them to take a seat.

Betty said it must be 'business' they were on when they were wanting a 'quiet' word. Jimmy said it was and the business involved her.

She knew what was coming but said nothing...

McBurnie asked her what happened to Sam and she said he must have had a fall but she knew nothing about it. Jimmy knew by the look on her face she was lying. She also knew what was coming next and her head went down.

McBurnie then told her he knew about McCarthy, a.k.a. The Grip, and his protection rackets and stressed to her there was only one way of getting him off her back. She looked at the floor and said, "I never said anything about paying protection money." Jimmy reiterated what he had said but Betty just kept looking at the floor. It felt strange for him to see Betty Syme, who had this no nonsense reputation, being so subdued.

He kept at her and this resulted in the first time he had ever seen her cry. She broke down and starting weeping inconsolably.

Jimmy went over to her and put his arm round her shoulder. He said, "Just tell me how he is threatening you and I will make sure he is out of commission for a long time."

Betty sighed, lifted her head and after wiping her eyes, confirmed what he already knew. She was paying McCarthy £400 a week to keep him from burning down her pub with her in it and inflicting any more pain on Sam. She said she was afraid of no one, but then explained...

When McCarthy and his cronies had first appeared at her pub about three months previously, it was before opening time. Only she and Sam were in the bar, preparing it for opening, when they knocked the door. She heard them knocking, but thinking it was some of her regulars just shouted to them, it was still half an hour till she opened.

They then kicked in the door, grabbed Sam and stuck a knife to his throat. Initially she got her shovel and threatened to pan them with it if they didn't get out and leave Sam alone. She also threatened them with the police but they just laughed before pointing the knife at Sam's eye.

One of them who the others called 'Grip' had a tattoo on his neck with what appeared to be an open scissors design. He then asked her how her niece Elish was getting on and did she enjoy having her stay with her above the pub. Before she could answer, he said it would be a shame if she was staying above the pub when it burned down. While his henchman still held Sam he told her about the shops she visited with Elish, about the nights her mother left the child with her and where Elish lived.

Grip said it would be a shame if something nasty happened to such a nice little kid.

For Betty, it was bad enough these neds were harming such a defenceless creature as Sam, but unthinkable any harm could come to her niece. There was no doubt they did know where Elish lived, knew who her mum was and when she stayed with Betty. She had seen what they were threatening to do and what they had now done to Sam and she couldn't risk anything happening to wee Elish.

She told McBurnie she paid them the £400 they asked for and they left, smiling at her. She had paid this cash every week until last week when she had refused to pay up. Three scousers, including, this animal called Grip, arrived as they normally did on the Saturday morning before opening time. When she told them she wasn't paying them another penny two of them grabbed poor Sam, took him to the toilets and gave him a beating. While this was going on Grip stood in front of her laughing, with a newspaper in one hand and a lighter the other.

She paid up and they left with the £400 after confirming this was her last warning.

McBurnie thanked her for eventually confiding in him. She then said, like Beardmore and Drummond, she would not be supplying a statement against them or going to court as a witness.

She asked McBurnie not to go near Sam who was terrified.

McBurnie and Green got up to leave and Jimmy asked Betty not to mention their meeting to the scousers. He said he would get back to her soon.

When they returned to the C.I.D. office Jimmy decided it was time to assess what they had. He knew there wasn't much to go on evidentially and definitely not enough to detain the scousers, but they should go through the assessment process anyway;
They had verbal confirmation from three victims who were all paying protection money on a weekly basis to McCarthy and his team.

McBurnie's touts, Bashful Girl, Wise Archie and Welsh Rarebit had all given him information about 'The Grip' and his buddies. The information included details of their drug dealing and violence but this wasn't evidence and he couldn't use his touts as witnesses.

McBurnie, was now getting really angry and resorted back to his racing terminology. He told Green all the scouse bastards were getting 'pulled up' for one hell of a long time and they would be there when it happened.

Both detectives reluctantly had to accept, little, or any, of the information they had could be used in court proceedings. The victims of the extortion had all refused to provide written statements or appear in court and he certainly couldn't compromise his informants.

Wise Archie had offered to infiltrate the scouse team but to date McBurnie had heard nothing from him. The fact he offered this at such an early stage continued to worry McBurnie. He told Green he wondered what Archie's motivation really was and what was his involvement with the scousers. He confirmed with Green they now needed to formulate a plan to ensure these neds demise and said he would meet with his Acting D.I. later that day...

While he was considering what his next course of action would be he went through his mail. Amongst it were details of the promotion process for applicants for the Chief Inspector's post at Stratshall. Like before, each candidate had to prepare a policing plan for the area where the post was becoming vacant. They then had to give a presentation of their plan to the promotion panel, made up of the Chief Constable, D.C.C. Flemington, A.C.C.Ramsden and Chief Superintendent Scott.

The plan didn't pose too much of a problem for Jimmy as he had served as an Inspector in Stratshall and knew quite a bit about its problems, its geography and its population.

The presentation of the plan however would be a problem as he wasn't a gifted public speaker. Nonetheless, he was determined now to give it his best shot and this time he hoped he might have some time to prepare for the interview in three weeks time.

When preparing for the last promotion interview he had to lead a murder enquiry and he was hoping beyond hope this didn't happen this time.

He didn't have a murder to deal with now but he still had the problem of getting rid of The Grip and his buddies. This was certainly going to interfere with his preparation but he told himself he would take a step back and let Green get on with it.

If he was honest with himself he didn't actually believe he could. He knew he had good detectives around him in Green, Allan and Starkey, who could all be trusted to give 100%. Whether he could take a step back from this investigation and leave it to them was debatable.

He decided if it meant working twenty hours a day he would attempt the juggling act, of preparing for the promotion interview and overseeing the investigation into The Grip and his cohorts. If the end result was he jeopardised any chance of promotion then he could live with it. It was more important to get rid of these evil bastards than him having three pips on his shoulder.

When he went home that night he explained his thought process to Doris. In her heart of hearts she wanted her husband to give all his effort and commitment to the promotion process. She would be delighted if he was successful this time, especially after apparently overcoming the previous 'hurdles' of Scott and Ramsden.

However, she was well aware Jimmy couldn't switch off from crime fighting, even more so now, when there were really evil neds threatening what he saw as his community of Newholm.

She was diplomatic, and told him it would be a difficult to concentrate on the promotion interview with these nasty scousers on the go but she was sure he could manage it. She was fully behind him and had every confidence in him.

This was all Jimmy needed to hear...

That week he made contact with all his touts again in a further attempt to improve his intelligence picture and hopefully convert information and intelligence into evidence.

At home he was sitting up to eleven o'clock at night preparing his policing plan and the presentation he would have to provide to the panel.

At work nothing new was coming into the intelligence team.

Thomason meanwhile made sure circulations about this team were going out regularly to all the forces and agencies as well as the home force, in the hope somebody had a 'wee gem' piece of intelligence.

Jimmy's touts came up with nothing albeit all the drug fraternity knew who was controlling the distribution, nobody was saying anything about them.

Neither Beardmore, Drummond nor Syme had been back in touch and any contact with them was instigated by Jimmy.

He was beginning to get despondent.

Time to ask for help from above....

Three days before the promotion interview, Jimmy had his policing plan completed. His contact in the training department had assisted him with his presentation and overall he felt as well prepared for the interview as he could be. There was no doubting however he was frustrated by lack of progress in his investigation into the scousers.

Help from above came that night when Welsh Rarebit contacted him and asked for an urgent meet. He said he had something about the scousers which might interest him...

McBurnie, perhaps unwisely, headed out for the meeting on his own. He was so eager to learn what Rarebit had to say, the adrenaline rush took over.

When they met the Welshman said he had found out the scousers had taken delivery of a consignment of high purity smack, coke and speed from Liverpool. He said he had heard through the grapevine the coke would 'blow your head off' as it was of such high purity.

Rarebit then told Jimmy the gear was being stored somewhere near a derelict farm known as The Steading about two miles outside Newholm. The tout said he only found out about this because of a conversation with one of the main dealers in North Wales, Gerard Davies. Rarebit said he knew Davies well. Like most of the drug dealers in the country, Davies sourced his gear in Merseyside. Now he had turned up out of the blue, in Newholm with the scousers.

Rarebit said it had been a real surprise when he saw his countryman in Newholm but it wasn't long before they were having a drink. Davies said he had something big going on and asked Rarebit if he wanted part of the action. He confirmed he had a stake in a consignment and Rarebit's muscle would ensure he didn't get ripped off. Rarebit confirmed he was interested if the money was right and Davies said it was and offered him £500 up front.

McBurnie interrupted his tout then and told him if he went with Davies and was caught with gear on him, he was on his own. Rarebit said he understood. He would not be in possession of any drugs.

Now that was cleared up McBurnie, almost dribbling at the mouth in anticipation of arresting the scousers, asked him to carry on.

Rarebit continued and McBurnie was frantically noting what he was being told...

The tout said Davies told him a large part of the shipment was being sold on the following night at The Steading to dealers who were travelling from Glasgow. One of these dealers came from the east end of Glasgow and was known as 'Milky', because of his fondness for white powder. This Glaswegian had spent some time in an English prison with Davies and they had kept in touch on their release. In fact Davies told Rarebit he had brokered this deal, spoken up for Milky with The Grip, said Milky could be trusted, and had the cash for a major buy.

It turned out The Grip was as suspicious as McBurnie and when Davies told him he wanted Rarebit with him as some back up, the scouser took some convincing, before he would accept Davies' fellow Welshman. Davies said after reluctantly agreeing to have Rarebit there The Grip threatened him. If things went pear shaped then he and Rarebit would be missing some fingernails, when their bodies turned up somewhere in scenic Scotland...

McBurnie privately thanked the man above and told his tout he would be in line for a substantial payment. It looked now like he was getting a chance to nab them with a large quantity of drugs, and the other bonus was he wouldn't be putting Beardmore, Drummond or Betty Syme at risk.

He wasn't going to miss out on this hit for anything, including possible promotion...

As he was leaving his tout McBurnie told him when he knew what time the job was coming down he was to contact him immediately. Then he warned him again. If he was going to be with Davies he had better not be carrying any drugs or he was on his own. McBurnie instructed him if he was with Davies when the drugs deal was coming down, he should wear his grey coloured flat cap with the dragon insignia. This would make him easy to identify, if there was an opportunity for him to make his getaway.

Jimmy then returned to the office and told Green he would have the responsibility of identifying Rarebit when he was making his escape bid.

Now he needed to get a hold of Detective Superintendent Melrose, the head of the surveillance unit in Glasgow...

When he phoned, Melrose said it was nice to hear from him again and wondered was it a social call. Jimmy confirmed it wasn't and passed the information he had about a guy called 'Milky' who he said supposedly came from the east end of the city. He told Melrose how Milky was due in Newholm the following day to get a consignment of drugs from the scousers.

McBurnie said he needed, at all costs, to protect his tout. He felt if the surveillance team from the city tailed Milky to Newholm they could legitimately say they were following a tip off but didn't have to say where that came from.

This proposal didn't pose a problem for Melrose who said he would find out about Milky and phone Jimmy back.

Before he had the chance to put the phone down Jimmy wanted confirmation Melrose fully understood what he was suggesting. Melrose said he understood but Jimmy nevertheless insisted that when it came to the court case Melrose or some of his team would have to confirm they received a tip off about Milky travelling to Newholm to collect drugs. This wouldn't be a lie but they wouldn't have to say where this tip off came from other than it was from a confidential source i.e. Jimmy. This would ensure Jimmy's tout's identity and involvement was protected and give a legitimate reason for Melrose's surveillance unit being in Newholm.

Melrose told McBurnie to relax. He fully understood and all they would be saying was the information came from a confidential source and it wouldn't be a problem.

Two hours later the Detective Superintendent phoned back and told Jimmy, Milky was Gregor White, a thirty four year old ned from the east end. He had form for housebreakings, serious assault and drug possession. Interestingly, he had spent some time in an English prison and maybe there he could have met Davies or the scousers.

Current intelligence on White suggested he was one of the main drug dealers in the east end but the Drugs Squad were having difficulty getting enough info on him to take him off the street.

Melrose said he had told the Drugs Squad about the planned visit the following day and instructed them to accompany his surveillance team. When it came to the court case they would be in a good position to produce local intelligence about White's drug dealing, which would also further remove any suspicion, the original tout came from Newholm.

Jimmy was relieved. He loved it when a plan came together!

Needless to say the promotion panel was no longer a thought in his mind...

Melrose confirmed they had identified three cars Milky and his buddies used and had covertly fitted them with 'bricks' (tracking devices). His surveillance team were now plotted up and carrying out observations on Milky's home address.

He confirmed with McBurnie he would give him the 'heads up' when they left Glasgow and his lead officer would keep him up to date with progress the closer they got to Newholm.

McBurnie contacted D.S. Jones of the Drug Squad and asked him what current information they held about The Grip and his team. Jones said they had a few 'anonymous' reports about this guy known as 'Grip' from Liverpool dealing heroin and coke, but none of his touts were saying anything about them. McBurnie then provided Jones with the information he had and in particular the information about the drugs drop at The Steading. He said his information was sound and he had a man on the 'inside'.

He never expanded on who this was...

He told Jones the whole Drugs Squad team would need to be involved along with C.I.D. detectives, traffic and uniform cops in this 'hit'. As it involved drug dealing and distribution Jones would report the case.

Jones was delighted he was to be the reporting officer, but as usual, Jimmy had another motive in passing it on. By getting the Drug Squad to report it he was not only distancing himself from the investigation, but with him overseeing it he was in a position to afford his tout some extra protection.

It was now time to brief the new D.C.C...

McBurnie ran up the stairs to the D.C.C.'s office in headquarters and told Flemington's secretary he needed to speak to the D.C.C. urgently. She went into his office and two minutes later she told Jimmy to go in.

Flemington could see Jimmy was on a high and told him to sit down. The Acting D.C.I. ended up being with the D.C.C. for over an hour telling him all about the scousers, their protection rackets, their drug dealing, violence, and the drugs distribution due to take place the following day. McBurnie could see now Flemington was as excited as he was and asked him how he was going to nab them.

Jimmy said the information pointed to the distribution taking place during the hours of darkness. Nevertheless, he planned to have trained observation men in place from first thing in the morning to 'clock' and identify any comings or goings at The Steading.

Flemington said he would have adopted the same tactic and asked Jimmy to continue with his briefing.

The more Jimmy told him the more excited he became.

McBurnie could see the detective in him, perhaps not quite experienced as Cobble had been, but with the questions he was asking, there was no doubt he would love to be involved in the 'hit'.

He asked Jimmy if there was any intelligence suggesting any of the neds would be in possession of firearms and Jimmy said it was rumoured they had access to guns but it was unconfirmed.

Flemington said in that case there would be a firearms team available. He told McBurnie with the violence this team used he would also need public order trained guys, and Jimmy nodded. The D.C.C. then instructed him to go and see Chief Superintendent Scott and tell him the D.C.C. had been briefed and he was to supply all the troops Jimmy needed.

As he was leaving the office Flemington said he would brief the Chief Constable and wished Jimmy the best of luck. Jimmy just nodded and the Deputy said he wouldn't keep him any longer. There was no doubt he had plenty to think about and prepare.

Jimmy then went straight to Scott's office.
Scott like Flemington could see Jimmy was on a high and he asked him to take a seat. McBurnie then blurted out a shorter briefing than he had given the D.C.C. but with what he felt was enough information for him to release troops for the 'hit'.

The Chief Superintendent couldn't be more helpful and told Jimmy he would get all the cops he required including both firearms and public order teams. Before Jimmy left Scott told him to come back with the exact numbers of officers he required once he had viewed The Steading.

As he was leaving his office Jimmy shook his head. He could still hardly believe the change in Scott's attitude towards him...

Back in the C.I.D. office he contacted Acting Detective Inspector Green, D.S. Allan and D.S. Jones. He told them they were going with him on a reconnaissance mission, to The Steading, and instructed Jones to get binoculars and a camera.

On the way there McBurnie briefed them all on the information he had. He told them, although the information he had suggested the distribution would not take place at The Steading till darkness had fallen, they would still mount a full scale operation from early next morning. For this reason they would have a look at these premises now, in daylight. This viewing would help when the adrenaline was running and it was dark.

As McBurnie, and his three colleagues were travelling on the main road they could see The Steading sitting some 200 yards back from the road in front of a wood. McBurnie thought if they could see it so easily then so could anyone else using this road. This left him wondering why the neds had picked this location when it would be difficult to get to the farm without being seen.

On Jones' advice they drove past the farm road entrance and parked in a lay-by half a mile from it. Jones who was trained in specialist surveillance work then left the car and entered the wood with the camera and binoculars. After half an hour he returned to the car and told Jimmy and his colleagues the following;

The farm building was in a poor state of repair. It consisted of two single storey cottages sat about 200 yards back from the main road, with fields on either side of the road leading up to it and the wood behind it. This potholed road was the only access to the building and only wide enough for one car. A barn in a poor state of repair sat about fifty yards behind the farm buildings. Behind the barn was the wooded area, where Jones had been, which was about a mile long and half a mile wide. There were no vehicles or any sign of life in or around the farm building or barn.

Jones had taken photographs of the location from different angles from the wood and he showed them to McBurnie and the rest of the team. These, he confirmed would come in handy at the subsequent briefing.

Jimmy and his colleagues were all pleased there was only one access road to The Steading. It would be easy to block if the neds arrived in cars, as it would be the only road out again. McBurnie couldn't get his head round why the neds had picked this location for a drugs handover but didn't dwell on it.

The big issue now was where they could plot up without being seen plus they didn't know if the scousers had 'friendlies' nearby who would contact them if they saw anyone at the farm.

It was vitally important the observation guys could get into the wood covertly. Jones, being as thorough as he was, had already identified a 'safe' route for them and they in turn would identify a 'safe' route for the other cops to get into position, unseen.

Jimmy told Green and Allan they and their troops would be with him and the public order team, in the wood near the barn at a point identified by Jones.

Jones was then tasked by McBurnie with getting the necessary surveillance authority signed by the bosses who were now well aware of the operation. It would also be his responsibility to compile an operational order ready for distribution at the briefing, which would be at 7 am the following morning, in the police gymnasium.

When back in the office McBurnie contacted Chief Superintendent Scott and told him about the briefing the following morning. He said he needed two firearms teams, a public order team, four double crewed traffic cars and he would use most of the officers from C.I.D. and Drugs Squad.

Scott said that was fine, he would get these officers and wished him good luck. He told him he would ensure the officers he required were in place for the briefing at 7 am. which he would also attend...

Jimmy didn't sleep much that night because his mind, like the rest of him, was working overtime. He spent the whole night tossing and turning, so much so that Doris had to go into their spare room to get any sleep. He couldn't wait to get these bastards off the street and in his mind he pictured various ways they could be 'taken out'.

At 5 am he was up, washed, shaved, and out the door. On the way to his car he momentarily dwelt on the promotion interview, but told himself he had completed all the preparation he could for it. Anyway what was more important, was getting rid of these dangerous neds.

He was in his office before the cleaners arrived at 6 am and was pacing up and down the floor waiting for his team to arrive.

He had told himself this would be the day when the scousers and their buddies got their comeuppance, and he was going to be there to see it, and make sure it happened.

At 6.15. am firstly Green, then Allan and Jones, came into the C.I.D. office, joined shortly thereafter by the firearms and public order team leaders and Chief Inspector McCann from the Traffic Department. McBurnie told them to join him in his office and they discussed Jones' operational order before the briefing to the rest of the troops began.

The order was comprehensive and Jones had been thorough, making sure everything had been thought through. In particular he described how his two obs men, who had been trained in rural surveillance were already on the plot. He explained how they got into the wood behind the barn without being seen and were now 'dug in' once there. They would identify safe routes for everyone and be the eyes and ears of any activity at the farm or the barn.

Chief Inspector McCann confirmed, when required, his four traffic vehicles would be deployed at different concealed locations on the main road, which ran past the farm. By being there they could quickly block the farm road if someone tried to make their getaway by car and also be in a position to carry out pursuits or controlled stops if required.

D.S.Jones, under McBurnie's watchful eye then passed out copies of the operational order to everyone who would be on the job, and copies to Chief Superintendent Scott and D.C.C. Flemington who had come to hear the briefing.

The D.S. then delivered the briefing, showing the photographs he had taken of the locus, supplemented by photographs of McCarthy and two of his team, a photograph of Gerard Davies, together with details of two cars The Grip was known to use. One of these cars was a silver Audi registered to Capo's mother.

When he was finished Jimmy spoke and left everyone present in no doubt this was a dangerous operation. Everybody should take great care because they would be dealing with guys known to use extreme violence.

Everybody was up for it and the two senior officers seemed well impressed.

As the cops were about to leave the gymnasium McBurnie told everyone to sit down again. He then started asking individual officers what tasks they had been given, and how well they understood their role. This was not just to make sure they knew what they would be doing, but by asking individuals questions he made sure he gained everyone's attention and focused everyone's mind on the task ahead.

There would be a bit of hanging about before darkness arrived at approximately 7 pm but Jimmy knew neds can change their plans at short notice and they might have to respond in daylight. As a result he asked the respective team leaders to go over their individual remits with their teams, ensure their communications were up to scratch, everybody was fed and watered and ready to go.

It was now just a matter of waiting on reports of any activity seen by the two obs men, and confirmation of the safe routes they had identified.

McBurnie couldn't content himself and double checked he had all the 'official' equipment he needed. He then disappeared into his office and retrieved his 'unofficial', lead weighted, leather finger bandage and strap, which he tied to his forearm and concealed up his sleeve.

This was the worst part of these jobs, the waiting, and Jimmy was at a loose end. He decided to phone Melrose in Glasgow and see if their was any activity at his end. When Melrose answered the phone he said his guys had 'housed' Milky at his home address and the 'bricks' were still on the three cars he used.

It was only 8am and laughingly the Detective Superintendent said "Do you not realise that neds in the east end of Glasgow don't get up before midday?" Jimmy laughed in response and confirmed everybody was ready and waiting in Newholm. Melrose told him to relax. He would notify him immediately Milky and his team were on the move.

McBurnie made himself a coffee and started to go through some of the paperwork in his overflowing 'in' tray but he couldn't concentrate. All he could think of was coming face to face with The Grip and his cronies.

It was 1.30.pm before anything changed...

Jones said his obs men had spotted a silver Audi car go up the farm road. It stopped periodically and the driver got out the car to drop something at the bottom of the fencepost's at either side of the road, before parking between the farm building and the barn.

He confirmed there was only one guy in the car and when he left it this time he made straight for the wood at the back of the barn. The obs men could see roughly where he went in the wood but had remained dug in until he left, which he did some ten minutes later. They had managed to get photographs of him and the car and it would later turn out the car was registered to Capo's mother and the driver was McCarthy, The Grip.

The two surveillance officers then carried out a search of the area in the wood where McCarthy had been and were careful not to disturb anything. They found a large forest green coloured polythene bag, which contained approximately forty individual bags of white powder. This was McCarthy's 'stash' and Jimmy knew the scouser had been checking on it to see it was still there.

Perhaps more importantly, the fact McCarthy went to the stash on his own, confirmed he, like McBurnie, trusted no one...

After McCarthy left the two officers noticed small pieces of fluorescent adhesive tape had been attached to the bottom of the fence posts on the road leading to the farm, but they couldn't give an explanation for this.

McBurnie knew now they were 'under starters orders' and even at this early stage felt 'The Grip' was one step away from the jail.

At 4pm McBurnie received a call from Detective

Superintendent Melrose, stating 'Milky' had left his house and entered a Grey B.M.W. being driven by another well known Glasgow ned. He confirmed his surveillance team and the Drugs Squad were following it. He then passed the registration number of the car to Jimmy, who passed it to his teams.

McBurnie was hyper now and after he briefed Green and Allan they were as excited as him.

Two hours later Melrose was back on, stating Milky's driver had been doing anti-surveillance manoeuvres in Glasgow, circling roundabouts five times, making sudden stops, jumping red lights and braking suddenly, all in an attempt to find out if he was being followed.

Thankfully he had not clocked the surveillance team, who were still on his tail. The other good news was, it looked like Milky and his driver were heading to Newholm.

McBurnie could hardly contain himself and quickly briefed all the team leaders telling them to get their troops into their locations following the safe routes identified by the two obs men.

Everyone was now on standby...

Unfortunately for the neds there was a clear sky as darkness fell and visibility was good. Having said this McBurnie was taking no chances. He and Jones had the only two night sights the force owned, with them. Once Jimmy had confirmed all the officers were where they should be, he and Allan joined the public order guys, in the wood behind the barn.

At 8 pm Melrose contacted Jimmy again and said his team, with some difficulty, had just tailed Milky's car to Newholm. At the same time the crew of a local traffic car said the other vehicle known to be used by McCarthy, a black VW Passat, had just passed them and looked to be heading to The Steading. They were able to confirm there were five occupants in the car but they were not in a position to say anything other than they all looked male.

From their position in the wood it wasn't long before McBurnie and the other cops saw the Passat turn into the farm road. As it entered this bumpy road its lights were extinguished but it still managed to reach the farm and the barn, quickly and safely.

McBurnie knew now why The Grip had put fluorescent tape on the bottom of the fence posts...

It was pitch black and difficult to identify the five occupants of the car as they left it. He could hear two men talking with scouse accents and one of the other three sounded as though he had a Welsh accent. None of the remaining two spoke but McBurnie knew one of them was Rarebit, because, with his night sight he could see he was wearing the flat cap with the dragon motif. The other guy looked familiar but because of the darkness and the fact he had a tammy pulled down to just above his eyes, further identification was impossible. McBurnie pointed to Rarebit and looked round at Green who said he had him in his sights.

Ten minutes later a gold coloured Mercedes arrived at the farm with two occupants and parked next to the Passat. Its driver too had turned off its lights as it entered the farm road. The arrival of this car was unexpected and McBurnie was just thankful he had the amount of troops on the ground he had.

A check on the Mercedes revealed it was registered to someone in the oil rich city of Aberdeen.

"This is getting really interesting" thought Jimmy and in a whisper he said to both Acting D.I. Green and D.S. Allan, "The more the merrier."

His wish was fulfilled five minutes later when Milky's B.M.W. entered the farm road with its lights switched off and drew up beside the other two cars.

Through his night sight McBurnie saw the two occupants get out of the car. The taller of the two, who McBurnie felt must be Milky, had a right 'gallus' swagger and he headed straight for the Welshman and then the two from the Mercedes, and they all shook hands. Jimmy thought these guys have met before by the manner in which they greeted each other. The only accent he could make out was a strong Glasgow accent which confirmed who he thought was Milky.

Jimmy knew these neds were clued up because none of them wore any bright clothing. In addition nobody lit up a cigarette and he didn't know many neds who didn't smoke. McBurnie whispered to Green. "They know what they are about these guys."

McBurnie was trying hard to hear what the content of their conversation was but it was difficult because they were keeping their voices so low. All he could make out was there seemed to be a consensus among all of them that the polis were, "A right shower of useless bastards." He almost laughed and leaned over to Green and cheekily whispered, "Which polis do you think they are talking about?"

Green could hardly contain himself.

Still no sign of 'The Grip'...

Ten minutes later another of the traffic cars spotted Capo's mother's Audi heading for The Steading and relayed the message to Jimmy. As well as the male driver there was a woman in the front passenger seat. Like the other vehicles at the farm when it left the main road and entered the farm road the driver extinguished the car's lights.

Both driver and passenger got out the car at the farm. The driver, who appeared to be McCarthy started swaggering about and Jimmy could hear him greet the others in his pronounced scouse accent. Jimmy, through his night sight could tell the woman passenger, who was done up like a dogs dinner, was Capo's mother, who he knew only too well.

All the cops in the wood were trying to be as quiet as possible. However, the adrenaline was kicking in and there was a lot of farting taking place which as well as making a noise was causing some hilarity among the troops. McBurnie told them all to, "Shut Up." At the briefing he had told everyone there would be no action till he called the 'strike' and he just hoped nobody alerted the neds before he made the call.

It was just a matter of waiting and seeing what happened next...

McCarthy then went face to face with Milky and one of the guys from Aberdeen. Jimmy was frustrated because he couldn't hear what was being said, but he couldn't risk getting any closer.

Shortly after this McCarthy left the group and walked into the wood to an area Jones had highlighted, carrying a small torch. He wasn't there long before he returned carrying what looked like a large, dark coloured carrier bag.

He then emptied the bag of its contents of smaller bags onto the bonnet of the Audi and gave equal numbers to Milky and one of the guys from Aberdeen.

Jimmy called the strike and all hell let loose...

Some neds tried to do a runner on foot taking off in all directions. Most didn't get far before the cops had (pardon the pun) a 'grip' of the situation. Others got into their cars but the cops soon smashed the windows and dragged them out. Two traffic crews had already blocked the farm road, so they were going nowhere anyway. Capo's mother had tried to run away which proved impossible in her high heels and mini skirt. Her position wasn't helped when she was jumped on from behind by D.S. Allen, who forced her to the ground. She told her she was under arrest and asked her if she understood, which was difficult for her to reply to when her face was pushed firmly into a cow pat.

McCarthy had managed to reach the wood with two other neds without being intercepted. Once in the wood he crouched low behind a large tree, trying to be as quiet as possible. While attempting not to move or breathe heavily suddenly he was smacked on the back of the head with something heavy, rendering him temporarily unconscious.

McBurnie's lead weighted finger bandage had come in useful again...

Jimmy had just bent down to handcuff the now prone McCarthy when he too was struck on the head from behind with a large tree branch held by one of McCarthy's buddies. He was only hit once, before Green appeared and felled this guy with his baton...

It didn't take long to round up the baddies although two got away, and one, strangely enough, was wearing a flat cap with a dragon motif. Twenty bags of heroin and twenty bags of high purity cocaine with a total street value of £400,000 were recovered.

McCarthy took a long time to rally round but not as long as McBurnie who was in a coma. An ambulance had to be summoned to take him to Newholm hospital urgently, to undergo emergency medical treatment.

It looked at one stage he was not going to pull through, and Doris spent eight long nights at his bedside before there was any sign her husband was beginning to come round. He had sustained a fractured skull and had to have an emergency operation to remove pressure from his brain.

When the surgeon who carried out the operation spoke to him, he told him he must have a guardian angel, because the odds of him pulling through were less than 10%. Jimmy knew who the guardian angel was and even found it humorous when the surgeon mentioned, in keeping with his penchant for horse racing, the 'odds' against his survival.

When he was able to speak to Doris he asked her to get him a mirror. When he looked in it he said he looked like something out of a mummy horror movie with all the bandages he had round his head. Doris was able to laugh but deep down she knew she could so easily have been a widow...

It was two weeks before Jimmy was allowed any other visitors and the first two there were Green and Allan. They told him all about the arrests. Green confirmed two neds had escaped but the rest were in custody. Jimmy asked if one of them was wearing a grey cap and Green, out of sight of Allan said, "Yes," which brought a smile to Jimmy's face.

When Allan told him about Capo's mother's arrest Jimmy started to laugh, but had to stop abruptly because of the pain he was feeling in his head. After getting every detail from his two colleagues he was pleased, nearly all the baddies were where they should be, in prison.

Green then showed him some press cuttings they had brought with them...

When Jimmy looked at them he saw the media had a field day praising the cops over the arrests of the drug dealers. Each paper's articles included details about Jimmy who they said was heroic but because of his bravery was now close to death.

There were photographs of Doris and his kids entering the hospital and when Jimmy saw this he nearly blew a fuse. His family life was private. He didn't want them to be put at risk by some stupid journalist's having them photographed and plastering their photos all over the papers.

He knew neds associated with McCarthy and other drug dealers could now get to them, leaving his family at risk. He could do little about it now, but asked Green to keep an eye out for Doris and the kids till he got home. Green said he had been visiting them every night and would continue to do so. In addition the Force had installed a personal alarm system in his house and Doris knew how to contact them urgently if required.

Jimmy thanked him but was still worried about his family's safety.

He said he would address the issue of the press when he got back to work.

Green said D.C.C. Flemington had been as annoyed as Jimmy when he saw Doris and the children's photographs in the newspapers. He had called representatives of the media to a briefing and in no uncertain terms told them how irresponsible they had been. He warned them to leave Jimmy and his family alone or face the legal consequences.

Jimmy didn't know Doris was also being plagued by the media, wanting an interview about how she was coping with the stress. Had he known he would have been out of bed and confronting the idiots who were behind it. That was probably the reason she never mentioned it or the photographs in the newspapers.

Green then asked his boss if he was aware he had missed the promotion interview. Jimmy nodded and said there may be other opportunities. He was just glad to be alive.

Green with some humour, then told his boss The Grip seemed to be 'losing his grip'. He was trying to work a deal with the Fiscal by claiming he was only a small fish in the drugs network and

Milky was the main dealer. As a result he had to be put on protection within the prison. He had totally underestimated the clout the Glaswegian had, both inside and outside the jail.

Green said Capo would also now be seeing a lot more of his mother and wouldn't have to rely on prison visits.

She was now in prison as well.

The other good news was Allan Drummond, Betty Syme and Sam Forsyth, when they heard what happened to Jimmy, decided to speak up. They had all supplied statements confirming they were being threatened by McCarthy and were paying him protection money.

The Acting D.I. confirmed both he and D.S. Jones had been in constant contact with the Procurator Fiscal. She had been regularly asking about Jimmy and was pleased when told he was now 'out of the woods'. She said she now had all the statements she required. If the trial went as she expected everyone who had been arrested was looking at a long period inside if found guilty of being concerned in the supply of £400,000 of Class 'A' drugs.

She confirmed she would not be accepting any deal from McCarthy's solicitor and would be making every effort to ensure he was convicted, not only of the serious drugs offences but with threats, serious assaults and extortion.

If convicted he could be going away for twenty years...

Jimmy said that was good enough for him because he was one evil bastard...

Green than asked D.S. Allen if she would get some coffee and biscuits for them. While she was gone he leaned over to Jimmy and whispered in his ear,"You know I am a keen fisherman, don't you?" McBurnie thought this was a strange thing to say, but replied, "I do and I am always grateful for any fish you give me."

Green then said he had been running short of lead weights for his fishing lines but had actually managed to source some, from a leather, finger bandage, which he had found in a wood...

McBurnie gave him a knowing look and Green responded with a wide grin. When Allan returned she looked totally puzzled by their cheesy grins but neither McBurnie nor Green were about to make her any the wiser.

As his two colleagues were about to leave Jimmy asked them who the bastard was who had felled him, and did they get him. Green confirmed he had decked this guy with his baton before he could inflict any further damage on Jimmy. This guy was also remanded in custody charged with the drugs offences and the attempted murder of Jimmy.

"Who is he?" McBurnie asked again, and this time Green gave him a name, which Jimmy knew belonged to 'Wise Archie' one of his own stable...

"Here we go again," thought McBurnie. "Now I am not only going to be a witness against one of my own charges but I am also the victim."

The trainer in him knew Archie would be put out to pasture for good now and the next time he met him, he would more than confirm his 'racing' days were through.

His next visitor was Mr Morrison the minister.

He spent a long time with Jimmy, saying how sorry he was to see him in such a state, but things could have been a whole lot worse. Jimmy nodded as he knew how close he had come to death and Mr Morrison said, "You know who is looking out for you, don't you?" Jimmy said he did and asked Morrison to, "Tell your boss not to teach me such a painful lesson next time." Both men laughed and before the minister left he said he would keep an eye on Doris and the kids and would visit Jimmy again soon.

D.C.C. Flemington had arrived shortly after the minister and told Jimmy what a great job he and his team had done, in getting rid of dangerous neds like McCarthy and his evil pals.

He informed Jimmy, Detective Superintendent Melrose had contacted him from Glasgow to say how delighted they were to get rid of Gregor White a.k.a. 'Milky'. He had been a thorn in their side for a while and this was the first time they had managed to get him 'dirty'. Melrose had told Flemington he would be sending a letter detailing Jimmy's part in detecting this drug dealer and he hoped it would lead to a commendation, this time.

The D.C.C. said he now had the letter and had spoken to the Chief who confirmed Jimmy would be commended for his actions.

Jimmy thanked him for his support but told him, in all honesty a commendation wasn't on his mind at this time. All he wanted was to get home and eventually back to work.

Flemington told McBurnie he hoped it wouldn't be too long before he got back but stressed Jimmy should ensure he was fully recovered first. In the meantime he had recalled D.C.I. Johnston from his internal investigation, which he had almost completed.

The D.C.C. then broached the subject of promotion and told Jimmy he was sorry he missed the promotion interviews but his chance would surely come. He should be proud of what he had achieved. He had not only taken some real nasty neds out of commission but he had prevented high purity drugs hitting the streets in Newholm and beyond. Jimmy just nodded and said it wasn't only him. He had a great team around him and they had all played their part.

Flemington agreed, everybody who had been on this 'job' were a credit to the Force, but said Jimmy had instigated this operation and led from the front. If it hadn't been for his input and information, these neds would still be wreaking havoc.

Before leaving he again told his officer to take his time getting back to work and not to return until he felt fully fit. When he did return he would find there were no obstacles in headquarters to any further promotion for him.

His next visitor was D.C.I. Louis Johnston who jokingly said he couldn't leave Jimmy alone for two minutes without him getting into trouble. Jimmy just raised his eyebrows and Johnston said he was really glad to see he had recovered so well. Surely it wouldn't be long before he was allowed home.

Jimmy told his boss he was in the hands of the doctors and as yet there was no indication when he would be back with Doris and the kids, let alone back to work. He and Johnston then had a few laughs about old times and the D.C.I. said in all seriousness, the arrest of McCarthy, Milky, and the others had been a great piece of work. Jimmy confirmed again it had been a team effort and without the team these neds would still be selling their wares and exploiting people. Johnston nodded and before he left he said he was really pleased he didn't have a mountain of paperwork to face when he was recalled to the C.I.D.

Jimmy confirmed it was one aspect of the D.C.I.s role he didn't relish, and jokingly said he knew why his boss had piles. They were caused by sitting on his arse too long in the office, going through drivel.

Johnston laughed, waved his finger indicating Jimmy was a naughty boy and then left.

The Chief called the following day and told Jimmy the local community were in his debt. In fact he had hosted a meeting with the media where he said he sang Jimmy's praises and responded to requests from them about his injuries. Before he finished the briefing he took the opportunity to stress what a safe community Newholm was when being watched over by officers of his calibre.

Like Flemington he told McBurnie not to rush back to work because his job would still be there for him.

It was another two weeks before Jimmy eventually was allowed home. When he got there he was totally spoiled by Doris, who wouldn't allow him to do anything in the house. She kept fussing over him and telling the kids not to tire their dad out with boisterous play.

Jimmy was just glad to be home even though he still had a personal alarm in the house which he felt he didn't need. Green was a regular caller, keeping him updated on activity in the C.I.D. and telling him all the guys on the shop floor sent their regards. There had also been numerous calls from people who refused to provide their names, asking how Jimmy was. Green told his boss he suspected these were some of the members of his stable.

The trial of McCarthy, Milky and the others including Wise Archie was set for four weeks hence and Jimmy got a phone call at home from Miss Scobie, the Procurator Fiscal. She was wondering if he would be fit to attend court or if he would be getting a 'soul and conscience' letter from his G.P. excusing his attendance.

Jimmy said he would not miss being there for any reason, including his health. If she wanted to precognose him (go over his statement) about the statement Green had compiled for him and which he had read and signed, she was more than welcome to attend at his home. She would be guaranteed cake and coffee.

She did attend and Jimmy confirmed his statement was accurate

Miss Scobie said the prosecution were likely to receive reduced pleas from most of the neds' defence agents, which depending on their level of admission, they might accept. However, there was no way they would be taking a plea from McCarthy.

She then went over Jimmy's statement again but he didn't know why. She asked him where the information came from about McCarthy and his cohorts in the first place. He said there had been many 'anonymous' reports about these scousers, their drug dealing, threatening, beating up people and eventually extorting money from them.

By doing some 'digging' with a 'confidential' source, he had managed to turn up Beardmore, Allan Drummond, Betty Syme and Sam Forsyth. He told her they were all in fear for their lives and would not complain or supply him with written statements when he spoke to them. He was aware now, other than Beardmore, they all had supplied statements against McCarthy.

She confirmed that was the case, and she herself had interviewed these witnesses. They told her the only reason they were prepared to be witnesses now was because of what happened to Detective McBurnie. She had interviewed Beardmore but he refused to make any complaint.

Jimmy told her the Drugs Squad had also received anonymous information confirming McCarthy was dealing both heroin and cocaine in Newholm along with Capo's mother. The information suggested that a major drugs deal was imminent involving both Capo's mother and McCarthy.

Scobie said D.S. Jones had confirmed this when she interviewed him and Detective Superintendent Melrose had also told her he had received a 'confidential' tip off about 'Milky' going to Newholm to collect drugs and about the subsequent 'follow' of him and one of his henchmen from Glasgow.

Jimmy then confirmed he too had received confidential information about suspicious activity at 'The Steading' and about a sighting of Capo's mother's car there. When he added this information to that of Jones' and Melrose he decided to put The

Steading under surveillance. Trained surveillance cops had seen Capo's mother's silver Audi turn up at The Steading and saw the sole occupant leave the car and head to the woods. After he left, these cops found a bag containing drugs at the location where this guy had been. McBurnie said by taking all these aspects into account and with Milky being tailed by the Glasgow cops this was the last piece of the 'jigsaw' or intelligence 'picture' and secured the downfall of McCarthy et al...

McBurnie felt he was being interrogated, but he didn't mind if it ensured Welsh Rarebit's involvement and identity remained secret.

Miss Scobie then left after confirming she was delighted to see him up and about again and looked forward to not only his court appearance, but his return to work.

McBurnie was only too glad he had managed to provide a sufficient 'smokescreen' to keep Rarebit's involvement hidden. The other bonus was that one of the Aberdeen neds escaped capture with Rarebit so this also again took suspicion away from his tout.

As usual before any High Court trial much 'wheeling and dealing' takes place between the Crown and the Defence. This case was no different and Milky, his driver, and the one Aberdeen ned who was captured, pled guilty to being concerned in the supply of controlled drugs.

The Crown accepted their pleas and similar pleas from McCarthy's scouse buddies and Davies. They were all sentenced to seven years imprisonment.

Capo's mother also pled guilty and probably because of her age received a sentence of five years imprisonment. Wise Archie pled guilty to the same charge and his solicitor negotiated down the charge of attempted murder against Jimmy to the lesser charge of serious assault. He was given a ten year sentence.

McBurnie made a point of being seated in the public benches in the court and never taking his eyes off him before he was sent down...

Archie knew when he got released from prison, McBurnie, if he was still in the job, would be waiting to 'speak' to him. Jimmy was in no doubt he would not be offered a place in his stable. If Archie could read McBurnie's mind, this would be confirmed to him in no uncertain terms.

McCarthy had offered pleas to reduced charges and tried to blame Milky as the main dealer. All his pleas were rejected by the Crown and he stood trial charged with being concerned in the supply of the drugs and with threats, serious assault and extortion.

Allan Drummond, Betty Syme and Sam Forsyth all gave evidence against him but Beardmore through fear, refused to complain or become a witness. When the jury heard the details of his threats and the violence inflicted on a poor soul like Sam Forsyth you could see both disgust and fear in their faces.

This was compounded when they heard Allan Drummond and Betty Syme provide graphic details of the extortion rackets he was running. Some members of the public and the press who were listening to these horrific details started shaking their heads, and this had a knock on effect on some of the jurors. They were also shaking their heads and drawing The Grip looks that could sink a battleship.

Not surprisingly they only took an hour to consider their verdict, which was a unanimous 'guilty'. Once he heard the verdict McCarthy forgot about the tutoring his lawyer had given him before the trial began, to show no signs of aggression and present a humble image.

He completely lost his composure and shouted at the jurors in his broad scouse accent, "You are all fucking dead people. I will see to that."

He then started cursing and swearing at the cops on dock duty, and the judge, Lord McClintock, had him restrained by them. Once he had calmed down it didn't take McClintock long to tell him just what a nasty piece of work he was and how society needed to be protected from people like him.

He sentenced him to fifteen years in prison and McCarthy then started threatening the judge, telling him he would rip his throat out. Lord McClintock remained calm and told the escorting cops to take him down and warned him he would be subject to an additional charge of contempt of court, if he continued with his abuse.

As he was being escorted to the custody area underneath the court he pointed to McBurnie, whom he had seen seated in the public benches, and shouted, "You will be the first."

Jimmy had been warned early in his career by some seasoned detectives not to sit in the public benches when a ned was being informed of the jury's verdict and judge's sentence. Their advice was once you gave your evidence get out of the court without delay. The last thing you wanted was for a judge or jurors thinking you were trying to influence them, and you may be even be recalled!

McBurnie had broken this rule with Wise Archie and did it again now with McCarthy. He wanted to make sure McCarthy saw him, because this scouser was one evil bastard who needed putting away. Seeing Jimmy in the public benches he would be in no doubt who was responsible for his downfall.

McBurnie was well used to threats from neds and knew it would be a long time before, or if ever he met him again, especially since he tried to incriminate Milky. The Glaswegian had many heavy contacts both outside and within the Scottish prison system and the likelihood was McCarthy would have to be moved to an English prison, for his own safety.

Jimmy still relished the thought of meeting him again, even without his finger bandage...

On leaving the court he was intending heading home. His doctor had told him he would be off work for another two weeks and to stay away from the C.I.D. office. He was told he needed rest, and certainly not the pressure he got being in charge of a team of detectives.

As he left the court building D.C.I. Johnston was waiting for him outside and asked him if he had time for a coffee. Jimmy said he was doing nothing else and would enjoy the banter and being brought up to date with the crime world in Newholm.

They went to a nearby cafe and Johnston ordered the coffees.

He asked Jimmy how the trial with McCarthy had finished and Jimmy said he was found guilty of all charges, by a unanimous decision. Lord McClintock had sentenced him to fifteen years in prison. Johnston said, "It's not long enough for a bastard like him," and Jimmy agreed. He then told his boss about McCarthy 'cutting up' in court, threatening the jurors, the judge and him with injury and death.

When Johnston heard this he said, "What an arsehole," and Jimmy said, "Not really, an arsehole is a useful thing." They both then had a good laugh.

Over coffee Johnston told McBurnie his work on the internal enquiry in the neighbouring force was nearly finished and just needed written up. While he was working on this enquiry, he was made aware by a senior officer in this other force, how pleased they were with the thoroughness of his investigation and his impartiality. So much so, before he returned to Newholm, one of their A.C.C.s took him aside. He told him there was a vacancy coming up for a Detective Superintendent and the post would be advertised nationally.

He told Johnston it would be in his interest to apply for this post...

The D.C.I. said he had now thought it over and put in his application. If he got the position it would mean leaving Newholm, but he had been in another force before. Moving wouldn't be an obstacle to him, especially when his kids were still quite young and changing them to another school should not be a problem. His wife also supported him, so he was going to give it his best shot.

Jimmy wished him well and said he hoped he got the position but he would be a great loss to both him and the C.I.D.

Johnston had the sceptics look now, not Jimmy. He said he wouldn't be out the door before he was forgotten about, especially when Newholm already had an Acting D.C.I. ready and able to take over.

McBurnie just smiled and said, "I have been through all this before. For me there are always going to be 'hurdles' I will not be able to get over." He then reflected on his previous experience of trying to get promotion. He told Johnston even when he thought he had a possible chance of a step up, without any 'hurdles', he still missed the promotion panel after being assaulted. He didn't think he would ever become the D.C.I.

Johnston told him to stop being so sceptical, his standing in the force was at an all time high. If he was honest with himself he would admit he knew he would be supported now both within and out with the force, for the position.

McBurnie remained downbeat saying,"I have heard it all before. I didn't believe it then and I don't believe it now."
"That's because you are a sceptic," replied Johnston and both men laughed.

Johnston paid the coffees and Jimmy returned home to Doris and the kids.

Over tea he told Doris about the court, about McCarthy and

what Johnston had said to him about possibly getting another promotion. She was more positive than he was and firmly told him if Johnston was successful in his promotion bid, he (Jimmy) would be applying for the vacant D.C.I.'s post. She was not usually as forceful as this, but to make sure he understood, she looked him in the eye and said, "Do you hear me?" He was a bit taken aback when she confronted him but did confirm he had heard her, loud and clear.

He returned to work the following week and got a round of applause when he entered the C.I.D. office. Johnston had organised a cake and over coffee he brought out the cake which had chocolate writing on top ' For the Sceptic/ Cynic' and underneath this a pair of pliers made out of icing...

Jimmy just smiled and before cutting the cake asked everyone to get a 'Grip'. This brought rapturous applause and roars of laughter. After going round speaking to everyone of his colleagues he headed for Johnston's office. Once inside he got straight back to business, saying he needed £1000 as a reward for his tout. Johnston just shook his head in disbelief yet confirmed it would be available the next day.

At 2pm he told the D.C.I. he wanted to go home as his head was hurting and he couldn't focus. Johnston offered to take him but Jimmy said he could manage.

When he arrived back at his house he told Doris he was going for a lie down and took some painkillers, before heading upstairs to bed. He couldn't sleep again because his mind was filled with what Johnston had said to him. The next morning, thankfully, he felt much better and when he got to work the reward money was waiting for him. Once he had it he told Green to get a car and he contacted Welsh Rarebit and arranged a meet.

The tout was delighted with the cash and signed for it using his nom de plume. He told Jimmy he had heard McCarthy was now in solitary at the local prison for his own protection. No surprise there thought Jimmy, who knew McCarthy would need to be shipped south for his own safety.

Rarebit asked McBurnie how his head was, and lying, he said it was fine, now he was back at work full-time. Cheekily the tout then looked at Green and 'tongue in cheek' asked him if he had left his running shoes at The Steading. Green just gave him a knowing look...

McBurnie queried if there had been any suspicion about his 'assistance' and Rarebit said everything was 'cool'. However, he had heard the Aberdeen guy who got away with him was now in hiding somewhere in London. McBurnie then told him to keep in touch. Rarebit nodded his head and left with his cash...

On the way back to the office Green said, "If he wasn't your tout I would be locking him up even if all he did was drop a sweetie paper." Jimmy just laughed.

McBurnie managed to see out his first week back at work and the following Monday when he arrived back Johnston asked him to come into his office. Once inside he said he had an interview for the Superintendent's position the following week. He was one of four candidates.

Jimmy wished him well but at the same time knew he would be

sorry to lose him. He told Johnston he was a good boss, a good ally and more importantly one you could 'maybe' trust. This comment just brought a knowing look from the D.C.I.

After he returned from his interview McBurnie asked him how it went and he said it was OK. He told Jimmy he had been asked the usual questions about policy, strategy, his strengths and weaknesses and what he would bring to the position, if he was successful. He felt he had provided comprehensive answers to these questions, but as always, you never knew what the promotion panel were expecting. He just had to wait and see.

The next day Johnston got a phone call confirming he had been successful and would be starting in his new force in three weeks time.

McBurnie was the first to congratulate him and then thought to himself, "What happens now?"

He didn't have to wait too long for an answer...

The following day an internal advert was circulated asking suitably qualified candidates to apply for the position of Detective Chief Inspector, with a cut off date at the end of the week.

When he got home he told Doris about it. She was forceful again and told him he would be applying for the post when he went to work the following morning.

Jimmy tossed and turned during the night and when he went into work he didn't apply and later lied to Doris, telling her he had put his application in. She knew he was lying and confronted him.

He 'burst' right away and said he would never be promoted again. There was no point in him applying, only to get another knock back.

He reasoned he still had enemies at high rank in Scott and Ramsden, who had accused him in the past of not having enough uniform experience. His only ally in a senior position was ex D.C.C. Cobble who had now retired. To add insult to injury the last time he had applied he ended up in hospital and nearly died.

He asked Doris if this wasn't an omen then what was?

She was angry and accused her husband, quite rightly, of being sorry for himself. She said it looked like Scott and Ramsden were no longer his enemies. The new D.C.C. seemed to be a supporter of his and had told him this to his face. What were his reasons for not applying now? More importantly, what would life be like if he didn't apply and somebody who he had no time for or had no C.I.D. experience got the position? Could he work with them and would he be coming home miserable and frustrated, making her and the kids lives a misery?

Jimmy knew she was right. He apologised, and told her he would apply the following morning.

He didn't submit his application till the last minute...

After handing in the application he wondered, "Would there ever be a D.C.I. Jimmy McBurnie. Is this part of the plan of the man above?"